The arm appeared first, the beautifully muscled, oiled arm that swung the bull-roarer. Then the dark head, a mighty knot of brow between angled horns with needle-sharp tips; the enormous snout, the eyes that seemed to be alive, focused on him. The shaved, glistening, copper-hued body was fully naked. He was a good six feet four in his bare feet.

Minotaur came slowly and grandly down flights of steps between the terraces, the bull-roarer moving tirelessly above its head in darting, elliptical flights.

What a show. All of it, Joe realized too late, intended to distract him. But he'd made the principal mistake of thinking of Minotaur only in singular terms. Disregarding—

"Nothing is more dangerous on this earth," the good doctor had said, *"than a deranged, yet calculating, mind."*

Joe didn't hear the footsteps, falling on thick sod behind him. But out of the corner of his eye he caught the gleam on the edge of the raised ax and whirled, pulling the revolver from his pocket.

He fired single-handedly wide of the target. The revolver bucked up just as the wide curved blade, one of two on the Cretan ax, sliced through his wrist. His hand, holding the revolver, tumbled into the grass. There was almost no pain; it had happened in the blink of an eye.

Then he looked into the eyes of Minotaur.

Further Titles by John Farris from Severn House

THE FURY
WHEN MICHAEL CALLS

MINOTAUR

John Farris

This title first published in Great Britain 1994 by
SEVERN HOUSE PUBLISHERS LTD of
9–15 High Street, Sutton, Surrey SM1 1DF.
First published in hardcover format in the USA 1994 by
SEVERN HOUSE PUBLISHERS INC., of
425 Park Avenue, New York, NY 10022,
by arrangement with Tom Doherty Associates, Inc.

British Library Cataloguing in Publication Data
Farris, John
Minotaur. – New ed
I. Title
813.54 [F]

ISBN 0-7278-4585-3

The quotation appearing on page 109 is from
Heart of Darkness by Joseph Conrad

Typeset by Hewer Text Composition Services, Edinburgh.
Printed and bound in Great Britain by
Redwood Books, Trowbridge, Wiltshire.

Minotaur

1. Classical mythology. A monster, the offspring of Pasiphae and the Cretan bull, that had the head of a bull on the body of a man: housed in the Cretan labyrinth, it was fed on human flesh until Theseus, helped by Ariadne, killed it.

2. Any person or thing that devours or destroys.

—*Random House Dictionary of the English Language*

Cast of Characters

LUCAS McIVER, M.D. Born in the hills of Kentucky, trained in the tradition of rough justice, he owes his life and vocation to

DR. VIOLA PURKEY, mentor and surrogate mother. Now an adventurer, a humanitarian, and an international fugitive, McIver is accompanied everywhere by

"THE LEPRECHAUN," a gentleman thief and would-be Shakespearean actor. Together McIver and the Leprechaun are constantly pursued by

BUFORD ELLINGTON, crippled patriarch of a rich Kentucky clan, and

BLAIZE ELLINGTON, his Harvard-educated daughter. Blaize has dedicated her life to hunting down and killing Lucas McIver, whom she saw shoot her beloved older brother,

JORDAN ELLINGTON, when Blaize was twelve years old. Blaize has been well-trained in her lethal quest for revenge by

PARD RANDOLPH, an oil-rich Texan with a colorful military career behind him. Another very wealthy man,

THE MARQUIS DE RIENVILLE, has befriended Blaize in her search for the elusive McIver. His only daughter,

ELIZABETH ROGER DE RIENVILLE, died tragically and mysteriously one day after her wedding to

ARGYROS COULOURIS, aging head of a powerful Greek family with deadly troubles of its own: the entity known as MINOTAUR. While MINOTAUR threatens from without, Argyros struggles with ambitious family members seeking power:

THEOS MELISSANI, whose dying father is a long-time associate of Argyros Coulouris. Theos's chief ally is

PLATO MELISSANI, his older brother, physically powerful but with the sensibilities of a poet. A cousin of the Melissani brothers,

KRIS ARAVANIS, is close to his Uncle Argyros and has his own ambitions, but plays a solitary game. Within the family Kris alone has taken the trouble to befriend

JOANNA COULOURIS, the only child of Argyros. She is socially inept and deeply traumatized by her father's lack of affection for her. Sexually promiscuous, her acquisitions include

AXEL STROH, scion of a wealthy German family; his macabre and twisted passions match Joanna's.

DEMETRIOS CONSTANTINE ARAVANIS, also related to the Coulouris family, has gone his own way and achieved distinction as a scientist. He has made a discovery that MINOTAUR desires to possess at any cost, even if it means the deaths of

OURANIA ARAVANIS, his wife, and

NIKO, their adopted son, a strange but unnaturally gifted child with emerald-green eyes who alone holds the key to the labyrinth of tragedy and revenge in which dwells

Minotaur

Part One

ATÉ

There is nobody who is not dangerous for someone.

—Madame de Sévigné

Chapter 1

Berzé la Ville and Arles, France

At five-fifteen in the morning, when he went downstairs in the cabinetlike *ascenseur* to have breakfast, there was just enough light outside the Chateau du Chatelin for the Marquis de Rienville to see that it was going to be a fine, misty morning, not too wet or foggy for his horses—particularly *the* horse—to work well.

He had slept his usual two and a half hours, retiring after midnight and arising at four to place a call to Australia, where he maintained a stable and his main hope for the Melbourne Cup, the fleet but emotionally erratic Pagan Shield. The report from the trainer of the four-year-old Irish Cup winner was encouraging; a slight malformation on the left foreleg had proved to be not serious, merely a bruise that was responding well to treatment. After the call, he dictated notes for the day's business, which would be transmitted to his offices on five continents when his secretaries arrived for work at seven-thirty.

The Marquis, who was nearing seventy years of age, had the diffident stoop and slight shuffle of an old family servant; wounds he had suffered while on bombing missions for the Free French during World War Two had caused a perceptible wasting of the muscles on the right side of his face, a quilting of the skin and flesh. But when he raised his head, smiled his hairline smile, he had the icy charisma of a Fer de Lance. He was dressed for the stables: riding boots and a cashmere hacking jacket with suede patches. He expected no company for his frugal breakfast and was pleasantly surprised to see that Blaize Ellington had preceded him to the garden room, which he favored in the morning, to watch the sun rise and break through the thick, churning mists that inevitably hovered over his Mâconnais estate at this time of the year.

"*Bonjour*, M'sieur le Marquis," she said, looking back at him over one shoulder, not smiling. But then he couldn't recall ever having seen her smile.

"Please call me Alex, my dear," Rienville reminded her, clearing his throat as if he were about to lose his voice. Rienville was four decades her senior but still he was stimulated, perhaps awed by her physicality, the aggressive nature of her beauty. She was tall, in stout hiking shoes standing just under six feet. A bulky long sweater and loose-fitting men's military fatigue trousers couldn't disguise the rawboned look of her, a legacy of her Kentucky forebears, who themselves came of excellent Scots-English stock.

She had hair like a wild horse's mane, mahogany-toned and nearly as *deshabille*. Her eyes, arrestingly wide in her large, almost classically English face, were a simmering, sultry olive color. Her mouth he would have died for at a like age (she was, perhaps, twenty-eight). It was a full mouth, sulky and demanding. Her high coloring denoted temperament; or perhaps she was host to sudden fevers of discontent, unexplained frustration. Her long nose had a charming bump and her eyebrows were heavy but shaped—so she had some vanity, although she seemed, during the brief time they'd been acquainted, artless, unaware of her sensual appeal. There was about her a prematurely old, bitter and sterile quality that reminded the Marquis of his late sister. Who, unfortunately, had been a lesbian. He somehow doubted this was true of Blaizè, but the possibility saddened him.

There was another thing that Rienville found disquieting, even neurotic, about his visitor from Kentucky: Blaize Ellington carried a gun.

She was wearing it now ("packing" it, the Marquis

thought; he had a good grasp of colloquial English and was a fan of the Louis L'Amour Western novels) in a holster on her belt, and the substantial lump of the handgun was obvious beneath her hip-length sweater. He would have to ask her about that. Surely she didn't feel endangered in his domain. . . .

For now, Blaize Ellington was preoccupied with the peculiar apparatus strapped to her lower left leg. Upon entering the garden room, Rienville had found her with her foot up on a window seat, her aluminum hand crutch leaning nearby. She was making adjustments in the straps of what looked like a hockey player's shin guard.

"May I ask what that is?"

"Sure." She tossed her hair back from her face. "Come have a look." She waited with her trouser leg rolled above the knee. "This gadget is called a Bi-Osteogen System. Around the tracks at home, the vets use it too; they just call it 'the boot.' "

"Oh, yes. I do remember seeing one like it. Shively was applying it to the fractured cannon bone of Galway Squire before the Royal Ascot."

With a long finger Blaize tapped the shield protecting her shinbone. "Inside the boot there's a device that creates a pulsating, timed electric current that travels through the leg and the bone. I wear the boot a couple of hours a day. It speeds up the healing process, particularly where there's a difficult fracture, an oblique crack like mine. But sometimes those never heal all the way."

"You're young; you will mend," Rienville said, admiring her leg, the length of her hand, the unadorned fingers. "You were wearing that awkward cast when we met at the Keeneland sales this summer."

Blaize nodded, rolled down the trouser leg over the boot and straightened, carefully putting weight on her left foot.

"I broke the leg almost a year ago. The horse took a spill. Serves me right for falling in with the Iroquois Hunt crowd again. Hell, I hadn't ridden jumpers since my school days. I don't know what I was thinking about, I couldn't have been *that* bored."

No, she didn't smile; but her mouth was capable of humorous, self-deprecating *moues*. Then she shook her head despairingly, a grandiose gesture. She had the flair of many fondly remembered stage actresses Rienville had possessed. Her cheeks flushed. She was annoyed with herself, thinking about the accident.

"A whole year lost," she said.

Lost? Rienville thought. But she was so young. That look of crucifying frustration again, the sterility creeping into vibrant, desirable young flesh. Hostage to monomania. But what was she pursuing? Or what pursued her?

Breakfast arrived on a rolling cart. They were served on an unimaginably valuable table of solid Baccarat crystal. Blaize knew what it was and praised it extravagantly, just as she praised the other treasures that had been in this room or another of the chateau for countless years, excluding those times when it had been necessary to hide them from invaders. There were medieval tapestries and Claude landscapes on the walls, gold-encrusted Sèvres porcelain on the table. But of course she would know and appreciate fine things. It was a humble state, Kentucky, except for those individuals who had made fortunes harvesting tobacco or taking coal out of the ground, and other fortunes breeding the world's best racehorses. Ellingtons had done both, with huge success. They were richer than he, and the Marquis de Rienville couldn't say how much his family was worth. They'd been well-off even before becoming involved in the grain business in the year of the Great Hunger in Ireland. Money had ceased to matter to the family long before he was born, and it didn't matter now, despite the stringencies imposed on the wealthy by the new regime in Paris. Wars and politicians came and went, but great fortunes were invulnerable. Rienville, and a very few men like him, had more power than the president of France or almost any nation one cared to name.

In measurement of power, the Marquis de Rienville was a pillar of flame, and Buford Ellington of Kentucky was a homely bonfire.

"You surprised me by being up so early," Rienville commented, watching with a feeling of envy as his guest tore through a hearty Burgundian breakfast that his weakened digestive tract couldn't cope with. He made do with brioche, pale coffee, a teaspoon of *confiture de groseilles*.

"I don't sleep much. Insomnia. Besides, I had something to look forward to."

"More coffee?"

"No, thank you, Alex." She sat back, looking contented, even sated. There was a gleam in her eye, and a gleam of light at the casement windows, striking fire in a bubble in the glass. Rienville smiled and nodded to one of the servants waiting silently in the room. The table was cleared.

"Good!" Blaize said, not waiting for assistance in rising from the table. Her crutch was handed to her. She leaned on it. The injured leg, Rienville thought, was weaker than she wished to acknowledge. She was pushing herself, looking for any sort of treatment that would heal her faster, make her whole again. She looked at him as he rose and signaled for the rest of his stable gear to be brought to him.

"Time to see my baby," Blaize said.

"You mustn't expect too much," Rienville cautioned. "After all, we've had him for only a few months."

"But it's happening," she prompted. "He's already showing that he's more horse than you bargained for."

Rienville smiled again. "You will judge for yourself."

A Mercedes limousine was waiting for them in the auto courtyard. Rienville had added a walking stick, a soft fedora and a full tweed cape to his outing attire, protection against the raw morning air. But Blaize seemed not to notice the November weather. She was nearly quivering with energy.

The stylish black and gold Excalibur she had driven from Cap Ferrat the previous evening was parked a few feet away on the cobblestones. She had arrived alone. She was not married. The very wealthy young women invariably traveled with entourages to protect them, mostly from boredom. He could not imagine Blaize Ellington as part of an entourage. She was a classic loner, although, from what he'd seen of them together, obviously devoted to her father. Enthralled by him, perhaps. It might explain the way she was.

There could not be, however, a suitable explanation for the

weapon. No need for it here. His security was unobtrusive but first-rate.

Rienville had a good look at the handgun as Blaize got into the Mercedes ahead of him, her sweater riding up over the holster. He was offended by it, and wary. Did the gun indicate something aberrant in her nature, potentially dangerous? He wasn't thinking of himself, but of his horses. This was no discreet hideout pistol, a purse gun of .22 or .25 caliber. It was a .45-caliber automatic; a single shot could destroy a large animal. He would just have a word with one of the security detail when they reached the barn. Then her every move would be closely watched. If Blaize reached for her gun, it would be taken from her before she could clear the holster with it.

Rienville settled back for the two-and-a-half-mile ride to the racetrack he maintained on the estate. They passed the estate vineyards, dormant following the harvest of the Pinot Noir and Gamay grapes in late September; they drove through autumnal pastures crowded with the white Charolais cattle of the region. But despite the excellence of his wine and beef, horses were Rienville's consuming passion. For a hundred years his family had been preeminent in European racing. He talked about his father, about Cup winners of a bygone era. Blaize listened politely, but he could tell she wasn't interested. She sat forward, almost on the edge of the seat they shared, ready to leap out of the car.

He thought about their first meeting, at the Keeneland yearling sales in July. A miserably hot day, even for Kentucky in the middle of summer. The prize two-year-old, the one all the owners had coveted, was Ellington Farms' High Drive, son of the richly syndicated Soberano. The bidding quickly topped four million. At that price, Rienville had his doubts; he was concerned about the fragility of the sire, weaknesses that had cut short Soberano's own racing career.

Instead, he bought two other yearlings of substantial promise, leaving behind a million and a quarter for the pair. He and his trainer, the elderly Jacques Mouraine, were satisfied.

Blaize was not.

She cornered him at one of the cocktail parties that followed the sales. Unkempt beauty, clumping sweatily around under the tent on a dirty walking cast. Hair fit for nestlings. But something about her attracted the attention of almost every man there. Men she ignored.

"M'sieur le Marquis, I want you to buy another horse."

Rienville was already dizzy from the parade of horseflesh, morning to night, the endless perusal of catalogs, the sales talks and the arguments with Jacques, tense bidding for prize bloodlines. He smiled politely.

"His name is Blaize Two. After me. I'm Blaize One." Her mouth twisted down at the corners. Not quite a smile.

Rienville recalled no such animal in the catalog. She shook her head, noting the expression on his face.

"No, he wasn't offered at the sales. He's been croupy and, well, my father thinks he doesn't make much of an impression. Sort of a disgrace to the family name."

"What are his lines?"

"His father was Glitter Gulch. He won a couple of stake races in Florida three winters ago. His mother—she had just average speed."

"And what am I to pay for this paragon?"

"You have to look at him first. You and Jacques."

"Indeed. I would have to look, if only I had the time and the stamina. But I'm afraid—"

She hung around. She cajoled and then insisted. She could be very stubborn. Not a quality he ordinarily admired in women, but—Blaize Ellington was different. Almost hypnotic in her intensity; or perhaps he was just tired, too tired to resist. It would take only a half hour of his time, she assured him.

"I know horses," Blaize said confidently. "I know this one will run. Maybe faster than High Drive."

The analogy was perverse; but he sensed Blaize Ellington was no fool. He was charmed, gradually, by her tenacity. They rounded up Jacques and went to see the horse that had not been at the sales.

At first glance he was depressingly chubby for a two-year-old. And not long on personality. He totally ignored the two Frenchmen. This didn't annoy them. Some of the best horses were proud and aloof. Not that Blaize Two had anything to be proud of. Perhaps, however, he was one of the exceptional mutations that occur but rarely; something in the genes, something calculating and intense, distinguished the truly superb horses from thoroughbreds whose bloodlines had been watered down through incestuous breeding patterns. What if he had the heart and machinelike will to win? That would be significant. He also had to be able to run. But, to some extent, running could be taught.

Blaize trotted him around a grassy paddock on a long lead. In the glare of floodlights they saw his head go high, observed solid muscle where it was most needed. He wheezed a little, but that was from the recent sickness, Blaize assured them.

"He's almost fully grained up," she said, but they could see it for themselves, all the promise, the controlled wildness out of the stall. Owner and trainer looked at each other. "What he needs now," Blaize said, "is to run and run."

"I suppose we could talk to Buford," Rienville said.

"He's not my father's, he's mine. Talk to me."

"What do you want for him?"

She was suddenly the hard bargainer. "Two hundred fifty thousand."

"Oh, my dear," Rienville scoffed, and Jacques rolled his eyes. "*Vous voulez rire*." Twenty minutes later they had a deal for one hundred thousand dollars less, and within a week Blaize Two was on his way to France.

Out of the car now, Blaize hobbled ahead without apology to the shed row where Blaize Two was being led out by his groom. Rienville walked more slowly, accompanied by one of the armed security men at the track.

Blaize greeted her namesake ecstatically; he deigned to recognize her. After four months' hard training the dark bay looked bigger, leaner.

"He's a prince," she said. "He's ready to win."

"Slowly, slowly," Jacques told her. "In the spring, he will race. Now watch him."

The track was cuppy in places, slow, but Blaize Two drove as hard as if he already sensed the hoofbeats of competing thoroughbreds behind him. His time was encouraging, his full potential still perhaps a year away.

Blaize lingered as the nerved-up, steaming horse was sponged and rinsed; then, with a last sad good-bye, she got into the Mercedes with Rienville. She looked suddenly played out, as if she'd run as fast and as far as the bay.

"Was he worth coming this far to see?" Rienville asked her.

"Yes! You'll be sure to let me know when he's going to race."

"Certainly. For the present, you know you are welcome to stay as long as you wish. Perhaps you will do some riding yourself."

"Thank you, Alex. I can stay only a few more hours."

"They will be most pleasant hours for me. We are invited to join friends of mine for a shoot this morning on their preserve, if you'd care for some sport. It would involve no strain on your injured leg."

"You mean bird-hunting?"

"The wild red-legged partridge. One of the most challenging of game birds."

"No, I'm sorry. I've never hunted with a gun."

"But you have an affinity, it seems, for firearms."

She raised her sweater to expose the holster and canted butt of the automatic, which was finished in satin nickel. The .45 appeared at a glance to have been extensively modified; there were finger-groove grips in a beautifully grained exotic wood.

"Are you talking about this?"

"Yes. I wonder why you carry it. The law regarding concealed weapons is very strict in this country."

"The laws are strict everywhere." Blaize shrugged and covered the pistol again. She had discovered early in life that if there were enough money, almost any difficulty could be smoothed over; and she had credentials. She was a nominal employee of a licensed international arms dealer and a special investigator for the Kentucky Bureau of Investigation, which entitled her to an eighteen-karat gold badge and a carry permit.

Blaize stared through a tinted window as they approached

the limestone chateau along an avenue of plane trees with branches as knotted as macramé.

"What do you know about my family, Alex?"

"Very little."

"I had two brothers." Her eyes, almost always expressive, *pétillant*, had dulled and narrowed. "Both are dead. Murdered by a man who seems determined to kill all of us. My father. Me. But at his leisure. He wants us to suffer first; repent of our supposed crimes against him. Is that reason enough for this?" Briefly she touched the bulge of the sidearm.

"Reason not to travel unattended."

"Not to live at all?" Blaize shook her head, eyes alight again, seething. "No man can do that to me!"

"Surely—measures could be taken—men can be hired who will, let us say, permanently remove the danger that seems to have scarred your life so tragically."

"Men have been hired. We've spent a fortune trying to track him down."

"You implied that he is known to you."

"I think I must know more about him than anyone living. But it isn't enough. Because—he's like a ghost from hell. Elusive. I last laid eyes on him when I was twelve. Sixteen years ago. The night he killed Jordan. But we'll find him. And when I see him again—"

She didn't continue; a cancerous pain seemed to take full possession of her. *C'est la folie pure*, he thought, but Rienville was moved by her suffering; and he understood the madness of obsession as well as any man. He reached out to take her hand in his. Blaize sat with lowered head, silent, seeing nothing but the scenes that haunted her. *Sixteen years ago*. . . .

She was his guest; she was in his charge. He devoted himself to diverting her. There was a tour, begun the night before, of the chateau, which was as richly endowed with treasures as any museum. The breadth of her knowledge of antiques astonished Rienville. Her mother's influence, which had ended even before Blaize graduated *summa cum laude* from Harvard. Not murder, but influenza, had taken the asthmatic Bliss Ellington. The death of Blaize's younger brother Lonnie had occurred two years ago, at the hands of the unnamed family nemesis. Since then, Blaize had spent part of the time with her father in Lexington, studied art and archaeology in London, Athens and New York, roamed the world in fear and anger. This morning everything she looked at was a reminder of earthly mortality, impending disaster: Dionysiac violence depicted in iconographs on a Macedonian interment krater; the marred faces of saints, their stoned gazes just a little shy of heaven; painted bronze vessels taken from ancient tombs.

The Shar-Pei puppies from one of the chateau's kennels distracted her for a half hour or so, but by noon Rienville knew he would not be able to keep her past lunch. There were distances in her eyes; she had the urge to travel again, fast and mindlessly, flaunting herself at Death.

"Where are you going?" Rienville asked Blaize, as she settled herself behind the wheel of the Excalibur. Earlier she had exchanged the boot for a cumbersome leg brace.

"Cap Ferrat, to return the car to Remy. Before that I want to stop at an auction house on the Rue Dieuzaide in Nîmes—"

"M'sieur Rapho's? Be careful there, they are swindlers."

"I always know what I'm buying," she said firmly. "There's a gold bull's head I want for a friend in New York. She collects them."

"*Au revoir,*" he said, and kissed her. He almost slipped then and called her "daughter," such was his regard for her. "Try to come back."

"I'll try," Blaize said and was away like the wind, her color high again, hair streaming in the pale sunlight.

Blaize traveled south along the Saône River to its confluence with the Rhône, pausing to take the top down, reveling in the highly charged ride on the N-6 autoroute to Lyon. From dour fall weather in southern Burgundy, the sun turned brilliant as she drove through Provence toward the sea; the air was noticeably milder. She seldom looked back, and so she was not aware of the three automobiles that had alternated in following her almost from the gates of the Chateau du Chatelin. The roads were full of them, cars fast enough to match her own: a butterscotch-colored turbocharged Porsche, a black Alfa Romeo GTV 6 coupe and a pale-green Citroen sedan.

The bull's head she was looking for was no longer available at the musty auction house, but the proprietor told her where she might find another one, he would just make a telephone call. . . .

The town of Gordes was an ancient place, once largely abandoned, revived in the 1960s by Provençal artists looking for inexpensive quarters. The buildings of the town rose steeply from terraced, silver-green hillsides. A winding road provided solitary access. There was a look of rain in the sky as Blaize drove up the hill. She left the car on the road and, reluctantly, feeling pain in her long-unexercised left leg, climbed an interminable crooked flight of stone steps to the town itself.

Several inquiries later, she arrived at a shuttered house with stone gargoyles at the eaves. The wind had risen, blowing leaves along the street. She was admitted to the house by a white-haired servant whose features had been neutered by age; the only clue to his sex were the trousers he wore beneath a full-length black apron.

She waited in a room unfurnished except for a bare library table with a brass-shaded lamp at one end. The house had an air of poverty, of dispossession. It was cold. Her leg ached. She wondered if she would eat tonight, and with whom. If she would sleep, and with whom. She had trained herself not to think about tomorrow.

A woman no more than four and a half feet tall came into the room on slippered feet. Pink and green bunny-rabbit slippers. She carried an object about the size of a croquet ball, wrapped in layers of jeweler's cloth. She sat it on the table and stood back.

"Greek," she said. "Very valuable."

Blaize grimaced noncommittally and unwrapped the artifact. It was not, as she had been promised, a bull's head, but the head of a calf. The style was Greek, of course, but—

She took time to look it over, although she didn't really want it. Heavy enough to be pure gold, but ony an assay could determine that. After a while she found the artisan's mark she had expected, turned to the woman who stood watching her with unblinking avidity.

"I'd say mid-fourteenth century, the Papal workshops in Avignon, copy of an original dating from about two hundred B.C. In that sense only, it's Greek."

"Authentic. Valuable. Twenty thousand francs."

"Horse puckey," Blaize said. "I'm not interested."

The old servant explained a short cut to her car. She was let out the back way. In the courtyard a loose shutter was swinging rustily in the wind; a cat quick-walked across the cobbles. Blaize walked slowly past a neglected garden. Thunder provided an overture to the storm beginning to mass overhead. By a dry fountain limbless statuary looked crudely menacing in the half-light of dusk. A few big raindrops splattered down. Her hair whipped around her face as she leaned on her crutch, adjusted the weight of the tote bag hanging from her other shoulder and pushed open the high iron gate, which was inclined at an angle toward the courtyard.

Facing her was another long flight of steps down the steep hill, with only a rickety iron-pipe railing for support. Many of the stones were cracked, and pieces were missing. It was growing dark quickly. The descent would have been difficult even for someone with two sound legs. But to get to her car the way she had come meant a much longer walk, and she was tired.

Blaize started down, carefully, right hand on the railing. Rain came with a gust of wind, subsided. There was a sullen flicker of lightning overhead. Five minutes, no more, and the storm would break.

She had to stop. She was breathing hard. More lightning, the flashes now vivid, at closer intervals. The steps angled sharply right and out of sight. She had a glimpse of the road below, through foliage. A van passed, moving slowly.

At her next step a piece of stone shifted, teetered, almost throwing her headfirst down the steps. Blaize clung to the railing and her crutch.

It was just no damn good; she was going to have to retrace her steps, take the long route.

In a glare that caused her eyes to narrow she looked up, and back.

Standing above her, on the top step, was a young man wearing a bulky dark sweater, trousers and cloth cap, and tinted eyeglasses so thick they resembled goggles. He was staring at her. Before he faded with the fading of the light, she felt something threatening about his stance, his silence, his magnified gaze.

Thunder jolted her; without thinking she started down again, hurriedly. At the next flash of lightning she had to look around.

He was following, one measured step after another.

Halfway down the tip of Blaize's crutch caught in a crack and it was wrenched from her hand, went skidding into a thicket. She clung to the railing to keep from falling.

The young man, methodical as ever, came into view behind her.

Gasping, afraid now, Blaize hurried, pushing through branches of olive saplings overhanging the steps, emerging into a grotto in which the torso of a stone maiden faced her, a pot of withering flowers atop the flattened head.

Thirty feet away, parked at a diagonal across the narrow roadway, was the van she had glimpsed earlier.

Above her on the road, a Citroen sedan pulled into view and stopped. Two more men, wearing the same odd-looking glasses as her pursuer, got out and stood several feet apart, watching her.

The sky cracked open above her head. Blaize screamed unheard. The man in the cloth cap walked toward her across the grotto; his right hand came up from his side and a stiletto blade flashed into view.

Rain poured down as she backed away from him.

And suddenly she was almost calm. There was no thought of what she must do next; it had all been drilled into her, hour after relentless hour, during the days and nights she had spent training in the West Texas desert. With her left hand she raised the sweater over the Bianchi leather on her belt; with her right hand she drew the cocked and locked weapon, which she had fired more than a thousand times.

The parts of the cut-down .45 ACP had been accurized for precision shooting—less than two-inch groupings at twenty-five yards—and tailored to her grip by Pard Randolph's team of gunsmiths. The six cartridges in the magazine were low-pressure rounds to reduce recoil. The muzzle velocity of a .45 is low, expanding rounds of little value. What matters in self-defense shooting, Pard had told her, is how big the holes are and how many you can make in a hurry. Her brightly nickeled Colt was ideal from both points of view.

Using the two-fisted combat stance Pard had taught her, Blaize went for the breastbone and blew the knife-carrier down from ten yards away. The sound of the pistol's firing was muted by the deluge of rain and thunder. The discarded casing was still in the air as she realigned herself for the next shot. Two men advanced on her from the Citroen, one a few feet ahead of the other. She hit him twice before he fell in a twisting sprawl, and Blaize noted without emotion a jet of blood as she lined up on the third man, who had turned tail and was running. Lightning; she saw him cleanly against the low bulk of the car and shot him between the shoulder blades at almost thirty yards. He appeared to dive headfirst into the side of the Citroen.

She was still watching him when, out of the corner of her eye, she saw the first man she'd shot sit up laughing.

"Whoo-whee!" he said. "Ol' Pard was right. You sure do know what to do with that thang, darlin'."

Blaize pivoted automatically to fire again.

He held his hands protectively in front of his face. "No, no!" he said. "Hey, once is enough. I'm *dead*, you got me, no shit. Don't go shootin' me in the head, now, that'd really smart."

"Smart?" Blaize echoed, her lips numb, her face full of rain. She was tingling all over as if electrocuted, but she continued to hold the pistol on him. Up the street, the other men she'd potted were rising. She was more confused than she'd ever been in her life. "What . . . is . . . going . . . on . . . here?"

"Final exam," Pard Randolph said behind her. "And you get a A-plus, honey."

Blaize puffed her cheeks, breathed out slowly and lowered the pistol. She turned. Six feet six in his boots, with a magisterial gut and a face that glowed in the dark. But he'd left his Stetson behind, and rain was saturating his dyed blond locks.

"Pard, you old buzzard," she said tonelessly.

"Piss your pants?"

She hadn't noticed before; now she did. "What does that get me? A C-minus?"

"We've all pissed our pants one time or 'nother." He put his arm around her and crushed her against his big chest. " 'Cause we've all been scared, like you was scared. But you came through. Not just cut-outs this time. Men. As far as you knew, it was real bullets you let fly. So I know now what I had to know. I guess you know it too. By the by, the one with the knife there's D.W., and this here's Hub and Paco comin' now."

"You bled," Blaize said to the man called Hub.

He grinned and pulled up his thick sweater. He was wearing a Kevlar vest beneath it; there was an expended squibb charge taped to the body armor.

"Tried to make it as realistic as possible for you, ma'am," he said in a pleasing Texas drawl.

"That you did. What was I shooting?"

Pard explained. "The usual 185-grain Remingtons, with wax up front instead of JHPs. Just in case something went wrong and somebody's head got in the way."

"And the glasses protected their eyes. How long have you been following me around?"

"Oh, 'bout a week now. Had to be real careful where we staged our shoot-out." Pard looked around. The rain had a sting of ice in it; thunder boomed. They were alone in the road. "Couldn't ask for a better place. Made the switch in ammo a couple nights ago when you were sleepin'."

"I don't sleep."

"Occasionally you do doze off," Pard amended. "And Paco here, he can steal a honeycake out from under a fly and the fly'll never know it's gone."

Paco smiled and extended his hand. He had wide shoulders and great teeth; Blaize wondered what else he was good at.

"What say we get in out of the rain?" Pard suggested. "Took the liberty of roundin' up hotel rooms for us in Arles; figured you wouldn't want to drive on back to the Riviera tonight after all the excitement."

It hit Blaize halfway to Arles, while she was still shaking from the surprise and the soaking she'd received; it hit her like a line of speed-laced coke, and the high carried her through dinner with Pard.

Before then, she jabbered on the phone for twenty minutes with her father in Lexington but couldn't remember afterward half of what she'd said.

"I'm proud of you," Buford Ellington had told her after she described her speed and accuracy with the .45. "I knew you had the stuff, little girl."

"Anything yet, Daddy? Any sign of McIver?"

"We had him traced to Switzerland two weeks ago, but he slipped out of the country again. I just have a feelin' we're close. We'll find him, rest assured. Then I know I can leave it up to you."

"Yes. Yes. I want you to leave it to me."

At dinner they celebrated with Pol Roger '71 at the little two-star Restaurant Chouinard, whose proprietor was a longtime friend of Pard's from the days just after World War Two.

Pard and M'sieur Benoit reminisced at length about another well-known patron of the famous restaurant.

"Summer of '48 I guess it was," Pard said. "A Sunday afternoon. Papa and I had been tyin' one on for most of the week. He'd had a lot of bad reviews on his new book, you know how it is with the literary types. Well, we was sittin' at that little table right there by the door, and we saw a man comin' down the street carryin' a dead horse. Big man, small horse, but still it was what you'd call a pro-digious accomplishment. His knees wobbled, his eyes was glazed, he was by-God pissin' sweat from every pore. Papa and me made bets as to just how far the man would get before he dropped, but he wouldn't quit. To this day I don't know where he went with that dead horse . . . we was both too drunk to follow him. But I know this: he was either the most dedicated man I ever saw, or he was the craziest."

Pard sat chuckling at the memory, then contemplated Blaize over the rim of his champagne glass.

"Might be what you call a cautionary tale. Mean anything special to you, honey?"

"It's a good story."

"I mean, is that all it means?"

"I get you, Pard. Leave me alone, huh?"

He steepled his hands over his bulbous, cheerful nose. "I've done everything your daddy asked of me, Blaize. More. But I've come to feel responsible for you, What I hope is, I haven't spent all this time trainin' the third victim in the Ellington family."

"What do you want, Pard?"

"Just take care of yourself, and leave the dirty work to the pros."

"I'm a pro now," she said.

Pard had managed to tone down her euphoria only a little. She was still highballing when she returned to her small suite at the hotel and, not unexpectedly, her second treat of the evening.

Paco was everything she'd anticipated earlier.

He got up off the bed as she closed the door behind her. He was brown and hard and naked, except for a black silk handkerchief that he'd knotted above his double handful of balls. It might have made him look swish, but she knew what it was for: to choke off the seminal vesicles so he could last all night if necessary. Blaize moistened her lips as she looked him up and down. Maybe she had finally found the man for her.

She had no pretense, no modesty. Her clothes she discarded randomly; the reloaded pistol she placed, with the hammer back, where it would never be far from her hand no matter what she and Paco were doing to each other.

Apart from the handkerchief, he had no devices. His hands were covered with the calluses of a karate master. He had oiled himself. There were tiny drops of oil on the black hair that feathered thickly over his ears and at the nape of his neck. His newness, his musk, excited her. Standing toe-to-toe, they mauled and kissed each other in the frenzy she had invited in her undressing.

"Take me from behind," she gasped.

With Blaize mounted, they made a single heaving shadow across the walls. And Blaize was transported . . . to the breeding barn at Ellington Farms, where she had been introduced at a tender age to the most primal of urges, heard the steely screams of stallions and mares in rut, watched their couplings. She remembered herself, little more than a child, long-legged but flat-chested, beneath a burly fifteen-year-old groom who was so frightened and intimidated by what they were about, what she had insisted on, that he wouldn't remove his pants and had scarcely pulled her own down far enough. But he couldn't manage it, straining and prodding and hurting her, finally coming on the inside of her thigh, coming in clotted spasms that were hot on her skin, that seemed to burn there for many days afterward, no matter how often and thoroughly she washed.

And she had wondered, gazing disappointedly into his clenched sweat-streaked face, why she could not feel what the young groom and her horses so obviously felt and enjoyed. The thoroughbreds she admired and loved deeply, more than her father, her mother, her brothers. Often she wished God had put her on earth as a horse and not a human. Her body was pathetically frail next to theirs, her two legs inadequate to carry her as swiftly as she dreamed to run. . . .

Paco was sobbing. How long had they been locked together?

"*Madre . . . Madre . . . Madre de Dios, estoy sufriendo*! Let me come!"

On all fours, Blaize was motionless, breathing hard, and he had frozen too, unable to endure the agony of another stroke. She was coldly aware that it had gone, the hope of orgasm vanishing behind the possibility of revitalization, while Paco clutched her and moaned in his great need. She reached behind her slowly, found an end of the knotted silk, pulled hard. The knot came loose, releasing him from torture.

"I need to be alone," she said dispiritedly, as soon as he was drained.

She lay curled on the bed, uncovered, while Paco showered and dressed. He came near her once, jaunty, whistling softly, smelling of generous applications of Paco Rabanne cologne, but when she didn't look up or acknowledge him, though her eyes were wide open, he took the hint and let himself out without a word or meaningless familiarity in parting.

"*Puta frigida*," he said, almost under his breath, as the door closed. Blaize understood the language, and the epithet ("frigid bitch") perfectly, but she neither blinked nor moved until, a little later, she became aware of the need to wash herself.

Much later she switched on a table lamp and sat next to it, a gold-latched Hermes case on her knees. She opened the case, took out a thin red-leather folder.

Inside was all that was currently known of the man who had killed her brothers. Some of the names he'd used, the passports, the countries he'd traveled through. Reports from half a dozen public and private investigative agencies.

Fraud. Con man. Thief. *Killer*.

Aided and protected by influential men as twisted and depraved as he himself was, Dr. Lucas McIver had never spent a day in jail anywhere.

Ten and a half single-spaced typed pages, all that was known or alleged of his activities since he had fled Kentucky in his teens. He was four years older than Blaize, having just turned sixteen the night he viciously shot down Jordan at Ellington Farms.

Only three photos of the undisguised McIver existed. The most recent had been taken eighteen months ago: a telephoto glimpse through the heavy wire enclosing the principal military airfield of a West African nation, catching McIver as he was about to board a twin-engine, French-built business jet. He was hatless, looking back toward the camera. Six feet two and a half, wide shoulders, a mountaineer's big frame. Long arms. His hair was now dark brown. He'd been a strawberry blond, crew-cut, with a hard face for a boy. His mother was a Youngblood: the Youngbloods had the worst reputation for combativeness in southeast Kentucky. His chin was still a bulwark of excessive pride, the violence-prone hubris of the hills. In the photo, his eyes were shielded by sunglasses, but she remembered them perfectly: light but dangerous, gray as granite. Wild with hate.

Jordan, with the back of his head blown away, lying there in the library, a fistful of blood and brains spattered across the spines of rare editions that Buford Ellington had collected. . . .

Killer!

Dr. Lucas McIver, who had taken the Hippocratic Oath with blood already on his hands; who continued to kill and enrich himself while supposedly serving the causes of medicine.

How could he have fooled so many people for so long?

The familiar saw-edged pain in her stomach, Blaize hunched over in her seat, not taking her eyes off the recent photo. Trying to see more of the man than the blurred exposure permitted, to mystically perceive his thoughts.

A million and a half dollars spent to date. They had come so very close before. Two attempts made to end his life. Traps set by supposed experts. Both had failed, and after the last attempt, Lonnie Ellington, age twenty-six, had been pulled from a noxious *khlong* that flowed through a Bangkok slum. So riddled with machine-gun bullets he was nearly chopped in half. And McIver had disappeared from the city like a morning mist. . . .

Fuck you, Lucas McIver, fuck you. I'll fuck you with this!

She came out of it aware that she was brandishing the cocked .45 too near her face. And her finger was on the sensitive trigger.

Blaize let out her breath a couple of notches, lowered the hammer of the pistol with her thumb, put it in snug leather and buckled it on, went out walking with her aluminum crutch.

Three a.m. on Les Alyscamps, the Street of Tombs. The night had cleared but was chilly. There were patches of stars. Along the road, the cypresses swayed in a river wind. Les Alyscamps was lined on both sides with broken tombs. In medieval times, coffins were floated down the Rhône, corpses clutching money for interment in Arles.

The last obstacle was out of the way. The question of nerve.

She had only to find him.

An hour before dawn, when tradesmen were coming into the streets, Blaize Ellington was still wandering, lost in her own limbo, in the City of the Dead.

Chapter 2

Kyūshu, Japan

"Tohru-san, please pardon my interruption. But we will miss our flight to Tokyo, and there is no other until after seven-thirty tonight."

In his closed study, Tohru Mukaiba heard but perceived no importance in the words of his longtime secretary. His left hand still rested on the receiver of the telephone, which he had hung up more than a minute ago upon completion of the typically terse call from his colleague in Greece.

Tohru Mukaiba was nearing eighty years of age, but the mind of the Nobel laureate scientist had not weakened with advanced age. Nor, despite certain infirmities one became accustomed to in the course of time, was his body incapable of withstanding the demands he made on it. He could still work around the clock, exhausting younger men, be refreshed at prayers and exercise, eat a frugal meal and continue his investigations for another full day without serious fatigue.

Since the advent of Cirenaica, he had maintained a killing schedule, afraid that he was working against time.

The word that he had hastily printed, in English, on the pad in front of him while he talked to Demetrios Aravanis, confirmed this suspicion.

The word was "mutated."

Came the knock again.

"Tohru-san, your address to the conference is scheduled for eight-thirty."

Ah, yes. The conference. Tohru Mukaiba, temporarily dwelling on the news from the ancient world of Cirenaica and the future this news proposed, wrenched his thoughts back to the here and now. Representatives from twenty-three Asian nations had been in Tokyo for three days, to be feted and lulled and reassured by the multinational companies who largely controlled the world's agribusiness that their technology and their innovations and their monopolistic patents could only result in a brighter tomorrow for all nations. *Leave it to us, and we will provide.*

Such folly. And now the delegates were awaiting him. His address, he supposed, with a slow pained smile, was to be the highlight of the Conference. More assurances. More platitudes.

Not tonight, my colleagues.

"*What is it killing now*?" he had asked Aravanis, afraid of the reply, sensing the chilling answer even before the word was spoken.

"I have called the airline," said Hijame Ujihara outside his door. "They are willing to hold the flight only so long, even for you, Tohru-san."

"It's all right. Please come in." He knew it was important now, crucial, that he reach the conference as scheduled. And to deliver the new address, the one he had not yet written; given his reputation, given the evidence he could provide at this point, his words might well be heeded beyond the confines of his profession.

I do not wish to alarm you unduly, but—

He was on his feet when Hijame came in. Despite the pressure of time, the secretary bowed and waited silently. His eyes went to the full attaché case on Tohru's tortoise-shell bamboo worktable. Tohru nodded. In a rush of nervous energy, Hijame crossed to the table and closed the case.

"Your luggage is in the car. Will you be needing anything else, Tohru-san?"

"Yes. All the research to date on Cirenaica from the computer." He gave Hijame a file code number and Hijame retrieved the floppy disk for him. Cirenaica itself was time-locked in a cold-storage unit of a vault used solely for the confinement of the rare, the deadly-prolific and the hitherto-unknown of the microscopic plant world.

The cassette tape with dictated notes for his upcoming speech was lying on Tohru Mukaiba's desk. The old man dropped the cassette into a pocket of his tobacco-brown traveling suit, nubby silk and years out of style. He seldom wore it anymore. Too much to do, not enough time—not even for his beloved grandchildren.

The sun was lying low across the waters of Aria Kai Umi as they left the traditional wood-and-paper hilltop house where Tohru lived and worked.

Just below lay the superb bamboo forest he had begun more than thirty years ago. Six hundred and sixty two varieties of bamboo flourished in the mild southerly climate of Kyūshu. For his work in bamboo herbal medicine Tohru had received the Japanese Order of the Sacred Treasure, which meant even more to him than his Nobel prize. The variegated splendor of bamboo and the terraces of mirror-perfect rice paddies reflecting pink-toned cloud contrasted with the shabby old corrugated iron research buildings and equipment sheds that lined the road down by the bay.

This part of the station, named for him, wasn't much to look at; government support for his studies was meager despite his eminence, and in order to keep the station operating, he was forced to accept grants from several of the corporations he had come to fear. But it had been his life's work, and to give it up was unthinkable. Almost every day he resisted both suggestions of retirement and offers from such megalithic companies as Actium International and Masunobu to do modest consulting work for handsome fees. What they wanted, of course, was his endorsement for their suicidally ambitious projects, which in turn were motivated by mindless greed.

They reached the airport, east of the city of Kumamoto, as the setting sun was turning the peaks and smokes of the nearby Aso volcanic range a brilliant mulberry red. They had five minutes to spare. For most of the journey Tohru had been silent, contemplative.

"Perhaps," he said to Hijame before they got out of the

chauffeured Nissan wagon, "we should schedule a news conference to follow my address tonight."

Hijame was surprised. Tohru explained.

"I believe there may be questions, many questions of interest to laymen, once I have spoken."

"But—there's so little time. And I know of nothing in your address that requires explication."

"I am making a last-minute change in subject matter."

"What—what will you be speaking of, Tohru-san?"

"Blight," Tohru said mildly. "Plague. Global catastrophe."

An official of All-Nippon Airways was at curbside to assist them. The ancient Buddhist temple in Kumamoto attracted many pilgrims, including a group of a hundred or more monks in saffron robes who had just deplaned from a charter flight; there was considerable crowding, shouting and confusion at the entrance to the terminal. For holy men, they had the manners of tyrants. Tohru received a buffeting that he endured with stoicism, although he was unused to the dehumanizing press of his countrymen. The combined efforts of the airline official and Hijame saw him safely through to the gate and the self-contained ramp of the Boeing 727.

There were only a few seats left on board. It was a businessman's commuter flight. Nearly all the passengers were reading high-tech newspapers or shuffling documents from their briefcases. Tohru and Hijame were separated by several rows. The plane left the gate as soon as Tohru had settled into his window seat.

Once they were airborne, climbing steeply away from the active crater of Aso and the streamers of fumarole gas issuing from it, Tohru took from a gold case one of the three cigarettes his doctor permitted him daily. He held it until the 727 reached its assigned altitude for the Kumamoto–Osaka leg of Flight 65 to Tokyo and the no-smoking sign was turned off.

When it was time, he relished the acrid cigarette, reclining with his eyes closed against the late glare of the sun magnified by the glass of the window by his head. He began worriedly to plan the speech he would make in a few hours, but his thoughts wandered; an annoyance. Perhaps it was time to meditate instead.

After more than half a century of practice he could meditate at any time, under any circumstances, in the special place he had set aside in his mind. In the time it took to recall one of the many poems he had composed as a young man, he was there.

On a mountain, a tree
alone in the wind.
From broken branches
an eagle flies toward
the sun.

One after another, he called upon the colors representative of the chakras of his physical self, gazed at his mountain fastness through windows of red, orange, yellow, purple, blue and green; and finally the color composed of all others, the color of pure energy: brilliant, foaming white light that ultimately surrounded him in his mind-mountain retreat, light that poured into him through an imaginary funnel at the top of his skull and quickly suffused every cell of his body. Revivifying, energizing light.

When he returned from his meditation and looked out the window again, Flight 65 was over the terraced islands of the Inland Sea. The bay and port city of Hiroshima, an earthbound constellation of lights, had come into view sixty kilometers to the north. Hiroshima, where on the sixth of August, 1945, at eight-fifteen in the morning, the mushroom-cloud symbol of an era of technology both lethal and wonderful had been visited on the world. Hijame Ujihara still bore scar tissue on his body from that atomic dawn, despite the many excruciating operations he had endured as a young man.

Not too many years ago Tohru had accompanied his grandsons to the reborn city of Hiroshima, the Peace Park cenotaph and the skeletal memorial to holocaust, which drew throngs of tourists and devout pacifists every year. Of course the boys were too young to appreciate what they saw, what he had to tell them about the war Japan had lost. It meant little to them; it was ancient history.

From devastation and humiliation, with the assistance of

their conquerors, the Japanese had surged back, staking their future on the brilliance of their scientists and technicians, spending ten billion in fees and royalties for foreign technology, stealing what couldn't be bought. From these resources, they had built a different kind of juggernaut.

Now Japan was the world leader in robotics and optical electronics. Forging ahead of the competition in genetic engineering, semiconductors, energy research. Artificial blood had been invented in Osaka. In modern plants industrial robots worked around the clock assembling parts for still more robots. His elder son, a software-company executive, lived in a modern home in which everything, from his bedroom drapes to the temperature of his sauna to the rice cooker in the kitchen, was monitored and controlled by a microcomputer. *His* sons played a vast assortment of video games on a different computer, spoke a language of time warps and hyperspace drives.

Tohru thought of his own quiet childhood, of the four hundred varieties of butterflies he'd collected, the ship models he'd constructed of rush and reed, the poems painstakingly brushed onto rice paper. But he had no quarrels with the entertainment and marvels of this day. His only quarrel was with the singlemindedness of a government obsessed by technology, with giant companies thinking only of profits five years in the future while ignoring all the signs that a famine of unprecedented proportions could lie just ahead.

All the distant early warnings had sounded. But Tohru was not pessimistic. He believed that, once the powerful men of industry were fully aware of the danger, once they saw, under stringently controlled conditions and through the use of computer-constructed models, what the Cirenaica spore was capable of, they would begin voluntarily to reverse policies and decisions that had brought the world so close to disaster.

The first move, Demetrios Aravanis had agreed, was up to him; and the forum was immediately available.

Tohru reached under the seat in front of him for his briefcase. Growing heavier and heavier with each day. He would need another one soon, if he felt compelled to carry so much work wherever he went.

In the right-hand pocket of his suit coat he groped for the cassette, which contained a record of everything he had thought and observed about the spore since receiving his portion of the core sample almost a year and a half ago.

He opened the case on his lap, took out his Sanyo recorder and the ear-button attachment, put the tape in the machine. The man sitting next to him had nodded off; his head was almost on Tohru's right shoulder. Tohru gently realigned him in his seat. The man blinked at him and went back to sleep.

The Boeing 727, now fifty kilometers due south of Hiroshima at twenty-three thousand feet, banked to the right over Yashiro Island as the captain made a course correction. Tohru listened to the tape.

"*This is Minotaur*," the unfamiliar voice said in his ear.

Tohru started nervously.

The voice, on what he had thought was the Cirenaica tape, had been altered electronically until it was impossible to say if it came from a man or a machine. But the words, in English, were understandable.

Minotaur!

"*It would have been simpler,*" the voice continued, "*if you had chosen to cooperate with me, and sold me the data I now possess despite your stubbornness. Hijame Ujihara believes the tape he has substituted is blank. His price for betraying you was three million yen.*"

Tohru twisted in his seat, disturbing the sleeping man, and looked around: he saw the frightened eyes of Hijame staring at him just over the top of a seat five rows back.

"*He has no suspicion that he is about to die. Nor will you live, Tohru Mukaiba, to oppose me.*"

Tohru stood up, the well-stocked attaché case falling from his lap. The slim black cord was pulled from the socket of the cassette recorder and dangled by the earplug.

Minotaur!

At the airport, he thought. Hijame must have passed the Cirenaica tape to someone in the crowd. All the monks looked alike in their yellow robes; an imposter easily could have joined their ranks.

His secretary for more than twenty-five years, a man he thought of, treated as, a son. . . .

Tohru's brains were boiling. "Hijame!" he shouted. "What else have you—"

At that instant the narrow tape in his recorder fed a signal, recorded at a different frequency from the rest of the tape, through the heads. The shrill signal no one heard was transmitted to a compact detonator, weighing a little more than two ounces. It was concealed in the attaché case, which had been taken from Tohru four days ago when he was busy elsewhere, disassembled and then rebuilt expertly, with the added weight of some thirty ounces of plastic explosive in sheet form placed between layers of framing and worn leather. Within an hour it was back on the spot on his worktable from which it had been removed.

The attaché case exploded, disintegrating Tohru where he stood, shredding seats all around. The explosion beheaded the man in the seat next to him, removed the face of the man on the aisle and caved in his chest, blew out two windows nearest the site of the bomb, cratered the floor and jaggedly opened the ceiling. Everything not belted down or stowed away within a radius of fifteen feet of the rent in the side of the aircraft was sucked into space, a streaming sewer of trash and macerated garbage that had been men.

Alarm bells sounded as the cabin was depressurized and became filled with dense fog. Oxygen masks tumbled from the overhead compartments. The captain put the plane into a dive; a flight attendant was thrown upside down against the ceiling and her neck was broken. One hundred twenty-seven surviving passengers and attendants screamed in the dark.

The plane dove at an angle of forty-five degrees toward the lights of the fishing boats bobbing off Yashiro Island.

Fanned by the fierce airstream, the small fires that had started in mangled and shorted wiring became a larger fire sweeping through the cabin as the captain struggled to maintain control of his aircraft.

At eleven thousand feet he changed the angle of descent and headed for an emergency landing at an airfield in

Matsuyama, twenty-three kilometers east-southeast on the coast of Shikoku.

For nearly five long minutes he was able to keep the badly damaged aircraft in the air and on course to safety. But in the cabin, those passengers who were not on oxygen were stifled by smoke and the numerous deadly gases, such as hydrogen cyanide, given off by the rapid burning of synthetic materials. And all of them were roasted alive. The lucky ones never knew. The unlucky, including Hijame Ujihara, remained conscious to the end.

Listening to their tortured screams, the captain went insane with horror at the controls. Still he kept flying. Until his hair burst into flame.

The 727, a hurtling pyre, slanted over on the left wing, grazed and then crashed thunderously against one of the far-flung collections of barren rockpiles four kilometers off Shikoku, six and a half kilometers from the end of the east-west runway at the field.

About two minutes' flying time at just above stalling speed.

Patrol boats and helicopters of the *Kaijo Huancho*, the Japanese Coast Guard, were on the scene within minutes. But nothing could be done. There were no survivors.

Chapter 3

Corfu, Greece

Demetrios Constantine Aravanis took the news of the death of his friend and esteemed colleague hard. When he heard about it, he stopped working on the paper he was revising for the *Institut National de la Recherche Agronomique* on the elimination of acid toxicity from his new variety of winter rapeseed and spent the rest of the day sailing along the Paleokastritsa coast. The boy went with him. The boy he could talk to, tell him everything that was on his mind and know that not another living soul would ever hear what he'd had to say.

"Coincidence?" Aravanis said above the hiss of the waves and the formidable spanking of the Ionian wind against his ears. "Possibly. It shouldn't take long to be certain."

He wasn't thinking of the months of labor that would go into dredging pieces of the shattered airliner from Kumomoto Bay and reassembling them in some vacant hangar so that investigators could justify suspicions of sabotage, conclude just where on board the explosion had taken place. Aravanis had his own criteria.

The boy looked around at him again, without expression, from his seat in the cockpit of the forty-foot trimaran yacht, which was four and a half streamlined tons of cedar, Cephalonian fir and teak. They were slicing through dark water at just under twenty-eight knots, one hull completely exposed, poised like a dagger above the bubbling, rushing surface of the fabled Greek sea.

It was a boat built for speed and excitement, more than most men could handle alone; it required the utmost in seamanship to sail a trimaran, particularly on a day of cold and tricky winds. But all of Aravanis's family had been sailors, going back three hundred years. Mariners' genes were a birthright. Reversing the final trek of Odysseus, who on the advice of a blind seer, had walked inland with an oar on his shoulder and planted it, thus achieving peace, his ancestors had forsaken the land and gone down to the turbulent sea to confront their ultimate destiny. They had been horn-handed fishermen (and pirates and smugglers when necessity demanded), then builders, first of simple fishing boats and inter-island caiques, and finally of larger oceangoing fleets. They'd become rich from the sea after World War Two, had grown richer still in the Byzantine game of diversification, acquiring and pyramiding companies around the world. Aravanis, Melissani, Coulouris. Intermarried, interlocked, the names represented immense power beneath a single banner: Actium International.

Demetrios Constantine Aravanis, virtually orphaned during the Italian and then the German occupation, had little to do with the cousins, although they were always on cordial terms. In his youth it was obvious that he had no business sense: any half-wit could cheat him out of his modest possessions. Nor did he seem to care about money. These were grievous failings in any Greek. He liked the sea but was happiest when breaking his back in the olive groves, stooping under the hot sun in a vineyard to examine the results of a stem graft. By the age of fourteen he had decided he wanted to be an agronomist. The family eccentric. His cousins gladly left him to his own pursuits. They supported him as he dawdled through universities, taking eight years to complete his studies, and provided him with funds he needed for his research. They expected nothing in return.

Even when he did his best to explain, they didn't understand what he was up to. Genetic pools? Cell fusion? Hybridizing agents? What was the use of it anyway? Poor Demetrios Constantine. But his experiments eventually had generated considerable profits for the Actium companies holding patents on the results. After so many years the cousins took notice of the many academic honors coming his way, as well as the hefty profits, and extended their full approval. Demetrios Constantine was oblivious to this change in his status. But then he rarely paid attention to anything that went on outside his hundred acres, the fertile estate he had created for himself in the eastern foothills of Pantokrátor, the great mountain of the north.

The wind shifted suddenly; he tacked across the foaming waves, and for a few moments they were all but soaring in the oddly shaped boat, at an angle to sky and water, skimming along at a breathtaking pace. He and the boy were drenched with spume. Aravanis laughed and shook his head; droplets of water flew from his salt-and-pepper beard in the sparkling sea light. There was always danger with this boat: acceptable danger, given his ability. But he knew the unpredictable wind could snatch control from him, cause the multihull vessel to capsize or pitch-pole, flip spectacularly end over end.

The boy was wearing an orange flotation vest with a safety line clipped to it. But when he showed his drenched face to Aravanis, his expression was untroubled. He had never shown fear of anything in the natural world. Which was why his sudden fits of hysteria and frenzied cowering, in response to some dark apocalypse of his disordered mind, were difficult for Aravanis and his wife Ourania to endure. Thank God they came less frequently these days. Their hope was that he would outgrow the seizures entirely, enjoy a measure of peace within his impenetrable world.

Although in the eyes of the cousins he had married beneath him, the marriage had been happy. But childless. After twelve years without issue, it was determined that he, not Ourania, was the barren one.

Demetrios Constantine was deeply wounded by his lack. He resisted all suggestions that they adopt children. Until the *Papas* from the orphanage at Pelekas had shown Ourania the ravishing infant with the cool, unblinking green eyes. Born with a caul, the *Papas* said. An auspicious omen. But there was a danger in cauls as well, and a virus had almost killed the baby twenty-four hours after his birth. He was free of fever now and had been brought to the orphanage fathers from the mainland, through arrangements made at the highest level of the church.

This was almost all the *Papas* knew, except for some whispered gossip. The boy was illegitimate, of course, but not the issue of peasants. Impressive bloodlines were hinted at, although it wasn't sensible to speculate on his origins.

For the second time in her life, Ourania was in love.

She was sure that Aravanis, once he fell under the gaze of this unusual boy, would not be able to resist him either.

She was right.

He was christened Nikolas Spyridon, after her father and the Corfiote patron saint. He ate well, grew strong and seldom cried. He was never sick again. He sat up early, began cutting teeth and was absorbed in his toys. He loved to pull his father's beard and mimic his mother's laughter. Occasionally a shadow would darken his green eyes and he would lie motionless in his bed, staring at nothing, for an hour or more; no amount of animated coaxing could prompt an answering expression. But when the spell passed, he was full of life again.

Not until he was nearly a year old did they realize that something was seriously wrong with Niko.

His hearing was tested by one specialist after another. They flew him to Switzerland, to Paris. Although he could hear certain high-pitched sounds, like the whistling of a teakettle, or birdsong, all the doctors said he was functionally deaf. It was a blow but not a catastrophe. He was still beautiful, loving, intelligent; his eyes were like emeralds.

Niko walked early. He had the coordination of a born athlete, the shoulders of a little bull. He could not speak at the age of two, seldom uttered any sound. But he seemed to substitute for language an intuitive, almost psychic, grasp of what was wanted, expected, of him; he communicated with them on a level beyond their understanding.

Then, almost overnight, he simply went away.

He walked back through a labyrinth to a cave in the darkest recesses of his mind, hunkered down and stayed there.

He no longer demonstrated interest in his toys, his picture books, the animals of the farm. He had frequent shuddering seizures, dark blood suffusing his face, the pure green of his eyes turning muddy from unspeakable grief. Either he huddled whimpering in a far corner of his room or he went running wildly through the house, breaking things, shouting incoherently. When they tried to restrain him, Niko bit and clawed. He made no further attempts to feed himself. Nor did he pay the slightest attention to where he made his toilet. He had become totally an animal, with only flashes of the old Niko to sustain them in their tragedy.

They learned the word for this sort of child, the aberrant behavior: autistic.

A school is the only answer, the experts counseled. Very expensive. But by then money was not a problem. They visited schools for autistic children, received encouragement from the teachers and saw children, much older, whom they thought were in far worse shape than Niko. Could he hope to improve in the company of children like these? They took him home.

Aravanis and his wife prayed daily to St. Spyridon and St. Gerasimos, who healed sick minds and bodies; and they set about making a new life for Niko and themselves.

The boy had not lost his coordination. One blessing. The more savage his behavior, the more beautiful he became. He was godlike in his tantrums, but when the peaceful spells occurred he could be loving and devoted, as they were to him.

They knew they would find a way to lead him out of the labyrinth that existed in his mind. They read everything they could find on autism, talked for hours to parents of other autistic children around the world. There were a few stories of nearly complete recovery after arduous years of retraining, unflinching dedication. Such stories strengthened their faith.

Niko's condition, it was agreed, was perhaps worsened by his hearing problem. As one doctor put it, he was an audiological enigma. But Demetrios Constantine learned that there were others, hearing-impaired like Niko, who were being helped through new technology.

Niko was flown, sedated, to New York in an Actium jet lent by the cousins. At Columbia Presbyterian Hospital he underwent the most thorough auditory testing of his young life.

The audiologist, whose name was Meyerson, gave them the first real hope they'd had in five years.

"Niko still has the capacity to hear, but only at very high frequencies. He is totally deaf in the lower registers."

"Would a hearing aid help?" Ourania asked.

"Not the conventional type. An ordinary hearing aid could result in acoustic trauma that would destroy what hearing he has left. But there is a device we've recently developed that translates low-frequency sounds, such as human speech and most music, into a range where Niko can hear them. It's a magnetic earphone with two channels. One channel amplifies high-pitched sounds; the other will shift lower pitches to the ultra-audiometric range."

Niko didn't like the looks of the battery pack and the tiny earphone. For a week he resisted all efforts to get him to try it. Meyerson suggested they place the phone receiver over his ear while he was asleep and play music, something soothing.

It worked beautifully. Except for high-pitched whistles, screams and hisses, the first sounds Niko heard were those of Elgar's Violin Concerto in B minor.

He loved music, and there was good music everywhere in the house: Demetrios Constantine had a collection of more than five hundred classical recordings, and Ourania played the mandolin. Niko heard her play for the first time and was fascinated. She had a sweet, wistful voice, but she had not felt like singing for several years. Now she sang all the time. Niko watched her lips carefully. While he was listening to music, he was calm, orderly. They enjoyed hours of peace in their home. Demetrios Constantine got his appetite back and put on twenty pounds, four extra inches around his waist. Niko began to bathe himself again, to play with his building blocks and to feed himself, at least with his fingers. All to music. He went to sleep to Brahms or Bartok, awakened to *kantades*, folk ballads. Evenings he would sit on the floor of the terrace, immersed in rhapsodic sounds, while his mother and father drank coffee, nibbled at Ourania's nut-filled baklava and sickle-pear preserves and talked.

By accident, Aravanis discovered his son Niko's gift.

That day Ourania had been to visit her mother at the cottage near Potomi and had returned with butter and cheeses, the best produced on Corfu, and rich helpings of gossipy news: betrothals, infidelities, feuds.

Aravanis was drowsy from his evening meal, trying not to nod as Ourania prattled on. He became aware that the stylus of the tone arm had stuck in a groove of the old recording that Niko was listening to. He got up to adjust it, deciding to replay the Mozart *Prague* symphony from the beginning.

After only a few notes of music, Niko spoke, loud and clear.

He was by then nearly ten years old. He'd had his hearing aid for seven months. To that moment he had never spoken an intelligible word. Suddenly they heard whole sentences, an outpouring.

". . . On the Feast of the Virgin, he took her to Athens. For three days! To visit his old sister at the clinic, they said. Ha! She is terribly spoiled by his attentions. She thinks he is so rich because he owns a *cafenion* and vineyards. But his vineyards produced only a hundred barrels of wine this year. And his children. They are up in arms. They should try before it's too late to tell him a thing or two about Thelxi. . . ."

Niko was simply repeating, word for word, inflection for inflection, what Ourania had been saying minutes before.

Ourania looked startled, then terrified. She screamed and ran from the terrace.

Niko looked solemnly after her, a hint of a frown on his face.

"*There is nothing nobler,*" he said, "*than when two people who see eye-to-eye keep house as man and wife, confounding their enemies and delighting their friends.*"

These were the words of Odysseus, written by Homer; Aravanis had just quoted them to his wife as a gentle rebuke before getting up to adjust the tone arm on the Bang and Olafsson turntable.

After that, Niko listened to the music and spoke no more, even when Aravanis knelt in front of him to claim his attention and said several times, sharply, "Niko!"

Then he went in search of his wife, who knelt trembling on the *prie-dieu* in their bedroom, having lighted a tableful of candles to the *Panagia*, the Holy Virgin, and all the saints and angels represented on their iconostasis and who, they hoped, favored them in their daily lives. The room was already stifling from candles.

"Ourania—"

"A miracle! You heard him! All of our prayers are answered, Demetrios Constantine!"

He wasn't so sure. But his wife was beside herself with ecstasy, weeping. Better to leave her alone for now. He returned to the terrace. Niko didn't look at him.

Aravanis said to his son, this time in English, which he spoke fluently: "No matter what this means, no matter where we go from here, you will always be the light and joy of our souls."

Silence, except for the music. Aravanis stared at the record on the turntable, then suspended the stylus. He moved the tone arm back slightly, restarted the movement. He heard the music they'd just been listening to. Then he heard the words he'd said to Niko. As he had suspected, they had no meaning for the boy. He could only repeat them.

Aravanis turned off the music again. Niko fidgeted on the mat where he was sitting in shorts and sneakers, and he touched the side of his head where the earphone was. Aravanis switched on the television. The satellite dish on the side of the hill near the house brought in more than a hundred channels from around the world. A fashion show, narrated in Swedish, appeared. He let Niko hear a snatch of the Mozart, then narration from the channel in Stockholm, then the same few bars of Mozart again.

Niko repeated what he'd just heard on the television. His Swedish was flawless (Aravanis assumed).

Eventually they learned what it was. Their hopes that Niko would someday be completely normal were severely blighted.

A neurologist at the University of Athens Hospital tried to describe Niko's condition to them.

The human brain, he said, was the most wonderful and complex object on earth. Investigators had gained some understanding of how it worked, but their knowledge was drastically incomplete. A surgeon could point to the area of the brain where memory was contained, a complete record of everything the individual had seen or heard in his lifetime. Just one day's sensory input was astonishing: the brain was capable of processing twelve hundred bits of information per second. As long as the memory neurons went undamaged, the record would remain intact. But, as Nabokov said, "Speak, Memory." Some people had eidetic recall of routine conversations from twenty years earlier, and others had trouble remembering their current phone number. The storage system was perfect; access to the storehouse was hit or miss. What keyed the retrieval process?

"In Niko's case, the music he hears prior to additional audio input acts as a kind of access code."

"Can he also remember what he sees?" Aravanis asked.

"Perfectly. But he hasn't the means to express what he sees. He can say the word 'chair' in twenty-seven different languages if he hears it. But show him a chair and he will make no connection between the object and the spoken word."

"Will he ever be able to do this?"

"I've looked at the most recent NMR scans. A fantastic diagnostic tool, by the way. There is no structural damage; his brain appears completely normal. It simply misfires, malfunctions in a crucial way. Perhaps a school devoted to—"

"No," Ourania said, and they took Niko home again, to his sunny room and his music, the open fields and mild, healthful climate of the valley where he had been raised. Miracles had happened thus far; the possibility of another blessing from the saints was not to be dismissed.

Now in the trimaran, Demetrios Constantine and Niko, having rounded Cape Falakron, slanted closer to the palisades north of Paleokastritsa, the most beautiful coastline in Greece.

The crags and precipices rose nearly nine hundred feet from the level of the roaring sea and numerous intricately cut bays and inlets along the shore. The wind was constantly shifting, requiring Aravanis's total vigilance to prevent a spill as he searched for a calm harbor he had visited before. Dolphins leaped abeam, attracting the boy's eyes; he mimicked their wave-top arabesques with his hands.

They had their lunch on a protected acre of crescent sand beach, an overhang of raven-haunted rocks at their backs, tidal lagoon for the trimaran in front of them. It was warmer here; the mid-afternoon sun shone directly on them through wisps of spray from the reef. The jutting lower cliff face, a roosting ground for seabirds, was white with bird droppings.

The boy ate what was handed to him: cold roast chicken and chunks of tender kid, bread and feta cheese. They drank red wine from a goatskin, wine from the best vineyard in all of Greece: Aravanis's own. Then they explored the small beach, which was unpolluted by either tourists, who had overrun the fine strands of Ermones Bay to the southeast, or tar from the oil tankers. On his Sony Walkman, Niko listened to Police and Duran Duran, to Bruce Springsteen and Elvis Costello. Demetrios Constantine stayed alert for messages on the radio in the small cabin located in the middle hull of the trimaran. He had dialed the volume all the way up, but because of the intervening cliffs, he had little hope that Ourania could reach him here, even if she received the news he was expecting.

Niko could reproduce his name now, with a large crayon or a stick to write with in the sand. And he knew what the marks he made stood for. He was twelve. It was a small breakthrough, a milestone of sorts.

"You are Niko," Demetrios Constantine would say over and over, and the boy obediently watched his lips, sometimes moving his own. "Niko, my son."

It startled him to hear his wife's voice, calling faintly from the farm through broadsides of static. He sat the boy down on a piece of driftwood and plunged toward the trimaran.

"Yes . . . yes . . . Ourania. Can you hear me?"

The farm was less than fifteen kilometers overland from

where he had anchored, but her voice was a flyspeck of sound.

"Mukaiba station . . . Norishige says . . . trace of Cirenaica . . . repeat, no trace . . . all samples missing . . . come in, Demetrios Constantine. Are you receiving?"

"I hear you, Ourania. Leaving now. I'll be home before dark."

Shuddering, he waded through a light chop back to the beach. The boy was where he had left him, sitting very still. A hermit crab picked its way slowly up one sleeve of Niko's sweater. The boy studied it with cool imperturbability.

Aravanis brushed the crab away and sat down beside his son. After a few moments, he took the boy in his arms. Aravanis had stopped trembling, but he was heartsick and afraid. There would be no more outings like this one in the days to come. Spores were missing. Inconceivable that such a thing could happen. They all had known the danger. Now nothing lay ahead but work, mind-numbing work. And what should he say to the others? He was reasonably certain that madmen had murdered Tohru Mukaiba, destroying a whole planeload of innocent people merely to ensure one man's silence.

But he had no proof. Only remarks that Tohru, perplexed by it all, had made to him on the telephone recently.

"Well, what have you heard from Minotaur?" Tohru had asked jokingly, only hours before his death.

Aravanis was certain that he himself was months ahead of the others in his research. Sharing what he knew with Pinto, or Ridgway in Iowa, might now prove dangerous if they were all being watched.

Minotaur.

Of what value was Cirenaica to anyone else, except as an instrument for the total destruction of humanity?

Tears rolled down his weathered cheeks and into his beard as he contemplated the face of his beloved son.

"I think they may kill me too," he said. "But the cousins will see to it that any man who tries will risk more than he can hope to gain. You and Ourania will be safe, Niko. And I swear that whoever they are, they will never get what they want from me.''

He picked Niko up in his arms and waded out to the trimaran.

''We have much to do, you and I,'' he said exuberantly to the boy. ''Tonight, yes; we must begin tonight.''

Chapter 4

San Juan, Puerto Rico

The woman for whom Cesár de Milagros Pagán had resolved to forsake all others was inflicting sweet pain on his body as the gale-force winds of tropical storm Hector lashed the city, crossing the island in a southwesterly direction, moving from the South Atlantic toward the Caribbean Sea.

Miriam, kneeling on her bed, was face down in his naked lap. She moved her jaws back and forth in a delicate grinding motion, a mock-decapitation that he felt, shuddering, to the soles of his feet, which made his heart beat so frantically he thought it might burst. Her hair was in abundant disarray, streaks of blonde, streaks of mahogany red, lipstick ear-to-ear. She liked to put on a lot of lipstick before sex, caking her lips, making a big, whorish mouth that eventually he nibbled down to a virginal primness.

Rafaela, through fourteen years of marriage and three children, had steadfastly refused to take him in her mouth. But Rafaela was seldom on his mind these days, even when he was in the same bed with her.

"You goddam great *machista, solamente tu puedes chingarme asi*!" Miriam celebrated, letting his *bicho* slip from between her lips. She now grasped it in both hands, beginning a new kind of desirable torture, a washerwoman's wring-ing motion that caused his lower jaw to sag and fried the roots of his hair.

"No, I can't last, be quick!" he begged, forcing her to lay back.

When they had both come they lay together exhausted, now feeling the storm that buffeted the building in which Miriam, professionally known as Yoélis, had the third-floor apartment. The wind was like a great sighing breath, exhaling, inhaling, threatening to rip the closed louvers from the window frames. The lights in the bedroom had dimmed several times and now were just a ghostly bronze radiance, incapable of casting shadows around the mirrored walls. Winds of sixty to sixty-five miles per hour, and gaining strength as the storm cut a swath inland. Rain came in sweeping salvos, in blinding sheets. But the old building that faced the harbor from the hillside street dated from 1750; it had withstood many violent tropical blows and was as durable as the pitted gray wall of earthwork and stone that partially enclosed San Juan Antiguo, the old city. The building, like many others on the narrow streets around La Forteleza, the Governor's residence, had been gutted and restored, and the apartments it contained were luxurious.

Miriam was twenty-six, a graduate of the Inter-American University. She acted frequently in many of the locally produced *novelas*, television soap operas, that were enormously popular throughout the Spanish-speaking western hemisphere.

Cesár de Milagros Pagán, like almost every Puerto Rican male, had a nickname. He was known as "Pinto." He was forty-three. He wore glasses, his scalp was bare in a little circle at the back of his skull, he had put on too much weight through the years. But he was her heart's delight. Miraculously, he had all her love. Alternately terrified or manic with joy, Pinto was going through his major mid-life crisis: wallowing in troughs of self-recrimination, climbing to peaks from where nothing of his old, decent, respected life looked good to him anymore.

His middle child, Eulalia, would be frightened by the storm. She would be asking where daddy was.

But Miriam was a little frightened too, he could tell. He

put a hand to her fluttering heart, sneaked a look at the cabinet clock in one corner of her bedroom.

Twenty-five after ten. Falkner had said ten-thirty, but he was driving in from Santa Maria. The ferocity of the storm, flooding in the low places of the road by Miramar, would delay him. Still, Pinto knew he should be getting dressed.

Miriam sensed his nerves. She opened her eyes, putting a hand on his shoulder.

"Pinto, you should not go out in a storm like this," she said. "And you promised, you said you would spend the entire night with me."

"I'll be gone only an hour. Less. It's important."

"What is important?"

"Business. A meeting."

"Where?"

He meant to be vague. It just slipped out.

"The castle."

Miriam sat up, wide-eyed. "El Morro? At this time of night, in this weather?"

"No, no, no, I meant—we are meeting with a man named Collins. A senior vice-president, from New York. He is in the Castle Suite at the Caribe, which is reserved for the exclusive use of company executives when they come to the island."

"It should wait until morning," she said, pouting.

Fifty thousand dollars, Pinto thought, his mouth drying up. *In an hour, I will have fifty thousand dollars. And no one has to know.*

"I—I think I'd better take a bath now."

"*We* will take a bath," she said, giving his earlobe a mischievous twist. Sometimes, when he'd disappointed her in an obscure way, she dug a fingernail in at the last moment. Tonight she was gentle.

They were soaping and scrubbing each other—he enjoyed the ritual of the lipstick, but it was damned hard to remove all traces after—when she laid her head like a child on his hairy shoulder and said, "Will you be mad if I tell you something?"

"I can never be angry with you, *negrita*."

"The rent is overdue. That pig Delgado has called up, and I just don't have the money this month." She explained in a rush, gesticulating, soapsuds flying from her fingers and stinging him in the eye: "The trip to New York was very expensive, and then Amparo, the *puta*, wouldn't let me stay at her apartment as she promised, her lover was in town too, and I had to go to a hotel. The prices in that stinking city—*coño*! —and then those bastards at the audition did not treat me with the respect I deserve. I have been acting in the theater since I was fourteen. Do they think we have no theatrical tradition here?"

"I know, I know, it's difficult for you," he murmured, his mind not on the explanation, which he was familiar with. He kissed her. "Don't worry about the money. I'll have it for you—tomorrow."

"It will be for only a few days! I'll pay you back. I always pay you back, Pinto."

This was true. She repaid him ten cents, twenty cents on the dollar. He didn't care. He wanted her to be well-dressed, to have the expensive Botello prints she coveted for what he thought of as *their* apartment. He only wished she would stay away from the casinos, where she played recklessly at roulette on those boring, interminable nights when they could not be together.

Bathing him, she took up a fold of midsection flab between thumb and forefinger. "You must spend more time at the health club."

"I know, I know. I'll have the time soon."

He had never worked so hard as he had during the past few months. Getting by on two or three hours' sleep a night. A stranger to his children. How simple it could all be, except for the children! Taking off Rafaela like a well-worn shirt, frayed at the collar. Dressing himself in the dazzling silks of Miriam, resplendent in his recalled youth. How he'd had the stamina to make love as often as she demanded he would never know. But the hours he had invested in the Cirenaica spore were about to pay an undreamed-of dividend. Thanks to Falkner.

Once more Pinto felt a twinge of conscience, of burning remorse. His discovery properly belonged to his company, to

Lortrex, by contract. By law. Very shortly he would be breaking the law. What if—

Fool.

All he could expect from the company, which surely would profit from his discovery in sums beyond his ability to calculate, was a bonus for Christmas. Twenty-five hundred dollars perhaps. Once he would have been grateful. Before Miriam came along and the scales fell from his eyes.

They would not name the radically new, bioengineered dwarf variety of seed after him. That was company policy.

He had always known that he was not brilliant, a trail-blazer who belonged in the distinguished company of Vavilov, Borlaug, Aravanis, the late Mukaiba. He was a plodder. He'd had some luck in his career, made some contributions, earned the approval of his peers.

This time it was more than luck: a combination of money and technical resources had produced, if not a miracle, a breakthrough in recombinant agricultural technology that was ten years ahead of its time.

Lortrex would snatch it all away. In another twenty years or so, he would have a gold watch and a pension to show for his loyalty.

In the meantime he earned thirty-eight thousand dollars a year. There were two mortgages on the house in Parkville that Rafaela had insisted they buy, tuition for two of the children in private schools. He had two hundred twenty dollars in his personal account at Banco de Ponce. In the past six months he had spent nearly eight thousand on his *inamorata*. All he had saved or could borrow. His car, a '76 Datsun sedan, was falling to pieces.

Fuck the company.

Miriam lingered in the bath while he got out and dried himself, holding his stomach in should she glance his way.

As Pinto was buttoning one of the *guayaberras* he kept at the apartment the lights went out, probably for the rest of the night. Miriam squealed in the tub. They had candles and a hurricane lamp ready. He lit the lamp and carried it to her.

There was a lull in the wind. Below, in the Plazuela de la Rogativa, he heard a car horn sound impatiently.

Falkner. It was ten forty-seven.

"You can't leave me now," Miriam wailed. "Not in the dark!"

"Courage." His hands trembled as he put the lamp down. "I will be back before you know it."

He had left the Duraflask on the shelf of the foyer closet. It looked very much like an ordinary thermos bottle; fully loaded, it weighed only a couple of pounds. He put the Duraflask in a plastic shopping bag and reached for a flashlight.

He had decided that fifty thousand wasn't enough. He was going to ask for more money.

His boldness, his greed, distressed him, causing stomach cramps.

Be a man, Pinto admonished himself as he closed the door of the apartment behind him. Under the circumstances, the contents of the Duraflask he held was worth hundreds of millions . . . who knew? A *billion* dollars.

"They know that," he said under his breath. "I know it. They will pay whatever I ask."

The skylight above the stairs was leaking badly, a drip that was almost a waterfall. The wind, renewed, moaned ferociously. He shuddered as he went down the steps, a metallic taste of fear on his tongue.

Pinto had a difficult time forcing the downstairs door open against the howling wind. Rain half-blinded him; he was almost blown down on the sidewalk as he made his way to the pale-blue BMW that Falkner was driving. The power of the storm was terrifying. Palm fronds lay in the street. The headlights of the car were obscured by the torrent. He clawed open the door on the passenger side of the sedan and sank into the seat.

"I've been leaning on the horn for ten minutes," Falkner complained. "What's the matter, your little *chingona* couldn't get enough tonight?"

Falkner was one of those continentals who never troubled to learn much Spanish except for vulgarisms, who treated all Puerto Ricans with thinly veiled contempt. He was almost fifty years old and slaved to look thirty-five. Short dyed hair, much flashy dental work. He'd had his eyes done in the past couple of years. He had been a hockey player in his youth and still kept his body in excellent condition. He was branch manager of Lortrex's island operation; middle-level management was as far as he was going to go. He was glib and hearty with his superiors, treacherous to subordinates. There was not a likable bone in his body.

Falkner looked at the Duraflask Pinto was holding in his lap.

"A goddam thermos bottle? Is that where you keep it?" He seemed a little suspicious. There were tension lines around his mouth.

"This is no ordinary thermos. It's lined with Pyrex and filled with liquid nitrogen. Very cold."

"The stuff survives in liquid nitrogen?"

"The cultures are inside aluminum ampules. And the theoretical life of embryonic tissues in such an environment is at least one hundred thousand years."

Two months earlier Falkner had become aware of Pinto's findings about the new, amazingly hardy strain that Pinto had dubbed *El Invicto*: The Unvanquished. Until that time Falkner had had little to do with the AgriTech Research Division, a blessing as far as Pinto was concerned. Pinto stuck to his lab and the fields and stayed out of everyone's way.

Suddenly there was Falkner in Building One-C near Humacao, buddy-buddy, effusively complimentary.

"This may be one hell of a thing you've come up with," he said. "Who knows about it?"

"No one." Pinto had full autonomy in his section. Research assistants had done many of the cloning and gene-splicing experiments for him during the past two and a half years, which was standard procedure. The cumulative results were known to Pinto alone. And now to Falkner.

Falkner had Pinto's report with him, the original. Pinto had put it together himself on a word processor.

"This is all in the computer?"

"Of course. As unorganized data."

Falkner tapped the edge of the bound report against his pearly teeth. He smiled and smiled, looking around the large humid lab facility.

"Nice setup. I guess I should be spending more of my time finding out what you do around here."

Pinto's reports to management were punctual and exhaustive. He looked puzzled.

"Keep up the good work," Falkner said. "For now, I'm not going to pass this on to Geneva. I want to study it for a while. By the way, let's have dinner one night next week."

Falkner took him to the Rotisserie at the Caribe Hilton. The best steaks and prime rib on the island. Falkner didn't care for spic food.

"How's your love life?" he asked Pinto as they finished the sixty-dollar bottle of burgundy Falkner had considered appropriate with Chateaubriand.

Pinto was afraid all his guilty feelings had flashed on his face at that instant. He lowered his head, shrugged noncommittally.

"Keeping that little *bombón* of yours must be *muy expensivo*. Huh? I know what those apartments go for down around La Forteleza." Falkner leaned forward in his chair, hands clasped on the tablecloth. He belched slightly and grinned. "Matter of fact, lately I have taken the time to find out everything there is to know about your income, and your outgo." He shook his head, commiserating. "The old balance sheet doesn't look so hot these days, Pinto. And there's the matter of that added tax liability. The meter just keeps running on that one, piling up interest and penalties."

Pinto swallowed hard in alarm and indignation. It was like being violated in public. He wouldn't look at Falkner.

Falkner said, "Hey, Pinto. You want to know something? I'm in worse shape than you are. I'm long past the point where I can even-up by jiggling the expense account around. Hell, everybody I know is living too high, spending what they haven't got. It's a goddam feeding frenzy, before the whole economy comes tumbling down around our heads. Now I say, if the opportunity presents itself for a man to lay some bucks by and nobody's the wiser, he's a fool not to take advantage. Want coffee?"

Pinto shook his head numbly. Falkner ordered coffee for

himself, Armagnac for two. When the drinks came he lit a long green cigar, not taking his eyes off Pinto.

"You and I are the lucky ones, *'mano*. The finger of fortune is pointing at this table tonight. We can fandango our way out of the financial minefield we've been trapped in. I have a buyer for *El Invicto*."

"A buyer? What are you talking about? It belongs—"

"Sure, sure. It's company property. That is, if the company knows what it's got in the first place. But they never will know. Does it matter to you or me which multinational markets *El Invicto*? Is it going to change the future of the world? Shit no. You're not a businessman. Let me tell you what business is, Pinto. Business is a whorehouse. You can let the head whores peddle your tail cheap if you want to. Or you can find out if your tail's worth a little more on down the street."

Pinto drank his Armagnac, which deadened his tongue. He didn't want to talk anyway. Falkner savored his cigar, paid the check, tipped generously and gave the maitre d' a hug on the way out. They stood for a couple of minutes outside the hotel's casino. Falkner used a gold toothpick. Judging from the noise, someone was having a great run at one of the crap tables inside. Falkner shook imaginary dice in a fist near his ear and glanced at Pinto.

"How much money are we talking about?" Pinto asked finally.

And now they were driving cautiously the last few hundred yards up to El Morro, an odd place for a rendezvous. Or perhaps the best, if secrecy was so important.

"They chose the meeting place, not me," Falkner grumbled when Pinto brought it up again. His manner didn't encourage further questions.

At the top of the hill they'd slowly been climbing, on the narrow point of land between the Atlantic and San Juan Bay, winds gusting to seventy miles an hour—nearly hurricane strength—hit them. The BMW rocked. The cypresses that lined the approach to the castle were dragon shapes in the screaming wet night, rearing, slashing, then bending almost double toward the center of the road to scrape and claw the roof and sides of the car. The windshield wipers were nearly useless in this much rain. Falkner swore under his breath; he couldn't see more than a few yards ahead. Only the great beam of the castle lighthouse, slicing through low dark rolling clouds, gave Pinto a sense of where he was, on firm ground and not suspended precariously by the wind above the solid, smashing sea. His stomach was knotted; he was sweating profusely.

They had to leave the car at the entrance to the bridge across the dry moat and make their way on foot to the door in the facade. There were no lights here either, but both men carried flashlights. Falkner was wearing a raincoat that couldn't keep him dry; Pinto's shoes were ruined and he was drenched to the skin by the time they had tottered, clinging to the side walls of the bridge, up to the bastion entrance.

The door was unlocked and swung inward easily. They were pushed through by the wind into the sally port. Both men leaned against the bulletwood door to close it behind them.

"Which way?" Pinto shouted.

"The museum."

They had to go out in the rain again, to the patio, which was ankle-deep with runoff from the ramparts above. But much of the wind was blocked here; they could move without having to inch along, their backs to the surrounding high walls. Far above the entrance to the museum the San Juan light cut powerfully out to sea; some of the light was reflected back and down to them by clouds. Surf thundered against the rocks a hundred feet below the castle walls.

The large vaulted room the museum now occupied had been used as an apartment for the Spanish governors of the island whenever San Juan was under siege. Which was frequently. The Spaniards, under Ponce de Leon, had arrived in 1508. The English, Dutch, French and then the Americans had spent the next four hundred years trying to take it away from them. The fortifications of El Morro, begun around 1539, were under construction for more than three hundred fifty years. The museum was thoroughly modern. It also had lights, a welcome relief.

Pinto shook himself like a dog inside the door and looked inquiringly at Falkner, who had laid a cautionary hand on his arm.

"Good evening, *señora*!" Falkner called, rain streaming down his face, accentuating the gleam of his overly white teeth.

Pinto stared in the direction Falkner had turned him. Tall display cases served as dividers on the museum floor. Through the glass of one of the cases he saw a rather small woman, five feet three or four, sitting at a table with a lamp on it. A book was propped up in front of her. She had taken off her reading glasses. It wasn't a face he was likely to remember in his dreams; too thin for Pinto's taste. An excess of makeup couldn't disguise her plainness. But she had rather nice dark eyes. The slight warp of the glass through which he viewed her had elongated her face and neck; her features were out of kilter, as in one of the early Picassos, or a Modigliani portrait. She was wearing a plain gray cardigan and a dark-green skirt. She might have been a librarian.

"Good evening," she said in English. No accent Pinto could place. He didn't think she was from the island. Too white. Spanish, perhaps. Or Italian.

"We have an appointment with, ah, Mr. Minotaur, I believe," Falkner said.

She smiled at that and closed her book.

"Yes, I know. Please come in. It's quite a storm tonight, isn't it?"

The air in the museum was chilly and a little damp, and Pinto had the shivers as they approached the woman. She noticed and indicated a small electric heater near her chair.

"This might help. You can put the goods on the table."

"Just hang on to that thermos," Falkner said quickly to Pinto. Falkner had looked around. As far as he could tell, the three of them were alone.

"It's after eleven, isn't it?" he asked the woman.

She looked at the Cartier tank watch on her wrist. "Six minutes past eleven."

"I guess Mr. Minotaur's been delayed."

"There is no Mr. Minotaur," she said. "I've been given

the responsibility of concluding the transaction. My name is Leda Watson."

"I see, I see," Falkner said, rocking on his heels while Pinto crouched in front of the little heater. Falkner had spotted an attaché case lying flat beneath the woman's chair. "That's the money?"

"Yes."

"Well, we have the—you know. Pinto, show her."

Pinto rose and put the Duraflask container on the table.

The woman leaned forward slightly in her chair to look at it. She raised her eyes to Pinto, whose teeth were chattering.

"I—I can't open it here. I s-suppose you know why."

"Yes. All the embryonic tissue is there, of course. According to our agreement."

Pinto didn't reply. Falkner looked at him, scowling.

Leda Watson smiled faintly, sadly.

"No!" Pinto burst out. "That's not all! I have other cultures! But I want—m-more money for the rest! Ten thousand dollars a month for the r-rest of my-my—"

"Shut up, *pendejo*!" Falkner said viciously. "Do you have any idea of what we're dealing with? You don't try to fuck *bichotes* like these!"

He turned to Leda Watson, who had risen from her chair. She put her reading glasses into a pocket of her sweater and took out a different pair, more like the goggles arc welders use to protect their eyes.

"It's okay, it's okay, *señora*. He doesn't know—I'll take care of—a deal's a deal. We have a deal, right? Just let me talk to him for a couple of minutes—"

Leda Watson didn't answer him. She put on the goggles. Then she reached beneath the chair, picked up the attaché case and walked away.

"Wait!" Falkner pleaded, showing his gums in an abject smile. He tried to stop the woman. She didn't look at him but changed direction deftly, took three quick steps and put her finger on a button in the center of a small wireless triggering device fixed inconspicuously to the wall.

The museum was filled with powerful flashes of light, as if the great mirror of the lighthouse had somehow been focused on them. In actuality there were seven compact xenon lamps, each with its own power source, mounted inside and on top of the display cases. They went off in sequence, each lamp firing twice a second. Falkner and Pinto were temporarily but effectively blinded.

Leda Watson, her eyes protected from the intense strobe effect, returned to the table, avoiding Falkner, who was stumbling around and grabbing at the air. She put the Duraflask in her attaché case and went to a barred gate in one wall. Cursing, Falkner encountered a display case containing antique weaponry and armor and sent it crashing to the floor; one of the xenon lamps exploded. Leda Watson opened the gate and went down a steep flight of stairs, the heels of her sensible shoes tapping stone. She cast multiple shadows from the pulsating light above and behind her.

Six seconds later all the lamps burned out, leaving the museum in darkness except for the glowing orange grille of the electric heater.

"Pinto, use your goddam flashlight!"

Pinto had clipped the flashlight to his belt upon entering the museum. He dropped it once before he could turn it on. He was nearly paralyzed with terror, but he managed to cast the beam around the museum. Falkner, his eyes streaming tears, was holding a bleeding wrist. He had cut himself on a shard of glass from the case.

"Where is the bitch?"

"I d-don't—"

The beam of the flashlight cut across the shadowy opening in the wall, revealing the iron gate.

"Give me that thing!" Falkner said. When Pinto didn't move promptly, he came over and snatched the flashlight from him.

"You know anything about this place? Where does that go?"

"Tunnels—beneath the c-castle walls. Escape routes for—times of siege."

Falkner turned and headed for the stairs.

"Where are you g-g—"

"After the money! You can get the fuck out of here for all I care! I'll settle up with you later, *mojón.*"

He had taken a small pistol from the pocket of his raincoat. Pinto had a glimpse of the .25-caliber Beretta automatic as Falkner swung wide the gate over the stairs. Pinto's bowels turned to a pruney liquid as he realized that Falkner might shoot the woman.

The money was almost in their hands. What had possessed him to take such a chance? Now he was in danger of losing everything: his family, his career, his mistress. He would go to jail for life if Falkner—

Pinto sobbed. His field of vision was filled with brilliant sparklers, but he could see nothing else. He groped his way through the museum and forced the door open, stumbled out into the rain, thinking only of the safe apartment in Plazuela de la Rogativa, Miriam waiting for him.

In his panic he fell twice on the plaza, and ended up crawling on hands and knees through the sally port.

The big door in the facade of the castle had been locked.

Hysterical, Pinto beat his fists against it until most of his strength was gone and it hurt him to breathe.

But there had to be another way out. Above, below.

Pinto had visited El Morro many times in his life. Now, in his raddled brain, he tried to visualize the plan of the castle.

From the parapet of the Austria bastion, where he now stood, he could perhaps leap down into the dry moat. The earth there, softened by rain, would cushion his fall. Then he could scale the wall of the moat by the road and be free.

He backtracked through the sally port and went to his left, past the alcove that contained the chapel of Santa Barbara.

The door stood open a few feet. There was a light inside, slanting from floor to ceiling above the altar and the painting of *La Patrona* on the wall.

A few benches near the front of the chapel served as pews for the devout who wished to spend a few minutes there in prayer. Someone appeared to be lying on his back between the rows, studying the vaulted ceiling with his flashlight. The hand that held the light was propped on a bench.

"H-help me," Pinto whimpered. "I w-want to get out of here."

He ventured closer. The man was wearing the uniform of the National Park Service: he had to be the night guard at El Morro. His campaign-style hat was resting on his chest. Pinto leaned over a bench to see his face. But all he took in was the man's opened throat grinning at him, the uniform blouse soaked in blood.

Pinto jerked back and fell over the bench behind him, bruising his elbow on the stone floor. His mouth was open, but he couldn't utter a sound.

Instead he heard terrible screams coming from one of the passages beneath the castle.

Falkner?

Pinto got up, poised to run. But he needed light to find his way, any source of light, even a dead man's flashlight. He forced himself to reach over the back of the bench and twist the flashlight from the stiffening hand.

Outside the chapel rain lashed his eyes and poured on his head. The chamber next to the chapel was used as a storeroom, and the doors were padlocked. The third chamber had been a powder magazine. He thought he heard screaming again, but the fierceness of the wind overhead and the splashing of rain obscured the sounds. Through the gate he shone the light inside the magazine, past pieces of rusting mortars, pyramids of fused cannonballs, to the gaping mouth of another tunnel.

Something moved in there.

Instinctively Pinto clicked off the flashlight and backed away from the gate, shielding his face with his arms against the rain. It was so heavy he could scarcely breathe without drowning.

He had to have shelter, he thought, a hiding place, until the worst of the storm passed. Then he could escape.

The old fort was vast: five levels, rising to a height of a hundred thirty-five feet above the sea. There were nooks and crannies everywhere, away from the reach of the wind, the punishing rain.

He felt the opening gate brush his arm, sensed a presence; he jumped, clicking on the flashlight.

Pinto had only a glimpse of the monster, all that he wanted. He saw the honey-dark, magnificently well-muscled body of a naked man, the weighty horned head of a bull with hot red eyes. He saw blood washing from the polished blades of a double-headed ax.

He ran like hell.

The opening of the tunnel to the Santa Barbara bastion, which overlooked San Juan Channel, was located in the center of the patio. It went steeply down to the gun emplacements below. There were steps on either side of the ramp, which was like a shallow river in the rain. Within the tunnel, the winds that ripped at the walls of the castle were intensified to full hurricane strength. They literally sucked Pinto off his feet and sent him bowling head over heels down the watery ramp.

Pinto lay unconscious for several minutes, still clutching his flashlight, which had not broken or shorted out.

He came to with a taste of blood in his mouth, a roaring in his ears. He got slowly and dizzily to his knees. For now the rain had slackened; it was like a fine mist swirling in the air, mixed with spray from the immense surf not far below this level of the bastion.

He looked at the eighty-two steps leading up to the patio and knew he was incapable of climbing that far.

The flashlight beam wavered through the murk, past emplacements of old cannon to a single larger piece, dating from the Spanish-American War, that was mounted on a semicircular iron track embedded in the paving bricks.

Something was draped over the eroded black muzzle of the eight-inch gun, aimed impotently at the winds. He saw the bare, muscular legs of a man, the pale undergleam of the soles of his feet.

Pinto's throat was thick with horror. But he had to be sure his eyes weren't fooling him, that he hadn't gone mad.

It was a naked man, all right. The ankles and wrists were bound. The head was missing. The great ivory horn of a bull, three inches thick at the base, was rammed into the rectum.

Pinto stood holding on to the breech of the cannon with both hands to avoid being flattened by the wind. He looked stupidly at the corpse, unable to accommodate any more shocks to his nervous system.

Down another flight of steps were identical vaulted chambers beneath the gun deck, each chamber approximately eighteen by thirty feet, with a single barred window overlooking the ocean. They had served for centuries as enlisted men's quarters. The latrines and kitchen were opposite, beneath the stairs. Pinto made his way into one of the empty chambers and slumped, exhausted, his back against a white plaster wall. He kept the flashlight on. He couldn't bear to be alone in the dark.

Was it Falkner? he wondered, thinking about the corpse mounted on the barrel of the artillery piece. If so, what fate was in store for him?

There was still a way out.

Another tunnel, descending to the so-called floating battery at the base of the castle. He knew of a path that he could take around the bay side to safety. But there was a danger that the waves would be very high, leaping over the rocks to the wall. He could be battered to death, or washed out to sea.

Anything was better than waiting here, shuddering, vulnerable, racked with pain from his fall.

Pinto got slowly to his feet and walked through one chamber after another until he came to the gate over the battery tunnel, which ran crookedly down beneath the massive outer wall of the castle.

The gate was not padlocked. He pulled it open and began his descent into a cavelike cell so deep in bedrock he could no longer feel the stunning power of the waves or hear the shriek of the wind.

His flashlight was failing; the yellowed beam barely reached the wall a dozen feet away.

And there, leaning against the wall, was the great double-bladed Cretan ax he had last seen in the hands of the monster. The handle of the ax, known as a *labrys*, was of solid bronze, five feet in length and intricately cast, a panorama of iconographs: bulls and bull-leapers from a fabulous age.

They had known he would decide to come this way. They were ready for him.

But the ax was a means to defend himself.

Pinto tried to lift it and groaned from the weight. He couldn't manage to cant the *labrys* above his waist and gave up in despair. The steel rang on the stone floor. He turned the flashlight on the walls again, looking for the exit to the rocks outside. He heard a footstep behind him and turned.

The light grazed her face.

She was painted in a bizarre way. It looked as if she had learned the art of makeup from an embalmer. She wore gold boots, a white kilt cinched with a gold-link belt from which hung huge peacock feathers. There were many jeweled bracelets on her arms. Her breasts were oiled and bare.

"Oh, it's you," Pinto said. His chin trembled, and he began to cry.

The woman gazed at him with opaque indifference, then suddenly bent her knees, keeping her back straight. While she continued to watch him, her hands went to the *labrys*. She raised it with an awe-inspiring ease.

Pinto couldn't believe the concentrated strength in that small body. Or perhaps he'd gone totally insane and was imagining this.

She straightened into a stance and swung the ax so smartly the scimitar edge of the leading blade was a blur; he barely saw it before honed steel cut cleanly through his neck and clanged against the pitted stone behind him, striking sparks.

Her arms were straight and rigid, muscles trembling from wrists to shoulders with the effort of holding the ax to the wall. The cords in her neck stood out, her breasts were hard and blue veins showed all around the upstanding nipples.

For seconds Pinto's head, separated from his body, was poised on the wide blade of the angled ax. His eyes were open, staring; in the seconds that the brain continued to function perfectly, he realized that he was dead. Then spewing blood greased the shining blade and his head began to slide, very slowly at first, then faster, until it toppled off the scalloped side and landed, upside down, on the floor.

* * *

On the fenced grounds of AgriTech near Humacao, forty minutes from San Juan, tropical storm Hector, flirting with hurricane status, was causing considerable havoc.

A major construction project had been underway for several months: a six-story building that would contain all the laboratories and departments of the experimental station, now housed in older, unsatisfactory quarters scattered around the two hundred sixty acres. There was a pedestal crane atop the new building. In anticipation of a major blow, workmen had spent the afternoon anchoring the long arm of the crane with additional cable supports. Engineers had confirmed that the crane could ride out steady winds of up to ninety miles per hour, indefinitely.

After five hours and gusts of more than seventy-five miles per hour that caused the huge steel superstructure to tremble and sway groaningly against its cables, the unexpected happened: a cyclonic wind of unprecedented ferocity struck the station. For more than thirty seconds, the whirlwind raged at close to two hundred fifty miles per hour.

The crane was whipsawed. Welds failed and girders twisted like putty. Cable bolts gave way, and the massive arm of the crane was hurled from the roof to crash against Building One-C forty yards away.

Building One-C was little more than a high shed with skylights and big louvered windows. It covered a dirt floor of more than two acres that was crisscrossed with plastic irrigation pipes. The growing areas were, for the most part, isolated inside Filon bubbles with airlock entry systems. The sides of the bubbles had project codes painted on them.

In a bubble the size of a basketball court, several strains of corn had been grown. The male plants were genetically sterile to avoid cross-pollination.

Of the genetic varieties under culture, six had been blighted before reaching maturity, ravaged by a disease that scarred both ears and leaves.

The seventh hybrid variety, untouched by the spore death that existed only a few feet away, was flourishing. The ears of corn, a pearly yellow color, were firm and healthy.

The falling crane arm spun into Building One-C and squashed two-thirds of the structure flat, exposing the rest to the elements.

The Filon bubble that contained Pinto Pagán's discovery, *El Invicto*, was quickly torn apart by the winds. Both diseased and healthy stalks of corn were uprooted and whirled through the air, carried well beyond the confines of AgriTech.

The black fungal spores, millions of them, were stripped from the leaves and sailed higher and farther still, across the island's central Cordillera, the semiarid south coast, and out over the Caribbean. They traveled for the most part in a west-southwesterly direction. Some of them reached the upper atmosphere.

When the storm faded two days later and the winds calmed, the scattered spores began to descend, undetected, on several of the most impoverished countries in the western hemisphere.

Chapter 5

Berzé la Ville, France

At five-fifteen in the morning, when he went downstairs in the cabinetlike *ascenseur*, there was just enough light outside the Chateau du Chatelin for the Marquis de Rienville to see that it was going to be a fine misty morning, not too wet or foggy for his horses to work well.

But his mind was not on his racehorses, and he had not slept. For it was the anniversary of his daughter's death.

He had spent most of the night listening to her recordings, privately made while she was still a student, with the finest symphony orchestras on the continent: the brilliantly sung arias from *Pelleas et Melisande*, *La Boheme* and *Adriana Lecouvreur*. They never failed to bring tears to his eyes.

Elizabeth Roger de Rienville. She would be thirty-four now, at the height of her powers. The world had been denied all but tantalizing hints of her gift, a voice that comes only once in decades.

She had thrown it all away—the years of rigorous training, the high promise—for a man who lacked refinement, the soul to appreciate her. Who betrayed her so vilely on her wedding night that she committed suicide the following day.

The Marquis de Rienville locked himself in a drawing room on the ground floor of the chateau. He sat at a flawless Louis Quinze table facing undraped windows that looked east. He could see little out there; the sun had yet to break through the mist that shrouded tall birch and chestnut trees. He was conscious of his own reflection in the leaded-glass panes. The face slack, no longer handsome; the eyes neither young nor old, coldly radiating an eternal, intimidating, almost supernatural power.

Almost no one saw him like this: eyes fully open, staring. He had learned from his father, another Scorpio, to smile often, avert his gaze, conceal his passion, control the oceanic flow of his emotions until just the right moment. Then use with care the power that was his by birthright—to seduce a woman, or utterly crush whoever was in his way.

There was a scrambler telephone on the table in front of him, one of the secure lines that came into the chateau. He looked at it once, then at a small gold and ormolu clock on the polished table.

He felt his daughter's presence, her sublime spirit, as he always did when his heart was filled with her music.

Dead thirteen years.

Now the days of reckoning were close. The scope of his revenge had expanded with time. They would all pay, the hated cousins. They would pay and pay, then die in the most horrible ways imaginable. His mind could not conceive of deaths appropriate for such arrogant peasants.

For that he needed Minotaur.

The call came at five forty-seven.

"Good morning, Alex." Only his closest associates, a few intimate friends, called him by his first name.

The language was French, the voice a strange, guttural combination of human and beast, further modified by computer-controlled equipment. Unidentifiable. Untraceable.

"Did it go well?" Rienville asked.

"Yes. The one called Pinto tried to blackmail us at the last moment. He said there was more of *El Invicto*."

"I expected that," Rienville said. "Did he tell you where?"

"Torture was impractical under the circumstances. And he may have been lying."

"In case he was not, try Ridgway. And Aravanis."

"All right."

"One more thing. Aravanis's family. Kill them all."

There were five seconds of silence.

"Even the boy?" Minotaur asked.

"Especially the boy."

The connection was broken; the line went dead.

The Marquis de Rienville hung up the receiver of the secure telephone and sat back in his chair.

There was no more music in his heart. Only the blackness of rage. His liver-spotted hands shook uncontrollably.

Especially the boy.

Chapter 6

New York City

On a blustery but glistening December morning when she would rather have been riding in Central Park, Blaize Ellington sat in Anthony Troy's office on the thirty-fourth floor of a Park Avenue building and said of the report she held, "You're paid to get results, Anthony. I don't want to see any more of this speculative bullshit."

Anthony Troy smiled forbearingly and adjusted the angle of a solid gold link on the right cuff of his blue-striped shirt. He never allowed anything to upset him, although Blaize Ellington could be more of an irritant than he cared to deal with so soon after his mid-morning tea, a well-aged (forty-year-old) Pu Er from Hong Kong. Wretchedly expensive stuff, but Troy was convinced that Pu Er and Shu Mal, the White Ebony tea he took upon arising, had kept his stomach in good condition for all the years he had plied a devious trade.

For twenty-one years he'd been with the Central Intelligence Agency, the last five as a deputy director; now he was in charge of the global operations of Troy Ransome Associates, an international investigative and protection agency that had contracts with multinational corporations such as Huntleigh Resources. And Huntleigh was Buford Ellington. He wasn't about to offend Buford or his daughter, though he didn't much like Blaize. Didn't understand her, actually. She seemed not to care that she was a beauty. Did she ever bother to comb her hair? Anthony Troy lavished time and attention on his own hair (thinning), his skin (deeply tanned), and his discreetly pinstriped suits, which were run up for him half a dozen at a time by Prince Philip's tailor.

"It isn't bullshit, Blaize. What you have there is, I think, the most exhaustive attempt we've made to predict a subject's future movements by programming every scrap of information about him and his associates. Included are all the psychological imperatives that subconsciously influence his decisions. Given sufficient analysis, a significant pattern emerges."

Blaize grimaced and flipped through the pages.

"You still don't know where he is."

"As of this morning, ten fifty-four Eastern Standard Time, no. The computer can only give us the odds on where Lucas McIver will appear in the near future. Say between now and the Christmas holidays."

"Thirteen days." Suddenly she was interested. "Where?"

"Chicago."

"Oh, hell." Blaize shook her head. "It's so obvious. Home for the holidays. He'd never take the chance."

Troy opened a folder on his desk and took out a sheet of paper, which he handed to her.

"Four weeks ago a quantity of an experimental drug called 4-LYTP was stolen from the lab in Basel where the Megadyne Company cobbled a small batch of the stuff."

Blaize glanced at the particulars. "So what?"

"4-LYTP is the only drug to date that's been successful in treating Meiner's disease, a motor neuron disorder that afflicts only about four thousand people in this country. It's totally debilitating and ultimately fatal. Dr. Viola Purkey suffers from Meiner's."

"And?"

"The disease and the drug are referred to in the pharmaceutical business as 'orphans.' It can cost up to eighty million dollars to test, produce and market a new drug. Break-even on a drug like 4-LYTP is a hundred thousand users. There are probably less than half that number of Meiner's victims worldwide. So the pharmaceutical manufacturers don't bother with orphans; even if a cure or palliative is known, it isn't available."

"He's a doctor, so McIver knew about 4-LYTP. He wanted it for Dr. Purkey. Like everything else he wants, he just took it. Okay so far. But he could mail it to her."

Troy shook his head. "Psychological imperatives," he said. "Keep in mind McIver's image of himself. The beleaguered loner, falsely accused of murder, hounded by a wealthy and powerful—"

"Falsely accused!"

"Consider his background, Blaize. To Lucas McIver, the murder of your brother was a pure example of rough justice, the code of the hills, beyond the judgment of the law."

She closed her eyes momentarily, knuckles white on the padded arms of her chair. After sixteen years it was still so clear in her mind: the smoking revolver in McIver's hand, her brother with his bloody face, lying on the floor. It hadn't stopped McIver from shooting him again, and again. While she screamed. . . .

". . . Denied the opportunity to realize his full potential in his profession, he roams the world, using his skills in those situations where any doctor is a godsend and no questions are asked of him. Getting his hands on money and medicine any way he can. That may be his true calling, and he's certainly learned a lot from the Leprechaun—"

"Whose side are you on?" Blaize asked hostilely.

"You know I'm totally sympathetic to the family, Blaize."

And goddam well-paid for your sympathy, she thought. But there was no point in antagonizing Troy by trying to chip through that beautifully barbered facade.

"Viola Purkey is the closest thing he has to a blood relation. Like all of us, he needs and wants approval. McIver hasn't seen her, we suspect, for more than three years, although they have been adept at keeping in touch. He'll want to see her now, and he'll go to Chicago for that reunion because she's in no condition to travel."

"He knows she's watched. Twenty-four hours a day. He won't go near her."

"He'll try to find a way. And then we'll have him."

Blaize sat up straighter in her chair and gazed thoughtfully at the cannel-coal fire on the grate in the Sienna marble fireplace.

Troy knew nothing of the oath she had sworn to her father and herself. He didn't know about the weeks of training at Pard Randolph's school for survival shooting or of her "final exam" on the hilltop in France. He was aware, of course, that she had a .45 automatic in her purse this morning; no one could enter the elegant offices of Troy Ransome Associates carrying a weapon without that fact being instantly known to Personnel. He had assumed it was a whim, an affectation, the latest accoutrement for scared, rich young women in the age of mobile terrorists, the high-profile snatch. He had not said anything to her about the automatic. If he knew she intended emptying the magazine in Lucas McIver's face, he would have pulled his operatives from the field and sent her father a closing bill. The money was excellent, but he couldn't approve of anything so reckless or condone an act of violence that could go drastically wrong, one that would in any event reflect on the integrity of his organization.

"I want you," she said slowly, "to stop all surveillance of Dr. Purkey's clinic. Pull your men out of Chicago, Anthony."

That startled him; he almost stammered. "But—this time I'm reasonably certain—"

"When it comes to traps, McIver turns to smoke. He blends with the air. It hasn't worked before, and Lonnie was killed in Bangkok. It won't work now. I want to try something else, something totally unexpected."

"What is that, Blaize?"

"Kindness," she said.

The world headquarters of Actium International occupied a sixty-two-story tower that took up a full block of Fifth Avenue close to St. Patrick's Cathedral, which it overwhelmed.

In the design of the building, the architect had blended Greek classicism with the new art-deco style of the eighties, and somehow it worked. The tower consisted of many marble-sheathed octagonal tubes of varying height that conveyed the strength of a single Corinthian column. The top of each tube contained a pleasant terrace large enough to accommodate a helicopter landing pad. At street level there were plazas, colonnades, reminders of the ancient Mediterranean world in frescoes, mosaics and sculpture walls.

Windows on each floor had been reduced to small studlike bronze-tinted rectangles. From a distance, at night, the tower seemed to have not windows but eyes, looking in all directions, like the eyes of Argus, the ever-vigilant giant. The tower cast a spell of power and plenty over a city that worshiped power before all else.

The building had not yet been open for a full year, and they were still celebrating its completion with a lavish gala-of-the-month for each of the twelve large corporations Actium had absorbed and now controlled: Actium was the largest private holding company in the world.

Blaize was seldom in town these days, and Joanna Coulouris, probably the best friend she had—although she was really close to no one—had promised her the party would be fun. Besides, Joanna was dying to show off her new passion, a sixteen-year-old high-fashion model from England. To ensure Blaize's presence, Joanna had sent her personal hairdresser, a makeup artist and a pedicurist from Elizabeth Arden, one of her maids, a masseuse and two chauffeurs to the twelve-room Ellington apartment in the Pierre Hotel.

This is overkill, Blaize thought resignedly. Joanna, at thirty-eight, still seemed to believe she had to buy and bribe people in order to have any friends at all. The terrible tension to please, to be liked, had caused Joanna to have several breakdowns, or at least drug-enhanced crises of nerves. She had spent a forbidding amount of time in the best sanitariums in Switzerland and was still, as she entered middle age, looking for clues as to who she was.

After a steaming, deep-scrubbed, flesh-pounding afternoon, Blaize was pleased with the results and decided to enjoy the occasion. Three days ago she had discarded for good the bothersome brace on her left leg. She got herself up in a severe black off-the-shoulder gown and a silver-fox jacket, took along a slender enameled walking stick and a handbag specially made to conceal the .45, and was driven to the party in a lemon and ebony Rolls that was almost as old as her father but a whole lot quieter.

The dinner-dance was being held in the topmost ballroom of the tower, a geodesic dome of bronzed glass so cleverly designed it seemed intimate despite its huge size. It was like a garden of the gods. Four levels of interior terraces surrounded the central atrium, which, at eight o'clock at night, was as brightly lit and aromatic as a spring morning in the foothills of Olympus.

On the main floor guests found carpets of real grass underfoot, embankments of fresh flowers, purling fountains, live tethered kids bleating forlornly, white doves in cages, embodiments of roguish Pan lolling on fake rock formations and playing shepherds' pipes. A strolling orchestra in the costumes of ancient Helena also was on hand. Food was served buffet-style from tables that formed a rectangle the size of a tennis court. Within the rectangle chefs labored, roasting racks of lamb and slabs of prime rib inside three hollow bronze bulls.

Blaize was met on arrival by one of Joanna's emissaries and conducted to the sheepskin-lined conversation pit just off the atrium floor, where Joanna was holding court.

Joanna hugged and kissed her enthusiastically. Even in a two-thousand-dollar designer's toga that was intended to conceal her faulty figure, she seemed endearingly frumpy. Her hair was always in the latest style of wretched excess, her makeup failed to get rid of the bags under her eyes.

Blaize was introduced to the hot new black comedian, who kissed her hand. Several of Joanna's clique she already knew. A daughter of the president of the United States. A dazzlingly successful actor-director who, in his mid-forties, was afflicted with paresis. It was said that he was considering a sex change so that he might be the only performer in the history of Hollywood to win Oscars for both best actor and best actress.

Lastly she met Dove, the English model. Six-one and probably still growing. Dove sat elegantly akimbo, staring in admiration at Blaize, and extended a limp hand. She had a willowy neck, a concentration-camp haircut and that ravishing sulkiness that could only mean big bucks in her trade, until she flamed out somewhere over the horizon of twenty-one.

"Darling, how is your leg?" Joanna asked her and explained to the group about Blaize's accident.

"About as good as it's ever going to get," Blaize said. "How have you been?"

Joanna had a smile that meant to be ingratiating but seemed only agonized. Yet Blaize found her less nervous and klutzy than usual, less inclined to paw and prey on people like an insecure child. "I'm working so hard. Papa has finally begun to recognize how indispensable I am. I have astonished him with how much I know about the business."

"That's good news," Blaize said.

"And where have you been? It's impossible even to phone you."

"Oh, I've been diddling around Europe doing some research. Nothing serious. I'm heading home for the holidays."

Joanna took her aside for a few moments. "We'll all be in Greece soon after the new year. You must come." Blaize reacted to the invitation with a raised eyebrow and pretended to gasp for breath. Joanna said, grasping her arm in supplication, "No, no! I promise. Nothing strenuous. We'll swim and sail and listen to good music and have a marvelous time."

"I'll try to make it," Blaize told her. She opened her handbag, reached inside surreptitiously although the pistol was fully concealed and took out a small gift-wrapped package. "I found this for you in Avignon. Merry Christmas."

"Blaize!" Joanna eagerly unwrapped the package. She had always had everything she could possibly want but never tired of the interesting little surprises Blaize brought her.

Joanna held up a pendant on a gold chain and turned, showing it off to the group. The object was bronze; it had the weight and dignity of many centuries.

"What is it?" Dove asked, squinting at the winged lionlike beast.

"A chimera," Theos Melissani said, reaching past Blaize and arresting the slowly revolving pendant in the palm of his hand. He kissed Blaize on the ear. "Hello, my dear."

"Hi, Theos."

''Etruscan, isn't it?''

''What do you think?'' Blaize said challengingly, looking Theos in the eye.

He smiled and studied the chimera. Joanna's lips had clamped shut.

''No sense of proportion, no purity of form. But powerful and dynamic, like the people themselves. It's Etruscan.'' He unfastened the clasp, put the chain around his cousin's neck. ''Good fortune, Joanna. And happiness always.''

Joanna paid only slight attention to Theos. So the feud was still raging, Blaize thought. But Theos Melissani was the wrong sort to tangle with, even if the family business was at stake. He was forty-six, of average height like his father but very powerful through the chest and shoulders. He had a large good-looking head carried a little forward of the rest of his body, and a chin that could clear paths for him. His luxurious tight curls were beginning to dapple with gray. Big dimples and a fond twinkle in the eye: but sometimes Blaize was too aware of the mechanism of his charm, like the never-idle pistons of a model engine in a bell jar. She once had agreed to a tryst with him, then suddenly decided to fly to Japan instead. He still sent her a wry note on the anniversary of her no-show but otherwise didn't pursue her. *Someday*, his smile insisted whenever he saw her. *Maybe*, Blaize thought. But Theos had many women. He also was the father of seven children, including four boys, and was raising them all to perpetuate a dynasty well into the twenty-second century—although it was a dynasty he didn't yet control.

''And who were the Etruscans?'' Joanna asked. ''Or is that a stupid question?''

Blaize said, ''They may be the only great people who had the foresight, or the humility, to predict their own downfall. They gave everything to the Romans: their culture, their religion. And the Romans destroyed them. I don't know if that word is strong enough. Because for fifteen centuries it was as if the Etruscans had never existed.''

''Obviously they lacked the durability of the Greeks,'' Theos said with a contented smile. ''Particularly the Melissanis.'' Looking at him, Blaize wondered if his head expanded, ever so slightly, like a tomcat's, whenever he had sex. Eventually it would be the size of a balloon in the Macy parade.

"I've lived before," Dove said for no apparent reason. "A psychic told me. I was a slave boy in Egypt."

"Know I seen you somewhere else!" the black comedian said. "Remember me? I was the undertaker to the royal family. All I ever did was gift-wrap. Keep it simple, I told 'em. What do you need with those gold chariots, those twenty-nine virgin handmaidens in that tomb with you? Man, you can't have no pussy after you're *dead*!"

Blaize left after another kiss on the cheek from Joanna; she hadn't eaten all day. She ran into the senior senator from Kentucky and his wife, then other people she knew, and didn't have a bite of food or a drink until nine-thirty. She polished off a plate of poached salmon and washed it down with Chardonnay.

Joanna wasn't there when Blaize rejoined the group. Dove said that she would be right back and invitingly patted the sheepskin next to her. Blaize sat down beside the girl, who was talking to a rock star with an evil face. He went elsewhere arm in arm with the actor whose brain was full of pus but whose body was still firm, and Dove turned her overwrought eyes on Blaize. She showed a bit of tongue at one corner of her mouth. Blaize winked at her.

"What d'you say, cutie? Had any calories today?"

"I hope you don't mind my telling you, Blaize, that I am absolutely barking mad about you."

"I don't mind."

Twenty seconds went by.

"Do you want me?"

"There're two problems. One, I'm not gay. Two, if I were I wouldn't take cunt away from a friend."

"Isn't that virtuous of you."

"I think so. Yes."

Blaize was bored and restless. She'd come to the party for Joanna's sake and now it appeared that Joanna had done a bunk, as the limeys put it. She didn't see Theos around either. Or Joanna's father, who still loved a good party and could be counted on to lead the dancing before the night was far along. Something must be up, she thought. A family emergency. Although she wasn't dressed for pub-crawling, Blaize longed for a good old-fashioned New York bar, something long, dark and crammed with neighborhood regulars. Dan Lynch's would do. Good blues there most nights. But it was on lower Second, not a neighborhood she'd want to appear in unescorted, even with a peashooter.

It would have taken her, perhaps, almost a full minute to select a date and cut him out of the herd—"Hi. I'm Blaize. Let's go somewhere"—but even that was too much trouble. She heard a helicopter above the hubbub in the ballroom, flapping thunder, glimpsed landing lights above the dome and thought for a moment it was coming at them through the roof. Then it faded off down the side of the building to land on one of the many terraces below.

Time to call it a night, she thought. She would write Joanna a note. And, with luck, they would meet again soon on the Sea of Poseidon.

Ten floors below the ballroom, the members of the business family known as "The Cousins" had gathered in the library of the apartment Argyros Coulouris called home when he was in New York.

Since his half-brother George had suffered a stroke more than three years ago, Argyros had been the head of Actium International. But his strength, and his resolve, were not what they used to be. With him was his faithful Joanna, who sat close to hand but slightly behind him; Theos Melissani and his brother Plato, George's sons, who occupied comfortable leather reading chairs opposite their uncle; and Kristoforos Aravanis, whose own first cousin was the botanist and agronomist Demetrios Constantine Aravanis. Kris, who was two years older than Joanna, was fair for a Greek, with blue eyes that could be chilly. He was always keyed up, but he seldom allowed it to show. He paced slowly around the huge astrolabe, recovered from the sea off Actium and restored to stand in the center of the onyx floor.

Except for Theos and Plato, who counted as one man, they

were bitter rivals within the company; but such was their dislike of publicity and their love of privacy that little was suspected, much less documented, of the determined maneuvering for control of Actium that had been going on for months. Because they seldom socialized and were rarely seen together in public, the bad blood didn't show. They came together only out of necessity: to strengthen the business, or to protect it from enemies.

The outsider in the library was Joe D'Allesandro, chief of security for Actium. Joe was a native New Yorker, a police-department veteran who had been deputy chief inspector of the busy Fourth Homicide Zone of Manhattan before moving over to Actium for more than double the salary he'd earned in the cops.

The helicopter sitting outside the doors to the terrace had just brought him to midtown from Kennedy.

"I spent close to two days talking with Demetrios Constantine. At this point we have practically nothing to go on, but I propose we take him seriously."

"Have you provided the protection he asked for?" Argyros asked.

"Yes, sir, we did that immediately. Some of our best men from the Athens and Thessaloniki offices."

"What is this 'Cirenaica' spore he's been talking about?" Kris asked impatiently. Kris was slender, small-boned. He favored dark suits and polka-dot ties. He had clever, soul-searching eyes and a somber pallor, a cool clerical distance in his manner; but his nose was hawkish, his mouth that of a flesh-eater. He had degrees from three universities and knew more about Actium's software and computers than anyone else in the room.

D'Allesandro consulted his notes. "It first came to his attention from a core sample routinely provided by ConStar Oil, which was drilling in Quadrant K-97 of their Libyan leasehold. That's in the northernmost part of the Sahara Desert, an area known from biblical times as Cirenaica. The core sample came from three thousand feet beneath the sand and showed traces of ancient artifacts—in other words, civilization. ConStar geologists looked the sample over, found traces of pollen and the spores, then shipped the sample to your cousin Demetrios for further evaluation."

"Why is it important?" Theos prompted the security chief. He got up to pour himself another retsina, smiled inquiringly at the others. Argyros raised one finger, a curt signal, and lighted another cigarette. Theos brought him a glass and resumed his seat as D'Allesandro finished flipping through pages of his notebook.

"Sorry, sir. I wanted to be sure of what I'm telling you. The, ah, fungal spores became active in the laboratory."

"After so many years?" Plato said incredulously.

"Time seems to have no effect on certain types of simple organisms. Demetrios told me that the earth may well have been colonized by spores that had drifted through space for billions of years. Anyway, the Cirenaica spores proceeded to damage or kill every growing thing they were exposed to. Four different varieties of cereal grains. If they were allowed to multiply unchecked, Demetrios says, the resulting blight could cause a catastrophic interruption of the food chain."

"Leading to mass starvation," Kris said.

Argyros's restless eyes flicked to him. He sipped some of the retsina. Argyros had a large head with a high-bridged nose, flaring nostrils, an astute, sideways squint that effectively concealed his thoughts and emotions, the pain that was with him for most of his days. At sixty-five, he still colored his full head of hair, leaving only a little white at the temples. His cheekbones protruded and his sensual mouth drooped a little at the corners, but he remained an unusually handsome man. He'd been a boxer in his youth, proud of his fists, his footwork, his ability to take punishing blows. In his late thirties he'd suffered a broken neck in a speedboat accident, and temporary paralysis. It was still difficult for him to move his head without turning his upper body as well. This gave him an unnaturally still, watchful quality that could be unnerving to others. He smoked incessantly, a cigarette in the hand that propped his chin.

"But he has the spore under control in his facilities," Argyros said. His was a commanding, almost operatic, voice.

"Yes, sir," D'Allesandro replied. "He did express concern that the sample he passed on to Mukaiba might now be in, ah, the hands of irresponsible individuals."

"In other words," Argyros said softly, "he believes Minotaur has the spores."

They all looked at him. "Who?" Kris said. At the same time Theos said, "What?"

"We don't know who or what," D'Allesandro told them. "Minotaur may be some kind of terrorist organization that's not on the books yet. But I'm only guessing. Someone identifying himself as 'Minotaur' has also talked to your cousin on the phone. This same Minotaur allegedly contacted the Japanese botanist Tohru Mukaiba several times before his death. Demetrios believes, without substantiating evidence, that Minotaur is behind the plane crash in Japan that killed Mukaiba and at least a hundred others. Minotaur, it seems, wants all the research on the Cirenaica spore."

"Has our cousin found a way to stop the fungus from spreading?" Joanna asked.

"He didn't tell me."

Theos said, "I'm certainly more than a little curious." He thought, *I shall give Demetrios Constantine a call.* Theos glanced at Kris, knowing what would be on his cousin's mind. How many million tons of grain and gallons of edible oils did Actium have in storage around the globe? Whatever the tonnage, along with the considerable and easily purchased surplus currently available in the U.S., it represented a potential windfall of at least a billion dollars. Within hours they would be going long on commodity exchanges everywhere: not only grains but oils, cattle, hogs.

"How did you know about Minotaur?" Kris asked his uncle.

Argyros took his time in replying, until all eyes were on him.

"I have received a phone call from Minotaur myself."

Joanna put a hand on her father's arm. He finished his drink and licked his lips.

"What did he—they—want?" Plato asked quietly.

Argyros smiled contemptuously. "Minotaur prophesied the fall of the House of Actium. The death of all of us."

Joanna withdrew her hand from her father and covered the lower part of her face.

"I think we can safely conclude we're dealing with terrorists here," D'Allesandro said.

"Yes," Theos said. "No doubt they will make it clear to us in time exactly what they want. In the meantime, Joe—"

"We behave as if we're at war. I'll be blunt. I'm leery of bombs." Joanna groaned, almost inaudibly. Joe went on: "None of you goes anywhere without extra security details. We just took delivery on three more attack-proofed Mercedes Pullmans; they can stand up to a direct hit from a rocket launcher. But I'd like the authority to hire an additional thirty-two men, effective immediately."

"Twenty additional men," Argyros said.

"Yes, sir. Now, I don't want any of you driving his own car, sailing his own boat, opening his mail or sleeping in strange beds—unless you check it with me first. And I think we'd better cancel the remaining galas."

"They were getting to be a bore anyway," Theos said with a yawn. "What do you think, uncle? Is it the Turks again?"

"Yes, it will probably have to do with the Turks," Argyros said with a remote smile. His eyes were introspective. He lit another cigarette for himself and withdrew further into a cloud of smoke.

"I had so much planned for the holidays," Joanna wailed.

"Patience, cousin," Theos told her. "We've lived with this inconvenience before. We can live with it again. It's better than being poor."

Shortly before two a.m., the last guests left the ballroom. As soon as they were on their way down in the elevator, Joe D'Allesandro had men with explosives-detection devices and a brace of bomb-sniffing dogs on the floor, sending the tethered kids into a frenzy, causing pandemonium in the dove cages. The searchers needed half an hour to make sure the ballroom had not been booby-trapped. There was a meeting of branch managers of Waldran BioTech scheduled for early that afternoon; the cleanup crews were due at six a.m.

In Security Central on the tenth floor, he contacted subordinates who were concluding similar searches of the living areas of the tower. They had found no explosives.

Joe relaxed for a few minutes and had a smoke and a drink, light vodka and a lot of tonic. He hadn't slept for forty-eight hours and probably would put in another twelve before pausing to catch a nap. Security chiefs at all Actium offices around the world were already being put on the alert: Communications was lit up and fully staffed at three a.m.

Counting servants and guests staying the night, there was an entourage of thirty-one people in the living quarters on three floors of the tower. At the moment, he knew exactly where everyone was, and with whom.

Argyros Coulouris was alone in his bed in his apartment, but probably not asleep.

Plato Melissani, who had been an Olympic-caliber weight lifter in his youth and still maintained a marvelous physique, was finishing a solitary two-hour workout in the executives' gymnasium. At fifty-two, he was six years older than Theos but distinctly subordinate to his brother, who had charm, ambition and guile in equal measure. The modestly named Theos ("Theos" being the Greek word for God) was Joe D'Allesandro's odds-on favorite to engineer a takeover of the company as soon as the old man showed signs of weakening.

Not that Kris was a lightweight, despite his youth and appearance. The old man depended on Kris more than anyone, including his daughter. George and Argyros had been empire-builders, shrewd in their day but now behind the times. Kris was visionary, constantly streamlining operations with the help of computers and his own philosophy of a rapidly changing world, which he called "Ecodynamics." Kris was, at this hour of the night, working on a conference call to the Far East. Theos was in his apartment, playing backgammon with his socialite mistress and friends.

Joanna, whom Kris had lately befriended, perhaps for strategic reasons, was bedded down with Dove St. Cyr in a third apartment. She was, Joe reasoned, much too unstable to be depended upon if things got really rough. But her father was now giving her every opportunity to prove that she had the fortitude to be his successor.

George Melissani, unable to speak very well or walk since his stroke, still was a force to be considered; he hated Argyros and was now desperate, realizing that his time was short, to see his son Theos succeed the older men as the head of Actium.

Three against three, a fortune countable in the billions of dollars.

But money wasn't the issue. They were all guaranteed plenty of money, forever. Dominance mattered. Absolute power.

D'Allesandro shook his head. He didn't understand, although he'd dealt with them all his adult life, people who couldn't be content with what they had, when enough, as his old grandmother used to say, was as good as a feast.

He could better understand the street kid, reduced by circumstances to animal instincts, ripping open an old man with a cheap steak knife for the two bucks in his pocket.

But he didn't have to understand the cousins, or sympathize with their ambitions. All he had to do was protect them, from envious, hostile outsiders or, perhaps, from each other.

Joe was carrying a revolver with him, a potent Colt Lawman, when at three fifty-five a.m. he took an elevator upstairs to the deserted ballroom.

Only a few lights remained on in the lobby and the ballroom. He threw a big shadow across the well-trampled greensward of the atrium, which smelled of stale booze, goat shit and the cold grease of a quarter ton of beef and lamb roasted in the great gas-fired bronze bulls. Doves rattled around their cages as he passed slowly by. The terrace levels above him were dark. Looking up, he saw only the revolving aircraft warning beacon atop the dome, which cast orange-toned reflections on the many panes of bronzed glass.

"Want to tell me where you are?" he said, searching the plant-filled terraces, hand on the butt of the revolver in the pocket of his coat.

No answer. Joe paused, smiling.

"I don't know the whole thing yet," he said. "I spent three weeks overseas, and I asked a lot of questions. Picked up one thread after another. Greeks are a closemouthed bunch, not to mention the Swiss, but I've had a lot of experience in getting people to open up. And I guess I've listened to a lot of bizarre stories in my time, but this one, well—it tops just about anything I've ever heard."

Joe cleared his throat, which was a little dry. He heard nothing but the bleating of kids, the fluttering of dove wings, the mild hiss of gas jets beneath one of the bronze bulls. Somebody had forgotten to turn the gas off. Fire hazard. He'd have to see about that, once he concluded his business with Minotaur.

"As I said, I don't know everything. Probably enough to stop you before it goes any further or gets any worse. I covered for you, with that stuff about terrorists, and wasted some time on bomb searches to make it look right; I guess I wanted to give you time to think. But you have to know I've got you. That doesn't mean you should be afraid of me. I think what you really want is help, and this—this kind of masquerade you've been putting on is an admission of how bad you want it. Or you wouldn't have had me come up here."

While he talked Joe was totally on the alert, eyes roving the huge room.

On the third level of terraces he detected movement, like a bird taking flight, and he turned that way, crouching, still not drawing the revolver.

Something *was* flying around and around up there in the dark. The swarming, singing sound of a primitive bull-roarer filled the ballroom.

"*You should not take the slightest chance with Minotaur*," Dr. Hoelscher had warned him. "*A mistake could be fatal.*"

"That's impressive!" Joe called. "Now why don't you come out?"

The arm appeared first, the beautifully muscled, oiled arm that swung the bull-roarer. Then the dark head, a mighty knot of brow between angled horns with needle-sharp tips; the enormous snout, and eyes that seemed to be alive, focused on him, although he knew it was just an elaborate mask.

The shaved, glistening, copper-hued body was fully naked. He was a good six feet four in his bare feet, Joe thought. Incredible proportions. Thousands of hours of dedicated work had gone into the making of that body, although God had been generous as well.

Minotaur came slowly and grandly down flights of steps between the terraces, the bull-roarer moving tirelessly above its head in darting, elliptical flights.

What a show.

All of it, Joe realized too late, intended to distract him. But he'd made the principal mistake Hoelscher had warned him against, thinking of Minotaur only in singular terms. Disregarding—

"Nothing is more dangerous on this earth," the good doctor had said, *"than a deranged, yet calculating, mind."*

Joe didn't hear the footsteps, falling on thick sod behind him. But out of the corner of his eye he caught the gleam on the edge of the raised ax and whirled, pulling the revolver from his pocket.

He fired single-handedly wide of the target, shattering a dove in a cage with the soft-nosed bullet, and the revolver bucked up just as the wide curved blade, one of two on the Cretan ax, sliced through his wrist. His hand, holding the revolver, tumbled into the grass. Blood pumped vigorously from the stump of his wrist. Joe stared at it, too amazed to comprehend the seriousness of the injury. There was almost no pain; it had happened in the blink of an eye.

Then he looked into the eyes of Minotaur.

". . . So deadly a compulsion, which for its own sake would loose terror and destruction upon the world. . . ."

Joe D'Allesandro screamed, but the sound was stifled by the nearness of the bull-roarer.

A hard blow to the back of his head sent him to his knees and his good left hand. He rolled over on his back and looked up groggily, saw his severed hand in the hands of Minotaur, saw the revolver pried from his fingers and discarded. There was a walkie-talkie in the left side pocket of Joe's coat. He tried to get it out.

A hand closed on his throat. He was lifted a good two feet off the floor. Fingers squeezed at the angle of his jaw and the bone snapped loudly. Joe's mouth sagged open.

His severed hand, wrist-end first, was stuffed between his

teeth. Blood trickled down his throat. Fingers, one of them wearing a diamond ring, dangled down his chin.

The eyes of the beast stared into his.

Then he was carried across the floor by the throat to one of the hollow bronze bulls.

Oh no oh no oh no Sweet Mary Mother of Mercy don't let. . . .

Pierced doors in the side of the bull were opened; he was stuffed inside on the warm, grease-blackened grate. Suit, shoes and all. His left hand was jammed beneath him, firmly pinned in place between the bars of the grate. The doors were closed and locked with a strong bronze pin.

He heard the hiss of the gas jets beneath a bed of charcoal briquettes. Now he was weakening, growing faint from loss of blood. He kicked frantically at the snug interior of his prison, but it was well-anchored to a concrete pedestal.

The jets were turned all the way up.

The last thing Joe D'Allesandro saw through the pierced curved metal was the head of Minotaur, bent over the bronze bull, a sanguinary false eye hovering like a malefic planet above him.

Dove, the teen-age model, turned in the bed she shared with Joanna Coulouris, stretched her long body and yawned, having slept the sleep of untroubled youth, and encountered Joanna fresh from her bath. Not unusual. Joanna bathed several times a day, at all hours. But there seemed to be tears on her cheeks as Dove snuggled closer.

"What's the matter? Aren't you happy with me?" Dove murmured.

"Unimaginably," Joanna sighed. After a few moments she put an arm around her lover, and pressed her lips to a small fragrant breast.

Chapter 7

Chicago

Blaize left at dawn for Chicago, flying commercial to O'Hare. There was no snow in the city yet, but the cold was like a blowtorch. Her nostrils were already raw at the roots and she was sniffling, feeling as if she might be coming down with the flu. Now all she needed was for her period to be a little early. She checked into the Ritz Carlton in Watertower Place, had two grams of vitamin C with her breakfast orange juice and then took a taxi to the South Side.

"Where you from?" the driver asked her. "Tennessee?"

"Kentucky."

"First time in Chicago?"

"No."

"I guess you don't know the city too good. That address you give me, it's near the university but the neighborhood is for shit, you don't mind my saying. Almost all niggers. Lot of drugs, you know. Rapes."

Blaize shifted her weight nervously on the broken-down backseat as the driver made a turn onto Lake Shore Drive and picked up speed. Morning rush-hour traffic had thinned out on the Drive. The sun low over Lake Michigan was dazzling. She was sorry now that she had eaten; the herb omelette wasn't setting well on her stomach. She was feeling lightheaded and a little disoriented from the pace she'd set during the past week. And she was heading into unfamiliar, decidedly unfriendly territory. Troy's men would not be around to protect her. But there was no other way she could hope to succeed, to finally come face-to-face with Lucas McIver.

Bozeman Street, off Cottage Grove Avenue, was a neighborhood of small stores and rank tenements. A spray-can bromide on a boarded-up window: *I must be somebody, 'cause God don't make no junk.* Trash in the gutters, spiritless holiday glitz wrapped around lamp posts. One of the four-story brick buildings, with a wheelchair ramp from the sidewalk to the basement level, looked better maintained than most. A small blue and white sign over the first-floor entrance identified the tenement as the Zacchaeus South Side Medical Center. There were a couple of dozen people lined up on the right side of the steps when Blaize got out of the taxi. Elderly men and women in tattered cloth and corduroy coats, earflap caps and ski masks. A bandaged head, an arm in a sling, an old-fashioned wooden crutch. There were young mothers with swaddled infants, only medallion-sized circles of chocolate faces exposed to the air. Blaize felt a little self-conscious as she went up the steps past those waiting on line, but few of the clinic's patients paid much attention to her. Probably they thought she was a social worker.

The narrow foyer was jammed. A couple of small scarred tables under the stairs, a young man and a gray-haired woman in blue sweaters and white jackets taking down information from new patients. Three telephones ringing at once. More patients waiting in straight-back chairs against the wall. Signs posted everywhere on the chipped plaster. PATIENTS WITH VENEREAL DISEASE MAY NOT USE THIS TOILET. Schedules of doctors' hours. Pharmacy regulations.

"I'd like to see Dr. Purkey," Blaize said to the young man. The receiver of a phone was propped on one shoulder as he went through a card file. He had a narrow Latin face, some fuzz on his upper lip and one gold earring.

"Be right with you."

He pulled the tattered card he was looking for and rattled off some Spanish into the phone. Blaize slowly undid the horn buttons of her coat; it was hot in the clinic. The windows were steamed over. A baby was crying. The young man hung up and smiled at Blaize.

"Is every day like this?" she asked.

"I'm not here every day. Saturday is probably worse. Case worker? You want to see Mrs. Castellano. Room six, upstairs."

"I have to see Dr. Purkey."

He shook his head. "She can't see anybody."

"I know she's been ill, but—this is very important. It's a personal matter."

"I don't know what to tell you. I don't think she's had any visitors for a month."

"It's very serious, then. What she has?"

"Meiner's? Yeah. I don't know much about it myself. There's no surgical procedure that helps. What's your name?"

Blaize told him. "It's in reference to Lucas McIver. If she'll just give me a few minutes—"

He picked up the receiver of the phone again and dialed three numbers. Waited. An old man with stubble cheeks and vile breath pushed past Blaize and sat down on the steps to the second floor. "Hey, my man, that's not permitted. Don't want you to get stepped on. Hello?" He switched to Spanish, looking up at Blaize. She heard her name. He stopped talking and listened for a long time. His eyes clouded over. He spoke briefly again, then hung up.

"Somebody'll come down in a few minutes, if you want to wait over there."

"Will she see me?"

"I don't know. Coni said to wait. Next? Eighty-four? Who has number eighty-four? Let's keep movin', now, it's cold out there on those steps."

Blaize moved to a vacant spot along the wall and stayed there while the ill and the infirm shuffled by her, first to sign in, then to chairs to wait, then to various treatment rooms as their names were called out down the hall. The front doors, sprayed with artificial snow and hung with wreaths, opened and closed continuously, letting in gusts of frigid air. Some-one had a ghetto blaster tuned to pop Christmas music on the low order of "Rudolph the Red-Nosed Reindeer."

Half an hour passed; Blaize fidgeted. After she'd memorized the signs there wasn't much else to look at. She thought of Lucas McIver going up and down the stairs for nine years, growing from gawky youth into manhood. She wondered what his life had been like here. Her jaw had begun to ache; she was grinding her teeth.

"Are you Mrs. Ellington?"

Blaize looked down at a short wide caramel-colored woman with flat features; she was wearing nursing whites and had a pair of black-rimmed spectacles attached with a chain to the pocket flap on her blouse. Her eyes were pools of bitter ink.

"Uh, no, I'm not married."

"My name is Consuela. Coni. I look after Dr. Purkey. You know that she has been very ill."

"Yes, I'm sorry. I heard."

"You here to cause trouble? Because she doan need any, the condition she is in."

"I'm not here to cause trouble. There's—been too much of that already."

"Okay. I am against it. But she say she want to see you. For her sake, please make it quick."

At the back of the building there was a small elevator in a framework that went up to the fourth floor through a dim stairwell. Everything about it looked handmade from junkyard scroungings. The elevator rose slowly, stopping frequently for no good reason. Coni punched the button that made it go and swore in staccato Spanish.

"Greased lightning, hey? We need to get this thing fixed. We need to do plenty else around here. All it takes is lots and lots of money which we don't have anyhow."

"Who is Zacchaeus? Am I pronouncing that right?"

"Dr. Purkey's husband, who opened this clinic in the first place. He has been dead a long time. Twenny-five years, I think. Also Zacchaeus in the Bible was a filthy rich money-changer or something, but he gave up his money and went with Jesus. That was the right move on his part, but I doan know if they ever made him a saint."

On the top floor there was cracking linoleum, exposed pipes, a cold radiator that two men in overalls were working on. Coni opened a door for her. Blaize went in and Coni slammed the door behind them. Blaize turned quickly.

The room was simply and neatly furnished. Black-enameled metal bedstead, patchwork quilt, a rocker, an armoire, a reading desk with a magnifying lamp, books in old glass-front legal bookcases. The wall above the bed was filled with odd-sized framed photos. A what-not held a collection of music boxes. Some green plants and a Christmas poinsettia on a stand soaked up the meager light from a single window. There was a second closed door, leading to the bath or an adjoining room.

Near that door a husky kid with slicked-back red hair was leaning, staring at Blaize, arms folded, his biceps flattened so they looked like horses' flanks. He had a lot of tattoos showing, some of them through the yellow cotton muscle shirt he wore with washed-out Levis.

"What we want you to do now is take off your coat, please," Coni said. "Give it to me. Then open your handbag and shake it out on the spread. Then I am going to give you a body search."

Blaize's eyes narrowed slightly.

"You doan want to cooperate, okay. This boy is Louis. He got his black belt a long time ago. He is expert. Louis doan mind separating your shoulder or something painful like that even though we are not into violence here; this is a non-violent place dedicated to the sick and the cripple."

"I'll cooperate," Blaize said, glowering.

"Only because we doan take the chance you have some kind of grudge against Dr. Purkey. This woman we all love, you unnerstand? There is nothing personal otherwise."

Blaize slowly took off her coat and handed it to Coni. Then, while the woman's hands went through the pockets and felt along every seam of the heavy coat, Blaize turned to the bed under Louis's watchful eye and opened her tote bag.

At the hotel she had debated the necessity for bringing along the .45 and at the last moment reluctantly decided to do without it, leaving the weapon, boxed so that no one could tell what it was, in the hotel's vault along with her few items of jewelry. She had left it because she didn't think she would be running into Lucas McIver all that soon; and because, although she hadn't anticipated a search, she could not very well have pretended to the doctor that she was there with the best of intentions, seeking a peaceful settlement to the old score, if she were armed.

When she had emptied her tote she gave it to Coni, who carefully sorted through the wallet and other things on the spread, putting them back one by one. Then Coni did a thorough job of patting her down, from ankles to crotch to the roots of her hair, before stepping aside and nodding to Louis.

The redhead went through the door he'd been leaning beside, leaving it half open. Blaize glimpsed a connecting bath, another bedroom beyond. Voices: the squeaking of a wheelchair. A new face in the doorway. Louis pushed the wheelchair across the room and turned it at the window, toward Blaize.

"Hello, my dear," Viola Purkey said.

The disease, a disorder of the nervous system, was a terrible one. The doctor slumped to one side of her wheelchair. She was partially covered by a heavy lap robe. She trembled uncontrollably, thin legs jumping beneath the robe, hands tapping on the arms of the chair. She wore a neck brace to hold her head erect. There could be no serenity for one who danced so aimlessly, with little hope of rest. Her brow was disorganized by pain, heavily puckered. Her skin was coarsely dried upon the bone and yellowed, nailed there with little brown hammer-marks of age. But her dark eyes had a stunning clarity and directness; her mouth smiled fiercely. Her hair was thin and gray, but she wore a flower in it, over one ear.

When she noticed the jaunty blossom, tears jetted into Blaize's eyes. She was confounded by her reaction and looked down, blinking, for a few moments.

"Hello," she said.

"So you're Blaize." There was a tremor in her voice too, but she wasn't difficult to understand. "I've always thought that you were strikingly photogenic. But photographs in newspapers don't do you justice. In person, you're simply stunning." Blaize shrugged and said nothing, wiping at an eye. The doctor cleared her throat. "Well. Why don't you sit down? I've often wished you'd pay me a visit. Instead we had to settle for all those detectives. Not that we haven't been grateful for them."

"Grateful?"

"Oh, yes. The neighborhood is busy, as you see, but homogenous, eighty percent black, the rest Hispanic. Everyone knows who belongs here and who doesn't. Quite a problem for maintaining long-term surveillance, I would imagine. One can't just loiter about the street without quickly being identified as the fuzz, or worse than that, I suppose, a narc. That might lead to sudden violence in an alley. So the solution was to have them work right here in Zacchaeus's clinic. Day and night, there's always something to do. We're totally dependent on donations, you know, volunteer labor to keep the clinic open. These past couple of years your private investigators have put in a staggering number of man-hours fixing up, painting, cleaning, looking after the old and the helpless. Now I understand they're all gone."

"That Eddie, he was a cute one," Coni said as she brought Blaize a chair. "Always telling a funny story. I will miss him."

"Why have you and your father decided to quit watching us?" Dr. Purkey asked Blaize.

"It was my decision."

"Yes?"

"Dr. Purkey, I want to make an end to it now."

"You want to end what?"

"The fear I've lived with. Fear of being killed because I was the last one left, the only one of us who saw him in the house that night. Revenge isn't worth dying for. I just want to get on with my life, to be free and at peace. Wherever McIver is now, I'm sure that's what he wants too."

"Why did you come to me?"

"I'd like for you to get in touch with him. Tell him I must see him. It'll be just the two of us. Alone. No traps. No police. He can set up the meeting any way he wants."

"Oh, child, I don't know where Lucas is," Viola said with

a dreamy smile. "Don't know how to get in touch with him."

Blaize watched her face closely. "Dr. Purkey, I have reason to believe he'll be here soon. Even before Christmas."

She took this prophecy too calmly, Blaize thought.

"That would be a blessing, to see his face again. But it would be no blessing to have him killed on our doorstep."

"It won't happen. I swear to you, the surveillance teams have been removed for good."

"Yes, you can take away the detectives you paid for. But you can't take away your father's thirst for blood." For a few moments old anger lived in Viola's eyes. Then she focused her attention on a small calendar painting of Christ on the cross opposite them, and gradually the anger was replaced with a more fulfilling emotion. She looked at Blaize.

"Unless you have a different story to tell now. As you say, you're the last one, the only one who knows what truly happened the night your brother Jordon died."

Blaize shook her head emphatically but sat back in her chair. Although she knew she had nothing to fear from the old woman, she realized, now that she had taken the leap, the extreme danger of the position she had placed herself in.

Viola seemed to perceive her state of mind.

"Lucas is the only son I've ever had. And I will swear on my Bible he was no cold-blooded killer while I had him under this roof. But how he is now—well, that would be a different story. A man learns to protect himself, any way he can."

"Do you think he wants to kill me?" Blaize asked.

"How can either of us know what's in his heart at this time? But I'll tell you this—he would do nothing to you if it would be hurting me. Child, let me see your hands."

It was very nearly traumatic for Viola to capture one of Blaize's hands between her own and hold on to it despite the palsy.

"Not soft like I expected. Hard. Such long fingers."

"I've been on a lot of digs—archaeology. And I ride almost every day."

"Where are you staying in Chicago?"

Blaize told her.

"There's an empty bedroom right through there. I'm not saying you need to look after an old woman, but I wouldn't mind the company of someone who's not too busy to share a book with me. Maybe we have a lot of waiting to do. Maybe not. Meantime, there are never enough hands for all the work to be done around here."

Blaize could scarcely believe it. She was being given the opportunity to stay at the clinic day and night until Lucas McIver showed up! But her first surge of excitement vanished quickly. Was it an opportunity, or a potential death trap?

He would do nothing to you if it would be hurting me.

Blaize wasn't fool enough to think that Viola Purkey had swallowed everything she'd been told, but apparently she wanted to trust Blaize. It would not be easy to put anything over on this formidable woman, despite her illness. Yet there had been something between the two of them almost from their first words: genuine empathy, a need for understanding.

Dr. Purkey knew she was going to die. And perhaps for her this was a final chance to close the books on a tragedy, to clear Lucas McIver's name.

"I-I'll have to get some things from the hotel."

"It isn't easy to find a cab on Bozeman Street," Viola said. "Perhaps Louis can drive you."

"Sure," Louis said.

His car was parked half a block from the clinic. It was a '57 Chevrolet that looked too pathetic to steal: patched, sanded, ill-painted, the right front fender and grille gone. There was a decal on the driver's side, a hard-faced man in a beret holding a submachine gun erect in one fist. MERCS, the legend said, DO IT FOR PROFIT.

"My brother," Louis explained. "He was with the Selous Scouts and the Angola Headhunters. Now he's in Guatemala." Louis took the car keys from a pocket of his black-leather jacket, then scowled at someone across the street. "Excuse me a minute. There goes a guy, owes me a bill for three months now. I need to rap with his ass."

"Take your time," Blaize said.

She was standing on the sidewalk in a sudden fit of lethargy, eyes half-closed against the sun's glare, hands deep in the pockets of her shearling coat, the collar up to keep the wind from her ears, when a white pimpmobile with darkly tinted windows cruised slowly by. Then it backed up, stopped a few feet from her. A back window of the Cadillac glided down. She saw a thin face with an oval of mustache and beard, a camel's-hair coat, a pinkish slouch hat with an ocelot-skin band. Long cocoa-colored hands and bejeweled fingers. He talked with his hands, and showed a rat-jut of gleaming long teeth.

"Hello, sweet thing. Ain't seen you on my street befo'. You be Louis's girl?"

"No."

"How come you be standin' there all by yo'self in the cold? You ain't no kinda workin' girl, is you?"

Blaize's lip curled. "Fuck off, pimp," she drawled.

"Oh, now. My, my. Lighten up. Thass no way to talk to Sweet Willie Wine. Come from the *South*, does you? Hey! You and me, baby, I know we could get along fine. Take a little willingness on yo' part, thass all. Sweet Willie is one generous dude. Hey! Ask anybody that know me. Too good fo' my own good. Now whatever it is you down here lookin' fo', score some dope, black cock or pussy, all you got to do is ask. I don't want nothin' in return. Jus' the pleasure of yo' company, dig?"

By then Blaize had reached into her purse and taken out the folder with her gold badge from the Kentucky Bureau of Investigation. She flashed it at Sweet Willie Wine. He withdrew into the interior of his dandified Caddy.

"Aw, hey. What'd I say? What'd I do? Jus' makin' conversation."

"Move your ass. Before I bust it."

"Shit! Try to do somethin' fo' somebody, they mess with yo' head."

The window slid up, the Sedan de Ville pulled away, made a U turn and picked up speed, missing Louis by a few inches as he hustled back across the street. Blaize put her badge away.

"What was that about?"

"Recruiting for the pussy patrol," Blaize said.

In the Cadillac Sweet Willie Wine took a last lingering look at Blaize through the cabriolet rear window. When he turned around he was scowling.

"Fuckin' cop."

"I don't know, boss," the driver said. His name was Snake Grace. He was six feet six, with no hips and almost no shoulders. He had a long bullet-shaped perfectly hairless head, little ears and lidless, Oriental eyes. Undressed, and from the right perspective, he looked like the world's tallest hard-on.

"You don't know *what*?"

"That tin didn't look right to me. Ain't what the local heat carry. Maybe she some kinda out-a-town fuzz."

"Or maybe it was jus' some tin she pick up at the fuckin' dime store." Sweet Willie Wine mulled over his own humiliation, and a lost opportunity, which as a businessman he most regretted. "Tell you one thing. She don't be no white trash. The bitch got some sweet licks in her. Hey! Ever see it 'round here again, I jus' maybe gonna teach it a lesson, have m'self some *injoys* at the same time."

Chapter 8

Bernardsville, New Jersey

Theos Melissani maintained his large family in a ten-bedroom, hundred-and-fifty-year-old mansion on the south bank of the Navesink River in Rumson, New Jersey. He spent an average of three nights a week at home, the rest of the time in the city. His brother Plato also lived in New Jersey, on a hunt-country estate. Two Sundays of each month the brothers and their families gathered for horseback riding or sailing, depending on the weather.

On the Sunday following the bizarre murder of Joe D'Allesandro, which had focused an unwelcome beam of publicity on the cousins after thirteen uneventful years, Theos sat with his brother in Plato's sunny corner library in the house near Bernardsville, discussing the murder and the subsequent investigation. The paneling of the library was a cheerful apple-green, with the grain of the wood showing through the paint. The carpet was a massive Bokhara. There were more than two thousand volumes in this particular library, half of them in Greek, some very old; Plato was intimate with them all. Plato loved his wife, his son and daughter, his daily workouts in the gym. But most of all, he loved his library and his books. Despite his great physical strength, he was by nature a contemplative man, direct in his dealings with others. He disliked the game of business, the subterfuge and deception, the groveling before profits. He did not appreciate his brother's powerful ambition for himself and his sons; but Plato forgave him for it and attended to the banking, which was his forte. He loved Theos uncritically, lavishing on him love that the boys had not received from their father, a temperamental man with jagged edges, given to rages that shackled the heart. There was sturdy weight in Plato's every emotion; you saw him laughing, but never gay.

The Sunday *News*, open on a nearby table, had devoted much of the second and third pages to the crime and the lack of progress in solving it; the paper also had rehashed an old tragedy, the death of Argyros Coulouris's young wife Elizabeth on the day after their wedding. As if one had to do with the other. It was disgusting, the brothers agreed. But the investigation would continue; the cousins would remain inaccessible; soon there would be nothing more to write about, and they would once again fade from public view.

Joe D'Allesandro had been well-liked and well-connected during his years as a New York City policeman; it was almost as if he were still working for the city and not for Actium, so his murder had caused much greater reaction throughout the police department than might have been expected. But four days later there were no leads. The *Post* had hinted, in two-inch-high headlines, that the style of the killing suggested a gangland reprisal, a judgment against the ex-cop for some unknown offense.

Plato doubted it. He was afraid that Joe's death was more directly connected to the current family preoccupation, about which they had said nothing to the investigating team from NYPD.

"Minotaur?" Theos asked.

Plato nodded.

"Why?"

"Joe was overseas for three weeks. He was making his yearly evaluation of our security arrangements in key cities: Frankfurt, Milan, Istanbul. But after the first two days, the business with our cousin Demetrios Constantine diverted him to Corfu. After that he canceled his itinerary. He went to Athens, then to France and Switzerland. We don't know why.

Let's assume his conversations with our cousin provided him with a lead to Minotaur that he felt he should investigate immediately. Whatever he learned, he made no report we've been able to find. But we may also assume that Minotaur knew what Joe was up to and considered him a threat, to be eliminated as soon as possible."

Theos listened to the sounds of collies barking on the lawn outside, children's voices. The young ones had been playing soccer. There was a rhubarb in three languages. He smiled faintly and looked into Plato's troubled gray eyes.

"You make Minotaur sound omnipotent."

"Just very well-informed. How did Minotaur know about the Cirenaica spore in the first place? Demetrios Constantine is not a talkative man."

"I see. You think Minotaur may be working from inside the company."

"It's a logical progression, Theos."

"No Turks?"

"I wish I could believe all of this is the inspiration of terrorists. But remember the phone call to Argyros."

"I didn't hear it."

"We have it on tape, of course. The sound of—Minotaur's voice is disturbing. Meant to be. We are all named. Marked for death. The question is, why? Who would gain from our deaths? Our direct heirs are all minor children. Actium International would be dismantled, sold piecemeal. Who gains from that? No one individual or organization. There are no logical political implications. It puzzles me. The call was no more than a cold-blooded promise of revenge."

"Revenge for what?"

"I don't know. It's possible Joe knew. We should make every effort to see if he left us any information." Plato's pipe had gone out. He relit it, sat staring at the birch-log fire on the hearth. "We need to name Joe's successor. Van Raburn is a good choice. Or we could bring in someone from the outside."

"I'm in favor of Raburn. And if the threat is from within the company, we must trace it quickly."

Plato nodded.

"The Cirenaica spore is important to Minotaur. Why? What does it have to do with the threats against our lives? We should start with Cirenaica."

"Where Joe started," Plato said forebodingly.

"Everyone who had the opportunity to know about Cirenaica is suspect. I'm excluding Demetrios Constantine."

"Who will investigate for us? Van Raburn?"

"His background is in security techniques; Joe relied heavily on him there. But Van isn't a trained investigator. Plato, I can't get out of my mind the way Joe died. It was savage. Primitive. An object lesson. We need someone who is equally ruthless and very clever, unorthodox in his thinking and methods. Someone who will be motivated not by a fee, but by ideological considerations. Cirenaica is a deadly threat to millions. Demetrios believes he has a friend who will be compelled not only by the challenge, but by the necessity of stopping Minotaur before the Cirenaica spore can cause widespread famine."

"Our cousin knows a man with these qualifications?"

"Yes. Demetrios met him while he was consultant to an agricultural mission in some godforsaken Latin American country. The man's name is McIver, Dr. Lucas McIver. A man of many skills, some of them tainted. There was an incident involving a small hospital ship operated by a Swiss foundation. The ship was seized in port by a brother of the president of the republic and turned over to a favorite of his, the swindler Rudolf Lasch."

"Ah, yes. In exile all these years."

"Lasch was about to marry into the ruling family to ensure his continued comfort and safety in exile. This McIver, pretending to be outrageously homosexual, caused a disturbance at a prenupital party. He realized his intention to be thrown into prison so that he might work from the inside to free the captain of the vessel and his crew. He smuggled a small pistol in with him."

"Difficult to believe the prison guards would not search him to the skin, and beyond."

"It seems McIver did a realistic job of makeup on his

genitals so that he appeared to be literally erupting from venereal disease."

Plato made a face, then laughed. "Go on."

"McIver was successful in engineering the jailbreak. The ship was retaken without much bloodshed and sailed beyond the reach of gunboats. The foundation was immediately three million dollars richer. Lasch had imprudently left the safe in the master bedroom stocked with some rare items of pre-Columbian jewelry intended for his bride-to-be."

"Interesting. A rogue-errant with a gift for theater, plus a social conscience. Still, I don't know that this McIver fits in with our needs."

"Demetrios not only recommends him, he is at this point unwilling to trust anyone else."

The brothers stared at each other while the birch logs crackled. Plato brushed at tobacco clinging to a lapel of his cashmere blazer.

"How do we find Dr. McIver?" he asked.

"That's the difficult part. He's a fugitive himself. He uses aliases. Demetrios may know how to reach him."

"A fugitive. We may be asking for more trouble than we have already. Can we depend on our cousin's judgment in this matter?"

"He was always a child among men. But I find him less ingenuous these days. The misfortunes with Niko have sharpened his perceptions of the world. If he's willing to trust McIver, he must have observed something of value in the man."

"There is a need for urgency," Plato said, scratching surreptitiously at his close-cropped, thinning gray hair. A few wiry strands fell through a mote of sun. Another time Theos might have joked with him about his rapidly receding hairline.

"I think we should try to find McIver, arrange a meeting, then decide for ourselves."

Plato nodded. He stretched himself in the glove-leather chair. He looked tired and a trifle feverish today; there was a cold sore at one corner of his mouth. But Theos, admiringly, saw only the huge arm muscles straining the sleeves of the blazer Plato wore. Once Plato had been able to ride his little brother around on his shoulders for hours, never tiring. Theos wondered what it would be like to fight Plato. A disaster. At fifty-two, he was immensely strong and still very quick.

And he thought of his brother dead. Prone, bloodless, unbreathing.

It was a quirk of Theos's nature, cold ink stealing into his veins. On the brightest, happiest days, a sudden pall over the sun. Death overtaking him or, worse, those he loved. Animus. Retribution for past sins so secret none living could recall. But somewhere there had to be a Fate keeping score.

Theos had a lump in his throat. At times he could sit by the hour drinking ouzo, and the lump wouldn't dissolve. Swallowing tears could not wash his throat clean. But he was luckier today. It all passed, he grinned, the sun was bright again, he felt secure in his wealth, his progeny. Immortal. The threat of Minotaur receded to a dim shadow at the back of his mind.

"A drink?" Plato asked him.

"Sure; Scotch," Theos said with a loving smile. They moved together toward the bar. "Then backgammon."

"First we'd better call Papa. Otherwise we'll play on and on, you'll never get even, and you won't be able to say anything nice to anyone."

"Papa first," Theos agreed. "Has Penelope said what she wants for her name day?" Penelope was Plato's daughter. The brothers were fully relaxed now, happy in each other's company, needing no others, reveling in talk about the children.

"Nothing elaborate. A few stars from Cassiopeia no one's going to miss."

The two men laughed. They lifted their glasses together, looked into each other's eyes. They drank.

Chapter 9

Chicago

The suboccipital craniectomy at Luminarian Brothers Medical Center in suburban Bathgate Village had been in progress for more than three hours before the surgeons uncovered the tumor, using a two-man microscope with a cable attached that fed a TV monitor and video tape machine. The patient, a forty-five-year-old man, was clamped in a sitting position on the table, his eyes and nose taped shut, a respirator breathing for him. A clear plastic tube dripped anesthetic into his bloodstream. With the back of his head open for the lengthy exploration, air could easily seep into his blood, so a monitor amplified the sound of that blood as it flowed through the chambers of the heart. The pump-action gurgling and whooshing had been a ceaseless accompaniment to the painstaking manipulation of the scope in an area where every minute piece of tissue was uniquely valuable to the patient.

The tumor, a brain-stem glioma, was as blood-swollen and glowering in appearance as a hammered thumb. It stuck out from the orderly red tissue of the stem from which it had grown. A doctor from pathology appeared within minutes to take away a piece of the growth for analysis, but the staff surgeons and residents on hand were already certain it was malignant; most brain tumors were. The chief of neurosurgery at Luminarian got up from the microscope. He was sterile from his neck to his waist, but his feet were bare; he had bad feet and preferred to operate with his shoes off. He had done more than three dozen of the difficult craniectomies.

"Doctor, care to have a look?" he said to one of the attendings, a tall young man with oxbow shoulders under his OR greens, a short haircut and close-trimmed reddish beard, piercing gray eyes beneath a rugged brow.

"Thank you, doctor," Lucas McIver said.

He took the neurosurgeon's place on one of the stools and peered at the glioma for almost a minute while the cauterer was made ready. Then the neurosurgeon took over with the long instrument, which had tips like a pair of tweezers. When the tips came together, an electric current burned the malignant tissue a little at a time. A thread of curling smoke rose from the depths of the brain through the opening in the skull.

McIver admired the man's skill, first on the TV monitor, then through the dual eyepiece of the microscope. The surgeon's patience and concentration were heroic. But as good as he was, he couldn't get all of the tumor. The patient would have radiation treatment and, with luck, would live for many more years. McIver itched to do some of the actual excision himself, but he was neither staff nor resident, just a visitor from a remote mission hospital maintained by the Luminarians, in town to soak up in a few days what he could from those more widely read in the literature and better trained than he.

The operation ended just shy of the six-hour mark. There was time for shoptalk in the crowded locker room, fresh popcorn and gallons of soft drinks; then the doctors went separate ways, McIver to the medical library to read everything the neurosurgeon had published on the procedure he had spent his day observing.

The Leprechaun came in at five-thirty with fresh snow on his boots and found McIver xeroxing pages from a thick book on angiograms. The Leprechaun had fumes of good cheer on his breath.

"Did you have yourself an enjoyable day?"

"I saw a beautiful supracerebellar infarctorial approach to a brain-stem glioma. It belongs in the Hall of Fame."

"Were you inspired to do one yourself, darlin'?"

"I have about as much chance of doing one myself as I have of hitting a major league curve ball without taking batting practice."

"Ratin' yourself low these days."

"I didn't say I couldn't do it. The fingers know, the hands know, the brain knows. It's instinctive. With training, hell, I could make the first team. But the training takes seven years. Using the kind of equipment we'll never see in the bush."

"I did hope that rubbin' elbows with your peers might be a tonic for your morale."

"My morale's okay," McIver snapped. The Leprechaun smoothed the full collar of his knee-length sealskin coat and smiled placatingly. He had been with McIver for many years, as friend and mentor, and was familiar with all of his moods. The Leprechaun was stage-trained, a gifted actor and singer who, unfortunately, had come from the womb undersized and so hopelessly ugly he looked as if his face had been squashed by a truck tire. He had a cast in one eye. His nose was pug. His tufted ears were attached to his head at almost right angles. He was doomed to playing secondary comedy roles in mediocre touring companies and on telly. Audiences never heard him sing, though he had a clear tenor voice that would stimulate the tear ducts of a slumlord. Until he was well past thirty he'd lived a life of shadows, both onstage and off. His other talents were for thievery, the elegant sting. The plots he composed, for no applause save his own, made up in some measure for the limited roles he played in the theater.

Now the Leprechaun was in his late fifties, still no higher than a tot and a half, but stouter. Age had helped his looks; he'd grown into the character he was always meant to be. There was green mischief in his gaze and the ladies loved it; his wide, gap-toothed smile was half huckster and half shark.

McIver finished his xeroxing. "What did you find out?" he asked the Leprechaun.

"Blaize Ellington has been at the clinic for a week. She and Viola are very nearly inseparable. All surveillance, electronic and otherwise, has been discontinued. Everything is bliss and serenity on Bozeman Street."

"Says who?"

"The always-dependable Louis."

"Has he tossed her room?"

"That he has. On a daily basis. She brought a gun with her. A .45 ACP. Accurized. Custom-fitted to her grip. A lovely weapon, sez our Louis. But unladylike. A man doesn't have a sportin' chance at less than forty yards."

"What did he do with the piece?"

"Left it right where Miss Ellington went to so much trouble hidin' it in the first place."

"What do you think she has it for?"

"Protection. The old neighborhood's not the garden spot it used to be."

McIver fingered a scar on his neck he'd had since breaking up a fight in the Zacchaeus Center when he was seventeen. He took off his reading glasses and put them in a pocket of his corduroy jacket. "She came around to blow my head off. More guts than good sense. But that leaves a couple of questions."

"If one accepts your explanation of her motive."

"Viola hasn't gone soft in the head, so she must know what Ellington is up to. Why does she let her hang around?"

"Perhaps Viola isn't as convinced as you that Blaize has murder on her mind."

"Second question. How did she know I was coming to Chicago?"

The Leprechaun smiled. "Easier to answer. We are never, at any time, as clever as we like to think we are. Consider the resources that have been mobilized against you, old darling. Do we always cover our tracks so well? Remember Bangkok."

McIver remembered. It was almost enough to give him a headache on the spot.

The Leprechaun looked around the medical library. "One might wonder if this is the best place for you to be stayin' whilst you remain in the States."

"It is," McIver said shortly. He lowered his voice. "Here I'm just another mission doctor on sabbatical, with all the credentials I need to prove I'm 'Robert Painter.' Look, it doesn't matter if Ellington is here or how she came to be here. We'll see Viola tonight, and every night this week if we want to, and Ellington will never be the wiser."

"With an assist from our ever-faithful Coni." The Leprechaun looked at his pocket watch. "We do have a bit of a drive ahead, and perhaps we shouldn't think too hard on empty stomachs. How about The Mother of Pearl?"

"Indonesian food? Yeah. I'm pretty damn sick of Burger King. What the hell, if we're going to live at all, we might as well live dangerously. And Viola always was crazy about Mother's *tom yam kung*. We'll get a pint to go."

* * *

> ("The mind of man is capable of
> anything—because everything is
> in it, all the past as well as all
> the future. What was there after
> all? Joy, fear, sorrow, devotion,
> valour, rage—who can tell?—but
> truth—truth stripped of its
> cloak of time.")

Because of her affliction Viola Purkey was unable to get much sleep, in spite of her medication. Blaize was an insomniac who never took pills, but she didn't mind a little unadulterated Bolivian blue diamond or some high-quality grass now and then. It had been noted that marijuana in moderation had a beneficial effect on sufferers of Meiner's disease; it wasn't a cure, but for up to an hour after she smoked a joint Viola's jitters were noticeably reduced. Pot and the potent muscle-relaxers she took could in sufficient quantity put her away for a full night, but the aftereffects made her groggy and surly, so she limited her drug intake. She liked to have a glass of white wine with her evening meal, which she ate at five-thirty. At six she and Blaize watched the news on TV, then Blaize read to her for nearly an hour. They were working their way through the short novels of Joseph Conrad. Following the night's pages of *Heart of Darkness* or *The Secret Sharer*, they had tea. Viola couldn't swallow pills, and her medication was in the tea. Then they each had a joint. While they smoked they talked, mostly reminiscing, staying away from the Heavy Topic that was always in the room with them like a black beast hunkered down in one corner, and Viola almost always nodded off before nine.

Blaize had time to herself then, until midnight or a little after. She devoted an hour to exercise, walking up and down stairs to strengthen her leg and pop a sweat. She never went out alone after dark and seldom left the clinic at all. After exercising she devoted an hour to her bath and usually dozed herself, up to her chin in suds, with a constant trickle of hot water running into the high tub, its chipped porcelain stained with rust. She had been constantly near Viola, except for two afternoons when Viola had been taken by invalid coach to Cook County Hospital for a checkup and treatment. Of course she might have met with McIver while at the hospital, but Blaize didn't think so; there would have been some sign of the fugitive in Viola's eyes, some magnetic imprint of him when Blaize met the coach on its return.

After midnight Viola was always awake and Blaize stayed with her until Coni arrived at seven-thirty with the breakfast tray.

In the small hours of the night they watched old Edward G. Robinson movies on a Betamax; Viola never tired of the actor because, as she said, he was the "spit 'n' image" of her late husband Zacchaeus. The cigars! "You have to truly love a man to put up with his cigars. Z never talked tough or carried a heater, you understand. But Z wouldn't take lip from any man. And when he wanted to charm you, his whole face shone like a harvest moon." They ate M&Ms by the bowlful, although Blaize became constipated from all the chocolate. And always, around three a.m., they each smoked another joint that Blaize made from the lids provided by Louis. Then, and only then, with time slow and heavy on their hands like skeins to be rewoven, was it possible for them to speak seriously, without rancor, of an old crime, of wounds that resisted healing.

"You were just twelve years old," Viola had said to her on Wednesday night.

"Yes." Each word stretched Blaize's mouth in such a way

that she had consciously to put it right before she could speak again.

"It was the fall of the year. Late October. Well after midnight."

"Yes."

"You were in your nightclothes."

"Yes. Yes. I could sleep then. Before. But never—after."

"Can you tell me what you were wearing? Describe it for me."

Blaize took a long drag on her roach and held the smoke deep and tight, staring with narrowed, hazy eyes at Viola. The doctor's tremors had lessened, but then Blaize scarcely noticed them anymore: Viola had become the central figure of Blaize's existence in a week's time, and subtly larger than life—respected, even loved, although Blaize's love was tempered with coolness, with the knowledge that Viola loved another more, and could betray her.

"It was—yellow. I was pretty in yellow then. Can't—wear the color now. I look like—death."

"Could it be there's another reason for your aversion to yellow?"

"I don't know—what you mean."

"There was blood in that library room of your home."

"God." Blaize squirmed. "God—yes."

"And some of it got on your pretty nightgown. Didn't it?"

Blaize looked blank for a few moments. Then she opened her mouth as if kicked by a horse; she gasped.

"Please, Viola," she whined. "I don't—don't want to."

"What we're trying to do, child, is strip away that cloak of time Conrad wrote about. See it differently—if different it was from the way you have it in your head."

"But it wasn't different!"

"You forgot about the blood all these years. You just knew you couldn't wear yellow, the reason being that blood got on your nightgown. Whose blood was it, Blaize? Yours? Your brother's? Or the blood of Lucas McIver?"

"Oh, Viola!" Blaize gasped, twisting hard in her chair, the forgotten roach hot beneath her nostrils, a scrim of smoke before her eyes.

"Tell it to me, child. Tell it the way it really happened, so you can finally have the rest you deserve."

"You want me—to say things. Things that aren't true. But I don't lie. I never lied. *He shot my brother*!"

The strong pot hit her the wrong way then; usually she giggled and gabbed, but there were times when she sulked up like a whipped child and wanted to hide her face from the world. She turned from Viola and went to her own room next door, threw herself down on the bed hard enough to break the old springs.

And stillness. But no regret on Viola's part for prodding raw nerve; because news had been whispered, and urgency possessed her. Viola was receptive to a vision of events about to careen out of control, with no hope for the future where either of them was concerned. If she'd had two children of her own, she could not have wished for better than Lucas and Blaize. She sat helpless, her ticking muscles like the seconds of a clock working toward self-destruction. She wept a little but kept her head high. And prayed to God.

The next evening Blaize finished *Heart of Darkness*. They were served their tea. This time Blaize got the doctored cup. A sedative. She was unused to heavy eyelids, the slowed rhythm of her heart, the heaviness in her hands. She got up a couple of times to splash water on her face in the bathroom.

"I feel strange," she told Viola.

"Why don't you lie down for a few minutes? I'll be all right."

"You look—wide awake as a bird."

"Leave the television on for me, Blaize."

"O-kay." Blaize found her way through a fog to her room and curled up on the lumpy bed. It wasn't much of a mattress, but tonight it felt as if she were floating aimlessly, like a character in a children's storybook, on a big goose quill.

Although her experience with drugs was limited, she had just enough presence of mind to realize what might have happened. Could she have drunk Viola's tea by mistake?

Blaize meant to get up and find out, but she fell first into a dreaming state that was not quite like sleep. She fretted and perspired. She was home again. It was a warm Indian-summer night. The full moon outside the windows brought shadows in, a complex cage of branches from the Rowan oak within which her collection of crystal horses gleamed, brainstorms in their unearthly heads, minute points of gemlike fire. Was she alone in the house? She felt uneasy. The servants had their own quarters, in two cottages on the other side of the garden. Her father and mother were away for the weekend, in the East, visiting Lonnie at Lawrenceville. His first year at prep school. Mother thought he was too young to be away from home. So did Blaize. She missed him badly, even their fights. No reason anymore to think of elaborate excuses for spending the night in his room. She could sleep in either of the bunk beds now, play with his toys anytime she wanted. But it was no fun. He wasn't there to talk to.

But Jordan was home. He'd taken her to dinner and the movies in Lexington. Just the two of them. No snooty girlfriend of his she had to be nice to. For once she wasn't sharing him. He was letting his hair grow long. He had curly sideburns almost down to his shirt collar. He looked like great-grandfather Boyce Ellington in his Civil War uniform. On the way home she asked Jordy if he was ever going to get married and he laughed. "Why buy a cow when you can get milk through the fence?" Blaize wasn't sure of what he was talking about, but she laughed too.

The house was so quiet, and she had a headache. An Alka-Seltzer headache. Prime rib for dinner, both sour cream and butter on the baked potato. Sneaking nips of Jordan's bourbon-and-branch when he pretended he wasn't paying attention. Then the tub of popcorn at the show; she had eaten almost all of it by herself. The back of her throat was scratchy and her stomach felt like she might throw up.

Blaize heard his voice, at a distance. He was always a loud talker, particularly on the telephone. A hearing problem, Mom said, but Jordan wouldn't admit it. Tonight he sounded angry. For months and months there'd been trouble at the coal mines down south. Strikes and explosions. Jordan had been spending a lot of time at Wolf Fork Number Two and Dublin mines, trying to get the strike over with, the miners back to work. She hoped he wasn't going to have to drive down there tonight. Better ask him, remind him to be sure and have Bertha or her daughter Scottie come to the big house and stay with her.

Blaize got out of bed, and her room looked funny. Cramped and boxlike. Cold wooden floor, a narrow bed, a beat-up dresser against one wall, a mirror as clouded as a sick eye. All of her nice things were missing. No crystal horses galloping shelf to shelf. A sob hung in her throat, her head went round and round like the head on a ventriloquist's dummy; in a panic she leaned against the iron bedstead

until

the dreaming crested over her again, a flood of silken memory.

Where was she going? Oh, Jordy. Needed to talk to Jordan before he went speeding off in the dark. *A long way to Harlan. A long way to Hazard.* Danger in the lonely coves and byways of the hill country. He'd been shot at before. He carried two shotguns in his Cadillac, a .44 Special crammed into one boot.

There were three stairways in the antebellum mansion, one in front, two in back. Her bare feet sank into the carpet of the front hall. The big chandelier suspended over the marble-floored center hall was aglow; its light drew her toward it. The chandelier had once hung in an Austrian palace. Austria, Blaize thought. Lipizzaners. Those gorgeous white stallions.

"Jordan?"

Blaize heard voices again.

"I never had your daddy taken care of. That's not my style, boy."

A more youthful voice. One of the grooms? Tearful. Nearly incoherent. She couldn't understand, from where she was, what the boy was saying to Jordan. But Jordan gave him very little chance to speak.

"You son of a bitch. You got a hell of a nerve, comin' into my house with a pistol in your belt!"

Fear closed Blaize's throat. She clung to the curved railing and half-slid, heels bumping, down the front staircase.

"I'll forget about this. I'll forget about it if you get the fuck out right now, 'n don't ever let me see—"

Jordan's voice stopped; there were choking noises, furious grunts, expletives.

"Little cocksucker, you—"

And a single loud popping sound froze her. It was like two firecrackers going off together. She heard an outcry, a strangled scream.

Silence.

"Jordan!"

Her cry hung in the air. She didn't know where the popping sound had come from.

On her left the living room was dark. She was afraid to go in there. To her right there were closed doors. A small parlor, a powder room. The center hall opened onto a dining room at the back of the house. Through the dining room there was a large library on one side; beyond French doors lay a brick-paved veranda, then a terraced garden with a free-form swimming pool with rock-ledge waterfalls on all sides.

Blaize crept toward the dining room. The double doors stood open. The black undraped windows reflected light from the massive chandelier at the front of the hall.

She puked without warning, all over the marble floor, splattering her feet. She sobbed and choked and kept going, through the dining room.

One of the library doors was partly open; light spread across the highly polished oak floor in front of her.

Breathing through her mouth because her nose was full of vomit, Blaize went on wobbly knees to the doorway. Her fingers were numb and prickly cold; she swallowed hard to keep more vomit from coming up and searing her throat and tongue.

Standing near the fireplace was a tall boy with a fair, freckled complexion. He was wearing a red cowboy shirt with fake mother-of-pearl buttons. His shirttail hung out. He wore Levis and motorcycle boots. He held in one shaking hand a revolver with a long barrel, the finish dulled to gray from age and handling. The revolver was pointed at her brother, who lay on the floor at the boy's feet. Jordan was on his back, his hands flung wide, the fingers clenching and unclenching weakly; there was an opened Buck knife near his right hand. Jordan's body was jumping like a catfish on a clay bank, eyes wide and staring at the ceiling, a great smear of red on his puckered forehead a trickle of red down one cheek matting his sideburn—

Blood. Jordy. Blood! *Blood*!

The revolver fired again, so loud this close. She saw a jet of powder, flame and smoke, and flinched.

Blaize didn't care about the gun anymore; all she cared about was her brother, lying helpless on the floor as bullets smashed into him. She tried to get to Jordan.

The boy saw her. He turned, pointing the revolver at her.

Blaize dropped into a crouch, long arms wrapped around her knees, head down, snot and vomit on her upper lip. She was conscious of one thundering heartbeat, and then it seemed as if her heart had stopped, unable to function in a chest turned to stone. All she could think of was how big the bore of the revolver looked, how near to dying she was.

He was walking toward her. She heard him yell at her.

"No . . . no . . . no . . . no!"

He grabbed her powerfully, lifted her from the floor. Blaize dangled, two-thirds as long as he, in his grip. She had to look at him. His eyes were fixed and dilated, like those of a zombie in a movie. The masses of freckles were like little wounds all over his death-white face.

The revolver went off again, so close it burned her ear. Expression of shock and rage on his face. He dropped her. She noted that the palm of his free hand was cut, blood soaking the cuff of his shirt.

He hurled the revolver through the doorway into the dining room. It struck a mirror, shattering glass.

They looked at each other. She would never forget his eyes. Then he stared at Jordan on the floor.

"I wasn't," he said. "I didn't—" He clamped a hand on his groin as if trying to get himself under control, but a wet spot became larger, and she smelled it. "Ittttt, shitttttt, just went offfff!" He thrust out his left hand while he stood there knock-kneed and pissing. The palm was jaggedly open. "Look," he said through gritted teeth, trying to make her understand. "He cut me. And the gun—hair trigger—"

"Go away," Blaize said primly. She was deaf in one ear from nearly having been shot. She could barely hear her own voice. "I'll tell Daddy."

He began to cry. He backed away from her, sobbing, big hands flapping uselessly in the air as he tried to conduct a symphony in his defense. Then, his bladder empty, he turned and ran and burst through the French doors into the night, and out there someone was calling, "Stop, stop!" And a little later a truck motor roared and there were more shouts. Finally someone came into the library ("Oh, my Lorddd!") but Blaize didn't look up to see who it was. She was staring at her nightgown and the blood streak his hand had left there over her right breast, the little nipple peaked in blood, and then

she

stumbled hard against the TV in Viola's room, turning the picture on the tube to sizzling diagonals, and fell down to her knees, crying.

"Can't wear *yellow*, Viola!"

But Viola wasn't there.

Blaize looked slowly around the doctor's room. There was a hard lump of indigestion against her diaphragm; her vision swam eerily; everything in the room had a bad case of the tilts. She yawned. Dream-time was trying to impose on her again but, shaky as she was, blood pulsing seductively at her temples, she knew that she'd been had tonight. Viola, Coni, *somebody* had deliberately tried to knock her out, and that meant—

She forced herself to her feet.

Get rid of it, Blaize told herself sternly. *Maybe it's not too late*.

She made it into the bathroom. She was like a dry reed swaying in a wind. Leaning over the toilet bowl, she jabbed the back of her throat with long fingers and retched until her stomach was empty.

She felt as if the temperature in the building had plunged to forty below. She was suddenly coated in icy perspiration. But she could think a little more clearly, had more control over herself as long as she resisted sudden moves.

Then she began to laugh, even as furious tears rolled down her cheeks.

Not get away with this.

She walked to the elevator, staying in the middle of the hall. The floor seemed warped—it was a little like balancing on a high curb—but she resisted putting out her hands to steady herself.

The elevator was down. She peered, blinking, into the poorly lighted stairwell. All the way to the ground floor. The elevator was seldom used, except to transport Viola.

Blaize gasped for air. She just wanted to sit on the steps with her head on her knees. But there was a cold draft in the stairwell; she heard the unmistakable sound of the fire door next to the kitchen bang shut.

Out the back way. Alley. Wheelchair ramp.

She turned and opened the door to the first room along the hall. The windowpanes on the alley were covered with what looked like thick cotton batting; snow had been falling since two that afternoon. She strained to raise the window, pressing close to the hot radiator for better leverage. The window squeaked up a few inches.

Blaize looked down into the alley, at the top of the invalid coach. The engine was running. She saw, through a plume of white exhaust and the steady snowfall, Viola, muffled to her ears in her wheelchair and rising on the power lift of the coach. Parking lights reflected from a tarnished pane of glass revealed a knobby, jumping hand.

There was a tall man in the alley with Viola. Dark hat, coat, gloves, she could tell nothing about him.

But he was holding tenderly to Viola's other hand.

Blaize knew it was Lucas McIver.

She almost cried out in rage. Stepping back hastily from the window, she lost her balance, jammed a thumb painfully against the radiator. She hurried back to her room, bumping from wall to wall, her vision still bleary, unreliable. She chewed her lower lip in a frenzy.

In the room she pulled the .45 automatic from the carefully slit mattress. The gun was cocked and locked. She grabbed her shearling coat, put it on, thrust the automatic deep into a pocket and went out again, adrenaline pumping, her head clearer now.

Kill the son of a bitch. Kill him!

Going down the stairs she fell twice. The heavy coat protected her from serious injury. But she lost track of which floor she was on and had to stop to rest, to get her bearings.

No time!

When she lunged through the fire door into the alley, she saw the invalid coach at the far end, making a cautious left turn. The snow was heavy, Bozeman Street unplowed.

Blaize ran after the brown and white coach, keeping to the deep ruts the snow tires had made in the alley.

Her left leg began to ache. Footing was treacherous. But the hours of tramping up and down the stairs in the Zacchaeus Medical Center had been good for her wind.

The coach was three-quarters of a block away, going toward Cottage Grove, when she reached the end of the alley. Her hand was on the .45 in her pocket, but she had no thought of drawing and firing at the vehicle. Blaize didn't know if McIver was driving, and besides, Viola was inside. She had no wish, despite her expanding sense of outrage, to harm Viola.

The light at the intersection with Cottage Grove was red. There was heavy traffic on the avenue, proceeding cautiously. She saw a bus and a couple of trucks at a standstill. Horns were blowing. Blaize hadn't stopped running as she left the alley, but the going was heavier now. Her steps were labored. It was dream-time again, almost, except for the lash of the falling snow, the fire-bolt of the wind deep in her lungs. She couldn't close the distance between herself and the coach. Would they see her if they looked back? It didn't matter. She was unrecognizable in the dark and snow. She might be running to catch the bus. The light was still red, and a snowplow was momentarily in the way, hampering the movement of traffic. If only the light would hold, she would be there in less than half a minute.

The light changed to green. Blaize groaned.

The coach began to maneuver its way around the front of the bus. The revolving lights of the snowplow were reflected from tinted windows. The coach angled right on Cottage Grove and started downtown as Blaize, staggering, reached the avenue.

She spotted a northbound taxi that was stationary behind the bus and waved frantically for the driver's attention, pointing down Cottage Grove. The driver, who was on radio call, ignored her.

Blaize stared in dismay as the coach picked up speed going south. It was already a block away. Then a car trying to pull out at a diagonal from the curb spun its wheels and stalled; the brake lights of the coach came on and stayed on.

Still a chance—

She dodged a barking Great Dane wearing a plaid overcoat and plunged into the street through banked snow that was bumper-deep between parked cars. She didn't see the lights of the oncoming tow truck until it almost ran over her.

Blaize spun away as the high, flat plane of the truck's front bumper grazed her right hip and sent her sprawling, skidding on elbows and knees out into the middle of Cottage Grove Avenue.

Shit!

Cars were coming at her in slow pinwheels, brakes locked on the quarter-inch of polished snow the plow blades had left. Enough patches of blacktop showed through the scraped snow to give the brakes of the vehicles a chance to hold. There were a couple of minor collisions. Blaize scrambled for her life, rolled, came up almost under the wheels of a passing bus and jerked away. Horns. Angry voices.

"Where the fuck do you think you're going?"

With tears in her eyes from the salt mush on the pavement, she reached the safety of the opposite sidewalk and looked south at the dwindling taillights of the invalid coach.

She was holding on to a parking meter, still too wobbly to stand up on her own, when she felt a hand on her shoulder.

"Hello, *Ken*tucky mama. Thought we might be seein' you again sometime."

Sweet Willie Wine's outrageous cologne had almost the effect of a popper under the nose. She saw his Sedan de Ville a few feet away, a door open, the faces of dark foxes, twinkle of jewels inside. Sweet Willie was a vision in a cashmere topcoat with a chinchilla lining and a chinchilla Borsalino to match, a rust suede jump suit with knee-high boots of ostrich hide.

"I—listen—need wheels. Catch up to—invalid coach. See? There goes. It's goddam important! Life and death!"

"Sho', sho', calm yo'self. Sweet Willie here to help."

"That way. Down Cottage Grove. Hurry! Follow—"

"Hear that, Snake?" Sweet Willie said to his driver. "Got us a desperate e-mergency here. Can you handle it?"

"Yeah, I can handle it."

To Blaize Sweet Willie said, "Jus' get on in now. Watch yo' step. Hello, ladies! Move over now, make us some room."

"She all wet, Sweet Willie," one of the foxes whined.

"Shut yo' fuckin' mouth! Ain't gonna hurt nothin'. What you think I got them leopard-skin throws for?"

Sweet Willie's big hand guided Blaize into the car. She was trying to keep an eye on the fast-disappearing invalid coach and was just conscious of her surroundings, the tang of pot, flash and dark luster of leather and silk, bracelets and rings, paint and pompadour. Hostile haughty eyes on her. She sank back in a tight squeeze between Sweet Willie's hard flank and a high-waisted transvestite with an orange afro and sequins on her black-net stockings. Another time Blaize would have died laughing at the carnival atmosphere. Two of Sweet Willie's South Side *soigné* paramours sat hunched on jump seats. Sweet Willie waved a languid hand adorned with eight big rings.

"Drive on, Snake." He looked indulgently at Blaize as the loaded Cadillac pulled away from the curb. "Ain't this *de*-luxe?" Too late she felt his other hand in her coat pocket.

He pulled the .45 free and held it up. Blaize made a futile grab for the weapon, and the Orange Queen hit her under the chin with a sharp elbow. Blaize's head jerked to one side, her front teeth struck sparks.

"Hm, hmm. Now what we got here?"

"Fuckin' cannon," one of the foxes said, and giggled.

"Whooo-whee! All cocked and ready to go off."

"Watch it, you son of a bitch! Look, he's getting away! *Give me that*."

The tough transvestite raised her elbow threateningly again. Blaize subsided. Sweet Willie handed the .45 muzzle-first over the front seat to Snake Grace. "Don't blow your jewels off with that thing." He turned to Blaize, smiling, showing all his crowned, gold-encased teeth. The Cadillac turned right, off Cottage Grove. Blaize stiffened.

"Where are we going?"

Sweet Willie's hand stroked the back of her head. Then he grabbed a hank of hair and twisted persuasively. As Blaize tried to resist, the nearest fox held up a hand and a stiletto lanced into view. Blaize stopped struggling.

"Where we headed? My place, of course. Look like you in a whole lot of distress 'bout somethin'. We'll get to the bottom of it. Sweet Willie is yo' man. *Mi casa es su casa*, as the fuckin' P.R.s tell it. Like I said, why don' you jus' relax yo'self? My place we'll have a drink, a little pop, freebase, what the hell, yo' choice entirely. Sweet Willie have it all. Hey! Relax, I said. We got us all night, and tomorra too. I be a lovin', carin' man, baby."

Sweet Willie opened his mouth wide and laughed from deep inside his throat; it was a cavernous, dark-toned sound, with just a nuance of menace. Blaize stared at him, her neck painfully crooked from the violence of his grip on her hair. She saw nothing but her own elongated, despairing reflection in the mirror lenses of the fancy French shades he wore.

She was ready to take her chances, kick at the hand that held the stiletto, fight them all, raise so much hell they'd be forced to heave her out into the street; but the Orange Queen pried her jaws apart while the fox with the knife leaned forward a little to touch the point of the blade against Blaize's Adam's apple.

"You look like you 'bout to jump out of yo' skin, honey; try one of these."

The Orange Queen popped a capsule onto the back of Blaize's tongue. Then she closed Blaize's mouth for her and massaged expertly under the jawline; Blaize was forced to swallow. When she did, her Adam's apple was pricked by the stiletto and a drop of blood appeared.

Sweet Willie yelled at the fox, let go of Blaize's hair and tenderly flicked the orb of blood away with a scented handkerchief.

"What—are you going to do with me?" Blaize asked Sweet Willie Wine as they glided through the snow.

"Why, baby, I am jus' gonna kill yo' fine white ass with kindness. Then I am gonna ship it out to the street and let it earn me a suitable *re*ward fo' my time and trouble."

Blaize began to laugh, and Sweet Willie laughed too; but her brain was already more than a little fuzzy, and there was something building behind her eyes, a fearsome dark tide that threatened to roll through her brain and carry her deep into oblivion.

It occurred to Blaize that, ludicrous as this situation was, she was going to have one hell of a time getting out of it.

At about the time Blaize's pursuit of Lucas McIver was taking an unexpected turn, United Airlines Flight 763 from Des Moines, Iowa, to Chicago was arriving two and a half hours late at O'Hare due to the weather.

Dr. Mark Ridgway of Iowa State University in Ames was one of the first passengers off the airplane. He had carried all his luggage aboard with him: briefcase, a small under-the-seat bag, a hang-up two-suiter. He was ticketed first-class to Corfu, Greece, by way of Rome on Alitalia. The connecting flight was due to depart at ten o'clock the next morning. He hoped it would leave as scheduled. He had urgent business with Demetrios Constantine Aravanis, the Greek botanist who had arranged for him to make this trip so close to the Christmas holidays. Ridgway disliked traveling and hated being away from his family, particularly during basketball season, when there were a lot of tournaments scheduled. All three of his sons and his daughter played for their high-school and college teams and, at six-five, Ridgeway had been a starting forward for three seasons at the University of Kansas, on a team that featured Wilt Chamberlain at center.

"Dr. Ridgway? I'm from Actium International. My name is Leda Watson."

The young woman who met him at the gate was small-boned, more than a foot shorter than he. She was wearing a black suit, white shirt and black bow tie, a peaked velveteen cap. She wore rose-tinted glasses and was overly made up, which didn't enhance her rather plain features. She had a stiff, lacquered, doll-like appearance. There was a slight accent he couldn't place.

"How do you do?"

"I have a car outside. How was your flight?"

"Seems there's only one runway open. We kept circling and circling. I thought we might have to go on to Detroit or Cleveland."

She smiled. "I'm certainly glad that didn't happen. Accommodations have been arranged for you. We'll see to it that you're at the airport in ample time for your flight tomorrow morning. I understand that the weather in Corfu is very fine for this time of the year."

"I won't be there long. A day or two."

"May I take this bag for you?"

"Thank you."

"This way, sir."

Ridgway followed her through the terminal, keeping an eye on the small bag in her hand. She walked briskly enough to cause him to lengthen his stride. Beyond the windows, snowplows were working on the field, a swarm of flashing yellow lights. An unseen jumbo jet took off overhead, sending back thunder through the steady snow.

She had left the small, dark-blue Aries wagon in the parking structure opposite United. She put all the luggage in the wagon, smiling again.

"I believe you'll have more legroom if you ride in the backseat."

"Yes, thank you. Where are we going, into the city?"

She nodded. "The company has a very nice floor of suites in the Castlebar Tower on the lakefront. Fully staffed with butlers and maids. You'll be quite comfortable."

"Sounds good," Ridgway muttered and settled back for the tedious ride.

Instead of taking the direct route to downtown Chicago, she got onto the southbound Tri-State Tollway outside the airport.

"You're not taking the Kennedy?" Ridgway asked. He knew the Chicago area. He had taught at Northwestern for five years in the late sixties, before accepting the McCambridge Chair of Botanical Science at Ames.

"There was a bad accident in the southbound lanes when I was coming out. Two overturned tractor trailers. It looked as if all the lanes were blocked. Might take them most of the night to clear it up."

"Where are you from?" he asked. "I can't place your accent."

"Greece," she said. "But I've spent most of my time in the States."

"Watson isn't a Greek name."

"Leda is. Would you like some music on the radio?"

"Fine."

She dialed around the FM band and settled on a good reading of the Liszt *Sonata* in B minor. Ridgway played the piano some and respected anyone who could really get the most from this difficult composition. The playing sounded to him like Rubenstein's. He closed his eyes, listening to the *Sonata* and the almost subliminal swish of the windshield wipers, a soothing counterpoint.

"Mr. Ridgway?"

"Yes?" He was nearly dozing.

"You did bring it all with you? The spores? And *El Invicto*?"

"Certainly. Demetri said—" Ridgway felt a sting of caution. *El Invicto* had been Cesár Pagán's code name for the new strain of hybrid corn that now existed only as embryonic tissue, meticulously dried in a gylcerine solution and stored in liquid nitrogen, in the Duraflask that Ridgway carried in his flight bag. He had thought that only Pinto, Demetrios Aravanis and he himself knew about *El Invicto*. And Pinto was dead, savagely murdered. Just who was this Leda Watson person?

Demetrios hadn't said anything about his being met in Chicago by a representative of Actium International.

Ridgway looked out the window, seeing nothing that was familiar. Some low buildings. Lights and a chain-link fence around an industrial park. Traffic wasn't heavy. He looked at his watch. The going was slow. They'd been driving for nearly twenty minutes. The Liszt had ended. He was now listening to a stodgy trio for piano, violin and cello that he hadn't heard before. Ridgway rubbed his high forehead. It was hot in the Aries; he was perspiring. His rimless glasses had half-moons of mist on the lenses.

"Could you, uh, please turn the heat down?"

"Certainly, sir."

"What is it you do for Actium?"

"Whatever they ask me to do." She angled the wagon to an offramp. He saw green signs through the steamy windows and the snow. Archer Avenue. Now wherethehellwasthat?

"You haven't got yourself lost, have you?"

"No, sir. I'd better find some gas. I didn't realize I was so low. We'll be only a few minutes."

Ridgway didn't say anything. He sat back, still perspiring. They drove west on Archer Avenue. A lighted Shell Oil emblem drifted by outside.

"That station's open." He had decided he'd better make a couple of phone calls.

"Oh, I don't have their card. I think there's a Texaco just a few blocks from here."

There seemed to be a lot of nothing where they were. Isolated side streets, a few dark buildings, occasional street lights. She made another turn, down an unplowed cross street. The wagon wallowed in snow.

"Oh, dear."

"What's the matter?"

"I think—I guess I made a mistake. I don't want to go this way. I'd better turn around."

Ridgway was about to say something sarcastic—he was famous for his cutting tongue and his willingness to exercise it on hapless students—but he swallowed his irritation. It was a free ride, after all. And he wasn't in a hurry to get somewhere.

He had decided there was no reason to feel so damned uneasy. All he wanted was the chance to call home before midnight and find out how Kerry had done against that all-state guard from Waterloo West.

Now they were veering sloppily down a long alley; goddam woman couldn't do anything right. He could see nothing on either side but walls with barred windows, doorways, trash bins with snowdrift heaped alongside them.

"Young lady, I really think—"

She was stopping.

Something was in the way just ahead, blocking the alley. She flicked on the high beams. He sat forward, trying to make it out through the windshield. High, boxy superstructure in back, like a—a—

"Is that a hearse?"

"Yes, sir. I believe it is."

"Better back up."

"I know."

She put the wagon into reverse. The snow tires spun and the light rear end skidded, nearly colliding with a dumpster. They had no traction. The headlights continued to shine on the rear of the hearse.

"Well," she said, "this looks like the end of the road."

"Oh, now, we can't stay here!"

"I think someone's in that hearse," she said. "Maybe he'll move if it's not stuck. Would you come with me?"

Without waiting for his reply she got out, gingerly; Ridgway joined her and she smiled a strained smile. They trudged together thirty feet to the hearse. Someone was inside, all right. A hulking brute. Ridgway could make him out through the scrim of snow on the window of the left side door.

Leda Watson scrubbed some of the snow from the glass and had to rap on it before he became aware of her presence. His head turned. He took a long look at her. Then he rolled the window down three-quarters of the way. Snow blew on him, spangled his knitted brows. The man had the curls of a Sampson, the deep-set ashen eyes of an existentialist philosopher and a mouth that was about as appealing as a pair of pliers; the crimped lips ruined his handsomeness, made Ridgway think uneasily of base passion, the monstrosity lurking behind the erotic nature of man.

Nothing was said. Leda and the large man stared at each other. Then the man reached through the window and handed her something.

In the glare of the Aries' headlights Ridgway saw a revolver with a six-inch barrel. And a silencer attached to the barrel.

She turned to face him, revolver in hand.

"We have nothing against you, Mr. Ridgway," she said softly. Never expressive, she now exuded all the warmth of a shrunken head. Terror rippled through him like a big, shiny crosscut saw. "Unlike the others, you haven't opposed us. You have to die, but it would be discourteous to leave you in this alley or a ditch by the side of the road. So we've gone to some trouble to see that you're promptly returned to your family. I promise that you'll be on the first plane in the morning back to Iowa. We'll arrange for shipment of your body direct to your door."

"What—what are you—"

She bit her lower lip and aimed for the forehead, a prominent expanse; but she wasn't a marksman and it wasn't an easy target even at ten feet, given the weather and lighting conditions. The barely audible shot struck him in the throat instead. Ridgway fell down in the snow, still amazed, and was rolling, choking to death, his hands clutching his shattered throat, when she thrust the gun closer and fired the next bullet, *phuttt*! through his skull a little above the left ear. He arched once, like a diver completing a back flip off the high board, and died.

The large man got out of the hearse. He was almost as tall as the deceased but massive through the chest and shoulders. He had a self-important way of moving, acute consciousness of his shaped bulk and martial strength.

In one hand he carried a bag of heavy-gauge polyethylene, which he unfolded while the woman walked a little way down toward the front of the hearse, the revolver at her side. The large man busied himself with stuffing the body into the bag, sniffing almost ecstatically at the odors of death, wiping his nose on the back of a glove. There was a disagreeable amount of blood and tissue in the snow. None of it had splashed on the hearse. The man was careful not to get any blood on his shoes or clothing. When the body was fully bagged and the bag tied shut, he went around to the rear door of the hearse and swung it wide. He trundled the coffin out. The lid was opened. Placing the body of the six-foot-five-inch Ridgway in the coffin was a matter of little more difficulty for him than pressing a plucked flower between the pages of a heavy book.

Meanwhile the woman who called herself Leda Watson had dropped the revolver on the front seat of the hearse, walked to the Aries wagon and opened the flight bag, which contained a Duraflask. She was satisfied with what she found. She kept the briefcase and the flight bag and carried the hang-up bag back to the hearse. The large man put it into the coffin with Mark Ridgway's body. The lid was closed. The rear door clunked shut.

"You have all the necessary papers for shipping?" she asked.

The man nodded. He knew the mortuary business inside out.

"Just leave the hearse in the airport parking lot. It won't be missed before morning."

She went up on her toes to kiss his lips, then returned a final time to the Aries wagon. He got in behind the wheel of the hearse, one of several he'd had to choose from in the garage of a Downers Grove funeral home, and started the engine. She followed him from the alley to the Tollway, then north on the Tollway to where it met the Adlai E. Stevenson Expressway. The hearse continued toward the airport. The woman turned right and headed for downtown Chicago.

"It's a trick," Lucas McIver said irritably to Dr. Viola Purkey. "I don't know why you can't see it."

"I truly believe Blaize Ellington means you no harm. Am I a fool, Lucas? Haven't I learned a thing or two about people in seventy-two years? Of course she's all mixed up, and burning inside; that's the way her father is, and he wants to make sure she keeps on feeling hate, nothing but hate. She's suffered. She's lost two precious brothers. And she's been afraid for her own life these many years. But I know you can convince Blaize you didn't kill those boys."

They were in a large ground-floor room in an Oak Lawn motel run by friends of Viola's, buttoned up away from the world with a gas log fire going on a small hearth. The Leprechaun, who had been McIver's companion for years, training him in the ways of a fugitive, had brewed coffee on a hot plate and laced it with Irish.

McIver pulled at his lower lip. "Lonnie Ellington's easy enough, if they'd only listen. I can put them on to a couple of U.S. narcs who operate out of Thailand and know part of the story. Lonnie was bored and couldn't resist getting involved in a little side deal while he waited around Bangkok for the chance to lower the hammer on me. I don't know why he needed another couple million, the family's supposed to be loaded. A girl named Chamnian had the most to do with it. I'd known her for a while. She set me up with Lonnie, then set Lonnie up with one of the big heroin processors, a Burmese warlord from Shan State named Lao Su. Chamnian had a lot of strings on her bow. Lao Su took Lonnie's table stakes and wasted him, and Chamnian implicated me in his death."

"Lonnie didn't need the money," the Leprechaun put in, "but he craved the excitement. And she was a very exciting young woman, was Chamnian."

"What were you doing in Bangkok?" Viola asked McIver.

"Drinking a lot. I was run-down and depressed. I lost fifty-five pounds in three months working with *Médicine Sans Frontières* in the border refugee camps. Two of them were razed by Vietnamese artillery. In Bangkok I couldn't seem to put weight back on. Thai food is tasty, but it goes right through you if you've had the bug. Anyway, I met Chamnian. She said she was studying architecture at Thammasat University. I fell in love with her feet and ankles. She also had a perfect oval face and hair with more highlights than a rainbow when she brushed it. She was so young and clean, and I felt like I was a hundred and six years old. I know what she'd been studying most of her life but it wasn't architecture, it was anatomy. She gave me a lot of love, and she cooked food I could retain. I told her more about my life than I should have. By and by there was good old Lonnie in Bangkok, with a couple of Anthony Troy's best men. Leprechaun spotted them hanging out at the Oriental. My brain was half asleep. I tried to convince him it was a coincidence.''

''Ah, but she was lovely,'' the Leprechaun said without malice. ''Such soulful eyes, m'dear.''

''So I didn't listen to you. Five million people jammed into Bangkok, I didn't think there was a chance they'd get a line on me. So I gave Chamnian all the time in the world to work her deals and weave her webs, trying to get top dollar for all our bodies. She had me by the nuts, then Lonnie; God knows how many other men in Bangkok thought she was in love with them. What a talent. She must be running the country by now.''

McIver fell into a brooding silence while the Leprechaun held a cup for Viola to drink. Viola, still slumped in her wheelchair, was showing the effect of the experimental drug Lucas had given her earlier. The tremors had lessened. Her eyes never left the tall man's bearded face.

''Lonnie . . . Lonnie was just too young and inexperienced. If the old man wanted me dead, he should have left it to the pros he hired. They'd come close a couple of times. Maybe, just maybe, the girl would forgive me for what happened to her little brother. But Jordan? Hell, she's right. I killed Jordan Ellington.''

''How can you say that, Lucas?''

''My father had organized the strike at the mines and because of that he was dead and my mother had half her left leg blown off and no fingers on her hands. Jesus, I just grabbed the first piece I could find at the house and went up there to waste Ellingtons, to blow them all to hell. Nobody home but Jordan, or so I thought, but it was Jordan I wanted most. Maybe I didn't put the revolver to his head, but it wasn't exactly an act of God, either.''

''The gun fell to the floor between you when he knocked it from your hand. It could as easily have killed you when it went off.''

"But if I hadn't gone to Ellington Farms, he'd probably be alive today."

"The Greeks had a word for it," the Leprechaun said. "*Até.*"

"The Greeks had a word for everything. What does it mean?"

"It means your judgment was blinded by circumstances. Fate took a hand. The Ellingtons, I believe, have not been above reproach in this life. Jordan was a thug when it came to dealin' with the miners. Lonnie met a temptress; his own judgment was blinded and he paid in full measure. Your culpability in the first matter is acknowledged, boy-o. But you've assumed too much guilt where none is deserved. It was *Até*. Let it go now, if you have the chance."

"It's not entirely up to me. I'm not gunning for them anymore, it's the other way around."

"Blaize will listen to you," Viola assured him.

McIver smiled painfully and glanced at the Leprechaun.

"I have a feeling," he said, "that this could turn out to be worse than Bangkok."

Chapter 10

New York City

Argyros Coulouris, the powerful Greek businessman who controlled Actium International, was working with his nephew Kris Aravanis in the library of the Fifth Avenue apartment when the call on his private line came at eleven-fifteen p.m.

"This is Dr. Hoelscher calling, from Davos."

Argyros, standing by a desk that had once graced the study of his friend John F. Kennedy, said nothing right away. His dark eyes went to Kris, who was leafing through a thick stack of documents on a low table, paying no attention to the interruption. Joanna Coulouris usually telephoned her father about this time from wherever in the world she happened to be.

"Just a moment." Argyros held the receiver against his chest, cleared his throat. Kris looked up. "I'm sorry. This won't take long."

"Certainly, uncle." Kris was glad for the opportunity to escape the cloud of cigarette smoke for a couple of minutes. He closed the library doors behind him.

Argyros ran a hand through his thick head of hair. There was pain in his back and neck; he felt the weight of his years tonight. He said harshly into the phone, "You have broken our agreement with this call, Dr. Hoelscher."

"I'm sure you will concur it was necessary when you—"

"I have paid you a considerable sum of money to be certain that neither I nor any member of my family—"

"You must listen to me, it's quite urgent! I am frightened—frightened, do you understand? He's back, Axel Stroh is back, although you assured me he was dead. And my life is worth no more than D'Allesandro's with those two morbid creatures in conjunction again!"

Argyros's face tightened, his jaw began to work; he turned stiffly and spat into the wastebasket, a Greek way of warding off Nemesis.

"Scum!" he said to Hoelscher. "You talked to my security chief, didn't you, Mr. Walk-on-water Holy Psychiatrist. Told Joe all of your damned absurd theories."

"Joe D'Allesandro knew a great deal already. He was very clever, that detective, well-versed in the pathology of the compulsive murderer. I felt an obligation to explain the mythos involved, the critical psychodynamics of—"

"*Don't say that word!* I will have you killed myself! It's all wrong, twisted, fraudulent: lies, lies, *lies!* from your pitiful cracked brains—"

At the other end of the line, Hoelscher was silent. Then he drew a shuddering breath. His voice quivered with emotion. "It's pointless defending my contributions to psychiatry; my standing in the profession is unassailable."

"You are a quack," Argyros said, his big voice dark with scorn. "You have betrayed my confidence. I say you are an unethical man, a traitorous bastard. Axel Stroh is dead, I made sure of that myself. Are you saying a dead man can climb out of the grave, Dr. Quack? Do you hold me in contempt because I have so little schooling, no distinguished university degrees like yourself? Let me say this, I am not the superstitious peasant you take me for. Is a dead man walking around this minute? What psychiatric theory gives you the right to say such a thing?"

"For God's sake, man. There is no doubt in my mind who, or what, roasted Joe D'Allesandro alive—"

"*I forbid you to say it!*"

"You are being a fool. None of us is invulnerable."

"Is it more money you want for your wretched clinic, your

wealthy child-molesters and drug-saturated film stars? Yes, I'll pay you, *again*. But I'm warning you, Mr. Big-Shot Untouchable Head-shrinker, you will in future leave me alone, or suffer the disastrous consequences."

"Mr. Coulouris, your money is meaningless in this instance. It won't buy me, it won't buy my silence when my life is in the balance. Minotaur was *my* discovery—"

"Shut up!" There was froth at the corner of Argyros's mouth. "I hold you responsible, *you*, for everything!"

"Show me Axel Stroh's body and I will admit I am wrong. Not before. In the meantime, I believe that only you can stop the inevitable. For my sake, for my family's sake, I'm leaving Davos within the hour. I'll be in touch with you. Because I do feel some responsibility for Joe D'Allesandro's death, I urge you to act before I must take matters into my own hands."

The connection was broken.

Argyros Coulouris stood for half a minute with the telephone receiver in his shaking hands, veins swollen and throbbing at his temples. Then he took a small in-house telephone directory from a drawer of the desk, looked up a number and dialed Van Raburn, the new chief of security for Actium International.

"Van? Argyros. I apologize for disturbing you at home. I must see you at once . . . thank you. In my apartment."

Argyros hung up and looked at the stack of documents he and Kris had been going through. He dialed another number, from memory.

On the third ring, a woman answered.

"This is Coulouris. I want the Actors. Yes. Two a.m., at the theater."

He hung up without saying good-bye. He always terminated telephone conversations in the same manner, abruptly; he considered closing pleasantries a waste of time.

He went slowly to the doors of the terrace and gazed out at two-thirds of Manhattan Island. It was a brilliant, cold evening. He could see south from midtown to the lights of the *Queen Elizabeth II*, outward-bound through the Verrazano

Narrows. Until his vision went bad from the sickening pressure of blood in his head.

He had pills to lower his blood pressure in a pocket of his silk jacket. He took one.

His nephew was knocking discreetly at the library doors. "Uncle?"

Argyros walked unsteadily to the doors, opened one of them a crack. "I can't work anymore tonight, Kris. We'll finish tomorrow."

Kristoforos Aravanis was curious.

He was reasonably sure the telephone call had not come from Argyros's daughter Joanna, who had flown to Palm Beach earlier in the day to attend a wedding. He had heard his uncle's angry tone, but not his words, through the library doors, which were of solid oak and iron removed from the ruins of a sixteenth-century Parnassian friary.

There were many hundreds of telephone lines in the Actium tower. Nearly all phone calls received day or night were automatically recorded by computerized equipment, including those business calls routed through secure lines. The telephone in Argyros's library was not part of a secure line; nor was it, like half a dozen other phones in the cousins' apartments, supposed to be connected to the recording/retrieval system.

Kris had always hated the idea that his uncle or one of the cousins might have something to say that would ultimately affect his own well-being or the balance of power within the company. He had made use of his extensive knowledge of electronic eavesdropping gear and the Actium computers to construct a private listening post in his own apartment, seven Spartan rooms almost no one ever visited. He cooked his own food, made his own bed and had no use for a valet. When he closed his door behind him, he was alone, inviolate. Through headphones he listened nightly to reels of generally boring chit-chat. He knew by now almost every detail of the clandestine erotic lives of his rivals. He had a file of secret bank accounts and brokerage accounts, a list of the psychiatrists and doctors they discreetly consulted. He knew just how bad

Argyros's heart was and the mournful diagnosis of Plato's prostrate trouble. Plato had yet to break the news of the cancer to his own brother. Kris had the names of the elite drug pushers patronized by Joanna and her wastrel friends. But Joanna he considered hopeless. He skipped most of her mewling, hours-long conversations to would-be friends, who seldom had the chance to say anything to her except in monosyllables. Joanna created boredom everywhere. She was sloppy, neurotic, obsessed by the desire to serve her father, who could barely tolerate having her around.

Kris was not married. He had no fondness for children. He was celibate by choice, because he disliked the touch of other human beings and because he believed celibacy gave him strength of purpose, powers of concentration otherwise unattainable. He excelled at fencing, where his only contact with his opponent was signaled by an impersonal buzzer. Fencing kept him slender and gave him stamina. He had few other diversions: a collection of medieval illuminated manuscripts and austere, abstract paintings done in pale colors, with a lot of white canvas left untouched; tropical fish that he raised in a two-hundred-gallon tank. There were just a few of them, but they were rarities, and exquisite.

After Argyros dismissed him for the night, Kris went straight to his apartment.

He changed from his blue suit to a short black-cotton kimono and, using the computer modem in his bedroom, quickly located the telephone call Argyros had received less than twenty minutes earlier. He ordered a playback.

"This is Dr. Hoelscher calling, from Davos."

Kris had not heard the name before. He made a note of it. He spoke good German and had no difficulty with the spelling. Davos, he knew, was in Switzerland.

"Mr. Walk-on-water Holy Psychiatrist. . . ."

Kris made a note of that too. And the name Axel Stroh. Then he became so absorbed in the conversation he forgot to take any more notes. His scalp prickled when the doctor mentioned Minotaur and Argyros's rage reached a peak of incoherence. Then, when his uncle could be understood, his voice was weaker, panicked. He was gasping for breath.

"I hold you . . . responsible . . . *you*. . . ."

The other two phone calls were of no less interest. Van Raburn was on his way to the tower. And, after consulting with the security chief, Argyros planned to go out, for a very late night of theater.

Kris wished he knew what that was all about.

He consulted the IBM mainframe computer to check out the last number Argyros had dialed. Then the computer told him how many times in the last twelve months Argyros had called the same number, and when.

Five times. Always late, sometimes very late, at night.

The number was listed under a false name. The telephone was located in an otherwise vacant one-room office on Eighth Avenue. Through a shunt it rang another number in the apartment of a woman who lived on West Fourth Street in Greenwich Village. Her name was Stefani Petriades. She was fifty. She made a living in summer stock and off-off-Broadway productions; she'd been an actress, director, producer, agent. Some experience in making and distributing porno films. She had been busted, many years ago, for running a call-girl ring in association with a cabaret theater troupe. The cops were no longer interested in her.

The theater that Argyros attended so infrequently was called, modestly, The Globe. It had housed some fairly distinguished plays over the years. Argyros, under another name, had purchased the playhouse two years ago and had spent seventy-two thousand dollars refurbishing it. The Globe was now permanently closed, except to Argyros. While he was there, no one else was allowed inside. Not even his chauffeur or bodyguards. The performances, or whatever it was he witnessed, lasted up to forty-five minutes. Never longer.

Kris was not the nervous sort, but he was almost jumping from the excitement and impatience of knowing instinctively that big secrets were about to be spilled. The trouble he'd gone to in bugging the family's private lines had paid off in just these three phone calls. He considered getting dressed and trying to find out what was going on down at The Globe at two a.m., but he didn't know how he could manage that without being spotted by Argyros, which would have serious repercussions. Nor could he hope to get any information from Van, who was good at his job and not interested in playing one family member off against another.

But when it came to investigators, Kris had several he could rely on.

He listened to Argyros's conversation with the psychiatrist again. Then he put a tape of Cretan *syrtaki* music on his stereo, dialed the volume low. He sipped a small glass of white wine and paced, studying the names he had printed on his notepad.

Dr. Hoelscher.

Axel Stroh.

Minotaur.

Something unnervingly dangerous in the very sound of it.

My discovery, Hoelscher had said, but what did he mean? Kris had heard the legend many times as a schoolboy. There once had been a king of Crete, named Minos, who had married Pasiphae, daughter of the sun-god Helios. She had fallen in love with a fabulous bull sent from the sea by Poseidon for sacrifice. Pasiphae enlisted Daedalus, a renowned artist and inventor, to make for her a hollow cow in which she could conceal and offer herself to the bull. The result of their unnatural mating was Minotaur: half man, half bull. Minos hid this amazing creature deep in a maze of passages called the Labyrinth and appeased it with offerings of youths and maidens, until the Athenian hero Theseus found his way to the heart of the Labyrinth and killed the minotaur.

Kris put it together this way: someone, probably a former patient of Dr. Hoelscher's named Axel Stroh, had adopted the name of Minotaur for reasons rooted in psychopathology and was dedicated to a reign of terror motivated by a desire for revenge against the House of Actium. Revenge for what? Both Argyros Coulouris and his half-brother George Melissani had made numerous enemies in their time. Axel Stroh must be one of them. Argyros obviously knew all about Stroh, but he had thought, he still clung to the hope or conviction, that Stroh was dead. It was also obvious that both the name Stroh and the symbol of the minotaur represented a past event of enormous unpleasantness. This Stroh must be something,

Kris marveled. The doctor was sufficiently terrified to flee from his home, and Argyros was reduced to shaking in his shoes, while denying all along that anything could happen. . . .

Good so far, Kris thought, drinking the last of his wine. Now all he had to do was substantiate his hypothesis and decide how best to use the information.

Five minutes after two in the morning.

The raked, thrust stage of The Globe was lighted softly, a morning radiance. Pale shafts of sun streamed through a disappearing mist. Boulders enclosed a grassy bower with a trickling waterfall on one side of a small, round pool perhaps three feet deep.

From offstage came the sweet, drifting notes of a shepherd's pipe. The same simple tune, repeated several times.

A man, a woman and a young girl came onstage, climbing over the fake rocks, laughing, helping one another. They were simply dressed, the woman and girl in white shifts and sandals, the man in a shirt opened nearly to his waist and loose-fitting trousers. He carried a basket of food, a goatskin of wine. The woman carried a lyre.

They were each masked. The young wife/mother wore the mask of Serenity. He wore the mask of Maturity, dignified middle age. The child, golden as a budding willow, wore the mask of Innocence.

They sat together in the bower and pantomimed eating and drinking.

When they had finished, the woman strummed her lyre and the young girl danced for them, a soaring, high-stepping dance, her pretty legs flashing gracefully, bare arms outthrust, fingers writhing in mime. Her balance was extraordinary; in moments of stasis she seemed to have no weight, and the mask smiled endlessly, a study in beatitude.

Then they all lay down to rest, the man and the woman side by side, the girl a little apart.

The light changed; shadows encroached. Only the pool was lighted, from above and within, a rippling blue-green in color.

After a few moments, the girl rose and went to the edge of the pool. Untied a sandal and dipped her toes in.

She looked back at the sleeping couple, then unfastened her shift and let it drop. Still masked, she stood naked in the single shaft of light at the water's edge, glistening from a dew raised by the exertion of her dance. The piping, haunted theme of the shepherd was repeated.

Honeyed hair fell evenly below her waist, partly concealing like a cloak her shapely buttocks. She held her firm, small breasts as if they were nesting birds. And turned, very slowly, downstage. The round cleft navel followed the orbit of her belly like a dim, mysterious moon. She had the waist of a child but ripening, womanly hips. There was a sprinkle of pubic hair fine as shaved gold on the virginal mons.

It was a brief revelation; then the girl clasped her hands together between her thighs in an act of concealment and stood quite still, masked head inclined slightly forward. The melancholy notes from the pipe filled the theater. She turned back to the pool and again tested the water.

Behind her the man abruptly sat up. He had changed his mask. He now wore the gross, leering red face of Priapus.

He got to his feet, his movements stylized, expressing lust. He dropped his trousers, revealing a considerable, realistically detailed but fake phallus in a state of erection. He approached the girl and seized her from behind. His struggle with her was brief.

The woman in the mask of Serenity rose in the shadows upstage and stood contemplating with lowered head the seduction of the virgin by the ancient fertility god. Then she turned and walked off.

The actor playing Priapus drew the girl down with him, and they began a mime of intercourse that was erotic and nerve-racking.

From his seat in the darkened house Argyros Coulouris felt, as he always did, as if he'd been shattered by a bolt of lightning. His pulse was too fast, his heart dangerously overworked. His mouth had dried up and his skin tingled eerily. He could scarcely breathe. He was filled with fascination, revulsion and dread. But he was not sexually aroused. Nor had he been capable of an erection for the last thirteen years.

The girl in the mask of Innocence, squatting over the bulge

of the phallus, screamed, throwing her head back in ritual ecstasy. The single spotlight on the pair went out, leaving the stage in darkness.

Argyros rose shakily from his seat. Another spot slashed through the playhouse, illuminating a gruesome figure standing in the aisle nearby.

It wore a wedding dress, stained and blackened by the grave. It wore a Death's-head mask. It held out its arms to Argyros.

Mouth working chaotically, he rushed to the embrace and exploded from grief.

Only in the arms of Death personified could he achieve the momentary release, which he so desperately needed, from the long agony of his life.

Chapter 11

Chicago

"So where is she?" Dr. Lucas McIver asked.

He and the Leprechaun had returned to the Zacchaeus clinic with Viola a little after eleven o'clock. Viola assured him that Blaize Ellington would be sound asleep in her room. But the room was empty. Blaize's luggage was there, and her tote bag, with her wallet inside. The wallet contained two hundred dollars and change, and some credit cards. There were no signs of a struggle, no evidence of robbery. The clinic was never unattended, day or night, and seldom broken into: the locks were good, lights were always on, and a youth vigilante group called the Bozeman Bravos had posted the place off limits to the neighborhood junkies. There were usually several of the Bravos playing cards or video games in a den on the first floor. Different Bravos came and went all night. It was an auxiliary clubhouse, particularly in winter, when many of the Bravos didn't have a heated room to go home to.

The Leprechaun had checked for Blaize in all the obvious places: bathrooms, the kitchen downstairs. The Bravos, smartly turned out in berets and turtlenecks, hadn't seen her leave. But her shearling coat was missing, and so was the .45 automatic that Louis had told the Leprechaun about.

"What did you give her that was supposed to knock her out?" McIver asked Viola.

"Thirty milligrams of Dalmane."

"Might not put her away. It depends."

"She's an insomniac. But she was curled up peacefully on her bed when Coni took me down to the coach."

McIver looked at the Leprechaun. "She could still be lurking around here somewhere. And she probably has that gun in her pocket. Which will make for a one-sided conversation if we come face-to-face. I think I'll call it a night."

"Lucas, I'm worried about her," Viola said. "I'm afraid something's wrong. She wouldn't go out by herself at night."

McIver wasn't convinced. "Wherever she went, she'll be back. If she swallowed a couple of uppers to get rid of the cobwebs, look out. I don't want to take any chances with her, Viola."

"But I'm responsible for whatever condition she's in. We must find her."

"Get hold of Louis and have him check around the neighborhood. Somebody must have seen her go out."

"Louis is entered in a martial-arts tournament at Fort Sheridan. He won't be back until all hours."

"Try the Bravos then."

The leader of the Bravos was a scar-faced kid who called himself Sir Cedric. He brought three of his cohorts with him up to Viola's room. Some of them already knew Blaize. Viola told them what was wanted. McIver tossed Sir Cedric the keys to the invalid coach he and the Leprechaun had rented for the night then walked down one flight, alone, to his old room, which Viola had kept locked during the years of his forced absence.

The room was small and narrow and disagreeably stuffy; he opened the window a couple of inches and sat on the bed, hands knotted between his knees. He looked around. There was a small study desk between the bed and the radiator, diagrams of the human body thumbtacked to the walls, a yellowed skeleton suspended from steel rods in one corner. Crammed bookshelves containing high-school and college texts, paperback editions of Hemingway, William Golding, Camus.

Stacks of well-worn books from medical school. He had memorized nearly every page. Third in his class at Loyola. There were several framed photographs from his high-school and college years. Team pictures: wrestling, lacrosse. A large signed photo from Janice. *Luke, I will love you forever*. She had a shapely face and a wide-eyed, ecstatic acceptance of life that the camera recorded poignantly. By now she must be living in a split-level in Glen Ellyn or Arlington Heights with three kids. Hips spread all over the place. Once she had caused him sweet sleepless nights, but he hadn't thought about Janice recently. Too many lifetimes ago. His eyes lingered briefly on each photo. There was nothing of him in his baccalaureate cap and gown on the triumphant day of his graduation from med school. On that day, half a dozen well-dressed goons hired by Buford Ellington had shown up to take him back to Kentucky, any way they could manage it.

McIver lay back on the bed, finding it inadequate, as always, for his length, and tried to remember what he had been like those months after his father's death, the culminating nightmare in the Ellington house. Emotionally paralyzed by shock, saved from certain death by Viola's gift of persuasion, her urging him not to sacrifice himself in pointless acts of violence to satisfy his demonic pride.

And she was a black woman, who had stopped one night on a dark road because she'd seen, in the throw of headlights from her old Ford, a boy so far gone he couldn't stagger another dozen steps, who, as she put it, "looked as if his angels were too long overdue." A badly cut hand and sick, unreasoning eyes—she could have been overpowered, killed. But there are moments in life when you know you have the authority, the will, to dominate almost any of God's creatures.

He was down on his hands and knees, swaying slowly from side to side.

"What have you done?" she asked him.

It was not a voice of Judgment; the quiet richness, the tone of compassion, caved him in.

"Killed Jordy Ellington," he sobbed. "They're . . . after me."

She was from out of state. She'd been to a reunion of her

class at Maharry Medical College in Nashville, and she didn't know Jordy Ellington, or any other Ellingtons; if she had, even Viola Purkey would have thought twice at that crucial moment.

"Did he deserve it?"

He looked at her as if she made no sense to him. But the question was like a barbed hook dragging fire through his chest. He screamed confirmation.

"Get in the car," Viola said then. It was more an invitation than an order.

She went to considerable trouble to smuggle him through a couple of roadblocks. Even then he didn't trust her completely for a long time. When they were across the Ohio River and temporarily out of danger, she took care of his wound and gave him a powerful sedative. He woke up on the South Side of Chicago, surrounded by ghetto blacks. Culture shock. He went around lean as a toothless rat from shadow to shadow: belligerent, defensive. A wonder he wasn't killed by some of the forerunners of the Bozeman Bravos. But Viola had passed the word on the street. Luke McIver had known his share of grief. Leave him to mend.

A knock at the door.

"Lucas?" It was the Leprechaun.

Sir Cedric and three of the Bravos were waiting outside in the invalid coach. It was still snowing. The streets were hushed and very nearly deserted at twenty minutes past one in the morning.

"Where are we going?" McIver asked the gang leader. "You find her yet?"

"There's somebody you best talk to."

They parked behind a garish all-night burger joint on Halstead. The Bravos took their time looking over the lot, watching the occasional car mush slowly by in the street.

"Your turf?" McIver asked Sir Cedric.

" 'Sposed to be the DMZ. Most of the time, that is." Cedric nodded, finally. They all got out.

The place was full of orange plastic tables and swing-out stools. Overhead fluorescence was dimmed to an acid yellow by a fog of cigarette smoke and cooking grease. A high thermostat made the air even more difficult to breathe. There were half a dozen refugees from the weather, including a hulking, over-the-hill whore who sat in one corner. She was so stoned she couldn't get her cigarette between her banged-up lips without the help of the boy sitting next to her. She complained in an obscene monotone about how rotten life was. She wore a satin jump suit that, up close, showed wear and tear and a fur wrap around her shoulders.

She looked up without delight at the appearance of the Bravos, McIver and the Leprechaun. Her eyes were blistered obsidian. Some of the bruises on her face were fresh. One eye was all but closed. She poked her tongue at a cut in a corner of her mouth.

"Which one you is the doctor?" she asked the boy next to her. He had an arm around her shoulders. He wasn't wearing the Bravo turtleneck, but McIver guessed he was one of them. He was about sixteen, with close-cut, rust-brown hair and a part like a scar on the right side.

"I'm the doctor," McIver said.

She tried to lift her head and focus on him. He was too tall. Her eyes wandered away vaguely. "Stomped me," she said. "Hurt some'pin. Give me a rupture, feels like. Can't hardly straighten up enough to walk."

"Who stomped you?"

The boy explained. "Snake Grace. Works for Sweet Willie Wine. This my momma. Name Dolores. She with Sweet Willie fo' a long time, but he throw her out las' week. Say she too old. Don't bring in the bread like she used to."

"Thass a fuckin' lie! I turn more tricks than any cunt he got on the street!" She began to cough and sagged lower over the table. "Fuckin' johns don't pay what they should fo' a woman of *my* 'sperience." Dolores coughed again, then began a tremulous whimper.

The boy held her tighter and murmured, "She really hurtin'."

"I can't do anything for her here," McIver said. "Bring the coach around, we'll take her back to the clinic."

"Won't 'low me on the street no mo', he says. Ha! I was here long time befo' Sweet Willie. I got rights of *enema domain*, thass what I got."

"Come on, Momma. Get you fixed up."

It took three of them to haul her outside to the invalid coach. Dolores collapsed inside, breathing hoarsely. She had a pulse near a hundred and was sweating heavily. McIver found in her purse what she'd been taking for her pain and distress. 'Ludes. She couldn't remember how many.

"You'll be all right," he told her.

"I know it. Been kicked lots of times. Snake don't have no muscle. Don't have the meanness for it, neither. I don't hold what happened 'gainst him. A hired man just do what he's told."

"What about Sweet Willie?"

"Get close enough, I'll fix him good. I knows how. See that little chrome straight razor in my bag?"

"I saw it."

In pantomime Dolores showed him how deft she was, the good wrist action. Her face squeezed up for a laugh but she couldn't come out with it. She held her stomach and one of his hands.

"They tell me you out lookin' fo' somebody."

"That's right."

"Tall white woman? Wear one of them sheepskin coats?"

"Did you see her tonight?"

"I did. They helpin' her out of the pussywagon at the Park Waldorf. I waitin' 'round there jus' to see if I could settle up quick with Sweet Willie. But he see me first and send Snake over."

"Helping her out?"

"She was stoned, worse'n me. Couldn't stand up by herself."

McIver glanced at the Leprechaun, who said, "Could be a coincidence."

"Does Sweet Willie have any white foxes in his string?"

"Not lately. Maybe one a year. He don't like to mess with 'em, 'less he be thinkin' they worth a whole lot of bread."

At the clinic McIver spent twenty minutes examining the aging hooker. She had a lot of things wrong with her, including an enlarged liver, but her blood pressure was okay and he didn't have any reason to believe her spleen or kidneys had been seriously damaged by the stomping. He couldn't find any broken bones. He decided Dolores should stay twenty-four hours for observation and X rays, and had her put to bed.

While he examined the woman McIver thought about Blaize and Sweet Willie Wine. He had no reason to assume she was in trouble. What the hell, there were white girls who liked to party with blacks, even black pimps. He didn't know anything about her sexual tastes, her kinks and darkest fantasies. Maybe after a week of hanging around the clinic she'd been bored silly and in the mood for some grins.

So she left her purse and makeup and hairbrush behind but took her .45 with her. It was shaping up to be a swell party.

Viola said, "That girl is in trouble, Lucas."

"Oh, hell."

"Just get her out of there. Then we'll find out what's going on."

"Why don't we call the cops?"

"Don't be ridiculous. They wouldn't bother."

From the black whore he obtained what he hoped was Sweet Willie Wine's up-to-date private number at his pad and the address of the Park Waldorf, where Sweet Willie had the fifteen-hundred-dollar-a-month penthouse. It was a short drive in the coach. The Leprechaun went with him.

The Park Waldorf was an old but well-maintained ten-story building at Lake Park and 65th Street, opposite Jackson Park. There was a silver and red canopy heaped with snow, a lot of glass brick used for trim, and terrace setbacks.

McIver made two slow passes in the coach. The penthouse was blazing with light, but all the windows were draped.

"Let's take the easy way out," he suggested.

"I saw a phone box two blocks from here."

"Do you have a quarter on you?"

"If you want to do this properly, you should make it a collect call."

McIver grinned tiredly and made a U turn.

By the time he had dialed Sweet Willie's number, he was in character. He conjured a vision of his late Uncle Edmond, so bad-tempered junkyard dogs didn't dare bark at him.

"Hel-lo," said a darling voice in his ear. There was music in the background, a relentless beat.

"This Sweet Willie Wine?" His refurbished South Kentucky accent slurred the syllables: "Wine" became "wan."

"I did see him a few moments ago. Hold on. May I say who is calling?"

"Buddy, it ain't none of your goddam business."

"Well!"

McIver held the phone, whistling metallically into the cup of the receiver, listening to the party in the background. It sounded like a lot of fun.

"Sweet Willie, who this?"

McIver gripped the phone tighter and said in his gravelly drawl, "Listen here, nigger. I don't repeat myself. You got my cousin Blaize Ellington there with you. I got me ten shotguns in two vans, and I'll be at your front door before you can hawk and spit less'n you do exactly what I say. Pull her pants up and put her coat on and give her a shove on out the door. I want her standin' on the sidewalk in front of your buildin' the first time I drive by, or I'm gone scatter your black ass and six more like it all over your purty velveteen walls. You son of a bitch, you got that straight?"

"Hey, m' man, I don't know who the fuck—"

"Shut up. You're standin' in shit up to your eyeballs already. That girl's daddy is worth four hundred million if he's worth a nickel, and if that don't give you somethin' to think about, try this: me and my boys are just the volunteer troops. Ol' Buford can hire a whole Special Forces platoon if he needs to, and you ain't the first nigger took to foolin' with his little girl. The last one, that television singer did the falsetto voice like a girl, well hell, he don't need to fake it no more. Uncle Buford pure-damn run his nuts up the flagpole. I'm on my way now. You know what to do."

Click.

Sweet Willie Wine, wearing a floor-length blue velour robe trimmed in ermine, stood in the living room of his penthouse apartment scowling at the telephone receiver in his hand.

"Now what the shit was that all about?"

Nobody heard him above the pounding beat of the music on his ten-thousand-dollar stereo system; but a nearly nude tigress with glazed ebony eyes reached out from a nest of silk pillows on the floor and stroked his ankle beneath the heavy robe. "Sweet Willie, ain't you gonna pay no 'tention to me tonight?" He kicked her hand away.

Sweet Willie was annoyed, but he was cautious too. The threats had an authentic sound. He'd had his new telephone number for only a week. Not just every dude knew how to get hold of Sweet Willie Wine. Chicago was crawling with hill apes, and only a fool, white or black, messed with them. They were worse than the fucking Mafia.

Fun time was over. Before it even got started good.

Sweet Willie picked his way through the crowd, most of them sprawled on the carpet, little red-hots of roaches glowing all around, the air hot and tangy; he went quickly down the hall to the double doors of his bedroom, calling, "Snake!"

Snake Grace came trailing after him out of another bedroom, barefoot, snapping up the suspenders of his trousers.

"Yo, boss."

"Have you a look out front and tell me when you sees a couple vans drive up."

He closed the carved, churchlike doors behind him.

There was a different musical beat inside the soundproofed bedroom: reggae. The lights in the smoked-mirror ceiling were pink and dim. The carpet was as thick as the coat of an Afghan hound. The bed was a high, square box of precious cocobolo wood, enclosed in stained-glass panels. Videotape cameras were focused on the bed from above, and a console monitor offered instant replays. On a low round stone table in one corner two naked women were dancing, revolving sensuously around each other, touching, gliding, toe-to-toe, hip-to-hip, cheek-to-cheek, slippery from each other's sweat and other essences. One body was solid, small in the waist, dark as aged bronze; the other was tall, loose-jointed, long-necked, pink as a fledgling devil in the toney glow from the ceiling spots. Her head was bobbing, twisting like a playful colt's as she gave her hair teasing flips across the face or breasts of her partner. From time to time she snorted horselike through her lips but kept moving, tirelessly. Her eyes had a curious quality: they were wide, dense as lalique glass, fixed and bizarre. The smaller woman, called Jamake, had a short haircut, no more nap than a sponge. On their confined dancing platform, she was agile as a gymnast, doing stylish torso rolls, splits and backbends in time to the music, using her head as an erotic revolving buffer against Blaize's high, firm ass and flat belly.

Despite the problems he was facing Sweet Willie had to stop and admire the action, then flip his robe open to give his erection room, and the swish of velour against the head of his cock made him both unbearably excited and cross; the lust in his throat began to feel like a hairball. He resented Blaize more than ever now that he had to part with her before he could teach her the lessons he knew she deserved. He looked regretfully at the little Japanese case open on his dresser, the gleam of exquisite cutting instruments, flagellant's tools. Then he dialed up the rheostat that controlled the ceiling spots and turned the music off.

The women went on dancing exactly as before, not missing the beat. Sweet Willie clapped his hands smartly.

"Hello, ladies!"

Blaize came to a swaying stop and Jamake leaned against her, an arm around her waist. Jamake looked over one shoulder at Sweet Willie. Blaize whinnied exuberantly and didn't look anywhere.

"Time to pack Blaize up and send her 'long home," Sweet Willie explained.

"Oh, no!" Jamake looked at Blaize. "You don't want to leave us yet, do you, baby?"

Blaize was tapping one bare foot. "I'm Blaize the horse. I can run all day. Run all night."

"Less don't hear no argument," Sweet Willie said to Jamake. "She got kinfolk on the way, make yo' average SWAT team look like the Upper Volta National Guard. Jus' put that big ol' coat back on her, she ain't gonna need nothin' else to wear."

Snake Grace was back, knocking. "Yo, boss."

Sweet Willie tied his robe and let Snake in.

"There's one of them big fourteen-passenger vans parked 'cross the street."

"See anybody?"

"Big mean-lookin' dude with a beard. He jus' standin' there with his arms folded, lookin' up here."

"Any others?"

"Tinted windows on that van. Couldn't see inside."

"One van? Probably got the other parked in the alley." Sweet Willie pondered his next move while Jamake helped Blaize on with her coat. Blaize's star-spangled eyes wandered. There was a little drool of clear snot on her upper lip. She continued to breathe through her mouth. "You get dressed," he said to Jamake. "Give Snake a hand with her."

"You gonna give her back with nothin' on under her coat? How that look, boss?"

"Ain't said nothin' 'bout givin' her back. Leave her to find her own way home, if she able. But she be some kinda Wonder Woman for sho', if she do that."

"What 'bout them waitin' down there in the street? Call a po-lice on 'em?"

Sweet Willie said with a smile. "Fuck the po-lice. When I need action, I knows who to call."

"From your mouth to God's ear," Blaize said, just as if she had full possession of her faculties.

While Snake and the other woman were getting dressed, Blaize sat humming to herself and petting the shaggy carpet. Sweet Willie went into his dressing room and closed the door. There was a safe behind one of the mirror panels on one wall. He opened it and took out an ampule of a drug he never touched himself and only, on the rarest occasions, gave to others. He filled a syringe with the liquid, then put the syringe in a small box for safekeeping. Reactions to the tiniest doses of the drug were varied, but almost always gruesome. He had observed a rival pimp sitting in a corner of a bare room, lunching on his fingers until he had the flesh nearly gnawed away to the second knuckle. He'd seen a woman do a swan dive through a plate-glass window on Rush Street.

Where Blaize Ellington would be spending the rest of the night there were no windows—and no walls, either. And it was twenty chilly stories to the ground.

* * *

Lucas McIver couldn't tell much about the figure that came through the front doors of the Park Waldorf and went briskly down the shoveled steps to the street. Puffy hip-length black parka, lace-up boots and a ski mask with red knitted circles around the mouth and eyes. Red Mouth could have been a twelve-year-old kid or a small woman. He didn't think it was Blaize Ellington.

Red Mouth hesitated at the curb and took a long look across the street at him. McIver, leaning against the side of the invalid coach, stared back. Then Red Mouth crossed the street on a diagonal, heading for the corner and away from the coach. The snow had tapered off to flurries, like white moths tossing in the penumbra of the street lights. It was after two a.m. There was no traffic.

McIver had been waiting for fifteen minutes. He knew he had been, was probably still being, observed from behind the drapes of the penthouse apartment. He was thinking that she wasn't going to come out on her own and Sweet Willie hadn't been sufficiently intimidated to bounce her out of the party on her ass. Maybe, as Dolores the hooker had implied, Blaize was very, very stoned. Even so, he couldn't buy Viola's assessment that the girl was in difficulty and unable to fend for herself. If she ever allowed herself to get in that condition, then it was incredibly stupid of her to carry a gun.

Red Mouth had reached the corner and was just standing there. McIver shifted his attention.

As he glanced that way the figure moved; Red Mouth opened the door of the pedestal fire-alarm box and pulled the handle inside, then turned and shot him a gloved bird before scampering out of sight down Lake Park Avenue.

McIver opened the door and climbed into the warm coach. The Leprechaun started awake and the pint bottle of Scotch he'd been holding between his knees slipped to the floor. The engine was running; McIver gunned it and pulled away.

"What's the matter?" the Leprechaun asked, groping for his bottle.

"Sweet Willie sent an emissary down. Turned in a false alarm. This corner will be swarming with equipment in five minutes, and firemen get very hostile about false alarms. I'm not in a position to discuss it with the cops, either."

McIver was thinking furiously. The move had been designed by Sweet Willie to clear the neighborhood of the hostile rednecks he'd been told to expect. But, just possibly, it was also meant to create a diversion while he had Blaize smuggled out of the building and dropped off somewhere a long way from his domicile. Then, if she wasn't in very good condition, it would be hard to prove she'd been to his party in the first place.

He went sliding through the blinking red light at the corner, straightened the coach out, turned toward the alley at the rear of the Park Waldorf.

A car was easing out of the basement garage into the alley, a white customized Sedan de Ville with much added chrome, dark-toned windows. It headed west, slowly; there were seven inches of new snow in the alley.

Distantly they heard the sirens of oncoming fire engines. McIver explained his conclusions to the Leprechaun.

"She may be in the chariot," the Leprechaun conceded with a frown. "Beautiful lines, don't you think? So graceful, and easily half a block in length. In this neighborhood, at this time of night, it may be only slightly less conspicuous than a tugboat."

"Too easy to follow?"

"Yes."

"We shouldn't be following it, then?"

"No."

"I hope you're right."

"Instinct, Lucas. Pull up there, behind the dumpster. It's high enough to conceal this brute. Lights out. Splendid. We'll just wait another minute or two."

"Those sirens are getting closer," McIver said uneasily. "They'll block the alley and go running around with flashlights looking for smoke. And here we sit, with no good explanation for what we're doing—"

"Ah," said the Leprechaun.

The automatic door was rising again, a red light flashing overhead as another car emerged from the garage. It was a mid-sized maroon Cutlass wagon, several years old. They had a glimpse of a tall black man wearing a stocking cap hunched over the wheel. He turned left, not bothering to look their way. He seemed to be alone in the wagon. But at the last possible instant, in the red glow of the light above the garage door, they saw a limp pale hand raised behind the tailgate window.

"Bingo!"

"There's no traffic. Stay well back, lad; if he's a careful man he'll make you in no time."

McIver waited until the Cutlass wagon had cleared the mouth of the alley before he pulled out, using only his parking lights. They were barely out of the alley themselves when the fire trucks began to show up. McIver followed the Cutlass leisurely through the snow, staying so far back that all he could see were taillights. They drove west on 63rd, toward Midway Airport. Then, abruptly, near Pulaski Road, where clouds of steam were billowing up from beneath the street, McIver lost sight of the wagon. He speeded up.

"Looks like he ducked into a rat hole."

"Cruise around. We may pick him up again."

It was a neighborhood of old commerce, warehouses and light industry. Near the airport land had been cleared for an office-building plaza, twin towers twenty stories high. One tower was nearly completed; the other was a skeleton. Overhead the sky had begun to brighten with stars. A Learjet flew across their path at three hundred feet on approach to Midway, which was two-thirds of a mile away. McIver followed some cars north on Pulaski, past the office plaza. He caught up with three of them. He didn't see the Cutlass. The Leprechaun was looking back, watching a jet freighter in the sky.

"Turn around," he said.

"Did you see the wagon?"

"No. Drive past the construction site again. Slowly."

A high board fence enclosed the site. There were locked double gates at intervals. The Leprechaun had rolled down the window and was studying the brown steel structure of the nearest tower, the open elevator shaft along one side.

"It appears the lift is at the top," he said.

"So what?"

"Dark in there, but I'm sure I noticed the lift rising a few moments ago, whilst that jet was flying above the building."

"Probably the night watchman, making rounds."

"Why would he want to go to the top of a skeletal skyscraper?"

"What difference does it make? We're looking for—"

"Fresh tire tracks, from an automobile that entered the construction site not five minutes ago. Never be fixated on the obvious. Ah, well." The Leprechaun sighed theatrically. "Will I never complete your education? Now you must try to find a way around to the back of the site."

McIver did as he was told. They came to the corner of the office plaza, where the east-west street was blocked by wooden barricades with yellow flashers. McIver stopped the van and turned the side spotlight on the barricades. The snow around them was trampled. A car had driven up, a barricade was dragged aside, the car had continued on. The driver had carefully replaced the barricade behind him.

The Leprechaun got out and removed the barricade again.

"What do you think?" McIver asked when the Leprechaun rejoined him.

He was trying to get a look at the top of the uncompleted building but could see nothing except for the red warning beacon placed there for aircraft.

"I don't care for the looks of it. We'd best hurry."

The sharp set of tracks they were following turned in at a high gate two-thirds of the way down the street. The gate stood open.

"No lights," the Leprechaun cautioned.

Once inside the fence it was impossible to go very far. But they saw the Cutlass wagon almost immediately. It was parked at the base of the steel superstructure, beside one of the trailers used as on-site offices. Floodlights were mounted on the front corners of each trailer.

Next to the wagon there were two sets of deep footprints. He was wearing boots. She was barefoot. For the most part she had gone along beside him willingly, but there were places where her feet had dragged, little squiggly ravines in the clean snow.

He had taken her straight to the elevator, and up. To the bare platform that would become the twentieth floor of the skyscraper.

They heard voices then, far above their heads; a woman's shrill cry of indignation, or pain.

McIver ran back to the coach. He turned on the spotlight and swept it upward; the diffused beam grazed the top girders of the building.

"Police! What's going on up there?"

He kept the light moving. Ten seconds, fifteen. A figure appeared, stumbling. His heart froze in horror.

The figure moved out of the light at the edge of the platform, tottered there inside a steel frame enclosing nothing but sky, then fell.

Forward.

Silently.

Down.

And down, turning over once in the air before smashing into the roof of the nearest trailer. Two windows shattered and the long trailer trembled on its concrete-block foundation.

For a long agonized time McIver couldn't move or look up at the roof of the trailer.

When he did, all he saw was the empty sleeve of a shearling coat draped over the crumpled edge.

Blaize began to come back from never-never land on the slow way up in the drafty elevator, when her wet feet started to throb and send daggers of chills through her body. Except for the unbuttoned coat she had on, she was naked. She jittered on the metal floor of the elevator and complained in a small dull voice to Sweet Willie Wine.

"Ain't no big thing, baby," he said cozily. He slapped a pocket of the Navy pea jacket he was wearing. "What I got here, warm you up like a furnace. Jus' hold on."

"Where are we going?"

"Seventh heaven. Nex' stop. I promised you somethin'

extra. Kind of a nightcap. Does Sweet Willie lie? You special to me, honey. *Very* special."

Blaize took a look around. "I don't like it up here." Her teeth chattered. Her jitters became a joyless tap dance. The snow had stopped, but there was a cold wind blowing; the chill factor was around zero.

Sweet Willie slipped an arm inside her fleecy coat, laid a hand on her breast. The nipple was like a lump of ice. He had taken off his rings and other jewelry and was, in addition to the pea jacket, plainly dressed in dark colors. He wore a seaman's knit cap, pulled down to his earlobes.

"Twentieth floor, all out!" he sang. The elevator jolted to a stop. Sweet Willie opened the gate and ceremoniously ushered Blaize out.

"Yes, ma'am, yes ma'am; we a little full-up tonight, but we can always squeeze in one more. Right this way, please!"

The wind sang dismally, drowning out the sound of a nearby airplane. The flashing runway markers of the airport were brilliant off to the right.

The platform they were on consisted of three-quarter-inch sheets of plywood laid over girders. The first few floors of the building had been poured, but there was nothing up here except for some odds and ends of cut steel, bundles of reinforcing rods, a temporary flight of stairs to the floor below. Blaize shuddered. Her heart was bucking erratically. She needed to pee. So she squatted right there and did it. Sweet Willie laughed. His laughter made her cry petulantly.

"I want to get down from here!"

"Patience, patience. You gonna get down okay. Sweet Willie bring you up here to teach you a new trick."

"W-what?"

He helped her rise. "Hasn't you always wanted to learn to fly?"

With a big grin he took the box with the syringe in it from his coat pocket. He was holding Blaize by the sleeve of her coat. She tried to pull away and the shearling coat came half-way off.

Sweet Willie made a fist with the hand holding the box and

punched her in the face. Blaize cried out, flinching and twisting until she was out of the coat.

What the hell, he thought, holding the coat in one hand. Too good to let ruin. Give it to one of the bitches.

He gave Blaize a hard shove. She stubbed her toe and went sprawling.

Sweet Willie looked at the upraised goosebumpy bare cheeks of her ass and hunched over to plunge in the needle.

A beam of light ghosted around the bare girders.

Huh?

"Police! What's going on up there?"

Sweet Willie was startled. The needle of the syringe jabbed Blaize at too shallow an angle. She yelled and jerked aside, crawling on her belly; she reached for the dangling needle and pulled it out. Sweet Willie, mouth open in a soundless yelp of displeasure, tried to grab it back.

Blaize leaped at him and plunged the syringe into his mouth, seating it deep in the meat of his tongue and, at the same instant, squeezed off all the drug it contained—all but the drop or two she had received herself, subcutaneously.

Sweet Willie bit down on the syringe, cracking it in half.

Within seconds the drug was in his bloodstream. Within a few more seconds it was rocketing straight to his brain.

Enough of the hallucinogenic DMT to turn an entire nunnery into bedlam. The Salvation Army into a howling Apache war party.

More than enough to dismantle one rather ordinary human mind and send it careening, neuron by blazing neuron, into cold stellar space.

Sweet Willie had ceased to exist, except as a puppet of flesh and bone, by the time he tottered to the edge of the platform a hundred and eighty feet in the air.

He was still clutching Blaize's shearling coat in his arms when the wind caught him just right and flicked him, like a scrap of charred paper, unknowingly to the ground.

As soon as he had made certain it wasn't Blaize who had plummeted from the top of the building, McIver dropped down from the trailer's roof and said to the Leprechaun, "It's the black guy. She must still be up there."

"What happened to him?"

"Who knows? But if the girl's stoned, she could be the next one to do a nose dive. I'll send the elevator down for you."

He took off at a lope through the snow toward the stairs in the center of the steel structure. Nineteen sets of stairs to the top. He wasn't looking forward to it.

On the twentieth floor Blaize should have been slowly freezing to death, but her body, in its reaction to the dose of DMT, was overcompensating for her nakedness in the numbing cold. Her heart and glands were working furiously; her body temperature had risen and she was sweating; her tongue dripped saliva onto her chin. She had received far less of the drug than Sweet Willie, but her eyes already were dilating to the extent that she could scarcely see. She fell down twice for every three steps she took, and shook her head in misery. The shocks that were hitting her brain were too much for any human to bear. She sat raking at her face and pulling out handfuls of hair, trying to get inside her skull and rip out all the wires, put a stop to the horror show.

She wasn't aware of McIver until he was almost on top of her, and then all she saw, smelled and felt was a demon come to carry her away into the violence of the hell she was trying to resist.

With blood streaming from the slashes on her face she attacked him; she was a madwoman, and her strength was beyond his reckoning. She was so slippery he couldn't come to grips and even then he was afraid to try one of the four Hwa Rang Do submission holds he knew for fear of breaking bones or accidentally killing her.

Blaize had McIver down and an ear between her teeth, almost gnawed through so that a hard jerk would have torn it away, when her overstressed heart stopped beating and she slumped, dead, against his chest.

Chapter 12

Marbella, Spain

Although the weather along the Costa del Sol had been on the dreary side, with haze and chill winds off the sea, the marina at Puerto de Banus was crowded with yachts as the lengthy holiday season came to its conclusion. The Marbella Club had been sold out for a year, and it was next to impossible to obtain reservations at any of the good restaurants.

The French aristocrat and horse fancier Alex de Rienville, who was expecting company, stayed to himself aboard a chartered yacht that was not identified with him or his shipping subsidiary, Polestar Marine. It was a ninety-foot motor sailer named the *St. Affrique*. Not as elegantly appointed as the ship in which he customarily cruised the Mediterranean, the Monaco-based *Elizabeth Cèleste,* which was nearly twice the length of the *St. Affrique*; but it had ample staterooms below decks, a crew of six and amenities that included rare wines and a *cordon bleu* chef. There were also six telephones and two telexes aboard. The smaller yacht fully satisfied his need for both privacy and security at this time.

The lovers came aboard at nine o'clock in the evening, arriving in a limousine from the Malaga airport. They had traveled by private jet from the States. They were snuggled against each other like Siamese twins, which coefficiently they were, despite the disparity in their bodies.

The Marquis de Rienville shook hands with the man and kissed the cheeks of the woman, who was wearing a lot of makeup over appliques of thin latex that served as a temporary face-lift, changing the shape of her droopy eyes and propping up her chin line. The effect was masklike, Oriental. It gave her a more youthful appearance, although she could not have been called beautiful.

"New York was bitter?" he asked.

"Terrible. My feet still refuse to thaw." She shuddered lightly. "But I thought it would be balmier here."

The man just smiled and looked around the broad teak bayonet of the deck, stared at the lights of neighboring yachts in this millionaires' maritime ghetto.

"It looks better for tomorrow," Rienville assured her. "Or we could sail to Tunisia."

"And how have you been, Alex, my dear?"

"Impatient to see you both." But not anxious to have them seen; they had already been too long in plain sight on deck. "Come, let's get out of this wind."

Dinner was at nine-thirty in the salon amidships. *Pigeon de Bresse* for Rienville and the woman, huge quantities of steamed vegetables and rice for Axel Stroh, who took fanatically good care of his immense self. He ate no meat or animal products, no salt or sugar; he disdained tobacco and alcohol.

This was among the reasons why Rienville proposed no toasts at the beginning of the meal: but primarily it was to be a business cruise, and their business together was far from concluded.

Also, although he respected their worth to him, he loathed and feared them; it was an ordeal for Rienville, cold-blooded and calculating in his own right, endowed with a merciless pragmatism and intelligence that precluded irrationality, to be in their presence without showing his true feelings. The mad wretches of the world he could readily accept and deal with. Functional sociopaths raised to a higher power through supernatural bonding of personalities were beyond his ken. It was their air of absolute normality, their good humor, their fawning passion for each other that was so unnatural and finally unnerving, given what he knew of their activities.

There was never a wrong word, expression or gesture to serve as a clue to mental dysfunction, a distortion of the psyche so extreme they might, in an oblique moment, reacting to subconscious but common impulse, murder him as he sat opposite them with a wine glass to his faintly smiling lips. With no surface perturbation to indicate the impulse as it came and went.

He found himself watching them too closely, talking to fill silences. He did not like the mood they created when they gazed lengthily into each other's eyes.

But, the Marquis reasoned, reassuring himself, they could not be dangerous to him. On the contrary, he had all of their loyalty. They could never trust anyone else, but they trusted him; because Rienville, once certain bizarre information became available to him, had arranged Axel's rescue from the cocoon of isolation, the limbo of mind- and emotion-numbing drugs to which he had been consigned by his family.

And if not for Axel, Joanna Coulouris, daughter of one of the world's richest and most arrogant men, might still be no more than a rancid vegetable, an incompetent also eking out her life in the bright dungeons of an expensive Swiss sanitarium.

Rienville had seen their psychoanalytical profiles, listened to tapes that revealed them in all their gross deformity, described their visions of a world the Marquis could not imagine, much less live in.

Axel Stroh, despite his wealth of curls, calm demeanor and a lazy, abstracted gaze that was as gray and cheerless as a winter twilight, had developed from a pudgy, unremarkable child into one of the most menacing creatures who ever walked the earth. He came from a well-to-do German family, morticians in Essen and Hamburg. From his earliest years he had shown no outward fear of death or reverence for life. But of course his compulsive body-building activity was an hysterical reaction to the prospect of eventual dissolution. Two older brothers, tired of his whining and interference in their games, had helped condition his subconscious responses by shutting him up in a coffin with a naked and unembalmed female corpse when he was barely four years old. He literally had been reborn from that experience—as a cold, dreadful, remorseless soul who revenged himself on his brothers, twelve years later, by setting fire to them in their sleeping bags while they were on a family camping trip. The incident was passed off as an accident—a windy night, sparks from the camp fire—and both boys had recovered, after eighteen excruciating months of plastic surgery.

On reaching puberty, Axel began to gratify his sexual urges with the dormant assistance of the youthfully deceased. He entered into the family trade as a convenience, and this perversion, among others, was not discovered for a very long time.

By then, Axel Stroh later admitted to his therapist, Dr. Max Hoelscher, he had become adroit at snapping the necks of young boys and girls so that their deaths appeared to have resulted from falls, or collisions with high-speed trucks beneath shadowy autobahn overpasses.

He politely declined to number his victims, or to identify any of them.

At the age of twenty-one, he took up flying. He was a natural. He could fly anything: hot-air balloons, gliders, helicopters, twin-engine jets.

He liked balloons and gliders best. He liked to go very high, up into the thin atmosphere above the European mountain ranges, where the brain hung giddily on the verge of blackout. This was his nirvana, to sail along silently, watchful, godlike, away from the hue and cry of human souls. He craved three moments in life: the sudden snap of bone and release of a soul into the boundless ether; orgasm with the silently permissive; the utter quiet in the mind that immediately followed these two events. With practice he could extend those moments into hours: it was a feat like balancing on the wind, wings spread, gliding effortlessly around the world.

When they found him one morning lying in his bed—bubbles of froth on his lips, his mind gone soaring—next to a decomposing teenager with pigtails, they tried to take him away.

After he had demolished half a house and several policemen, he was finally subdued with a tranquilizer dart fired into his naked back by a veterinarian from the zoo.

He was then locked into the most rigidly secure unit of Dr. Hoelscher's Davos clinic, to await Joanna.

Her life had been dominated by her father, who cared nothing about her. The anger she felt toward him turned into a psychosis, triggered by one dismal act that Joanna chose to interpret as suicide.

When she met Axel Stroh, she was convinced that she had been dead for eight months. She was a mass of corrupt sores that did not respond to medication. Her skin had an almost luminous, corpselike pallor. He was attracted to her immediately.

And their slow fusion into one powerful, symbolic individual began.

Rienville was delighted when the lovers began to yawn soon after dinner, indicating their desire for an early bedtime.

By mid-afternoon of the following day, he hoped, he would receive the information they needed to get on with the final solution of their problem. In the meantime, on the open sea, they could entertain themselves, with only a few words and a smile from him now and then.

The *St. Affrique* set sail at dawn for Ibiza. Weather reports were good. The sun rose sharply over a jade-green sea, with lazy swells and a following wind. The lovers turned out at seven-thirty for a brisk hour of pumping iron in the stern.

They were naked. The crew had been warned, and tried to keep their backs turned. Rienville had no compunction about staring as they toiled so obliviously with their nickel-finished barbells flashing in the sun. He had ordered the mini-barbells for them and knew they weighed from fifty to seventy pounds apiece.

He was amazed at how shapely Joanna had become under Stroh's tutelage. And strong. She could pump a fifty-pounder overhead half a dozen times with one hand. She exhibited muscles he'd never before seen in a woman's body. As for Stroh himself, his proportions were difficult to believe. Mounds of muscle everywhere but on his earlobes. Even his horse's cock and pendulant balls seemed densely packed, made of metal, buffed to the same honey-dark shade as the rest of him. He could hold Joanna rigidly aloft, horizontal, with one hand, steady as a tree trunk himself in spite of the gentle rolling of the yacht on the surface of the sea.

It was hotter now, and they were sweating. Joanna had appeared on deck in the same makeup she had worn on arrival the night before. Rienville assumed that she never removed it when she was with Stroh. In the bright sun, in contrast with the rest of her body, the theatrical paint job gave her a grotesque, tribal look. Not of this world. But Stroh apparently liked her that way. When they were finished with their workout the necrophile ran his hands over her glistening body a few times and achieved a powerful erection, which they celebrated in a rattan chaise longue that eventually began to fall apart from the pounding it took.

Like children reveling in the first splurge from the wellsprings of their sexuality, they indulged twice more on deck during the day. Between times they ate, played and napped, and baked in the sun until they glowed. Stroh dove into the sea a couple of times without informing the crew, and they had to double back smartly to pick him up. Rienville, who disliked the sun, stayed below, attending to business by telex and edgily anticipating the one message that was so slow in coming.

In his business, excellent information and speed of communication were the difference between success and, not mere failure, but disaster. Rienville's principal business was grain, which Lenin suitably had called "the currency of currencies." Grain was more important to the world than oil. And five enormous, monolithic companies were in control of the world's grain trade. His own company was based in Monaco, with subsidiaries around the world. He bought and sold grain, and he sold the patented seeds to grow it.

At this time, while human beings in Third World nations, and even in the impoverished rural areas of the United States, were dying of malnutrition and related diseases at the rate of more than forty-eight thousand a day, world grain production was steadily declining, and surpluses, mainly in the U.S., where tillable land was disappearing at the rate of three million acres a year, had shrunk to levels of the worst famine years in modern times.

And grain wasn't like oil. It was subject to spoilage and infestations, even under the best storage and transit conditions. Until recently there had never been a surplus of rice, the staple food of two and a half billion Asians. A continuing adequate supply of oil and feed-grains depended on such a long list of variables that in any growing season a region's crops could be almost totally destroyed. Weather was one variable, disease another. Poor weather conditions always caused an explosion of blight. Rienville knew all the statistical projections by heart, and he knew that there was one constant factor that would cause the world's irreplaceable storehouse of food to be depleted almost overnight: human anxiety, and the hoarding instinct. A few bushels of grain per family, in a hundred nations. Easily concealed, but it would be consumed eventually. And if the Cirenaica spore had done its work in the meantime—

After that, the dead, those from hunger and those from bloody insurrections, would be literally beyond counting. They would rot in dense piles reaching halfway to the sun.

Let them. He had no enthusiasm for the human race. For Rienville, the light of this earth already had been extinguished; it had died with his daughter. Now let the earth suffer for that tragedy! If men could not see her face, hear her magnificent voice, rejoice in her purity, they would see Death in her place, breathe the smoke of war and not cleansing air, feed on their own rotten hearts instead of nourishing bread.

He was old, with only a few years left. But there was enough time. The engine for such a global disaster was already in place, ticking over almost unnoticeably. And the engineer was his other guest aboard the yacht, the entity known as Minotaur.

The need was for concealment until his plans could fully evolve; the danger lay in the inherently unstable nature of Minotaur. Each time Minotaur took action against their enemies, the danger was multiplied. Rienville had not fooled himself into thinking that he controlled Minotaur. But so far he had known just how to persuade Minotaur to want what he wanted.

Above all, Minotaur desired to survive, and to grow ever more powerful through the elimination of those who might threaten exposure.

In the late afternoon Joanna and Axel Stroh retired below to bathe and dress; Joanna spent the better part of an hour renewing her makeup. At sunset they joined Rienville for drinks.

Axel, wearing a blue sailcloth jacket and a commodore's cap, accepted Apollonaris and lime, excused himself with his crimped smile and sat leafing through a paperback omnibus of Nietzsche. Joanna and Rienville sipped Dom Perignon in the salon and had a quiet talk.

"It would seem that we now have more than ninety percent of the *El Invicto* tissue culture in our possession," Rienville said.

"Yes."

"The salvation of mankind. Should we decide that what is left is worth saving."

She nodded regally, like some queen of the outer darkness.

"Aravanis, of course, has, or did have, the remaining stock of *El Invicto*. I think we should be more than moderately concerned that he not have the opportunity to give any of it away to his fellow agronomists, or a government seed bank."

"He asked for our help," Joanna said, speaking of the cousins. "Now he has well-armed men with him day and night."

"It presents a problem."

Joanna glanced lovingly at Axel Stroh, who was speed-reading the Nietzsche, a blunt finger smoothly tracking down each page.

"Axel says they're looking for trouble—if it comes—to come from the outside, most likely by way of that long stretch of beach northeast of Róda. They will not be prepared for friends bearing gifts."

"But the exposure level, doing it that way, is quite unacceptable."

"We have no intention of leaving anyone alive."

"Numerous guards, plus the family members and servants? It's a formidable task, even for—"

She shrugged, then sniffed as stray bubbles from the champagne shot up her nose.

"Let's forget about Demetrios Constantine for now. I'm not angry with him. I am very angry about Dr. Hoelscher," she said.

"He has covered his tracks quite well. Utterly disappeared. The excuse he gave to family and friends is that he has an important manuscript to complete."

"He's probably writing about us," Joanna said.

"Better writing than talking."

She whanged her glass with a fingernail; the crystal chimed. She did it again. With kohl-darkened eyes she stared at Rienville in a way that infuriated him, made his skin crawl.

"A little more patience," he urged her. "I have a dozen investigators checking everywhere. He'll be found."

It was two hours later when a member of the crew approached Rienville; they had nearly finished their dinner.

"Excuse me, sir, but a coded telex message has just arrived, marked 'Urgent.' "

Rienville left the table immediately and took the message into his stateroom.

Dr. Max Hoelscher had been located; he was staying at the Goldener Bruck in St. Sebastien, Austria. The Marquis returned to the salon with this news.

"He is using the name Rolf Steiner. He is booked for an indefinite stay, and he seldom ventures from his suite except to ski the Vauluga. But today, for much of the afternoon, he had a visitor, who we can assume has also gone to considerable trouble to find him." Rienville looked at Joanna. "His visitor was your cousin Kristoforos Aravanis."

Axel Stroh, who spoke no French, said in clumsy English, "How soon we can be in Malaga? The plane is ready there."

"In four to five hours." Rienville paused, clearing his throat with a little Montrachet. "We must be in agreement on one thing. We cannot afford a sensation. Dr. Hoelscher has chosen to disappear; very well, let him disappear forever. As for your cousin—does he ski?"

"Yes. Usually alone. But Kris and I have been on very good terms lately," Joanna said.

"Then you will find a way to handle it so there is no suspicion of murder."

Axel Stroh held up a hand with fingers like shapely bananas: thumb and middle finger made an impressively loud popping sound in the salon.

"I had better notify the captain to change course for Malaga," Rienville told them.

Part Two

HUBRIS

Power of blood itself releases blood.
—Robert Frost

Chapter 13

Chicago

As for Blaize:
In her slow swings around the universe amid the constancy of the stones she managed to clear up some misconceptions from childhood.

[A.] At one end of almighty space there was an empty eye socket. God lived in there, sly as a rat.

So much for what she had been taught Sundays at Wescott Baptist Church, and during Vacation Bible School under the big shade oaks.

[B.] Her brother Jordan wasn't dead. Nor was Lonnie. Nor were her mother, Granny Bill and the slew of relatives she had once counted among the dear departed. She had come across them down South floating in the deluxe houseboat on Kentucky Lake with all the universe ahead of them.

It was a fine day and the lake had the color and sparkle of vintage champagne. They had changed their shapes somewhat. Granny Bill looked nice with her original teeth. Jordan was a stallion, and no hole in the head. Blaize made a hammock of his mane and they all floated together, speaking of the strategies of Time, Fate constellated, holy orders, sidereal effects and the precise geometry of bees, until long after the sun had set.

A colossal moon made faint the night. It nearly blinded her. Blaize knew she couldn't stay. She was still being born and reborn, several times around the earthly clock. And it hurt, each time she stepped onto her tongue and swallowed herself, went squirming and howling down into the light, filling the slack body that hung in tubes with the pain of relocation.

God the rat was swimming, huge as a submarine, beside the house-boat.

I don't want to go back, she pleaded. *Make me a horse, like my brother.*

But we have too many horses already, said God the rat.

Then he flew up out of the lake, terrifying in his aplomb, and bit her lovingly in the neck.

"Ohhhhh, miigoddddd!"

"Blaize? Blaize?

Dr. Viola Purkey was still in a wheelchair, but she sat up straighter and didn't tremble anymore.

Blaize stared at her through the bars of the criblike bed for almost half a minute. Then she said, "Hello, Viola."

Viola's face tensed. She smiled.

"Thank the Lord."

". . . What?"

"Those are the first lucid words out of your mouth in nearly two weeks. I believe you're going to make it, child."

Blaize was conscious of the sounds of medical monitoring machines; her eyes felt grainy and dry. She blinked.

"What do you mean? What happened to me?"

Viola wheeled herself a little closer to the bed in the intensive-care cubicle. "Your heart stopped beating after that unspeakable pimp gave you DMT. It stopped twice, once on the way to the hospital."

Pimp? she thought. Nothing came to mind. *Hospital*? She said it aloud. Her voice sounded to her as if it were coming from another room. "That's—where I am?"

"Salve Regina. Near Marquette Park. My husband and I were both on staff here. I'm still friendly with most of the members of the board and the nursing Sisters. Otherwise they wouldn't let me in here."

"I'm thirsty," Blaize complained. Her lips felt swollen.

"We'll do something about that. How is your head? I mean inside."

"Oh—I've—had weird dreams. Dreams," she repeated uncertainly, aware of how inadequate a description that was. She felt a chill. "What day is it?"

"The fifth of January."

"*What happened to Christmas*?"

"You missed it, child. But you're back with us again. That's the important thing."

"Guess so," Blaize said sadly. "But I was going to spend Christmas in Lexington with Daddy, and—"

"Mr. Ellington was here on Christmas day. He's been here every day for two weeks. He's staying at the Drake."

"What was it you said I had?"

"No kind of sickness. Worse. An overdose of DMT. Do you know what that is?"

"Like LSD. You mean I—I've been tripping out all this time?"

She had a taste of it just then. Her mind told her that her toes were falling off. She couldn't see them, nor could she raise her head or her hands; she was restrained in the bed as effectively as if she wore a straitjacket. Panic. She meant to scream, but it came out a scalded hiss. She looked into a flashing mirror of the mind and saw her face hideously scarred. Her tongue protruded from her mouth like a long-dead, festering fish. She tried to bite it off, ranting and cursing incoherently.

But as quickly as the seizure had occurred, it passed away. She gasped for breath. "Ohmigod," she said weakly.

"What happened?"

"Badddd trip. It was like—leafing through an old horror comic book when I wasn't supposed to be reading in bed."

"It may go on for a few weeks," Viola told her. "But the

episodes will become progressively weaker and you'll be able to cope with them."

Blaize wasn't so sure. "You said—my heart stopped. Just about freaked out all the way, didn't I? I can't remember—anything. Tell me what happened. How did I get here?"

"We'll talk later," Viola promised, glancing at the doorway of the cubicle. A nurse had appeared there. "Your father will be along soon. I'll phone him now, let him know that you're back with us for keeps."

"Is it morning? Night?"

"Eleven o'clock in the morning."

"I wish I could get out of here," Blaize moaned. But she was feeling too tired to talk anymore, and Viola's features were blurring. The nurse made some adjustments in the drip time of the medication and liquid nourishment coming from bottles upended on stands around the bed. The nurse spoke to Viola, but Blaize was adrift and couldn't understand what they were saying.

At a little after two o'clock she was awake again in the dimness of the cubicle, where day and night were exactly the same. She felt her heart beating, licked her dry lips.

"There's my baby-hon!"

Blaize couldn't move her head more than a couple of inches to either side, and it took her a little while to find and focus on her father's wind-reddened face. He was at the end of the bed, peering at her with a wide and over-anxious smile.

"Oh, Daddy," Blaize said, her eyes stinging from tears. "I sure fucked up!"

Buford Ellington clumped toward her. He walked with the aid of a pair of aluminum hand crutches. His legs had been in braces since a bout of polio when he was fifteen. He was wearing a French-cut, double-breasted gray pin-striped suit that Blaize didn't care for; all French clothes were designed for the willowy types. Totsie Graham's influence, Blaize assumed. Now she was picking out his clothes. What next? Totsie and Buford had been keeping company for a couple of years. She was one of those women always identified in the papers as "prominent socialite." Four ex-husbands had provided her with a tidy pile. She said she wasn't interested in a fifth marriage. Blaize didn't believe a word of it.

"Where's Totsie?" Blaize asked. "Is she with you?"

"Not today. The cold weather's got her down with a sick headache. You know she's usually in Hobe Sound this time of the year. But she was so excited when they called and told us you were coming out of it. Little girl, you don't know how I've been praying!"

When he was emotional, Buford Ellington dripped tears with the eyes of an abandoned hound. He was a homely man, a mouth like a picket fence, braying laugh: a lovable lummox, until he sat down to cut a business deal. Then he was lit from within by hellfire; he could be profane and brutal.

"Totsie's been such a tower of strength for me, Blaize. I swear to Jesus, I don't know how I would have got through the past couple of weeks without her. It's a good thing you didn't see your own face, all scratched up. But the doctor says there'll only be a couple of little scars and makeup will cover them." His heavy eyebrows came together forbiddingly. "There's still plenty of questions to be answered. The D.A. in this goddam forsaken city better understand I mean business! I'm having dinner tonight with the governor in the Pump Room; he'll get the investigation going."

"Investigation?"

Buford leaned against the bed, freed a hand from one of the crutches, reached through bars to grasp her hand. His palm was sweaty.

"What do you remember, little girl? How did you get in this fix? McIver set you up, didn't he? Hell, they want to blame it all on that black pimp! I know you better'n that; you'd have *shot* the nigger tried to get next to you."

"Wait, Daddy, I—I'm trying to think. It's really hard."

She closed her eyes. There were disturbances in her mind, flashes of light that illuminated a tumultuous and ongoing masque, images of such violence and filth and cruelty they turned her blood to cold slush. But she wasn't helpless anymore, trapped in the blasted areas; she could steer her thoughts to small islands of calm, focus on a kind of gray twilight sea until the mists cleared and memories welled up. There. She had a fix. The days and nights spent with Viola, getting acquainted. Waiting for—

"McIver," she said faintly.

Buford squeezed her hand too tightly; Blaize let out a squawk and a nurse came to the door of the cubicle.

"You saw him, didn't you? Finally caught up with the murdering son of a bitch."

"Yes, I—I—almost—"

"Mr. Ellington. Five minutes is what I said, and five minutes is what I *meant*."

Buford wheedled and cajoled, but the charge nurse was adamant. He leaned over awkwardly to give his daughter a kiss and went swinging out of the cubicle on his crutches, promising loudly to bring Totsie on his next visit. Blaize could hardly wait.

She was all slept out and her vital signs seemed to please everybody, including Viola when she came back that evening. Blaize spent most of her time mastering the trick of keeping her thoughts away from the nightmare areas of the mind: mentally she would just throw a big American flag over the unwelcome image and veer quickly away from it, toward images of home and horses and bluegrass rangeland, of a resplendent houseboat floating in a bucolic haze down there on Kentucky Lake, all the womenfolk dressed for teatime, the guys lazing on the roof deck, bullshitting and trading good-natured insults with Godtherat. Maybe it was all the tranquilizers they'd pumped into her to try to counteract the effects of the nearly lethal DMT, but Blaize had a definite sense of peace and hopefulness that was a rarity in her adult life. She knew that, wherever they were going on the houseboat, Mom and Jordan and Lonnie were happier than they'd ever been in this world. Godtherat, in his scruffy wisdom, had put her off the houseboat because it wasn't her time yet. She still had a few things to learn before school was out.

She missed them all terribly but it was a sweet ache, not a corrosion of the heart.

Blaize felt like singing, but she'd never been able to carry a tune. She felt like having sex. She wanted a big steak, charred on the outside, bright pink on the inside. She wanted to go home and ride a fine horse for miles in the January weather, until her blood flowed with its old clarity and she was purified by the cold fire in her lungs.

Then Viola told her how Lucas McIver had saved her life,

in the subzero wind atop the skeletal office building when her heart had stopped beating.

"He gave you CPR for nearly twenty minutes, until a paramedic ambulance could respond. On the way to the hospital your heart stopped again. But by then Lucas had all the right stuff to kick it back on course again."

Blaize just stared at the ceiling, scarcely blinking, too shocked to think straight.

"But he could have—just walked away," she said after a long time.

"Darling, I've tried to convince you! That man you've been after all these years? That's not the man he is."

"Well, goddammit, how should I know—my brothers are gone, but you keep telling me—Viola, you wouldn't lie to me. You wouldn't, you *wouldn't*!"

"No. And believe me, if there was anything he could have done for Lonnie in Bangkok, he would have—but your brother just got himself into an awful mess out there. Part of the story is on record, you just have to ask the right people."

Tears rolled down Blaize's cheeks. "Oh, shit. What do I do now? I don't know what I'm supposed to think anymore!"

"You don't have to think; you don't have to act. Draw a deep breath and be grateful you're alive. The rest will take care of itself, in time."

Blood was pounding in Blaize's temples and Viola's voice seemed faint to her.

"Viola!"

"I'm right here. Not going anywhere as long as you need me."

"I—I want to see McIver. I have to talk to him."

"Child, I can't help you. It's been two weeks, and Lucas is long gone, I'm afraid."

"Doesn't he come to visit you?"

"Since your father has been in town, the police have been showing more interest in the clinic than they have in years."

"Where, then? Where can I find McIver?"

"You ought to know I don't have that information."

"He can't be gone! He can't just leave me like this! Don't you understand how important—"

"What's important is that you get better. Get all your strength back. That'll take time. Now calm yourself. Your blood pressure's way up and your arteries aren't used to handling it."

True to his word, Buford brought Totsie Graham with him on his second visit of the day, although only members of the immediate family were allowed in the intensive-care unit. But Buford could smuggle daylight past a rooster if he wanted to. Totsie was in a holding pattern somewhere around fifty-five. Her face had been through so many tucks they had left her gaping like a fish. She had a golf-links tan that had begun to yellow in the Chicago winter and, as Blaize recalled, a disposition spotty as measles. She made a fuss over Blaize, who was unaccountably cold to both of them.

"As soon as they let you out of here, I want you to promise you'll come down to Hobe Sound. The whole place is *yours*, just as long as you need it."

"She means it," Buford exulted. "She really means it! And you know how Totsie feels about having houseguests. That's her hidey-hole. Her refuge from the world."

"My refuge from the world. When I'm home, I'm *not* at home. I don't accept invitations. I don't extend invitations. The *Bugaboo*'s yours too. A cruise on the inland waterway, that's just the tonic when you've got the blahs."

"Is that what I had? The blahs?"

"Oh, you know what I mean."

Either their voices were too loud, which made her cringe, or else there was surf in her ears and she had to strain to make out what they were saying. Blaize was tired of having company.

"They're probably going to move you to a private room tonight," Buford said. "You'll have nurses right there with you, 'round the clock."

"That's swell."

Her feelings of hostility passed almost as soon as her father left. She cried a little because she missed him. She was rude to one of the nurses, who paid no attention. Then she felt a surge of euphoria. Wished she had some decent music to listen to. Tried to remember the word that had knocked her out of the finals of the spelling bee when she was twelve. Dissension. That was it. Jesus Christ, she thought, angry with herself, *anybody* could spell dis—dess—disi—. She started to cry again. The hospital's resident psychiatrist popped in and caught her at it.

"I don't know what's the matter with me! I'm going crazy! I want to get out of here."

"Anybody who wants to get out of here can't be crazy. What's that from? *Catch-22?* We haven't been introduced. I'm Sid Fromkiss. I love your name. Blaize. Where'd it come from?"

"Old family name."

She was still restrained; he freed her hands and gave her a tissue. Blaize dabbed at her eyes.

"I have these fantasies about what I'd change my name to if I wasn't resigned to Fromkiss and scared stiff of being cut out of my old man's will. Tyrone Steele. Rory Benedict the Fourth. Dirk Cromwell. That's my favorite this week. I'm dying to look some tall, well-groomed blonde in the eye at a cocktail party and say to her, 'Hi. I'm Dirk.' Tall, well-groomed blondes are my other fantasy. It sends shivers up and down my spine. So what do you think? Do I look like Dirk Cromwell to you?"

He wore thick glasses and only a few tufts were left of his hairline. He had a pale egg-shaped face and bit his nails.

"Frankly, uh, no. Why did I have my hands tied?"

"Assaultive episodes are common with overdoses of hallucinogens. Also you might have been inspired to dismantle your own body and put it back together again, which is practicing surgery without a license. How are your mood swings? Sunny one minute, weepy the next? Thinking about suicide when you're in the pits?"

"*No*."

He was evaluating her chart. "Let's see. You've had a pretty good day. Tox screens are looking better. The other docs think you're stable enough to come off the machines. You don't require continual observation, in my opinion. I think we can skip the obligatory stopover in the psychiatric unit."

"Thank you," Blaize said humbly.

"By the way, some flatfoots are semi-anxious to talk to you. How's your memory?"

Her feet were cold. Freezing. Going up and up in the slow elevator beside the building empty as dinosaur bones. Stars swarming around and inside her head like jeweled insects. Sweet Willie Wine's saber-toothed smile detached from his face and walking all over her bare skin.

"Not—so good."

"Okay. I'll keep them on hold for a few more days. You may want to talk to your father and have the family lawyer present when the time comes."

"Am I in trouble?"

He shrugged. "I don't think so. You got taken for a ride. But be sure of what you're saying before you say it."

"Thanks . . . Dirk," she said.

"Hey! Did I almost see a smile there?"

"I don't think so. I was born a solemn child."

Before dinner they trundled her out of the ICU to another room in a newer, more cheerful wing of Salve Regina. She had her first solid meal at the hospital. Bland potatoes, a little well-done chopped meat, butterscotch pudding. She managed to eat a few bites. There was a TV mounted on one wall and she watched the evening news hour, which was too brightly colored. The news seemed to be taking place on a planet with which she was totally unfamiliar. Sometimes sentences in plain English made no sense to her. It was very irritating. She hated the way the anchorwoman did her hair. With the help of a middle-aged Irish LPN who had forearms like Popeye's, she got up and walked to the bathroom. Ten short steps. They had taken the catheter out. Urination was painful. Her feet were swollen and sore. Her heart pounded, but she insisted on walking a little way down the hall and back again.

She got into bed and dozed through various visitations by the nursing staff: medications, keeping score on her pulse and BP. The first LPN was replaced by another, more elderly. Her name was Peabody. She had with her an accordianlike plastic folder, which, when fully extended, was three feet long and chock-full of pictures of her grand- and great-grandchildren. After showing Blaize the photos, she sat and silently read true-crime magazines in a corner where the light was low. Blaize tossed and turned and dreamed despondently.

The racehorse Blaize Two had fallen in front of a capacity crowd at Churchill Downs. Broken leg. Had to be destroyed. Blaize was on the track trying to draw her .45 from her belt holster, but it was stuck. Her father coming after her on crutches down the straightaway; old swivel-hips, feet flopping, he was shouting angrily. The gun was almost too big to hold in both hands. Each time she pulled the trigger, it blasted a big crater in the ground around the horse. How humiliating. Her father fell into one of the holes. He raved and cursed trying to climb out. She had no control over the weapon in her hands. It fired again, but the bullet came out of the barrel like a horse's dick and hung limply over the edge of the crater, pointing at Buford's livid forehead. Blaize had an orgasm in front of a hundred thousand people. At least she guessed that's what it was, it was her first. Totsie Graham was down on her at a thousand to one and cashed in for another quick fortune. Then she placed a huge horseshoe of flowers around Blaize's neck, burying her to the eyebrows. Blaize was suffocating and panicky—rose fever—the sweat dripping down while they led her into the winner's circle.

As she came out of it she felt a cool washcloth moving over her hot, damp face. She blinked to clear her eyes. It wasn't Peabody standing beside her bed.

He was tall, with wide shoulders, a short and shapely beard that had reddish highlights. He wore a dark-blue turtleneck and a corduroy jacket. His hands were large, his touch delicate. But the eyes had all of her attention. They were stone-gray and remarkably humane. Not at all unfriendly. But watchful, a little tired from the strain of always being on his guard.

Blaize gasped.

"Hold it," he said quietly. "What do you want to do, start screaming? Then I'll have to stuff this cloth down your throat and make a fast exit. We're on the second floor. I've already plotted a way out. I'll be driving away from the building in less than fifteen seconds. Or maybe you'll just be sensible, for once in your life."

"Oh, Jesus, I don't believe it! I don't—"

"Would you mind telling me what you're so afraid of? If I ever meant any harm, I'd have left you right where I found you, with your butt frozen and your eyes bulging out of your head." He touched his right ear. It was still tender. "Twenty stitches," he said. "To keep it from falling off in a high wind."

"What? What are you—"

"You nearly bit my ear off. Would have, but your heart stopped just in time."

Blaize stared at him. Lucas McIver stared back. Then he cracked a smile.

"That was a joke. I think."

"Oh."

He had a way of tilting his head to express mild surprise, or cynical amusement. "I don't know what it is with you and me. I ran our names and birthdates through a computer dating service. We're not all that incompatible."

"We're not? Is that a joke?"

"Not if you're not laughing."

Blaize looked surreptitiously around the room. They were alone.

"Peabody's off having a nosh in the nurses' lounge. We've got a few minutes."

"Viola said that you—"

"What Viola doesn't know can't hurt her, and it keeps her honest. I stuck around Chicago for a couple of reasons. I was filling some gaps in my education, but also I had to know if you were going to make it or if too many circuits were lost in that blast of DMT."

"Why care about me, though?"

McIver ran a slow hand across his bearded chin and mouth, a gesture of delay while he tried to put his emotions into words.

"I sure as hell didn't want you spending the rest of your life in a loony bin. You're the last of the line. Not that I hold any of you in such high regard, but I'd be judged responsible for the loss of all three of Buford Ellington's children, and he'd never let up on me. He could leave a hundred million in his will just to pay for bounty hunters. Not much of a prospect, and my life is difficult enough already. That's one reason I was concerned about you. The other is conscience. I see you as even more of an innocent than Lonnie was. You've wallowed in money all your life and think you know what the world is about. I have some advice for you—"

"Who needs *your* fucking advice!" she croaked.

"Hey, quiet down or I'll gag you." McIver looked around

at the closed door, then leaned over her. He had a physician's photo ID pinned to his coat; the name on it was Robert Painter. Blaize's stomach contracted. Simple fear, but there was an unexpected after-effect, a kind of lowdown warmth and tingling sensation. The fear couldn't hold out. No, he wasn't going to strangle her in the bed. His eyes held hers. Were they the eyes of a born killer? *How the hell was she supposed to know?* Pard Randolph had killed a lot of men, yet he had the kindest blue eyes she'd ever seen. You wanted to curl up in Pard's lap and hear a bedtime story. Would McIver try to touch her again? Thinking about it gave her a sensation of danger, an accelerated heartbeat. Anticipation. But he didn't touch her. She was *this close* to him after all these years. No use yelling for help; and then she realized with a little start of perfect awareness that she didn't want anyone interfering just now. Her avid interest, her pent-up excitement, were a kind of rapture that no one else could understand, much less share: but *he* could. She sensed that it wasn't just mercy that had brought McIver so late at night to her room, but a kind of reckless unfathomable curiosity.

"I'll be quiet," Blaize promised.

His face relaxed, subtly. After so many years of staring at blurred or out-of-date photos, half-realized images, she couldn't take her eyes off him: so disturbingly real, yet a more complex face than she had been prepared for. He looked resourceful, but not savage; nor jaded from misadventure, his time on the dodge. And the ghost of the half-wild, terrified boy she remembered lingering inside the man. She felt, unwillingly, attentive to the other side of the tragedy, his side: she was unnerved by intimations of the tyranny of circumstances.

"You're the lucky one," he told her. "You have your life back. Don't waste any more of it. Don't let your old man push you into settling a score that can't be settled. It's already lopsided."

"He's never pushed me into anything!"

"He hasn't tried to stop you, either."

"Because he—I don't know—because there was nobody left he could really depend on!"

"And you *wanted* to do it. You wanted to track me down

and fill me full of lead for your daddy's sake. Because he can't handle the job himself."

"It's not his fault he had polio."

McIver looked away, eyes cooling; in profile he seemed older, painfully demoralized.

"Blaize, we're all crippled. I'll be on the run for the rest of my life. Don't think I came up here to try to talk you into letting me off the hook. Your father recognizes no statute of limitations; as far as he's concerned, the charge will always be murder; and I'll always be a fugitive. But you don't have to be a hostage to my situation. Just think about it. Then go back to doing something useful with your life."

She blinked, dumfounded; and he was already halfway to the door, moving soundlessly.

"No, wait!"

McIver paused and looked back at her.

"There's nothing more to say."

"But I—I need—I've never talked to you. And—we might never have another chance."

"I know. So what?"

"I—I want you to tell me—everything that happened the night you ki—that Jordy was—"

The hand to the beard again, the thoughtful, almost profound hesitation. "No. We'll just start tearing at each other. When I think about tonight, it would be nice to believe we halfway got along. So good-bye, Blaize."

All of her frustration and anger were concentrated in a tone that wasn't loud but stopped him like the pop of a blacksnake whip an inch from his nose.

"*You wait.* The last time you ran off and left me I was twelve years old, I had blood all over my nightgown and I want to know once and for all *what happened to Jordan.*"

McIver said, with a look of interest he hadn't revealed before, "You mean you're not sure?"

"I saw you point that revolver at Jordy while he was on the floor and shoot him. But—"

He returned to the bed so abruptly that she was frightened again and did a girlish thing: she pulled the sheet up nearly to her chin. But he seemed elsewhere, looking at her but not really aware of her.

"That wasn't the bullet that killed him. Jordan was already dead."

"Would you help me sit up?" Blaize said timidly.

She had to ask him twice. Then he nodded and cranked the bed for her. She felt a little dizzy as her head was elevated. And something ghastly was starting to happen in her mind. Blaize closed her eyes tightly and waved a voluminous flag at the ghastliness. She began to sing, in a small quavering voice, "Ohhhhhh say can you see—"

McIver stared at her. "What's the matter?"

"One of those—flashbacks they warned me about."

"Are you over it?"

"I think so. Yes. I'm all right. So you were saying—the bullet—"

"Let me tell you about my Uncle Loyal's old double-action Colt's. The sear was stoned way down to a sliver, didn't take a long pull to fire it the first time. Just a touch of the finger, a moderate jolt, would do it. Understand?"

"I know about guns," she said impatiently.

"The hammer was cocked over a round when I walked into your house with the Colt's in my belt."

"Why weren't you carrying it?"

"I needed both hands to get the outside door, the door to the garden, open; then I wasn't more than three steps inside the library when Jordan walked in and sprang the lights on me. I had my hand on the butt, but I didn't draw the revolver. We just looked at each other. Jordan didn't seem scared of me. But my knees were knocking together."

(You son of a bitch. You have a hell of a nerve.)

Her heart, flopping like a fish in a waterless pail as she crept down the wide staircase in her bare feet.

After all these years, she could hear her brother's voice perfectly. Blaize shuddered.

McIver said, "He could have talked me into laying down my piece and walking away. But when Jordan saw I was—maybe not losing my nerve, just facing up to the actuality of what I was there for, and thinking about it for the first time—he started to bully me. Edging a little closer all the time until there wasn't five feet between us. Then I saw the Buck knife in his hand. Open. He must have heard me just before he came into the library, and took the knife out of his pocket."

Shaking, shaking, Blaize couldn't control herself. She wiped at the warm, wet spot she felt over her left breast. The nipple stood up. Her teeth chattered.

"I tried to pull the Colt's, but it hung up in my belt and he went after my gun hand with his knife."

McIver held up his right hand; she saw the timeworn scar across the ball of his thumb, angling toward the center of his palm.

"The Colt's hit the floor butt-first and went off; Jordan was off balance after lunging at me and looking straight down the barrel. That big sucker of a hardball hit him almost dead center in the forehead and tore out the back of his skull."

She put her hands over her face but the shaking wouldn't stop.

"Why—*why* did you have to shoot him again?"

"Didn't intend to. I just picked up the revolver and looked over at Jordan, and I was so stunned, so sick to my stomach I couldn't feel anything else. My finger must have grazed the trigger and the Colt's went off again. The next thing I remember, you were there in the library. I don't know how long you'd been watching. I never knew if you saw him die. You didn't, did you?"

"No!"

"And I still had the gun in my hand when I picked you up; it went off a third time, past your ear. Then I threw the gun the hell away and ran. That's all; ran. The truck broke down, somewhere, maybe it was out of gas. I don't know. I ran. I ran. I've lived through that night ten thousand times in my mind, in my sleep. Running, not getting anywhere. Wishing it had been different. . . ."

Blaize got out of bed with the swiftness of an attack, but she had no strength, she only fumbled against McIver when her legs wouldn't hold her up. In desperation she put her arms around him, stared him full in the face, her teeth bared.

"I don't want to believe you—no, no, I don't—!"

He looked unhappy, and threatened. "What *do* you want from me, Blaize?"

"B-but—if it's true—" She whipped her head from side to side in savage denial. "No. Not true." Shaking her head harder, hair flying across her face. Whip, whip, she was sobbing for breath. "But—why do you go on lying? Pointless. Don't you understand—we can't be like this—the rest of our lives!"

"Blaize, the worst I was guilty of was involuntary manslaughter. But I never had a witness to my name. All either of us ever had was—you."

She had exhausted her strength. Her head sank heavily against his chest. He picked her up and put her back to bed but stayed close, continuing to hold her.

Blaize said, "If you came back—"

"Back home? To the Commonwealth of Kentucky? I've already made that mistake. It got me where I am today. There was my picture in the Chicago *Trib*, honors at Loyola, all that. I wanted to see my mother one more time and brag just a little, let her know I'd come out okay. She'd been dying for six months by the time I got to her, sneaking downstate, scared shitless all the way. She was so deaf she couldn't hear me. Barely able to make out my face. But Jesus, Goddamn, I never saw her so happy before! I shouldn't have left the clipping with her, though. I know she had it in her hand when Aunt Chessie found her dead a few days later. And when the undertaker pried the clipping from her hand down at the funeral home and saw what it was, he went straight to the sheriff."

"No. He went—to my father. For the reward, you see."

"Oh, sure. The reward. It must have been a potful. Fifty thousand big ones? A hundred? I had a residency in surgery waiting in Houston, Blaize."

"Am I supposed to be—sorry?" But she was. And astonished at the relief she felt.

"At least the headhunters your father hired waited until I got my diploma. I guess they figured I couldn't go anywhere. But I had the Leprechaun on my side."

"The what? How *did* you get away?"

McIver backed off. "That's another story. But I'm getting a strange buzz at the base of my spine. Like somebody's taking dead aim. Is it you? Do you still want to kill me, Blaize?"

"Are you—going to do something to try to help us?"

"No."

"You stubborn son of a bitch, you don't know what my life has been *like*!"

"Get well."

"God! How I've *hated* you!" She felt glowing iron, white heat in her chest, as if the vessel of her father's wrath, which she had carried for so many years as a sacred trust, had tipped over. Blaize held her breath until the searing pain had ended and McIver, lingering, watched her. Twenty seconds passed; half a minute.

"No," he said. "That buzz isn't you anymore. Small miracle."

"I'm going home—with my father. And then maybe—I'll see you again."

"Not a chance."

"I'm *going* to see you again. Like it or not."

He shrugged, unable to follow whatever she was using for logic. He tried to look at her as—still—the enemy, but he couldn't follow the logic of that anymore either. He didn't know what to make of her.

"I might," he said, "like it. That would depend on the circumstances."

Blaize smiled.

It started slowly, hesitantly, and turned into a sunrise. McIver was dazzled. Then warmed. His eyes glowed momentarily in response.

Blaize caught it before she closed her own eyes.

"Goddam right you'll like it," she promised him with what was left of her voice, then settled herself for a long winter's nap.

Chapter 14

St. Sebastien, Austria

As soon as he saw his cousin Joanna coming out of the Goldener Bruck hotel, Kris Aravanis knew he was in deadly trouble.

He recognized the daughter of Argyros Coulouris just as she paused to slip on dark glasses to protect her eyes from the afternoon glare. She was wearing a full-length amethyst fox fur coat with a floppy-brimmed hat to match.

His first impulse was to leave the village immediately, not try to slip into the hotel by the side entrance and return to his room for his clothes. He was carrying his passport with him, and some travelers' checks, all that he needed to be back in the States by morning after an overnight run to Paris on the Arlberg Express.

Fortunately, though he had been walking toward the hotel on the other side of the Radstadplatz when Joanna appeared, she hadn't noticed him. The cobbled square was crowded with holidayers; it was the weekend following Epiphany in this popular Austrian resort, and Fasching, the winter carnival that went on for the six weeks until Shrove Tuesday, was about to begin. Already there were costumed mummers in the square, along with skiers who had returned early from the slopes of the mountains that rose to six thousand feet above the medieval village. Kris stepped quickly into a shop specializing in handmade lace and petit-point; from the window of the shop that offered a view of the hotel he watched Joanna.

She stood just outside the entrance, looking around the crowded square but not as if she were in a hurry to go anywhere. Rather, she seemed to be waiting for someone; and, folding her arms, it looked as if she had resigned herself to a lengthy wait.

She would be waiting for Axel Stroh, of course. Despite his apprehension Kris was filled with curiosity, hoping he would have a glimpse of this monster. And while he waited his mind began to work rationally again.

From his cousin alone he was sure he had nothing to fear, if what he'd been hearing from Max Hoelscher was correct. And despite the bizarre nature of Hoelscher's story, Kris had no reason to doubt the man's conclusions. Kris didn't need a psychiatrist to tell him that there were no apparent limits to the abnormal behavior of which many human beings were capable.

How, Kris wondered, could Joanna have known he was in St. Sebastien? He'd told no one of his plans. Which meant it had to be Dr. Hoelscher Minotaur was stalking. Undoubtedly, if Joanna knew where the doctor was staying, she also knew the alias he used. Hoelscher was skiing this afternoon, probably one of the difficult trails of the Vauluga, the summit of which was reached from the village by cable car. In the company of a couple of thousand other skiers, he should be safely anonymous until he returned to the hotel.

Kris would have to warn him that at least one-half of Minotaur's outlandish persona was currently haunting the Goldener Bruck. If anything happened to the doctor, Kris would have a difficult time proving what he had learned about Minotaur. The lives of all the cousins were in the balance; the fate of Actium International also depended on the action that Kris would take in the next hour or so, before the sun went down. And that, aside from keeping his own skin intact, was what concerned him the most.

Kris had spent close to ten thousand dollars to locate Hoelscher, but once he confronted the man, coolly confident and insistent, it had been surprisingly easy to get him to talk, to betray a professional trust. Kris had come to St. Sebastien knowing a little, from the telephone call his uncle had received; he pretended to know a lot more, always a valuable interrogative technique. Joe D'Allesandro probably had used the same technique to get the frightened but egotistical Hoelscher to open up—which of course had led to Joe's being barbecued alive. Kris was determined to be more careful. He had skillfully offered the doctor bribes, reassurances and praise while he painstakingly penetrated the psychological labyrinth that had formed around and protected Minotaur. Much of what he heard made the misanthropic Kris want to vomit; and Max Hoelscher could talk about the secret heart of Minotaur only when he was one drink away from falling headfirst out of his chair in his suite at the Goldener Bruck.

"Can anything be done to stop Minotaur?" Kris had asked.

"They must be separated, and locked up for the rest of their lives. Or else—"

"Destroyed?"

The doctor's face was flushed from the excessive heat in the room, from his days of skiing, from Lowenherz, the clear brandy that he drank exclusively. His eyes, behind drooping lids, were as swollen as feeding ticks.

"Your uncle has already tried," he said hoarsely.

"You mean he attempted to have Axel Stroh killed? At your suggestion?"

"*My* suggestion? No, no, I could never—"

"What happened?"

"I said to him—I said only—that as long as the two were together, there was no hope that Joanna could be cured."

"So Argyros determined to eliminate Stroh. He thinks, to this day, that Stroh is dead. Do you know what happened?"

"I only know—Stroh is a clever man. He is strong, quick, alert—all of these attributes are heightened fantastically by his paranoia. He obviously realized that because of his relationship with Joanna Coulouris he was a marked man. And that, in the long run, your uncle's resources would wear him down. Perhaps the assassins Argyros hired had already attempted, and failed, to kill him. Once, twice—until Stroh resolved to put a stop to the attempts on his life."

"How?"

"By faking his own death. I've given this matter a great deal of thought. He is a pilot, remember. It seems that Axel Stroh rented a small plane at an airfield in the south Tyrol. He used his own name. He took off from the field alone. Two days later the plane was found, wrecked, in a high meadow some thirty miles from the airfield. No one saw the plane go down. One body was found. The body of a strong young man like Axel Stroh. Severely mangled, of course. The face all but obliterated. But he was—identified through his dental charts."

"Then what reason do you have for believing it was not Axel Stroh?"

"Don't be naive. The man is a body-builder. He would know another man of similar age and size, with the same muscular development. In need of, let us say, much dental work. And pleased to accept Stroh's offer to fly him to, Hong Kong perhaps, to have the necessary work done, including the addition of the beautiful implants that give Axel Stroh such an arresting smile. How much would it cost Stroh, whose *inamorata* has countless millions of dollars, to have his own dental work duplicated in the mouth of his friend?"

"Then, having set it up, he arranges for his friend—whom he also has chosen because there will be few family members or friends to know or care where he is—to be found in Stroh's place in the crashed plane. And how would Stroh have worked that out?" Kris answered his own question with a slight, grim smile. "Simple enough. A quick landing in an isolated spot. He picks up his friend, then circles leisurely at ten thousand feet while he dopes the other man and then renders his face unrecognizable with blows from a heavy spanner, taking care not to wreck the valuable dental work. Then he parachutes from the plane, opening his chute only at the last minute to avoid being seen. Perhaps a long twilight free-fall while the plane, with the unconscious or dead man at the controls, crashes several miles away. Stroh buries the chute deep, meets Joanna at a prearranged location."

Hoelscher nodded. "Plausible. Now do you see what we are all up against?"

"He's intelligent, strong, utterly depraved—but still a man."

"Don't be a fool! Minotaur is *not* a man. It is inhuman, unearthly, a devastating force. Your security chief Joe D'Allesandro made the mistake of underestimating Minotaur."

"I won't," Kris had said to the psychiatrist, but now as he stood uneasily watching his cousin through the frost-rimmed window of the lace boutique, he was indecisive about his next move. Axel Stroh had not yet made an appearance. Joanna was restless, or agitated, turning one way and then another, peering around the Radstadtplatz.

As long as she was by herself, Kris thought, she was powerless, the Joanna he knew well, with whom he had dealt so persuasively in the past.

An elderly woman bent over a cane had been browsing near him; she asked him brusquely in German to move aside so she could examine more closely the petit-point bags in the window. Kris made up his mind at that instant and left the shop. He crossed the square, skirting some members of a village band on their way down to the shore of the larch-lined lake, where the Fasching celebration would begin at dusk. The only vehicles allowed in this part of the old town, from Christmas to Easter, were sleighs. Joanna's back was turned when he reached the opposite end of the square. She kneaded the fingers of her gloved hands and scuffed her booted feet, hating the cold.

"Joanna!"

She turned with a shocked intake of breath. He couldn't see her eyes, but her complexion, as always, was pasty. Her plump lower jaw was slack with surprise. He gave her no chance to speak but took her firmly by one arm and turned her away from the entrance to the Goldener Bruck and walked her back across the square, where all the narrow streets of the village met. Crowds, crowds, he knew he must stay with the crowds. He saw his face briefly in the polished brass of a band instrument, ducked a pair of skis angled across the shoulder of a husky youth, encountered a child wearing one of the carved wooden masks typical of this season in the Tyrol.

As he pulled Joanna along with him, he chattered. "What a

surprise! How long have you been in St. Sebastien? Let me buy you a hot drink, you look half-frozen, poor girl."

"But—Kris—I—what are you—I'm waiting—"

Lowering his voice, Kris, still on the offensive, dragging her away from the hotel, said, "Yes, I know who you are waiting for. We must have a talk, Joanna. You see, I've been with Dr. Hoelscher for the past two days, and I know everything. I know what happened aboard your father's yacht the night he married Elizabeth Roger de Rienville."

He heard Joanna gasp as if she'd been clubbed, and her resistance to his determined effort to get her across the Radstadtplatz lessened. She stumbled on iced patches of cobble but otherwise was easy to manage, as light in his grip as a child, despite the bulky fur coat. He guided her into the coffeehouse across from the Gothic parish church and they sat at a small table from where he could keep an eye on the doorway. A rectangle of sunlight dimmed slowly to a shade of orange on the wall behind their heads. Joanna had removed her dark glasses. Her face twitched, her eyes watered, she couldn't look at him but buried her nose in a handkerchief, smothering sobs.

"Poor Joanna. No one can really blame you. But you know that you must go back to the sanitarium at once. You need Dr. Hoelscher's help."

She shook her head mutely, without force. A waiter appeared. Kris ordered *mazagran*, black coffee with rum, for both of them. He sat back, gazing at his cousin. Axel Stroh would be looking for her. But Kris felt in control now. He would have her out of town within the hour, and before midnight they would be on a Zurich-bound train.

"Kris—please don't make me go back to Switzerland."

"What choice do I have? To be murdered?"

She lowered the handkerchief slowly; her eyes rounded from astonishment. "Why would I want to hurt you, Kris? I've never hurt anyone."

"Minotaur has. It's no use, Joanna. There's nothing either of you can do. I have protection—tapes of my conversations with Hoelscher." Unfortunately, they were in his hotel room. "And the doctor is safe—out of Minotaur's reach." Kris's eyes went from Joanna's face to a party of dusky-looking Middle-easterners coming in the door to two girls at a nearby table who were casting covetous glances at the fur draped carelessly over the back of Joanna's chair. "Where are you staying?" he asked Joanna.

"At Baroness Friedborg's chalet. In the valley near St. Anton." Joanna seemed to have a better grip on herself; she had dried her eyes and stopped sniveling. She looked dully across the table at Kris.

"You came here with Stroh to kill Hoelscher, didn't you?"

Joanna swallowed hard, then nodded like a chastised adolescent. Contempt for her was beginning to dilute his other feelings, depress his heightened sense of caution, although he still kept a close watch on the door of the popular coffeehouse and all he could see of the village square outside. The shadow of the mountains had fallen across the Radstadtplatz; the sun had disappeared from the wall behind them.

"When did you arrive in St. Anton?" he asked.

"A few hours ago. From Innsbruck."

"Where is Stroh now?"

She shrugged, distressed. "I don't know. I suppose—at the kinesthetist's in St. Anton."

"Kinesthetist? What's that?"

"Like a chiropractor, but with pressure points. Axel is sometimes bothered by a weakness in his lower back. Travel causes it to stiffen; he has such pain." She leaked another small tear, thinking about poor Axel's sacroiliac. Kris's lip curled slightly, he couldn't help himself. Seeing this, Joanna cringed.

"What are you going to do to Axel?"

Kris hesitated. "Stroh doesn't concern me. Interpol will see to him."

"Oh, God. Oh, Goddd!" Her voice had begun to rise.

"Stop that!" Kris wanted to slap his cousin; instead he leaned toward her, staring into her eyes. "My interest is the family's safety, and putting an end to this—atrocious business. With the two of you permanently separated, we shouldn't have much to fear."

Their drinks came. Joanna fumbled in her purse for a

plastic vial of tablets, nervously popped two of them into her mouth, sipped the steaming brew. She kept looking at Kris, trying to smile appeasingly.

"Joanna, do you have the Cirenaica spore?"

Joanna nodded. She bit her lower lip, then was transformed by the slyness that crept into her eyes. "I'll let you have it. All of it, Kris. Only—don't put me in that terrible place again."

"Perhaps something can be worked out," he replied, taking a more kindly tone. "You know I've always cared for you, Joanna."

She nodded again, eagerly, and picked up her mug of *mazagran*. Kris took a notebook out of a pocket of his sealskin jacket, opened it to a blank page, wrote quickly with his gold ballpoint pen.

"What are you doing, Kris?"

He was too preoccupied to reply. When he had completed his note to Hoelscher, warning the psychiatrist of Axel Stroh's presence in the area, he looked at the two girls who were getting up from the table nearest them, putting on their coats. The tall one, with close-cropped reddish-blond hair, gave him a passing glance; he caught her eye and spoke to her, smiling. She came over. Kris took a hundred-schilling note from his wallet, folded it into the note.

"Would you mind delivering this message to the Goldener Bruck? It's for Herr Steiner, suite three hundred."

"Certainly. Thank you very much." The girl's leather coat was scuffed and worn; there was a small hole in one of her knitted gloves. She beamed at the windfall, which would more than pay her bill. She returned to her companion, who was smaller and darker but similarly dressed, and conferred with her.

"Give me your purse," Kris said to Joanna. She looked puzzled; curtly he held out his hand. Joanna handed over the purse. He was dominating her now, pressing his advantage ruthlessly. *I know what happened aboard your father's yacht the night he married Elizabeth Roger de Rienville*. The impact these words had had on his cousin was impressive. His mind raced ahead, assessing all the possibilities of what he now saw as a coup, a heaven-sent opportunity to place himself firmly in control of Actium International.

Her passport was in her purse. Good. He kept it and handed the purse back to her.

"I have to make *pipi*," Joanna said apologetically.

The coffeehouse had begun to darken as the shadow of the mountains fell across the village. Kris knew that buses ran frequently from the shore of the lake to the railroad station in St. Anton six kilometers away, but he was less sure of the train schedules. He nodded to Joanna, who got up hurriedly, bumping the little table. Some of his untouched coffee sloshed from the mug.

"Oh, I'm sorry, Kris!" She reached across the table with a napkin to soak up the spill; he brushed some drops from his sealskin coat and said irritably, "Never mind. Go on." As she was leaving the table he added, "Take your coat and other things with you, Joanna. I'll pay the bill. I want to get out of here."

Kris had trouble getting the waiter's attention. New arrivals jammed the small coffeehouse. He drank most of his coffee and kept an eye on the alcove where the toilet facilities were. Joanna was taking her time. The waiter came with the check. Kris saw at a glance that the man had added it up wrong. Kris tried again to get his attention.

One of the girls who had been at the table next to theirs came out of the women's toilet in her shabby ankle-length Alpine coat. The short, dark girl. She was wrapped to the ears in a wool muffler, with a crocheted cap that didn't quite match the red of the muffler jammed low on her head. Shoulders hunched, she pushed through the crowd waiting for tables on her way to the door. Kris looked at the swinging door of the toilet, wondering what was delaying Joanna. Nervous stomach? He gave up in disgust on the incorrect check, left enough money to cover it and made his way to the alcove, thinking uneasily of the girl in the leather coat who had just left, wondering what it was about her that bothered him. He shouldered past two women waiting to use the toilet and knocked on the door.

"Joanna!"

He gave her four seconds to reply, then with a cold twinge of alarm knew he had been fooled. To the consternation of the women behind him he entered the toilet. The single stall inside was occupied. He glimpsed the hem of Joanna's expensive amethyst-toned fur above cheap boots and wrenched at the door of the stall.

The dark-haired girl inside was trying on the hat Joanna had been wearing. She looked in dismay at Kris and started to jabber.

"She *made* me take it! She said she had to have my coat and muffler! What was I to do?" The quaking girl put one hand to her throat. "I thought she was going to choke me! She was so strong!" Her hand fell away to the luxurious fur she was wearing, and stroked it. "I can keep it, can't I? I don't have another coat."

"Yes, keep it," Kris snarled. He wheeled and ran from the toilet, pushing everyone aside, ignoring their protests, his cheeks flaming from anger. He went flying out the door and onto the Radstadtplatz, trying to look everywhere at once for his cousin. The square was more crowded than ever, but almost everyone seemed to be moving in the same direction, down to the shore of the ice-covered lake. He heard a brass band. The shops along the square were closing. The church doors stood open, revealing mellow light inside, a realistic Christ agonizing over the heads of the revelers. A quick look satisfied him that Joanna was not among the half-dozen worshipers kneeling before the altar.

The village was small, its few streets crooked and narrow. It would, he reasoned, have been instinctive for her to go with the boisterous crowd toward the lake, one dun-colored leather coat among many. He fell in with the crowd but moved quickly, weaving in and out, searching for a glimpse of the scarlet crocheted cap Joanna had been wearing when she slipped out of the coffeehouse. He was convinced that she was only trying to get away from him, that she had no other plan in mind. Once she reached the shore of the brightly lighted lake half a kilometer away, there would be no place for her to hide other than the small bus depot. Already, as the crowd surged downhill, he had glimpses of skaters, a huge bonfire at one end of the lake, a torchlight parade forming. Horse-drawn sleighs with silver bells. Mummers in costume and the wooden masks. A tradition many centuries old, the first night of Fasching.

Kris found himself, as he neared the lake shore, surprisingly out of breath. As the crowd spread out among the food stalls, he stopped by an oil drum in which a wood fire burned briskly and took a more careful look around. His pulse, he noticed, was very fast. There was a numbness at the root of his tongue, spreading slowly to the muscles of his throat. The air seemed filled with vapors: smoke from many barrels and torches, an icy fog he hadn't noticed before on the surface of the lake. He licked his lips and swallowed hard, but the numb feeling persisted.

Check the bus depot first, he thought.

He had taken only half a dozen steps before he realized, astonished and indignant at the failure of the body he kept so finely tuned, that he wasn't going to make it. He needed a place to sit down, and fast. The fog was thicker, obscuring faces turned curiously his way. Skaters were dim shadows in the mist that now rose above the clean branches of the larch trees encircling the lake. A brass band paraded across his path. He stumbled, went down on one knee. He was lifted to his feet, he heard a girl's merry laughter. He was offered a drink from a silver flask.

Kris shook his head and tried to speak, but his throat was paralyzed to the root. He couldn't swallow anymore. Saliva flowed from the corners of his mouth. He went around and around, clownishly, in aimless circles, and found a tree to lean against. Noise everywhere. Sleigh bells and cowbells with big clappers and trumpets and drums. It became a tumultuous wash of sound like a giant cataract in his ears.

He knew he had been drugged. In the coffeehouse. Joanna had done it. She had a plan after all.

He pushed himself away from the tree and tried to run but was capable of only a spastic lurch and fetched up on his knees, unable to rise.

A hand on his shoulder. A firm grip, not helping him to get

up but pinning him there against the snowpacked ground. He was just able to lift his head. He gazed up at her.

Joanna wasn't smiling. There was a look in her eyes he'd never seen before. He thought, fleetingly, of pale Christ with his crown of thorns, and bowed his head.

"Don't try to get up, Kris. Help is on the way."

He only half understood because of the roaring waterfall in his head. She slid her hand under his wet chin and elevated it. He tried to tell her that she couldn't get away with anything. His lips moved sluggishly and more spittle washed over her gloved hand. Whatever sounds he made were ignored as Joanna turned her head expectantly.

A sleigh drawn by two powerful black horses came up behind her. The air was filled with snorted steam, the music of tinkling harness bells. He looked beyond the handsome heads of the fiery-eyed horses to the creature at the reins. The bulging, dark-bronze, well-oiled torso, naked in near-zero weather. The massive, thickly haired head, over-slope of brow, needlepoint tips of horns.

Minotaur.

But just another mummer to the crowds around them: *none of them could know what was going to happen to him!*

"Let's go, Kris," Joanna said, bending toward him. Using both hands, she raised him to his feet. He found her strength shocking, irresistible. Minotaur sat motionless on the sleigh, watching them. But Joanna needed no help. She lifted Kris bodily into the seat and covered him with a lap robe, held him upright. She smiled now, nodding to the friendly crowd as the horses walked, then smoothly trotted, and the glittering lights of the lake shore receded behind them.

Kris's throat swelled with the effort to scream. But his vocal cords were paralyzed. Spit froze on the lapels of his sealskin jacket and lap robe as the sleigh jangled on into the dark. He sank down in the seat, staring at his cousin, and shook his head as forcefully as he could. His eyes were glazed with terror.

She understood his meaning. "No, Kris; Dr. Hoelscher won't be able to help you."

There was a wicker picnic hamper at her feet. She lifted the hamper into her lap, undid the brass catch and opened it.

Kris saw, by moonlight, a grimace on the face of Dr. Hoelscher that nearly matched his own expression. Joanna's face was thoughtfully grave as she gazed at the trophy head, neatly severed a blunt inch below the jaw, that she was displaying. Then she slowly lowered the lid and replaced the heavy hamper at her feet.

Above the heads of the spirited horses Minotaur's whip cracked smartly; to Kris's dimming eyes the whip seemed to strike sparks, entire constellations in the air that pivoted timelessly and shed a melancholy light on the glacial peaks of the surrounding mountains. Then his field of vision narrowed until it was the width of the liquid pupil of Joanna's cool, remorseless eye.

Chapter 15

London, England

"Lucas, you've fallen asleep on me," April Hanley complained, reaching out with a sudsy bare foot to give his shoulder a nudge.

Dr. Lucas McIver's eyes opened and focused through the mists hovering above the bathtub he was sharing. "What? No, I'm listening. What about Aravanis?"

"Demetrios would only tell me that he seems to be involved, through no fault of his own, in something extraordinarily sticky—and potentially fatal. It has to do with some research he's been engaged in of late."

"Research? He's a botanist. What's dangerous about that? Or has he gotten himself involved with growing a hardier strain of poppy?"

Lady April gave him a less gentle push with her small foot, then turned around at her end of the sybaritic tub, which was of pale-blue and cream porcelain in the shape of a gigantic cockleshell, and took the bottle of Cheval Blanc '61 they'd been working on from a silver ice bucket. "Pass your glass, dear," she said to McIver. Her auburn hair was bound up. There were suds at the nape of her slender neck, in the hollow of her throat, around nipples still erect and reddened from lovemaking. She divided the last of the vintage for each of them, put a glass back into his outstretched hand, lowered her head to give him a playful love bite on the back of the hand. She frowned up at him, but not as if she were angry. "Demetrios Constantine Aravanis is utterly devoid of criminal intent."

McIver shrugged slightly. "I hardly know the man."

"Take my word for it, darling." Lady April turned her attention to a complicated assortment of brass faucets, valves and levers attached to exposed piping on the bathroom wall, peered nearsightedly at a temperature gauge and ran more water in the tub. She was one of those small-boned, almost delicate women who never weigh an ounce more than they should and by virtue of a good draw from the family gene pool, always look ten years younger than their true age. McIver didn't know how old Lady April was. He knew she had married before she was twenty, buried two husbands and raised three children, two of whom had young children of their own. In bed she was proud of her body, playful and mothering and sensually authoritative.

Steam hissed alarmingly from an opening above their heads. McIver looked up warily. She laughed. "No, it isn't going to explode. My great-grandmother knew the value of a good steam bath long before the sauna became popular outside of Scandinavia. Now then. Demetrios Constantine was mightily impressed, as were we all, with your ability to combine ingenuity with action in wresting our ship away from the abominable Mr. Lasch. You could legitimately have walked away with a great deal of money from the coup—I only wanted the ship back, and certainly was in no position to deny you the contents of Lasch's safe."

"Your check was enough. I never saw that many zeros before. I didn't have any trouble cashing it. And there have been other rewards, Lady April."

She lowered her eyes briefly, and smiled, and drank to that. "Indeed. Well, as for Demetrios Constantine— Lucas, it is difficult to stick to the subject when you have your foot where it is, and when your toes are, um, doing what they're doing—so skillfully—one might think you were born without hands—"

"I'm good with my hands too."

"I need no reminder; but for the moment—could we just—you see, it's obvious to Demetrios that you and he share a common concern, the plight of the helpless of this world. A plight, he contends, that is rapidly approaching a devastating climax. And even the most favored nations will suffer this time, not just the chronically stricken countries of Africa and the Indian subcontinent. It all has to do with the recent huge crop failures in the grain belts of Brazil and Argentina."

"I hadn't heard about that."

"Some new, or perhaps very ancient, natural phenomena has been introduced into the food chain. Our Greek friend has been investigating. But apparently his interests are opposed to the greed of a small group of entrepreneurs who stand to reap almost unimaginable profits from a world famine."

"*World* famine?"

"Haven't you been paying attention? No, no, no, don't stop—why did you stop? You're teasing me. You can be madly exasperating, Lucas."

"Why don't you crawl up here in the shallow end with me? I'm madly lonesome."

"Yes, darling. Well, as I was saying—Demetrios thought you might be willing to pop around and hear what he has to say."

"Pop around to where?"

"He lives and works in Corfu. It can be very pleasant there this time of year, actually. And London is so dreary right now."

"How about going with me?"

"If only I could! But the directors of the foundation will be in town all next week, and, umm. Ummmm."

"Don't try to talk with your mouth full," McIver said when the lengthy kiss ended.

"So beastly of you, weeks and weeks without a *clue* as to your whereabouts. I really should make myself unavailable to you when you treat me this way. Ummmm."

"If we stay in the water much longer we'll atrophy."

"Just what I was thinking. What are you looking at?"

"A gray hair."

"Where?"

"Right here."

"Pluck it. Will you go? Had you something else in mind?"

"No. But I don't promise I can be of any help to Aravanis."

"*Now* what are you doing?"

"Looking for more gray hairs? How about a four-leaf clover?"

"*There*? Fool." She rose from her knees and stepped over him and out of the tub, draped herself in a bath sheet. Looked back over one shoulder at McIver, smiled slightly. With a hand over the side of the tub he massaged a slim ankle, slid his hand higher beneath the towel. Her smile was bigger, her eyes full of him, her brow as clear and untroubled as a girl's.

"But you needn't rush off tonight. Daresay the fate of the world can hang in the balance for another day or two."

"I reckon it will have to," McIver said complacently.

An hour before closing time McIver went looking for his friend the Leprechaun, whom he hadn't seen for the better part of three days.

The high street in Kilburn was a sharp contrast to the terrace of beautifully preserved early Victorian townhouses in Sumner Place, where Lady April Hanley lived. He stopped in at several Irish workingmen's pubs. In each they'd seen the Leprechaun. But not lately. In the Stag and Fox he reportedly had passed out in the gent's. Leprechaun was having a right rave-up this time, McIver thought, annoyed and worried.

On the street a girl wrapped in a wool shawl thick as a layer of sod fell in beside him. She had a high-bridged nose and lips a little raw from the weather.

"Lookin' for the wee green-eyed man, are you?"

"Do you know where he is?"

"I might. I could take you. Provided it was worth my time."

"What's your time worth, this hour of the night?"

"Shall we say a fiver?"

"Say three."

From beneath the shawl she produced a tall can with a slot in the top and a crude red cross on the side. "It's not for me

I'm askin', sir. It's for my charity. I'm collectin' for poor babes that have no milk."

McIver grinned. "What the hell. Four quid."

"Right, sir. God bless. Two down, two on delivery."

"What do you mean, delivery? What kind of shape is he in?"

"Nobody's done him any harm, if that's what you mean. He's well-liked here, for the quality of his tongue."

McIver tucked a couple of coins into her can. "Let's go."

"Thank you. And it's Bridget, sir."

They left what passed for the bright lights of Kilburn and took to side streets; Bridget led him down a dismal mews. No one else was around. Their footsteps echoed. McIver looked at the dark fronts of row houses, slits of light around drawn shades, and wondered if he was being set up for a more meaningful contribution to the milk fund. Bridget, sensing his doubts, put an easy hand inside his elbow.

"Nothin' to fear, sir. Not familiar with Irish London?"

"I know a couple of local boys. One of them's starving himself to death up at the Maze for the good of the Liberation."

She almost stopped. "And where would a fine gentleman like yourself be meetin' up with the likes of the INLA?"

"Treating gunshot wounds. I'm a doctor."

"And you made a full report to the coppers, as is your sworn duty."

"Quit busting my chops, Bridget. I didn't turn Gabriel in. And I don't take sides in anybody's tribal war. Just do what I can to help clean up the mess after the butchering stops."

Her grip strengthened on his elbow. "Does it ever stop?" she said, but not as if she needed an answer. They turned another corner. "Just there. The door beneath the awning. I'd like to know your name."

"McTavish."

There was a fan of leaded-glass panes at the top of the stout door, faint light showing through. No sign to identify the address. "What's this?" McIver said, wary again. "One of the societies?"

"Nothin' so sinister as that. More of a social club. For those Ulstermen and their ladies who prefer not to be seen hangin' about in London pubs.'' Bridget uncovered a door buzzer behind a small square panel in the door frame. The panel was so cleverly inlaid she could not have found it if she hadn't known it was there. She pushed the button three times. They waited. A spot of light appeared at peephole level. They were observed. Bridget held her chin up, her face catching the meager light from the top of the door. They heard the latch click and the door opened.

''Bridget?'' He was slender, dark and plain-looking, except for sparkly hyperthyroid eyes that gave him a dangerously bent look.

''Ah, Desmond. And this is Dr. McTavish, friend of the green-eyed man they call the Leprechaun. Still here, is he?''

''Upstairs.'' They were standing in a small blank antechamber. A TV camera, mounted at the ceiling on one concrete wall, scrutinized them. The door opposite the entrance was steel-clad.

As soon as that door was opened to them they were met by a wave of cigarette smoke and heat. And McIver heard the Leprechaun. They climbed a short dark flight of stairs and went down a hallway to a large room crowded with men and a few women sitting at small tables or standing all around the bare, gray walls. There was a bar. The Leprechaun was walking up and down on it. And the only lights in the after-hours club were focused on him.

He carried a gnarled black walking stick in one hand. He was wearing a tawdry, cut-out paper crown. From his unsteadiness, his flushed face, the glass of his eyes, McIver knew he was fairly well potted. But his voice was clear, his speech as well-shaped as a cut-crystal vase. There was scarcely any other sound to be heard in the room.

''*You see me here, you gods, a poor old man,/As full of grief as age, wretched in both. . . .*'' He was acting Lear. Seated on the other end of the bar was an actress McIver recognized immediately. Still in her twenties, renowned for her Shakespearean heroines and notorious for her headline-making, anarchistic politics. She watched the Leprechaun over one shoulder, arms folded, visibly distressed by his senile tirade. ''*I will have such revenge on you both/That all the world shall—I will do such things/What they are, yet I know not; but they shall be/The terrors of the earth. You think I'll weep./No, I'll not weep.*" The Leprechaun looked up, eyes wide, nostrils flaring dramatically as if he smelled the approaching tempest, saw the lightning flashes of chaos that illuminated his mortality. He raised his short arms slowly, imperiously; and in this movement, by the tilt of his head, he seemed to gain in stature. Momentarily he was a king, despite the bowed legs and the squashed features of a born stooge, a low-comedy figure. And his tough audience continued to give him the respect of their silence, spellbound by words magnificently spoken.

The paper crown slipped precariously, his voice sank to a quaver. Little by little he collapsed to his knees on the bar.

"*I have full cause of weeping, but this heart/Shall break into a hundred thousand flaws/Or ere I'll weep. O Fool . . . I shall go mad!*"

The actress swung herself up on the bar and stood looking at the frail king, her eyes now filled with foreboding and, perhaps, pity. "*O sir, to willful men/The injuries that they themselves procure/Must be their schoolmasters.*"

Silence. Then the crowded room was filled with heartfelt applause, cheers of approval. The actress, who was a head and a half taller than the Leprechaun, reached down and helped him to his feet. They bowed together; it was impromptu, but they seemed as if they'd been rehearsing together for weeks. "*Kate, the prettiest Kate in Christendom!*" The Leprechaun declaimed in his commanding voice. "*Kate like a hazel twig/Is straight, and as brown in hue/As hazel nuts, and sweeter than the kernels.*" Laughter. The actress bussed him on the forehead. Drinks were handed up to them and they toasted each other. Seeing his friend standing there, half in the bag but in his glory, still swelled and seething with the magnificent poetry from the great roles he would never be asked to portray on a real stage, McIver felt a pang of deep regret.

He offered Bridget the rest of her money, but she declined with a shake of her head. "That's all right. It was worth a couple quid to hear him."

The Leprechaun saw McIver coming. He held up his double whiskey in a mock salute and smiled a crooked smile.

"Was I a treat to the ears, laddy?"

"You know you were."

"But never to the eyes, of course." His knees were weak. He had anchored himself to the bar by an elbow. "Dr.—ah—McTavish, may I introduce Katherine Larne."

She had been looking steadily at McIver through rose-tinted glasses. McIver smiled. "Howdy do."

Her eyebrows went up a notch. "American, are you? Tell me, when is your effing CIA going to get out of Nicaragua?"

"Well, honey, I reckon that will be when the effing KGB stops trying to run the country through its Cuban military advisors and so-called technicians."

"The Sandinista government must call on its freedom-loving friends to defend the rights of the people against Washington's official policies of terror."

McIver scratched his head and looked baffled. "The last time I was down that way—and I couldn't wait to leave, believe you me—there were more than four thousand political prisoners. The economy is in the shithouse, and the people the Sandinista *junta* loves so much have no right to strike, no right of habeas corpus, no freedom of assembly. Did I mention persecution of the Catholic church? During World War Two, when the Germans occupied France and all those same restrictions applied, the Frenchmen who objected to the Nazification of their country did something about it. They were called the Resistance. The same thing is going on in Nicaragua today, but now they're called Contras."

"Mining harbors is an illegal act of international terrorism!"

McIver sighed. "Let me tell you about a village I visited. Some of the locals came sobbing and screaming over to the medical mission that they needed a doctor fast, so I hopped in a jeep and went up some bad roads to this little place in the middle of fields that weren't producing anymore, where the chickens were so scrawny they walked sideways and fell down a lot. Okay, I found three Nicaraguan counterrevolutionaries who had been captured and interrogated by a government goon squad and its Cuban advisors. The technique the interrogators used is called 'the vest cut.' "

"Vest cut?" the actress said with a slightly dubious smile.

"Yeah. Each of the victims had had his arms and legs hacked off with machetes. The heads and torsos were left there in the *zocalo* where the flies were so thick they clotted the wounds right away. So the Contras hadn't bled to death; they died more slowly, screaming until their larynxes were ruptured and their guts were in their mouths—as an object lesson for the rest of the peasants who might be feeling a little dissatisfaction with all the peace and freedom they were enjoying under the Sandinistas."

The actress choked on her drink and spit a little of it up on her expensive sweater. She stared at McIver, her cheekbones shining like chalk in the bar's light.

McIver said pleasantly, "Now I've gone and done it. I guess you don't want to fuck me anymore."

"You—you're a right bastard!"

"Honey, forget about the theories and the doctrines. Politics smells the same everywhere you go. It smells like spilled blood."

"The Revolution is just! The Revolution is—"

"*Then God be blessed, it is the blessed sun,/But sun it is not, when you say it is not,/And the moon changes even as your mind.* Act Four, Scene Five, *Taming of the Shrew.*"

She clenched her teeth, seemed about to impulsively empty her can of ale in his face, caught a look in his eye and decided against it, glanced around the club room hurriedly for someone else to talk to and pushed off, squaring her shoulders toughly. McIver gave her a brief glance and looked down at the Leprechaun, who said, "In a scratchy mood tonight, are we?"

"Why make me come looking for you?"

"You were having such a delightful tryst with the Lady April, I never thought I'd be missed. Have a strengthener, old sweetheart."

"Sorry. Last call, Leprechaun."

"Oh, laddy. Are you going to be mean to me?"

"Just polish that one off and let's get out of here. We may have something to do."

Chapter 16

Lexington, Kentucky

When Blaize came in from her long morning gallop there was a Metro sector car parked by the south barn at Ellington Farms, and a lanky sandy-haired policeman was leaning against a front fender, arms folded, watching her.

"Mornin', Miss Blaize."

Blaize waved to him and dismounted, handed the sweating bay mare over to one of the grooms for hot-walking. They were enjoying a spell of mild winter weather in the Bluegrass, daytime temperatures in the upper fifties; the seasonal mist that had obscured the pastures and woodlands at daybreak was burning off as the sun rose higher. She stripped off her riding gloves and put them in a pocket of the snaggled old Lawrenceville athletic sweater she'd inherited from her late brother Lonnie.

"Hello, Lanier. Did you find it?"

"You know, I told you right off, Miss Blaize, I didn't think there was a hope in hell. That case is more than twelve years old, and when the city-county gov'ments merged, ever'thing that was considered closed before the merger didn't make it into the computers. And then they pretty well cleaned out the evidence room at the old sheriff's department. All the weapons were trucked up to the Ohio River and dumped off the back end of a barge."

Blaize groaned. "The Colt's is gone?"

Lanier passed a hand over his mouth to partially hide a grin. "Well, I didn't exactly say that."

"Lanier!"

"Thought I'd have me a talk with the deputy who was clerk of the evidence room back then. Retired now, but old Hooter's mem'ry's still sharp. He knew that Colt's; said it was a classic piece and in fine condition, although he wa'nt too partial to the hair trigger. Anyway, Hooter was friendly with a couple collectors, and they had a chance to buy what they wanted from the county 'fore the rest of the confiscated firearms was sunk in the river."

"Somebody bought the Colt's?"

"Fella named Steiger, lives a couple-three miles from here off the old Frankfort Pike. Went around to talk to him. Told him 'bout your theory. Now he wa'nt familiar with the case, but he offered to help. Said to come over any time. Licensed gunsmith. He's got him a pistol range right there in the house."

Blaize threw her arms around the policeman, smelling of horse and countryside. "Thanks, Lanier. You give Judy a big hello for me. When's the new kid due?"

"April."

"What are you calling this one?"

Lanier grinned sheepishly. "We're callin' it *quits*."

Rupert Brett Steiger was an eighty-five-year-old, ninety-eight-pound weakling who, he gleefully admitted, had been in failing health since the day he was born. He had recovered from several serious illnesses of childhood, including polio. He had been gassed in World War One, riddled with bullets in an Australian range war in the twenties and thrown off the roof of an opium den in Macao. He had survived six weeks aboard a raft in the South China Sea after a freighter he had served aboard as ship's cook was torpedoed out from under him by the Japanese. He had outlived most of his peers and all of his wives.

He shook his bald head over a shot glass of Wild Turkey and said to Blaize, "No, I can't account for it. By all rights, I should have been in the grave long ago. I don't take particular good care of myself. Why bother, when eminent physicians have been predictin' my demise since the crash of twenty-nine. 'Can't give you more 'n six months, Rupe, in your condition.' Solemn to beat hell. All of 'em long gone to their reward, I do believe. Well, the only thing I have come to accept as out of the ordinary about myself, that may have some bearing on my longevity, which now is truly biblical in its extent, is the fact that I still wake up ever' mornin' of my life with a good stiff hard-on. I hope you don't think I'm bein' indelicate, honey."

"Oh—well—no. 'Thy rod and thy staff, they comfort you.' "

Rupert Brett Steiger laughed and coughed and turned such a threatening color that Blaize was alarmed, but the spell passed and he survived yet another crisis. "Amen," he whispered, and poured himself another shot. "Well then. You wouldn't mind refreshin' my mem'ry as to why we're havin' this delightful conversation?"

Blaize told him about the death of her brother Jordan, as she had witnessed it, as it had been revised by Lucas McIver.

"So his contention is, the gun went off by accident when he dropped it. That ain't entirely out of the realm of possibility, but let's see for ourselves."

The gunsmith's workbench was cluttered with pieces of firearms; two walls of his shop were lined with cabinets that contained dozens of drawers loaded with pistols. He had no apparent filing system but went unerringly to the drawer that contained the double-action Colt's revolver Blaize had last seen the night her brother died.

"Never had time to do any work on it, but I recall that the sear is so touchy a cricket's hind foot could kick that hammer down."

He held out the revolver, butt-first, to Blaize. She wouldn't touch it, and licked her lips. Steiger glanced at her, nodded and carried the Colt's to his workbench, where he pawed through boxes of ammunition looking for reduced-powder blanks to fit the big bore. When he found them, he dropped several into the pocket of his soiled khaki shooting vest and beckoned for Blaize to follow him into the firing range adjacent to his shop.

"Your daddy's looking for you," Hiram the houseman told Blaize when she got home that afternoon. "In his office."

There was another man with Buford Ellington in the sunny, cedar-paneled room that took up most of the west wing of the rambling mansion. He wore a three-piece suit now, but he had the jutting, hawkish features and the firm carriage of an ex-military man who amuses himself in his leisure time by entering iron-man competitions for the slightly senior citizen.

"Blaize," Buford said, "I want you to meet General Bealer Stout, of Action for Americans."

The general rose and favored her with a million-dollar smile but didn't offer his hand.

"Action for Americans? What's that?" Blaize asked.

"We specialize in no-nonsense security arrangements for individuals and corporations, no matter where in the world they happen to be. My organization maintains a very extensive network of informants. In the five years we've been in business, we haven't lost anyone to the kidnappers and terrorists who make life miserable for our executives posted overseas. But several terrorists have paid dearly for stepping over the line we draw."

Blaize turned to her father and said flatly, "Anthony Troy's out?"

"Troy is out," Buford acknowledged.

"And you're going after Lucas McIver," Blaize said to Bealer Stout.

He nodded. "We'll treat him like any other terrorist we've set our sights on."

"Bealer says he'll nail McIver within thirty days or it won't cost us a thing," Buford said, chuckling.

Blaize felt a shudder begin at the base of her spine. "No."

Bealer Stout's smile faded. Buford sat straight up in his Eames chair and looked in astonishment at his daughter.

"What's that, Blaize?"

"No more. I want the whole sorry business laid to rest. I want to get on with my life."

"Honey, you don't know what you're—"

"I didn't tell you this before. When I was in Salve Regina in Chicago, he came to see me one night—"

"McIver—?"

"We talked. Daddy, he's not what I thought he was. He didn't kill Jordan and he didn't kill Lonnie. He told me how it happened with Jordy. Here's the Colt's, I brought it with me."

Blaize took the unloaded revolver from her big leather purse and laid it on the corner of Buford's desk. He stared at it, paling.

"Take a look. Both of you. It has a hair trigger. Lucas McIver dropped it that night he came to this house—he dropped it when Jordy cut him with a knife, and the gun went off accidentally. It just about blew the top of Jordy's head away. I was with a gunsmith most of the morning. We tried it. Loaded the cylinder with blanks, dropped it. Over and over. Eight times out of ten, the gun went off. Like Lucas said."

"*Lucas said*—"

"Daddy, please. I feel sick. I'm sick because of all the hatred and the wasted years and the blood that's been shed. None of it was ever really necessary. I just want some peace now. Tell the general here to go home."

Buford tried to get up. Without his crutches he was forced to cling to the edge of his desk. "What the hell has got into you? What did that goddam drug do to your mind? Lucas McIver murdered my sons, and by God he's going to pay the supreme penalty—"

"Then we'll all pay, Daddy. Because when the general here finds McIver, I'll be with him."

"You *what?*"

"I'm in love with him."

"You've gone crazy!"

Blaize began to cry. She couldn't stop the tears, no matter how many she wiped away. "Oh, Daddy. Why did you have to make me do this?"

Buford sprawled across his desk, lunging for the Colt's revolver. Ink from an overturned well stained his expensive silk jacket as he painfully pushed himself up from the surface and with the other hand hurled the revolver at Blaize. She turned away, catching it on the hip. The revolver fell to the carpet.

"Daddy, Daddy."

"Miserable—slut. Did you—sleep with him too? You're not my daughter anymore."

"*Don't!*"

"Get out—*out,* Blaize, and don't ever let me see you again!"

He fell back into his chair then, and sat there sobbing. "Jordy . . . Lonnie . . . and you, you were all I had . . . now I don't have anybody . . . I'll see you in hell with Lucas McIver, I swear it!"

Blaize turned away from her father, horrified and nearly paralyzed. She met, for an instant, the stern gaze of General Bealer Stout and thought she saw the beginning of a contemptuous, dismissive smile. She willed herself to walk out of there with what dignity remained to her after Buford's dreadful curse; but panic set in like a flash fire and before she reached the office door she found herself running, running for her life.

Part Three

NEMESIS

Chapter 17

Corfu, Greece

The farm of the botanist Demetrios Constantine Aravanis, properly called an estate because of its size, was situated in the foothills on the east side of the mountain known as Pantokrátor: Christ the King. Aravanis had begun with a few spring-watered acres of clay and marl, marginal farmland at best, and a grove of olive trees, many of them more than three hundred years old and looking as gnarled and twisted as witches in some perpetual Walpurgisnacht, and gradually added to his holdings worn-out hillsides and thicket-filled ravines no one else wanted. Through innovative agricultural methods and the time-honored conservation technique of terracing, the botanist had turned his own acreage and that of many of his neighbors into some of the most productive land on the island. The river that flowed from hillside springs through heath and the silver-green olive groves to orchards of a denser green and aromatic blossoms, through fields of beans and wheat and corn, never ran dry, even at the end of a rainless summer.

With royalties from his patented discoveries, Aravanis had built a spacious new home for his wife Ourania and his adopted son, two stories of local limestone with a traditional gallery that ran the length of the house in front; the gallery was shaded by a sloping tile roof and offered views from the

Alps-like mountains of Albania to the subtropical aquamarine waters of the Gulf of Kerkyra, and the lights of Corfu Town far to the south.

His farm was a complex of the ancient and the modern. The Dacron-covered paddles of conical, thatch-roofed windmills provided electricity and mimicked the shape of a satellite microwave dish nearby. Near the neatly terraced arbors, a purple-rimmed stone trough was still employed for trampling grapes to make wine; and there was a computerized, climate-controlled growhouse, half an acre square, alongside whitewashed storehouses that had been on the property for three centuries. In one wall of her kitchen, the wife of the old caretaker baked her bread on a hearth that was only a little less primitive than a cave. But in her own kitchen, Ourania had a state-of-the-art convection range with a ceramic top. Some of the tenants who lived in cottages nearly hidden by climbers of wisteria and clematis still rode in donkey carts to church or the *tavernas* in the little hillside villages below them. But Demetrios Constantine owned, among other vehicles, a thirty-thousand-dollar customized four-wheel-drive Caravan and a three-wheeled Kawasaki motorcycle with doughnut tires; he was patiently teaching his son Niko to operate the bike.

Altogether there were thirty-seven people in residence on Aravanis's estate, fifteen of them recent arrivals. These men had been sent by the chief of security of Actium International to protect Demetrios Constantine and his family. They were experts in guerrilla tactics and terrorist assaults and had done a good job of making the estate, particularly the house in which the family lived, unapproachable at any cost. They had set up perimeter silent alarms and defense bunkers in unused outbuildings, checkpoints and carefully laid out "kill zones" through which invaders would be routed day or night, no matter what direction they came from. The protectors could, with the aid of covert infrared light sources called "fireflies," kill in the dark as easily as in broad daylight. They had good communications, an attack helicopter and other weapons ranging from stun grenades to M-60s and long-range, high-velocity assassins' rifles.

There were no dogs. Demetrios Constantine and his wife were both afraid to have killer dogs, no matter how controlled they might be, around their son and the children of tenants, and they feared that some incautious or inebriated visitor, accustomed to coming and going as he pleased across low stone walls and through unfenced groves, might be set upon.

Ed Nikitiadas, the Greek-American from Rochester, New York, chief of mission at the farm, regretted the absence of dogs, but overall, he was confident that the arrangements he'd made could handle up to two dozen infiltrators. A larger force was unlikely to be sent against them, given the nature of the terrain and the formidable mountain behind the estate. There was only a single unpaved lane that wound up through the foothills from the corniche road along the shoreline from Ýpsos to Kassiópi, where there was a heavy concentration of tourist hotels and beaches. But there weren't too many vacationers in this off-season, and Ed had informants watching every marina. His major challenge for now was to make himself and his men as inconspicuous as possible because Ourania Aravanis hated having them around. Crime, particularly violent crime, was rare on Corfu, and guns, though not so rare, generally were seen only during the fall in the marshes and again during the spring bird-hunting season. Gossip about the guards' presence on the estate had spread far and wide. Ourania, unable to come and go as she pleased, stared at in church, felt like a pariah in her homeland. And then there was the problem of the retarded boy, twelve-year-old Niko.

Not retarded exactly, Ed reminded himself. Just—different, in ways no one could explain very satisfactorily. Of course there was the matter of his deafness; the kid needed a special device to hear the music from the Walkman he always had with him. But he didn't talk and he didn't go to school. Spent a lot of time with his father in the growhouse lab, but when they weren't together, Niko liked to roam around outdoors in the generally mild February weather now that the winter rains and cheerless damp days had almost ended. That was a problem; none of the security men assigned to keep an eye on Niko could keep up with him. He was just damned clever at eluding them, without seeming to make any special effort to do so.

When Ed pointed out the potential danger in this to the boy's parents, Demetrios Constantine wasn't disturbed.

"He has a need to be alone," Niko's father explained. "Wherever he goes, he always comes back. I don't worry because he's a good rock climber; he stays out of trouble. He knows the mountain; he knows this valley as if he's lived here for a hundred years."

"Well, could we at least put a homer on him so we have a reasonable idea of where he is at all times?"

"If you wish," Aravanis conceded.

And so the signaling device, smaller than an aspirin tablet but with a range of more than ten miles, was added to the Walkman radio when Niko was asleep.

Dr. Lucas McIver and the Leprechaun arrived at the international airport south of Corfu Town on a direct flight from Heathrow and were met outside the small customs enclosure by Ed Nikitiadas and two of his men; Aravanis had been in his growhouse laboratory for twenty-seven hours straight and could not be interrupted. Both McIver and the Leprechaun had Costa Rican diplomatic passports. Consequently there were no customs formalities to be observed. Ed didn't know who McIver or his companion were; Demetrios Constantine hadn't bothered to enlighten him. He treated the newcomers with deference and courtesy but made sure their luggage was checked for explosive devices and weapons before the unostentatious but fully armored Chevy Caprice he'd had air-freighted in from the States left the airport beside the Halikiopoulou lagoon. He observed, during the hour-long drive to the farm, that McIver and the Leprechaun were adept at carrying on a conversation while deflecting any questions that might have given him insight as to just who they were and what they were doing there. Even before they were well settled in at the manor, Nikitiadas was on the scrambler telephone to Actium International's chief of security at their New York headquarters.

Ourania Aravanis was uncustomarily cool to McIver and

the Leprechaun when they arrived. She was tired of visitors and upset by the tension she saw in her husband, the exhausting hours of work he was putting in; she was cross because she felt constantly spied upon, and worried because it had not been satisfactorily explained to her why they were endangered. What did the deaths of Aravanis's colleagues in Japan and America have to do with them?

The tall, bearded houseguest was a doctor, which automatically entitled him to Ourania's grudging respect. But upon seeing the bandy-legged Leprechaun, she drew in her breath noticeably and had to resist fingering the blue bead, secretly sewn into her dress and every other article of clothing she owned as a protection against the evil eye. She related him to the *kalikantzaroi*, a kind of Grecian gremlin and a very bad omen. But it was the Leprechaun who smoothly, without obvious flattery, ultimately won her over. Though he was as ugly as Socrates, he had a surprising lilt to his voice that, listened to long enough, could cure headaches and melt stone hearts. He praised the beauty of the isle of the Phaeacians and the beauty of its women, implying, with a disarming glance, that Ourania was the fairest he could hope to see on Corfu, as fair as white-armed Nausicaä. He quoted Homer in the classical Greek and knew the exact spot at Ermones Bay where Odysseus reportedly came ashore following his ordeal in crossing Poseidon's "unspeakable sea" on his frail raft. The Leprechaun admired the workmanship of the eight-string mandolin that Ourania's great-uncle had crafted for her and asked if he might play it.

He played and sang like a god on the gallery in the rapidly cooling dusk. Ourania excused herself to hurry off to the kitchen, where she canceled the rather ordinary evening meal she'd set the cook to preparing and composed a new menu, fit for a wedding feast or a favorite saint's day: the rare *kalógaros*, two huge live lobsters from the saltwater tank, fresh red mullet spiced with the pickled buds of caper flowers, the best nougats and cordials in her larder.

To themselves for a while, relaxing over glasses of retsina, McIver and the Leprechaun admired the evening star above the rose-washed gulf and the white mountain peaks beyond the Albanian coastline, less than five miles away. But McIver's eyes continually strayed from the tranquil view.

He said, "Unless I'm seeing things, that helicopter down there is armed with a thirty-mm. cannon. Besides Nikitiadas, there're at least half a dozen security men on the place. The really competent ones: full-dress black belts, lethal as samurai. The kind that can field-strip twenty-seven different kinds of weapons blindfolded and hit a moving target at five hundred yards. I get a little jumpy around those types. They move around. They work for this outfit and that outfit. One of them may have been employed by Troy Ransome Associates a year or two back. Maybe I'm beginning to wish I hadn't come."

"Excellent retsina," the Leprechaun said, pouring himself another. McIver, having just nursed him through a bout of alcoholic gastritis, winced. The Leprechaun pretended not to notice. "*Pánta chará*. Have you seen a better view in your lifetime of bumming around this old planet?"

"No. But I still wonder what I'm doing here."

The Leprechaun picked up Ourania's *bouzouki* again. "Have I ever sung this one for you, laddy? It's a lament I translated from verses scrawled on a very old wall of a crumbling temple of Delos. Let me see now. Ah, yes. *'To golden Delos Pontus sailed,/violence the coin of his realm./Where gods have fallen,/vipers rule—'* "

"Jesus, how about something a bit more rollicking? It's been a long time since I've heard you do 'My Old Woman's An Awful Boozer' or one of those old Edwardian music-hall showstoppers."

"The mandolin, m'darlin', is an instrument of sorrow and regret, of lost love and tragic misunderstandin'. As pure as a falling tear."

"Some mood you're in."

"I think I have a crush on our hostess," the Leprechaun confided, bracing his heart with one hand. Then he arose, smiling at Ourania's reappearance with a tray of *mezédes* and a burlap-wrapped bottle of dry white Cephalonian wine.

Demetrios Constantine, his hair and beard beaded with drops of water as if he'd walked through a brief rain, came up to the villa a little before eight with Niko, dead for sleep, riding on his shoulders. They settled into a rattan chair on a heated porch, the night air having become too cold for socializing on the gallery outside. Niko curled up in his father's lap and acknowledged introductions with a noncommittal stare. Ourania soon hustled him off for supper in the kitchen and then a warm bath.

"Good of you to come," Aravanis said to his guests after a couple of restorative swallows of *Soumáda*, an almond-flavored cordial. McIver noticed that his hands were trembling.

"Our pleasure," the Leprechaun replied; McIver didn't say anything. Aravanis gazed at him for a long time, his eyes muddied by fatigue.

"You see the state we are in."

"You're living in an armed camp. It sort of spoils the view."

"My cousin Kristoforos has seemingly disappeared—nothing has been heard from him for more than three weeks. The headless body of a prominent Swiss psychiatrist, Dr. Max Hoelscher, was found near a mountain ski shelter in St. Sebastien, Austria, several days ago. Kristoforos is known to have checked into the Goldener Bruck in St. Sebastien at the same time Dr. Hoelscher was there, under an assumed name. I—I'm afraid the worst has happened."

"To your cousin? Why? What's the connection?"

Aravanis shrugged despondently. "I think Minotaur may be involved. Why—how—I don't know where to begin, Dr. McIver."

"Lucas. Maybe it'll keep until you've had the chance to clean up and eat something."

"That is a good idea."

"Is Minotaur some sort of code name?"

Aravanis hesitated after getting wearily to his feet. "I don't know yet. None of us—the cousins—can be sure. Perhaps this is what you will be able to find out for us. And quickly."

"I hope Lady April hasn't given you the wrong impression. I've been in a few scrapes and I think pretty fast in a crunch. But I don't have any particular aptitude for detective work."

Aravanis gave him another long, level look and said, "I go

by my instincts—Lucas. After dinner I will show you what I have to show you, tell you all that I know.'' His face crumpled then; it seemed, astonishingly, that he might burst into tears in front of them. ''We are faced with something—so dreadful—'' He waved a hand vaguely, as if grasping for something solid to hold onto, failed to find it and walked quickly from the porch with a muttered apology.

''Handsome lad,'' the Leprechaun remarked of Niko.

''He has your eyes.''

''I believe there is a significant difference. Mine are more of a hazel shade enhanced by whatever bit o' green I may be wearin'. But Niko's eyes are purest emerald—the shade of a brilliant mind gone catastrophically awry. Unless I'm far off the mark, he is an autistic child.''

''Now that you mention it—damn shame.''

At dinner the problems that were consuming Demetrios Constantine were not mentioned, but he ate ravenously and seldom looked up from his plate. The Leprechaun and Ourania did most of the talking. Her formal schooling had been minimal, but in the years since Niko's improvement, she had begun to educate herself in the Greek classics. The Leprechaun, who might have been a star on Aristophanes's stage, entertained with passages from *The Frogs* and *The Birds* that had her laughing and blushing at the same time.

During the course of the meal the turbo helicopter took off and circled the area several times. Its powerful spotlight, probing the woods and upland coves, was visible through the silk drapes of the dining room. Conversation was suspended. Tableware rattled. Ourania scowled.

''Haven't we asked them not to fly at night?'' she complained to Aravanis. ''The vibrations will wake Niko.'' She excused herself to check on her son and returned, satisfied that he had slept undisturbed through the nighttime reconnaissance. This time she said accusingly to her husband, ''He's so exhausted, blue circles under his eyes. You have worked him too hard.''

Aravanis looked up and snapped, ''There is no strain on Niko. And I cannot do without him now.''

Dessert was fresh fruit and *moustalevria*, a gelatin made

from the juice of vineyards that rose in terraces behind the Aravanis's yellow and white stone villa. Afterward the men walked down a path hedged with forsythia in full bloom to the lighted growhouse, accompanied by guards carrying automatic shotguns. There was a tang of eucalyptus in the night air, the heavier odors of oil from Aravanis's olive presses, which had been busy all winter. Skops owls hooted plaintively in the net-shrouded groves. There were numberless stars above the dark gulf, the nearby Balkan coast, from which direction had come hordes of invaders in the first thousand years after Christ. Stars "drenching arrogance in silence," the Leprechaun murmured, now paraphrasing Pindar. Aravanis drew a heavy breath and opened several doors to the growhouse with a magnetically encoded card. They passed into a changing area equipped with showers, as clean as a hospital's operating room.

"I apologize for the inconvenience," Aravanis told them. "But you must strip to the skin now, and wear coveralls and plastic boots and caps. Dr. McIver and I will shampoo our beards after we come out of the growing areas." The Leprechaun looked slightly alarmed. "No, no, there is nothing harmful to humans inside. Only spores, virtually impossible to detect with the naked eyes. But they attack such a variety of plant life that even the figs, the olives, the grapes that so many Greeks depend on for their livelihood could be endangered."

As soon as they were all properly dressed they passed through one more secure passageway to the floor of the growhouse itself.

The air inside was mild and clean; there were no detectable odors. The half-acre floor, artificial turf weighted with sand to allow for quick drainage, was filled with translucent Filon domes, perhaps two dozen in all. It looked like an uninhabited village on another planet. Each dome, ten feet in diameter and eight feet high, had its own grid of full-spectrum lights trained on it, a network of piping inside that controlled temperature, humidity, artificial rainfall. In some areas the lights were extinguished, the domes bathed in moonlight. Others were as bright as noon on a midsummer plain; still others glowed with the fading light of sunset.

"Many of these are hybrid plants, growing in marginal soil or salty water, an experiment to expand the world's agriculturally productive areas," Aravanis explained as they walked slowly among the domes. "Each dome has its own growing and dormant season; a computer is responsible for the cycles of light and dark, of heat and humidity. Here we have hard red winter wheat, sprouting now as it would be in the early spring of north central Texas. And here is the same variety of wheat, a high-protein staple of the world's food supply, fully ripened and ready for cutting, as it would be in early September in southern Canada." He pointed to another dome. "The Ukraine." Another. "The *cerrado* of Brazil, where now, in the southern hemisphere, it is high summer."

"The Brazilian wheat looks as if it's dying," the Leprechaun said.

"It has died. Nothing is salvageable. Edible." Aravanis turned his face away, as if the sight of blighted plants was both sickening and terrifying. "And over here we have varieties of corn, the most prolific sterile hybrids, which now account for half of the corn grown in the world. Then barley, oats, soybeans. And rice. The dwarf variety known as IR-8, which is highly pest-resistant, and drought-tolerant. Because of the miraculous IR-8 strain, the Philippines, Indonesia, Malaysia and Sri Lanka have become self-sufficient in recent years, and net exporters of their rice crops. But look closely. You can see, even in the poor simulated light of an Indonesian dusk, what is happening to the IR-8 rice pods."

"A plague has set in," the Leprechaun murmured. "But a controlled plague, is it not?"

Aravanis didn't answer. "You see here, these grapes? The finest Gamay rootstock. But the vines have begun to wither and blacken. The past fortnight my suspicions have been confirmed. Everything that grows and can be, must be, consumed by the human race is vulnerable to Cirenaica."

"That's the spore you were talking about?" McIver asked.

"Yes."

"What kills it?"

"Nothing kills it. Cirenaica has endured for . . . perhaps eons, who knows? Periodically it may have ravaged the earth so severely that entire civilizations died out, and before them, species of animals that roamed in prehistoric times. It cannot be killed. But it can be resisted. That is our only hope. This way, let me show you—perhaps I'm premature, perhaps I'm only hoping for a miracle, but—"

The botanist led them down a path to his laboratory and workroom, where the environment was cool and dry. The room hummed with the energy of some tireless, high-priced machinery, including a pair of IBM PC/XT computers. There were two big walk-in refrigerators, and a solid table holding electronic microscopes and other sophisticated scanning and analyzing equipment. A smaller Filon bubble at one end of the oblong room was filled with amber wheat glowing in full, artificial daylight. Only when they were closer to the bubble could McIver and the Leprechaun see that part of the wheat, each stalk of which was tagged and coded, had withered and turned a brownish-black color.

"The healthy kernels have been immune to the Cirenaica spores for almost two weeks now," Aravanis explained. His hands trembled again as he unzipped one side of the bubble and reached inside to slice off a fat handful of wheat with a pocket knife. He held it out for them to examine. "You see? There is no trace of the fungus on the *Niko-B* samples. The affected wheat"—he zipped the bubble together again—"was grown with the most commercially popular varieties of sterile hybrid seed available, seed that accounts for more than one-half of the world's wheat crop."

"Agent Orange was nothing compared to this," McIver said, crunching a kernel of wheat between his teeth. "What's *Niko-B?*"

"A quantum jump in genetic engineering; a disease-impervious type of red winter wheat. I have worked on it for nearly three years. Using the older methods of crossbreeding and grafting, it might have taken up to twenty years to develop *Niko-B*. The seeds can be cloned from existing embryonic tissue. A marvelous technological, perhaps lifesaving, advance. Together with *El Invicto*, which is to high-yield seed corn what *Niko-B* is to wheat, a formidable barrier to the spread of Cirenaica may be erected in time to prevent incredible famine and plague. *El Invicto* was developed by a colleague of mine, Pinto Pagán. Pinto was murdered this past November in San Juan. Beheaded, possibly by a single stroke from an ax."

"And you think he was killed because of his discovery?"

"I am sure of it. Another colleague who received samples of *El Invicto* and a dossier of test results from Pinto was Dr. Mark Ridgway, of Iowa State University. He also was murdered, shortly after Pinto's death. As far as I know, Pinto entrusted only one other sample of *El Invicto* to anyone. It is here, in this laboratory. But I have been busy with my *Niko-B* and have not had the opportunity to verify Pinto's conclusions. Nevertheless, if we now have strains of wheat and maize resistant to Cirenaica, then there is sufficient hope of developing blight-resistant varieties for the other vital feed grains. But we face a very narrow deadline. Through a freak of nature, it is probable that Cirenaica is now widespread in the western hemisphere, although its dangers have not yet been recognized. Eventually, however—let me show you something on the computer screen."

Aravanis turned on one of the machines and located the software he wanted. Soon they were looking at a map of the Caribbean basin, from the island of Puerto Rico to the republics of Central America.

"Pinto Pagán worked for a corporation known as AgriTech, near Humacao, which is a small city in eastern Puerto Rico a few miles from the Atlantic Ocean. On the night he was killed, a fierce, out-of-season tropical storm had hit the island." The picture on the computer screen changed, showing a storm churning over the island, with arrows indicating the prevailing wind direction. "The facility where Pinto developed *El Invicto* resembled my own, but on a much larger scale. The main building, where Pinto was observing under rigorously controlled conditions the effects of Cirenaica, was partially destroyed when a construction crane collapsed. I believe a great many of the spores were released into the air when the roof caved in, and the spores by now have been disseminated over a wide area, not only in the western hemisphere, but as far east and south as Japan and Australia."

New graphics, concentrating on the principal agricultural regions of Brazil and Argentina, appeared. "The brown shadings indicate the worst damage that has been done in the breadbasket of the Argentine. And during the past few days I've had reports of corn crops partially destroyed as far north as the rich farming states of Mexico. Here, between the Sierra Madre Oriental and the sea."

"Not far from the Rio Grande," McIver commented.

"There are no boundaries that matter to Cirenaica. Here you have the western United States and the wheat-producing provinces of Canada. Nowhere are more wheat and feed grains grown. What is not mountain or desert in your West is, or should be by midsummer, one vast sea of grain. But this year's growing season, I'm afraid, will be quite different. The seeds of hard red winter wheat were planted months ago. They lie now in frozen ground, covered by snow. But at the solstice, when the weather turns warmer and the ground thaws, Cirenaica will be waiting. Believe me when I say there will be virtually no harvest in America this year. The Soviet Union? A hopeless situation, given its unfavorable geographical location. Even when weather conditions permit, the Russians will always fall short of what they must produce to prevent mass starvation in their own country."

"But what about all those vast stores of surplus food one hears about?" the Leprechaun asked.

"Yes, the U.S. and the western European economic bloc have surpluses: dairy, grain, a little meat. But can we depend on their generosity in a time of widespread crisis? And remember this: no one has yet devised an efficient system of distribution to those people already at or near the starvation level. We are talking about supplying millions of tons of food to countries whose political leaders have neglected to build roads or provide necessary means of transportation while they squander all the money they can borrow on weapons and munitions with which to destroy their enemies. Many nations of post-colonial Africa, already ruined by shamefully inept leadership, are now in the fourth year of drought—the entire continent is becoming a Malthusian disaster of unprecedented proportions. Forty nations of the world are dependent on grain imports; and the U.S. supplies sixty percent of that grain. Wheat and corn are in imminent danger. Beans, rice, perhaps not for two or three more years at best. That gives us a little time, possibly just enough time—''

Greeks were habitually a smiling people, even in the face of danger, at the worst of times. But since their arrival McIver hadn't seen a smile on the face of Aravanis. Now the botanist tried to smile, but it was a dismal effort.

''There are additional complications, as you might expect. Only small supplies of *El Invicto* and *Niko-B* exist. I have both. I am unique in this respect. You might say this makes me the most powerful man who has ever lived on this earth.'' He wiped the back of his hand contemptuously across his mouth; the smile was gone. ''Power. Ideology. Cant. Of what value is any of it when there is no harmony in nature; what man has stature, except in his own twisted mind, on a wracked and bleeding earth? I am a Christian, you understand; yet nothing to me is more holy than the power in a single seed. It is a living force and awesome in its symmetry. Without it, all the earth is a 'sickness-haunted plain.' But seeds cannot be stamped out in a factory, manufactured in millions of units like toothpicks. They must be grown, or cloned. If we begin quickly enough, if plant geneticists and bioengineering complexes have access to the capsulized embryos, then we may produce enough seed to counteract the almost certain deadly effects of Cirenaica on nearby harvests. Meanwhile research will continue. Perhaps, at worst, the chemical combines may come up with an antifungal spray sufficiently powerful to retard the spore even as we spread more poison throughout our atmosphere.''

''What about other types of seeds in stock?'' the Leprechaun asked. ''It occurs to me that I have read that there are dozens of seed varieties; mighten one not commonly in use be effective against this spore?''

''Unfortunately, in recent years the seed business has become concentrated in the hands of a few businessmen who operate conglomerates and who hold essential patents on the hybrid seeds they have developed. All other varieties have been neglected, or crowded from the marketplace. Some, known since biblical times, are now virtually extinct. A great tragedy. The same few types of seeds have been extensively produced and promoted and sold, year after year, to the world's farmers. Nature is intricate, and ingenious in her genetic adjustments to changing and frequently hostile environments. A fact for you to remember always: a truly healthy plant will resist any disease or insect. But seeds that are treated chemically as a barrier against insects, sprouting in soils abused and weakened by repeated applications of chemical fertilizers, eventually betray serious deficiencies. Think of the fate of the offspring of incestuous human dynasties through several generations. Dominant-recessive genes that produce dwarfs, madmen, hydrocephalic monstrosities. The modern seed merchants have become very rich and powerful through virtual monopolies—but at the expense of the agricultural community's ability to survive a blight. It's as if you and I had been bred to resist all forms of cancer, only to be fatally vulnerable to the common cold."

Except for the ticking and whirring of machinery, it was quiet for a long time in the laboratory. Then Aravanis turned off the computer and inserted a tape into a cassette deck on the workbench. There were several good speakers unobtrusively mounted around the lab. The air was filled with the whiskey-rough voice of Bruce Springsteen shouting out "Born in the USA."

Unexpectedly Aravanis laughed. He turned the rock music down, but not off.

"One of Niko's favorites," he explained to McIver and the Leprechaun. "He spends many hours with me here. Often when my assistants have gone for the day, there is just Niko and myself. And the work, hours and hours of data to be recorded. We always have music while I work. There is—there is a bond between my son and myself I could not describe, even to my sainted wife. But he is not a normal boy; there are problems with Niko that will never be solved."

McIver nodded sympathetically. "What about *El Invicto*

and *Niko-B*? Do you keep the tissue cultures here, in the lab?''

''Not all of them. I couldn't take such a chance. There are guards, as you have seen, and we are not in an easily accessible part of the island. But then—there is Minotaur. And it is Minotaur, I am convinced, that blasted my good friend Tohru Mukaiba out of the sky over the Sea of Japan; Minotaur that was responsible for the delivery of the body of Mark Ridgway to his unsuspecting wife and children in Iowa; Minotaur that left Pinto Pagán without his head in an old fort overlooking San Juan harbor. What madness! Now Kristoforos is missing. Minotaur again? I don't know. Weeks ago I spoke briefly to Kris, on the telephone, about Cirenaica. The very mention of the spore seems to inspire the most hideous forms of murder. I am fearful for my own life, I admit it. For the safety of my family. But no matter what happens to me, I swear that Minotaur will not get *Niko-B*, or what remains of the *El Invicto* cultures. Nor will the sum of my research to date ever be available to those who would use it for the wrong purposes.''

McIver pointed to the computer terminal. ''If the information is in there, then it's accessible. All anyone needs is the proper retrieval code. And if you're carrying an access code in your head, it can be extracted easily. Either through chemical persuasion or by one of the old reliables, such as wiring up your testicles and plugging you into a convenient electrical outlet.''

''Of course, I know that. I would be a fool if I trusted this machine, any machine, with such crucial data. You see, almost all of my research, and the location of the tissue cultures I've concealed, is stored in a far more complex and inaccessible computer than man has conceived.''

Aravanis was laughing again; his laughter veered to the outer edge of control. His eyes were wild and pain-filled. McIver thought he might be about to drop from strain and fatigue. He put a steadying arm around the Greek.

''I'll need to hear everything you can tell me about Minotaur. But it'll wait until tomorrow. It's more important for you to get some rest, my friend, or you won't be any good to anyone.''

Chapter 18

Berzé la Ville, France

"You've been very kind to me," Blaize Ellington said with a hint of a shy smile as dinner was concluded.

"Not at all. I remind you that you are always welcome in my home at any time; and I'm delighted that you're here. But if you were having difficulties, you should have called me sooner. If there's a way in which I can help—"

The elderly Marquis, Alex de Rienville, had been observing the difference in Blaize Ellington since her arrival at his Mâconnais estate earlier that afternoon. He found her much changed from their last meeting in November. For the better, he thought. She seemed no longer as taut, grim and haunted as on her first visit. And (he had made sure) she no longer carried a weapon. Clearly Blaize, instead of inflicting lethal damage on another, had been wounded herself, although not physically. That recent wound, while carefully concealed, was causing her a great deal of pain.

"Is it," he inquired, "the murderer who has brought so much grief to your family?"

Blaize lowered her head slightly, hand on the stem of her brandy snifter. But she didn't drink. "Yes, I found him," she said in a low voice. "And everything I believed to be true for sixteen years turned out not to be true. He's no murderer. In fact, he saved my life. He is—no longer a threat to me."

"Not in the way you have always believed," the Marquis said with a flash of prescience.

She looked up, lips tight. She shook her head. "The killing of my brother Jordan was an accident. Lonnie's death—well, I think we all share the responsibility for that. Lonnie was too young, too full of himself, he—he thought he could get away with anything. But my father won't quit now. The price on McIver's head is higher than it's ever been. The hunters are the best. I couldn't stop Daddy. He won't talk to me. Won't listen. I need to find McIver again. But I don't know where to look. Viola said—try London. But that's as far as I got. Not a trace."

She was talking too fast for him, her words running together. Rienville held up a hand placatingly.

"I'm sure I can help you. I have many resources."

Blaize took a deep gulping breath. "You would?"

"But of course, my dear. At once. You will tell me all that you know about this man—McIver—?"

"Dr. Lucas McIver. But he won't be using that name."

"You said that you found him once. Then you can perhaps describe him."

"Perfectly," she said, and her tone, the *pétillance* of her olive-colored eyes, left Rienville no doubt that she had become infatuated with the man to whom she had dedicated so many years trying to kill. A perversity of human nature—but the Marquis had long ago accepted perversity as the norm, and he was, as always, charmed by his houseguest. Her obvious sexual excitement aroused him poignantly; his heart was full. He would do anything, pay anything, to ensure Blaize's success in finding the man she wanted.

"Tomorrow we will drive to Paris. A computerized portrait of Dr. McIver will be constructed from your description. Is he a doctor of medicine?"

"Yes. He's been all over the world, doing volunteer work where no one cares much about credentials if you have the skills. War zones, refugee camps. He may be on the continent now, trying to set up something for himself."

"It becomes simpler. We will find him, and quickly. I swear that to you, my dear Eliz—"

Rienville was stopped by the quizzical change in Blaize's eyes. His own startled expression was that of a man who has bitten hard on a false tooth filled with cyanide. Color drained from his seamed cheeks. He was shaken by a spasm. He clung to the arms of his high-backed chair and attempted to smile.

"Forgive me. I didn't mean to—sometimes I forget myself. I have such compassion for you, it's as if I'm talking to my own daughter."

"Oh, you have a daughter! Her name's Elizabeth?"

"Yes. But—she is no longer with me."

Blaize understood. "I'm sorry."

Rienville nodded slightly. His face was composed again, too tightly composed, the only color the dark blue of outstanding veins. His eyes were lowered, but Blaize felt an impulse to draw back slightly, as if the palpable aura around him would be lethal to anyone who intruded upon it.

"Elizabeth would have been thirty-four this past November. She was not yet twenty-one when the—when she—it was called an accident. The car in which she was driving, alone, ran off a narrow road along a cliff on the island of Rhodes. But I know it was not an accident. Elizabeth committed suicide."

"Oh, God."

"She was a skilled and careful driver. And she had too much to live for, until her one fatal lapse of judgment, her—insatiable hunger to be with the Greek swine whom she married."

And suddenly Blaize knew what the Marquis was talking about.

"Your daughter married Argyros Coulouris!"

Still his ravaged face was immobile; his eyes, what she could see of them, were misted obsidian. He reached out with one hand to lift a tiny hothouse flower from the small vase at his place setting. "*Though she fell and died that night, she was the plant and flower of light*," Rienville murmured, paraphrasing Ben Jonson.

"I was only about fifteen—I didn't know Joanna then—but I remember reading all about the wedding and the—the—"

"Tragedy," the Marquis concluded. "Yes. It was all made to look as if *Elizabeth* were at fault. She didn't know the road; she was immature and recklessly high-spirited and should not have been going so fast as darkness fell—ah, the outpouring of sympathy for the bereaved husband! The tragic mask he wore, his melodramatic collapse at her funeral! But there was so little notice of the *real* loss: Elizabeth's beauty; her superb voice."

Rienville relaxed slightly, distant in contemplation. He raised his glass to his lips and sipped brandy. "Not everything was lost. I have many recordings. Lately I've been so busy I haven't had time to listen to her. But now that you've come—perhaps you'd like to hear Elizabeth sing."

"Yes."

"Shall we say ten-thirty, in Elizabeth's music room? I have some telephone calls to make before the close of business in São Paulo, and I know you want the opportunity to visit your namesake at the stables. While you're there, you may choose any of my horses for your morning ride."

"Thank you, Alex."

As they were leaving the leather-paneled drawing room where the Marquis preferred to take his meals when there were only a few guests to entertain, he said casually, "So you are acquainted with the Coulouris clan."

"Joanna's a friend; well, it's been kind of an on-and-off thing. She's had a lot of problems."

"So I have heard."

"I've met her father and some of the cousins. We went cruising in the Cyclades last summer."

"Aboard the *Archimedes*? Ah, yes, he who formulated the laws of equilibrium. If only the dynamics of physics applied so neatly to human behavior. My daughter was married in the grand salon of the *Archimedes*. Some two hundred guests were invited. I refused to attend. Elizabeth was—deeply distressed, but unfortunately the weight of my disapproval failed to dissuade her in her *grand folie*. She may have died still angry with me; but I like to think that before that awful moment, the truth of her situation effected, at least, a spiritual reconciliation. I know I have forgiven Elizabeth. She was, I'm certain, a virgin when she married Coulouris. And he was still in his prime, a bull of the Aegean in full rut. An experienced and callous user of women. Of course I am not blameless in that regard; yet I never was so lacking in scruples or elemental decency as to take another woman into my bed the same night I married Elizabeth's mother."

"Argyros did *that*? How could he do such a thing?"

"Most of the wedding guests spent that night aboard the yacht; if you know Greeks, then you know what the postnuptial celebration was like. Elizabeth never touched spirits, but Coulouris—and among the guests were many beautiful and famous women, some of whom undoubtedly had been his lovers in the past. All rats from an Attican sewer, in my estimation. But he had his pick, and instead of going to Elizabeth's bed at the proper time, he fell drunkenly upon a whore instead. I have irrefutable evidence of that."

"You know who she was?"

"Who she was no longer matters. I also know my daughter found them together. A woman of less delicate sensibility, of, say, the appropriate Latin temperament, might well have shot them both. But poor Elizabeth, who had such illusions about her charming, powerful, *devoted* new husband—Elizabeth was shattered in an instant. The crashing of her car against the rocks of a churning sea was an anticlimax."

"I'm so sorry, Alex."

He took her hand and patted it, as if it were she who needed comforting.

"We both have had our sorrows, our share of tragedy. But you are so young; you have a chance for happiness that is forever beyond my grasp."

Blaize smiled wanly. "Right now it doesn't look so good. Alex, tell me—haven't you ever wanted to—to do something about Argyros?"

"Seek revenge?" In the hallway he turned to her, eyes wide open, staring into hers. She felt as deadly a shock as if she'd opened an ordinary closet door and found herself facing the farthest reaches of a demon-haunted hell. "Revenge," he said slowly, "has never left my mind for one moment—for these thirteen years. But what would be right for such a man?

Simple emasculation? I could have arranged it. To arrange the ultimate took longer, much longer."

"The ultimate?" Blaize echoed, feeling cold where his hands still held hers. Feeling as naked as a little child in the grip of a remorseless god.

"To nullify all of the accomplishments of his life. To take away his power, his success, his fortune, his family. To close all the books, so that the life of Argyros Coulouris is reduced to a few words chiseled on a cheap headstone in an arid island cemetery, where nothing shall visit but ravens and the wind. That is the ultimate of revenge." He lifted a hand to signal a footman waiting at the other end of the hall. "Allow me to ring now for a car to take you to the stables. I look forward to your company tonight at Elizabeth's recital. Be well, my beloved American daughter."

Blaize didn't enjoy her visit with the racehorse Blaize II as much as she had anticipated; her postprandial conversation with the Marquis was too much on her mind. She thought she had known the fullness of hatred for another human being—the psychic fruit she had devoured for so long had only increased her hunger. But the revenge she had plotted, which she allowed to govern her life like a variation of "Dungeons and Dragons," seemed now to have been a bored child's play, only a wistful fantasy compared to the monolithic stature of Rienville's desire for retribution. Blaize was warmly dressed, but she still shuddered uncontrollably at the stables; the wind was high, her emotions roiled, the skittish racehorse shied from her touch and otherwise refused to acknowledge her. She wept and her nose ran and she soon returned to the comforts of the chateau.

An antique ball gown had been brought to her suite by one of the maids; the gown was accompanied by a note from Rienville suggesting that she might wish to wear it for the musicale he had planned. The gown, he said, had been his mother's before the turn of the century. Since she also had been quite tall, perhaps it would fit Blaize well, but she needed only to ring for a seamstress to make minor adjustments. The gown certainly was grand enough for the *Belle Epoque*, Blaize observed, and contained so much satin and so many seed pearls that it weighed upward of thirty pounds. The color, mauve, suited her well enough. But it seemed a curious, somehow obsessive, request by her host. She wished she could spend the rest of the evening alone by the fireplace in her sitting room, with the cache of M&Ms she'd brought with her from the States and several archaeological journals she needed to review before she departed for Greece. She had planned to spend a day or two aboard the *Archimedes* (and was glad she hadn't mentioned that to Rienville) before being dropped off at Thera, one of the Greek islands, perhaps to spend a relaxing fortnight visiting the sites of some recent discoveries pertinent to the Minoan culture.

But promptly at nine-thirty, maids appeared to help her dress. The cumbersome ball gown, once she had it on, was more flattering than she had anticipated. Very little alteration was necessary to make it a perfect fit. It may have been the weather or her mood, but her color was high and she needed only light touches of makeup. She pinned up her hair and was delivered by a manservant to the fourteen-foot, amber-colored oak doors of the music room at the appointed hour.

The Marquis was waiting for her. He wore white tie. He smiled and raised her gloved hand to his lips.

"You honor us," he said simply, and taking Blaize's arm, he walked leisurely around the music room with her, explaining how it had been meticulously reconstructed until it was a room within a room and acoustically close to perfection. Yet there was nothing of Elizabeth Roger de Rienville to be seen. There were fresh flowers on the immense grand piano, annotated opera scores in glass display cases, drawings of the famous opera houses of the world, and a few framed, handwritten notes from generous fellow artists who had recognized Elizabeth's talent.

"Sutherland," Rienville said, pointing to one of the letters. "She was twenty-six before she found she could reach an F over top C. But of course she never had perfect pitch. Elizabeth did."

Blaize wondered why he had no photos of his daughter in the music room. Because of Elizabeth's romance with Argyros Coulouris, her face had been all over the world's news magazines when Blaize was a teenager, and Blaize recalled, vaguely, that Elizabeth had been a looker, with just a hint of regal minx about the eyes. And, always, she seemed to be aloof from the celebrity turmoil around her, cool as a lemon popsickle.

An overture began without warning. Full orchestra. She seemed to be surrounded by the music, but there were no speakers in view. Blaize looked in astonishment at Rienville.

"Tonight," he murmured, "Elizabeth will be performing two of my favorite arias from *Lucia di Lammermoor*, which were recorded in London at Wigmore Hall with the orchestra from Covent Garden two months before her twentieth birthday. It was a remarkable achievement for one so young. You must be familiar with the demands that bel canto singing makes on coloraturas; and Donizetti was very much influenced by the style and tradition of the castrati, whose vocal techniques were known to be formidable."

At one end of the music room there was a small stage with a red-velvet curtain. Two comfortable Queen Anne chairs faced the stage. A servant had appeared with a bar on wheels, carrying chilled white wine. Blaize had drunk more than was her custom at dinner, but she was thirsty. And there was a hot patch in her throat that threatened a bout of ill-mannered coughing if she didn't cool it down. She sipped her wine too quickly and stared at the curtain, which as the overture ended was drawn quickly and noiselessly aside.

Blaize nearly dropped her glass in her lap. There was Elizabeth Roger de Rienville, in subdued, dusky lighting, staring out over their heads. She wore white chiffon, a loose, flowing shift. Her pale blonde hair flowed down over her shoulders. She wore a coronet of tiny blue flowers. Not exactly the costume for the opera's setting, the Scottish Highlands, but she—whoever she was, of course it couldn't be Elizabeth—was gorgeous.

"That is how I choose to remember Elizabeth," the Marquis said quietly beside Blaize. "Unchanged by time, untouched by tragedy."

Blaize nodded, recovering from the jolt. So he'd hired an actress to portray his daughter, to lip-sync the arias. But she didn't seem to be a very good actress. For long moments she was motionless. Then her hands rose slowly from her sides. Pretty stiff and stagey, Blaize thought. But after all, this was opera. It was obvious the young woman had been chosen solely for her close resemblance to Elizabeth.

Blaize forgot about the minor inadequacies of the impersonator when the singing began; the first great aria was "*Regnava nel Silenzio*." It was instantly thrilling, the voice a pure, high coloratura, with a top range that seemed to have no limits. Aside from astounding natural talent, Elizabeth Roger de Rienville had learned considerable technique for one so young. Her arpeggios were beautifully paced; she trilled with equal virtuosity on both high and low notes. Blaize drained her glass of wine without taking her eyes from the small stage, and instantly accepted another.

"My God," she said worshipfully as the upbeat *cavatina* ended. In the sudden silence she glanced at Rienville, whose eyes were slightly moist but fixed on the face of the impersonator. He had no comment. How many nights since Elizabeth's death had he sat here, watching, listening, absorbed, hating? The figure on stage had lowered her hands; but otherwise there was no significant change in her remote stare or her stance. The lip-syncing had been only fair, but in the subdued lighting, that remained a minor distraction.

The music began again; it was the Mad Scene.

Blaize drank a third glass of wine. Even without histrionics, the effect was engrossing. A high E flat that pierced the heart, and the first part of the long Mad Scene ended. Blaize dwelled on what might have been happening now, thirteen years later, in Covent Garden or some equally prestigious opera house. The wild applause, the numerous curtain calls. The second part began: "*Spargi d'amaro pianto. . . .*" The white dress slowly became stained with blood over one breast. Blaize, gasping, rose from her chair. She was seized by the hard hand of Rienville.

"But that's not—"

"Sit down! Of course she isn't real. Where could I hope to find anyone to match Elizabeth's beauty? It is an audio-animatronic figure. But now listen—listen as she dies!"

He forced Blaize back into her chair. The blood onstage continued to flow. The famous aria reached its peak of emotion. The Marquis's hand was hurting her—hurting her. Blaize sobbed quietly. The figure on the stage suddenly pitched forward, awkwardly, and began to vibrate, as if it were having a seizure. The coronet of flowers had tumbled from the pale hair. One of the bright, blank eyes popped from its socket and rolled off the stage. It continued to roll, toward Blaize, growing in size until it was like a glass beach ball.

She recognized that she was tripping out. At times of extreme stress, the DMT she had absorbed weeks ago could still cause weird dislocations in her brain. Pain helped to control the hallucination—she thought the Marquis's grip on her wrist would snap her bones. She shut her eyes tight and gave a harsh, explosive cough; then her stomach heaved and before she could do anything about it, she had vomited down the front of the antique-satin ball gown.

The weather wasn't too cold, but the woods were full of early fog when Blaize went out for her morning ride. She was unfamiliar with the estate grounds and soon strayed from the bridle paths. This didn't concern her; she preferred riding cross-country, and she knew that her horse, an eleven-year-old chestnut gelding with a dark ring around one eye, would find his way back to the stables when he got tired. But the fog was troublesome and failed to dissipate as she had thought it would. Riding across wooded hills where she had never been before, she was afraid of an accident, of a sudden precipitous slope or hidden gully.

When she could barely make out low-hanging limbs ten feet away, she stopped and dismounted, began walking with the reins in her hands, certain she would soon come to a road. Except for the sounds of her boots and the crunching of the gelding's hooves through layers of frost-hardened leaves, his mild snorting and blowing as he breathed companionably over her shoulder, the silence in the woods was absolute until Blaize heard the car coming.

She stopped and listened. It was not possible to tell where the car was coming from, or how far away it was. She looked around, trying to see more than the halftones of eerily unfinished trees in the mass of fog surrounding her. Then to her right—she barely turned her head in time—and downhill, perhaps a hundred yards away, there was a flash of amber fog lights, the low silhouette of a light-colored Mercedes sports coupe before the lights vanished abruptly at a turn in the road. The driver, she thought, was going too fast considering the visibility; and, seconds later, she heard tires grabbing the dirt-and-gravel lane, the sound of a collision. Car swiping stone, but nothing catastrophic. A five- or six-hundred-dollar repair bill for a crumpled fender.

The Mercedes stopped, a door opened, the driver got out from behind the wheel whining and swearing in French about her bad luck, but not her bad driving. Blaize, who had begun to move on down to the road with the gelding, stopped again, mouth open slightly in astonishment.

She had never heard her friend speaking French before, but she would have known Joanna Coulouris's voice no matter what the language.

And in a few moments Joanna was answered, curtly, by the Marquis de Rienville.

"You have driven this way many times. The wall has always been there."

"I don't know why we had to come out here. You are going to Paris today. We could have met in Paris, and who would know? I'm cold. I hate the fog and the damp."

"I should think you would have many pleasant memories of your long stay with Axel here in the gamekeeper's cottage."

"Axel is not here now. I haven't heard from him in four days. What if—"

"Nothing will happen to Axel. You will be together soon. Patience, Joanna. Above all, we need to have patience now."

"Why don't you want me at the chateau?"

"The reason is obvious. I told you I have a houseguest."

"*Look* at this place. It's dark and cold; I'll bet there hasn't been anyone inside since—"

"I'll soon have a fire going. And then we are going to talk sensibly, Joanna."

"I refuse to hear another word about Dr. Hoelscher!" Joanna replied sulkily.

"We need to be more in tune with each other. A mistake was made, I believe a very bad mistake. You know I disapprove of the way—"

His voice stopped abruptly, as if the two of them had passed into another dimension of the fog and vanished. Then Blaize heard the creaking of old hinges on a massive door. Open, close. And silence.

Shuddering, she remained where she was in the shrouded woods above the road, absently rubbing the muscular neck of the chestnut gelding, feeling the throb of a deep, vital pulse. The surprise—no, call it rightfully what it was, the shock—of discovering that her host, the Marquis de Rienville, and a member of the family he loathed were on edgy but apparently familiar terms was slow to fade, and the conversation she'd overheard filled a space of her mind like part of a complex equation in advanced physics, scrawled, too dimly, on a chalkboard. She'd just never been any damned good at solving equations, and she had always hated innuendo, circumlocution, the deviousness in human relationships. Now, unwittingly, she had been made aware of a conspiracy (*The reason is obvious. I told you I have a houseguest*) that perhaps was of little importance, that concerned her not at all. It was apparent that at some point in the past, Joanna had spent considerable time in this secluded part of the estate with a man named Axel, a lover whom she had never mentioned to Blaize. But then Joanna had had many lovers of both sexes. Perhaps the Marquis too was a lover—but Blaize scrubbed the thought as soon as it occurred to her. His tone of voice, everything he had said to her (*You know I disapprove*) indicated a different arrangement. And this arrangement, whatever it might be, involved the missing Axel.

Blaize's shuddering was threatening to get out of control, like a grand-mal seizure. Then the horse urinated, a strong, hot stream that made her nostrils swell with the sting of it and her own bladder to signal a need for relief. The fog seemed to be thinning now; there were tentative trills of birdsong in the still-topless trees. Blaize could see the outline of the road emerging, the dim shape of the Mercedes left where Joanna had damaged it against a stone gatepost and wall, and beyond the low wall, the steep slate rooftop of the gamekeeper's cottage, an organ-pipe chimney with a plume of wood smoke. The air was less oppressive; there was a hint of morning radiance.

She and Joanna were friends, and Blaize remembered telling the Marquis this the night before. Yet he did not want Joanna to know that Blaize was here. He did not, in fact, care to have anyone know that he was having this meeting with Joanna.

The equation scrawled in her mind became longer and weightier, more annoying; she felt a nagging sense of urgency about solving it.

Revenge, the Marquis had said to her, *has never left my mind for one moment—for these thirteen years.*

There could be only one reason why Joanna was here this morning. But as soon as Blaize had this thought, she didn't want to think about it anymore. With clenched teeth she mounted the gelding and walked him downhill to the road that would, she hoped, take them back to the stable area. Then she galloped the horse through overreaching lancets of trees, through a frothing whiteness that was like the mind of a ghost. Tears of cold streamed from her eyes, her hair whipped furiously, inches from the arch of the gelding's neck, his dark and fragrant mane. But though she had tried to force it from her mind with the danger of momentum, the headlong, reckless gallop, the equation suddenly was boldly understandable.

If Joanna were here, then, willingly or unwillingly, she had become a part of the Marquis's grand design to destroy Argyros Coulouris. To destroy her own father. And, inevitably, she would doom herself in the bargain, join him grave by grave on that island where nothing visited but ravens and the wind.

Chapter 19

Corfu

Niko Aravanis had climbed high that morning, leaving the estate of his father far below. The security guards no longer attempted to shadow him in his winding path among flocks of sheep on grazing land, green from the winter rains, and on to brushy slopes, through steep ravines so confining only the slender Niko could negotiate them with ease. He threaded his way through this open-air labyrinth and forded rills that trickled from hidden copses, then came together and fell as a river, in leaps and bounds, to the marshes on the seacoast plain. The sky had the searing blue intensity of midsummer, but the air was sharp. Gusts of wind were strong enough to pluck him in an unwary moment from uncertain perches on the rocks as he made his pathless way up the northeast face of the mountain. He did not hear the wind, only the taped music from the radio on his belt. He wore tough-soled hiking boots, a white woolen sweater knitted by his mother's mother, a woolen cap. He carried a small knapsack on his back. He drank from the clear waters of the little streams when he was thirsty, munched crystallized fruit and doughnuts when he was hungry.

By eleven o'clock he was near the summit of Pantokrátor, a landscape of gray and rust-colored sandstone, of thistle and Christ thorn and the tall mast of the State television network.

Here there was a small neglected shrine to an obscure saint, and a rocky path that led to the abandoned monastery on the other side, and the transmitter for the television tower.

The boy stood on a boulder next to the shrine, only a boot's length from a drop of two hundred feet down the steep slope, and gazed for a long time at the eagles and hawks circling slowly in the mountain thermals. Then he raised his arms and mimicked the slight, stabilizing movements of the wings of the predatory fliers.

But he was tired from the morning's climb and soon sat down, near the simple wayside shrine. Removing his knapsack, he unzipped it and took out a tablet of plain white paper.

He sensed then that he might be observed and turned his head slowly to look for the black-robed figure he had become accustomed to seeing the past few days at the shrine. But no one else was there. If he felt disappointment, nothing showed in his face. His brilliant green eyes watered from the sting of the wind, and drops fell on the tablet of paper in his hands. Placing the tablet on the rock between his spread legs, Niko opened it and tore out a sheet. This he began to fold, slowly and with difficulty, into the shape he thought he wanted. But the first effort did not go well. Looking at the shape he held in his hands, he knew it was wrong. He crumpled the paper and dropped it into a crevice between boulders, where there were other wads of paper from previous efforts. Days spent in the painful attempt to learn to do what another's hands achieved so easily—though they were large and powerful hands, the middle finger of each almost as long as the longest bone in Niko's forearm.

The boy tore out a second sheet of paper, began folding. When his hands trembled from the effort, the feeling of suffocation filled his throat, he stopped and waited, eyes on the distant indigo of the wind-roughened sea. He waited for the cooling in the brain that was better than explosive redness, the violence that sometimes still set him to flopping helplessly out of control, like a bird with a broken wing going in mad circles on the ground. It was better to fix his eyes on the sea, the wind-borne birds between himself and the water, and imagine soaring with them. Until the coolness came, until fingers that were adept at climbing could handle the fragile paper without crumpling it.

On his next attempt, it seemed to Niko that he had made what he wished to make. He held up the paper airplane between thumb and forefinger and, tremblingly, cast it aloft to catch the wind. But instead of sailing gracefully around and then downward in a long spiral, the unsymmetrical airplane sideslipped in a lull and dropped too quickly, a mockery of flight. Niko watched it fall and noiselessly crash. His expression did not change, except for a slight tightening of the lips. His green eyes watered copiously, and he wiped the tears from his cheeks, dried his fingers on the rough wool of his sweater. The tape in the Walkman—a Van Halen album—had ended. He took another cassette from his knapsack, removed the earphone for a few moments and rubbed the flesh where it had been pinching. Without the earphone, his world was one of total silence, of sky and sea and the buffeting wind. He was facing north and looking down at the long, empty strand east of Róda, and yet he knew, from the pressure of some deep instinct, that the man had come again along the path from the monastery and was behind him, in his ankle-length black robe and black monk's cap.

Niko selected another cassette from his collection, not one of those his father played for him these days in the growhouse, and put it into his Walkman. He replaced the two-channel magnetic earphone that was his link to the energizing world of rock music, then turned and stared up at the black-clad, bearded figure some fifty feet away. Prompted by the first ominous, quavering bass notes from the Kiss album, Niko said, in perfect Manhattanese, "So who you want Friday night, the Knicks or L.A.? Here's the kid again. Hello, Niko. What'ya suppose he listens to all day? Niko, give my best to your mother and tell her I think she's got a peach of an ass on her. Think it's true all Greek women want it up the ass so they don't have so many babies? Can't wait to find out, we better get some goddam rotation soon. The Knicks and three, that's my best—"

Niko stopped abruptly because he knew nothing more to say: by then he'd been out of earshot of the patrolling security guards. He continued to stare up at the huge man on the rocks nearby, to whom he had spoken inadvertently. But the man's understanding of English was limited. He lifted a hand in greeting and then came toward Niko, black robe flapping in the wind. He smiled down at the boy.

"A good day for flying," Axel Stroh said in German. "But I would fly every day if I could. Like the eagles." He indicated the birds in the sky above them. "So you try to make more paper airplanes. That's good. It's hard for you, but you will learn. Axel will show you again." He made another motion with his hand, symbolizing flight. Niko turned quickly and picked up the tablet he had weighted with his knapsack and held it out to Stroh.

Axel Stroh took the tablet and placed his hand lightly on Niko's shoulder. "Come. Sit down. Over here, where the wind is not so strong."

He made himself as comfortable as he could on a kneeling block beside the shrine. The false beard he wore was gray and white, and the spirit gum irritated his cheeks; he resisted scratching. He opened his robe and let the strap of a camera bag fall from one shoulder. On his right side he wore a 9-mm. MAC-10 in an SMZ/X holster. He took a case containing powerful Zeiss binoculars from around his neck, placed these beside him on the worn kneeling block. The boy showed no interest in the stubby weapon, but he liked to watch the hunting birds through the binoculars.

During the week Stroh had spent on the mountain making his careful reconnaissance of the Aravanis estate, Niko had been up there three times. He had shown no fear of Stroh, who had approached the boy out of curiosity. But during this Lenten season Niko went every morning with his mother to early mass at the Greek Orthodox church in the village nearest their home. And he'd grown up among black-clad village priests and monks. Stroh was bigger than almost any Greek, but otherwise he looked the part of a lonely ascetic to the boy's unsophisticated eye.

Now for a pleasant half hour, Stroh helped Niko construct simple paper airplanes that stayed lazily aloft, often for a minute or two, in the shifting winds around the summit. They paused only when Stroh heard the helicopter.

He took the boy into his lap then and held him gently, taking out the prayer book he couldn't read. He lowered his head and pretended to study as the Aerospatiale-built Gazelle helicopter rose almost directly in front of them and hovered less than two hundred feet away while those on board satisfied themselves that Niko was in no difficulty. Niko shaded his eyes and stared at the heavily armed chopper, and finally Stroh looked up and waved an admonishing finger, as if their noisy presence was disturbing the solitude he had sought in this sacred place. Like most pilots of fixed-wing aircraft, the German didn't care for helicopters, although he knew how to fly them; choppers were too frequently victims of the air currents that gave lift and momentum to the silent gliders he preferred to any other means of flight.

When the Gazelle had circled around behind the TV mast and the transmitter shack on the west side of the summit and disappeared in the direction of Spartylas in the southern foothills, Axel Stroh got up slowly, still holding Niko, who weighed perhaps ninety pounds. A feather in Axel's hands. A feather he could launch from this aerie with a flick of his wrists. Then Niko would know, for a few glorious moments, the exhilarating freedom of weightlessness, of tumbling head over heels through the turbulent air. The impulse gave Stroh prolonged, exquisite sexual pleasure. He smiled. The Grecian boy was looking at him, untroubled, though his feet were off the ground. The finely modeled face as fervently bronzed as if it had just come from the foundry of Praxiteles. The green-eyed stare alluring, enigmatic.

Axel Stroh loved him deeply, and just as deeply yearned for him to die.

Farewell, little Niko.

The muscles in the great shoulders bunched, his chest swelled.

Stroh lifted Niko higher and set the boy lightly on the boulder between the shrine and the steep crevasse on the other side. He turned to retrieve his binocular case and hang it around his neck, and closed the voluminous black robe. When he looked around again he saw only the rock and the bird-flecked sky, heard no sound except for the keening of the wind; the boy had gone.

Chapter 20

Lexington, Kentucky

"This is what he looks like now."

General Bealer Stout, U.S. Marine Corps ret., and now chief executive officer of his own multi-million-dollar corporation, Action for Americans, laid the photographed drawing of Lucas McIver on a green desk blotter in front of Buford Ellington.

Buford took out his reading glasses and hunched forward in his chair, gripping the edges of his desk with both hands as he studied the bearded face of the man he had hated and feared for sixteen years. Until this moment he had seen only a few blurry photos taken at intervals during the course of his expensive but futile hunt for the fugitive doctor.

"Where'd you get this?" he demanded. "It's too good to be true, like he posed for it! You sure this picture's authentic?"

"Computerized drawing. Constructed from details supplied by your daughter five days ago, in Paris. I had a copy within forty-eight hours."

"Do you know where the murdering son of a bitch is?"

General Bealer Stout smiled, just a little.

"Give me another forty-eight hours, Buford."

"And where in *hell* is Blaize?"

"She flew from Paris to Athens. She's staying at the King George. She occasionally sees friends from the university's archaeological department but otherwise stays in her room reading. Or takes long walks. It's as if she's—"

"Goddam well-told! She's waiting—waiting for him!" Buford's color was high. He seemed to have trouble breathing for a few moments. He dropped his half-moon reading glasses on the desk and stared at Stout for confirmation of his hunch.

The general nodded. "It figures they'll be getting together soon. Now, I've got six men keeping track of your daughter. And six more on the way, including myself. I'll be handling this matter personally, Buford."

"Count me in too, goddammit!" Buford shouted and reached for the receiver of the big telephone console on one side of his oak desk, which was a scarred but talismanic relic, Buford's lucky piece. It had been handed down to him from his paternal grandfather, a telegrapher on the old Louisville & Nashville Railroad, who had invested his meager savings in some eastern Kentucky land beneath which lay the first great black seam that was the basis of the family fortune. When his secretary came on the line Buford said, "Glenda, I want to lease a private residence in Athens for an indefinite stay. No, not Georgia, I mean Athens in the country of Greece! Get it done by tomorrow, then book me on the first goddam flight out of Kennedy tomorrow night."

Buford hung up and rubbed the shiny rounded corner of his desk where the luck was strongest. He sat back in his Eames chair, looking out at snow drifting down past his windows.

"We're gonna get him," he muttered. "I ain't had this good a feeling since Jesus made corporal. This time—*finally*. But Blaize—God, she's all mixed up now. I don't know how McIver got to her, but I do know he must have taken *un*fair advantage when she was sick there in that hospital in Chicago. Or maybe she's just purely cracked under the strain. What the hell, she has her share of Ellington moxie, but she's just a woman after all. Maybe I wasn't usin' my best judgment when I ran her out of the house like I did, but you know something, Bealer, it could've been the best thing under the circumstances. If McIver thinks he's gonna sneak around again somewhere and use my little girl like she was some kind of common snot-rag, well shitfire, he's in for the terminal surprise of his misbegotten life. Only we can't let anything happen to Blaize." Buford pounded his fist on the old desk. "Understand my concern?"

General Bealer Stout helped himself to more of the gritty Louisiana coffee Buford drank by the gallon every day, and sipped thoughtfully from his mug.

"You have to think of it as a surgical operation, Buford. And we're the best surgeons in our business. I guarantee that for Blaize it won't be any more of a risk than having a tiny wen removed from the back of her hand. And when the operation has been concluded and she's fully recovered from this—shall we say—little attack of irrationality, well, I'm confident that she'll be more than grateful to her daddy for saving the day, and her self-respect."

Chapter 21

New York City

Theos and Plato Melissani, chief contenders for control of the giant multinational corporation Actium International, had lunch at a French restaurant in an East-eighties brownstone near Lexington, a place that had always been known for its excellent food without becoming ragingly chic. The proprietor could seat only fifty guests at a time in the three small dining rooms, the most intimate of which, upstairs, overlooked a sculpture garden enclosed by high, ivied brick walls. The garden was exquisite in summer, austere in winter. Monkish pigeons, puffed up against the extreme cold, waddled listlessly around the cloister amid twisted fluent shapes of bronze. A pinkish sun glazed the diamond panes of the window where the brothers shared a table. The other three tables in the room were empty. One of the reasons the Melissani brothers favored the House of Augureau was the isolation it provided: on the days they came to lunch, the proprietor reserved the lemon-yellow room with its tall flecked mirrors for them alone. In addition to ensuring their privacy for serious conversation, it made life easier for their bodyguards.

"We are in severe difficulty," Theos said, finishing his frothy soup of lentils and herbs.

Plato nodded slightly, having put down his fork after a single mouthful of seafood quiche. He was gazing down into the garden at weathered forms he had seen a hundred times before. One was a bust tilted precariously forward on a block of granite. Restructured by an accumulation of winter ice, today it somehow resembled he who was on both their minds, their Uncle Argyros Coulouris, who dominated both of their lives. There was an enormous, perfectly round hole in the otherwise elongated, unsymmetrical head that suggested, not brainlessness, but a man without a soul.

"He has not left his apartment in more than two weeks," Plato said. "He does little work. He grieves. He thinks that our cousin Kristoforos is dead."

"Don't you?"

Plato was a long time replying. He had a sip of wine. He stared at the yellow blue-tipped flames of the gas log in the marble fireplace. "We don't know enough at this point," he concluded.

His brother contradicted him. "We know too much. And so does Argyros. More, I think, than either of us knows. That is why he refuses to discuss the implications of Kris's disappearance. I'm telling you, Argyros is terrified."

"Or terrorized," Plato suggested. "But"—he had to smile—"what is there to fear from little Joanna?"

"She may not be the pathetic near-incompetent she has portrayed so successfully for so long. Perhaps only her psychiatrist knew the answer to that. But Dr. Hoelscher is dead. Beheading is an ancient and dreadful form of punishment—or retribution. Former mental patients can be notoriously ungrateful to the doctors who have treated them. Do you find it coincidental that Joanna was staying in the vicinity of St. Sebastien when Hoelscher was murdered? She does not ski. She hates cold weather. Is it a coincidence that Kris was last seen, apparently in a drunken stupor, in the company of a woman who might have been Joanna—and a huge, muscular man wearing the mask of a bull?"

"A little retsina or white wine on ceremonial occasions," Plato conceded. "That's all I have ever seen Kris drink."

"Then he might well have been drugged."

"But not by Joanna! She loves Kris like a brother."

"I think she has never truly loved anyone but her father.

Call it love, or obsession. But he—listen, Plato. I was with the old man this morning when Joanna called from the *Archimedes*. She was on the speaker phone in the library. Whining, as usual. He had promised to come, to go cruising with her, why wasn't he there? Argyros put her off with lame excuses, but the look in his eyes as he listened to her voice—"

"He feels guilty for neglecting her."

"Guilt?" Theos said derisively. "He was stricken with fear. He cannot bear to go near his own daughter. He has convinced himself that not only is Kris dead, but that it was Joanna and her accomplice in the bull's mask who are responsible. And what does the mask signify?"

"Minotaur," Plato said heavily. "Theos—it is—a *sin* against our cousin to speculate this way. We have no proof."

"I believe Kris found out from Dr. Hoelscher what Minotaur is—what it means. Therefore he had to be killed."

"I can't believe that. If Kris is dead, where is his body? *Proof*, Theos. Otherwise we may not discuss this any further."

A waiter appeared to take away the nearly untouched quiche and Theos's soup plate. The brothers avoided each other's eyes. Theos sipped another glass of wine and glanced at his handsome reflection in one of the mirrors, trying to decide if his hair needed a trim. Plato sat with his head bowed in contemplation, hands clenching and unclenching on the table top.

"Proof," Theos said at last. "Very well. If Joanna yearns for company aboard the *Archimedes*, she shall have it. You and I will join her."

"I thought you were taking the entire family to visit Papa. And I'm to meet with this man McIver at Demetrios Constantine's estate."

"The children will be content at the villa on Iconis until school resumes. As for Dr. McIver, if he's all that we have heard he is, he should be useful to us. Bring him with you to Athens. Understand me, Plato, I am not above using unorthodox methods to persuade Joanna to reveal her true self to us in this—grave state of emergency."

"I don't know what you mean."

"Perhaps it's best you don't know." Theos changed the

subject at once. "Brother, you have not looked well to me this month. I think you have lost weight. It's nothing serious?"

"No—no," Plato lied. "Only the strain. The constant worry."

"Of course." Theos reached across the little table to grasp one of Plato's powerful hands in his own. Just before bearing down, he noticed the worrisome trembling. "Take care of yourself. You are my rock, Plato. You know that, don't you?" He stared beseechingly at his brother until he was rewarded with a weak smile, a small nod. "Our foremost concern will always be our families. Then there is Actium. And together, with God's blessing, we will preserve the business that is rightfully ours."

Chapter 22

Athens, Greece

"Son of a gun! Thought my old eyes was a-goin' back on me, but scrape me off the sidewalk and call me sticky if it ain't Blaize Ellington! How in the world are you, honey?"

"Pard? Pard *Ran*dolph? Why, I haven't seen you since Tipper McLeod married that Swedish count down there in Corsicana! Was that four years ago? Gosh, couldn't been *that* long! What're you doing in Greece, babycakes?"

"Just takin' in all the ol' ruins, Miss Blaize, 'fore I turn into a ol' ruin myself. You here all by your lonesome?"

"I sure am. Sit down a spell, Pard, let's get caught up. What would you like to drink?"

"Reckon whatever's the next best thing to George Dickel they got around here."

Pard Randolph, all six feet six of him, sat carefully on a rickety metal chair at Blaize's round table, one of eight on the little terrace of the cafe on Thólou Street. He pushed his tatty black muleskinner's hat back on his blond head and squinted up at the mighty Acropolis, dominating the northern skyline of this area—the Plaka, one of the older districts of Athens. There was perspiration on Pard's reddened brow: the temperature was only in the mid-sixties, but the glare of the sun was intensified by a sky without a fleck of cloud. Pard smiled at Blaize, whom he had not seen since that rainy night in France when he had staged a faked assassination attempt to test her shooting ability, and she looked back at him with lowered lashes in a pleased, catlike way before closing the thick book on Mycenaean culture from which she patiently had been making notes for the past two hours while drinking diet Pepsis. The square just below them was a small one, the narrow streets filled with razzing motor scooters and buses with noisy brakes, but she had adjusted to the cacophony, to the *bouzouki* music from a ghetto blaster perched on a nearby table. The fumes from the traffic were dissipated by a fresh breeze before they reached the second-floor level of the terrace. There was a fragrance of jasmine from the creepers covering the sunny wall behind her. The Greeks who had been staring curiously at Pard, that authentic specimen of Western Americana, and admiring Blaize again, slowly went back to their chess and backgammon, their newspapers and worry beads.

Blaize said in a quieter tone than she had been using, keeping her face down as she spoke, playing with the ballpoint pen in her hands, "Thanks for coming all this way, Pard. It's really great to see you. I needed . . . somebody objective to talk to."

"You know you can always count on me, Blaize . . . I'll just have a beer, George," he said to the unshaven waiter who had appeared. Pard called all Greek waiters "George." "Whatever you brew up local is fine with me." When the waiter had gone inside Pard turned his attention back to Blaize. "Well, I took a couple days to look the situation over, and it's plain they've got you hemmed in like a calf in a brandin' pen, honey. They're workin' four men per eight-hour shift to make sure you don't pop off to someplace unexpected-like. Now I think General Bealer Stout is an asshole, but your daddy didn't do too bad by hirin' him. Bealer's always retained the top talent. These ol' boys followin' you around got that lean and hungry look, like that crouchin' hound in marble up there in the *A*-cropolis museum."

"Where are they now?"

"I could point out who's workin' this shift on you, but then you start to gettin' edgy and self-conscious about bein' watched, and you ain't about to lose 'em anyhow without a pretty good plan in mind. But if there ever was a easy place to disappear from, Athens is it. Let's just sit and think on what to do next while I enjoy my beer."

"Pard, I'm really at a dead end. I don't know yet where McIver is, and Daddy's spying on me, and like I told you on the phone, if I do find McIver, I'll likely just get him killed."

"Must be someplace you can lay low for a while without gettin' bored out of your mind."

"I was planning to go up to Levkas. There's some work going on at that new temple site they uncovered recently."

"Umm-hmm. What's Levkas?"

"One of the Ionian islands. Close to the mainland and maybe forty miles south of Corfu."

"What's the best way to get there without Bealer Stout's coon-dogs sniffin' right along behind?"

"The only way is by boat. There's a ferry, or you can sail your own, but I don't sail."

"You could maybe find somebody who does; that harbor down there at Piraeus is full of good-lookin' yachts, probably some of them for hire."

"Wait a minute, you gave me an idea! No, skip it, that's a terrible idea."

"Won't know 'til I hear it. And you put on a sweet smile now, for all the pryin' eyes, like you are havin' one hell of a fine time sittin' here gettin' caught up on all the gossip from down home."

Blaize grinned immediately, reached out and tapped Pard's wrist with her fingertips, then threw her head back and brayed laughter. Pard joined in, his ample belly jogging up and down. He mopped his steaming brow with a yellow and brown bandana. His beer came. Pard sipped some of it, approved of the quality with a nod, and chuckled.

"So let's agree that gettin' clear of the city is your biggest problem. I can he'p you there, ain't no hound dog I can't misdirect when I've got a mind to. Then what?"

"Well—there's this friend of mine, Joanna Coulouris—"

"*The* Coulouris?"

"Yeh. Joanna knows I've been here in Athens awhile, and

I've been kind of, uh, ducking her. She calls a few times every day from the boat, the *Archimedes*."

"That's the yacht, it's maybe a little smaller than the *Nimitz* but better appointed than Buckingham Palace?"

"Right. Anyway, Joanna's been begging me to go cruising with her. She doesn't have anything more constructive to do with her time, and I could probably get her to drop me off at Levkas; they own an island up that way. Iconis. But it's always a heavy party scene around Joanna, and right now there're probably two dozen people on that fucking yacht I don't want anything to do with now or ever."

"How long would it take the *Archimedes* to get up there to where it is you said you wanted to go?"

"Levkas. Overnight through the Gulf of Corinth."

"Sure throw them Bealer hounds off the scent. They wouldn't be able to track you through some yacht charter."

"Yes, but—there's a pretty good reason why I've been avoiding—I need to think about it."

Pard chuckled and slapped his thigh as if he'd just heard something outrageously droll. "Well, honey," he said loudly, for the benefit of everyone within two hundred feet, "she was better-lookin' by far than any two of my best palomino parade horses, but I told her straight out that marriage wasn't in the picture. 'Jody Danielle,' I said, 'the woman ain't been born that can wipe her feet on the welcome mat of *my* heart.' "

Blaize laughed perfunctorily and then in a quiet voice said, "I've thought about it. I'll do it."

"Good. You make the arrangements with your friend Joanna, and I'll see to it you get to her boat without anybody the wiser."

"Thanks, Pard."

He had another long sip from his glass of beer and beamed at her. "Well, young lady, you surely don't have to tell me nothin' if you don't want to, but I am curious to know what changed your mind about this McIver fella."

Blaize explained how she had tracked her quarry to Chicago, only to have him save her life. And then she talked at length about the consequences, to her, of their meeting in the hospital.

"So he turned out to be totally different from that evil son of a buck you had all built up in your mind. And he convinced you he was tellin' the truth about your brothers."

"Yes. But—that's not all of it, Pard."

"Reckon not. Or else you'd just put paid to the whole sorry business. But he's been such an essential part of your life for so long, it's like somethin's missin' you gotta have back, for better or worse."

"Think I'm wrong, Pard?"

"Wrong or right don't matter, it's just human, Blaize, and that *does* matter."

"I swear, I can't put him out of my mind for five minutes! I just keep daydreaming about what it would be like—if he—if we could—oh, hell." Blaize reached for a tissue in her woolen *tagári* bag and blew her nose lustily.

Pard sat back, using his bandana on his forehead again. "There's been quite a change in Blaize Ellington since we last met. Back then, honey, you was all hellfire and on the prod, self-righteous too, like God Hisself pinned some kind of deputy avenging-angel badge on you. Now you got this kind of a—a softer, more womanly way of lookin' at a man, even a ol' ruin like myself, and I do believe I like you better this way."

"I like me better too," Blaize admitted. "And you're the sexiest thing ever walked out of Neiman-Marcus in a pair of pointy-toed ostrich-skin boots."

"Hoooohaw! You keep up that Texas sweet talk, honey, and I just might have to apply for a pacemaker."

"Want another beer, Pard?"

"Don't mind if I do. Now, Blaize, maybe it's time for a few words of caution. Supposin' you do meet up with McIver again. Just because you've had a big change of heart don't mean he's gonna trust you; there's still your daddy to reckon with. Guess I'll have to reckon with him too, sooner or later, for he'pin' you out."

"Daddy's got too much respect for your clout and your money to fuss with you, Pard. As for McIver—maybe it's like you say. I don't know how he feels about me. But he *came*, Pard. He came to the hospital, and that was taking a hell of a chance. He came because he had to see if I was going to be all right. That must mean something."

Pard nodded thoughtfully.

"There's just one way I can end this—get Daddy to call off his hounds forever. I can't stop him from hating McIver until the day he dies. But I can stop Daddy from trying to kill him."

"How, Blaize?"

She looked hard at the Texan, and then softness appeared around her mouth, her cheekbones reddened, there was both heat and humor in her vivid eyes.

"I think I know what Buford Ellington will do and what he won't do. So if I can't arrange a truce that's satisfactory to both sides, then I'm not worth a gob of warmed-over cowflop, am I? Now let's put our heads together and figure how you're going to smuggle me out of Athens tonight."

Chapter 23

Corfu

Dr. Lucas McIver was restless.

He had spent a week at the farm estate of Demetrios Constantine Aravanis and made himself, by his standards, minimally useful, treating a donkey bite and a bee sting and the sore throat with accompanying fever that had kept young Niko, who was even more restless than McIver, in his bed for two days. He had talked at great length with Aravanis as news came more rapidly to the botanist about the effects of the Cirenaica spore in a dozen countries of the western hemisphere; the presence of the spore, the fate it portended, was now being reported in the world's press as more of Aravanis's colleagues conferred about it. Aravanis received calls himself, from Stillwater and Guadalajara, from Winnipeg and Leipzig. He pretended ignorance. He believed he was the only botanist or agronomist who knew for a certainty what Cirenaica was: a deadly menace that threatened human life on the planet. He had, he told McIver, reached a decision about what he must do, but he needed a few more days of preparation.

"At first it was merely, how would you say, a 'scientific curiosity,' a plaything, really, to be investigated within the rigorously controlled environment of our laboratories. Sooner or later our findings would be presented in papers before seminars and conventions like the one in Tokyo in November."

"Where Tohru Mukaiba was going when he was killed?"

"Tohru was to be the keynote speaker. Because of his eminence in our profession, a Nobel laureate, we had agreed that it would be prudent, I suppose I should say imperative, for Tohru to release our initial conclusions about Cirenaica."

"There hadn't been any leaks to that point? Not a word about Cirenaica in the media?"

"No."

"But Minotaur knew all about Cirenaica."

"Apparently."

"You were the first to have samples of it."

"The spores were discovered by ConStar geologists at a drilling site in the Libyan desert."

"ConStar Oil is a part of Actium International."

"Of course."

"So you gave a few of the spores to Mukaiba, Pagán and Ridgway. Then all of them were murdered within about a month of each other, presumably for the spore samples, which would imply a link with Minotaur."

"The spore samples and, I'm sure, the *El Invicto* tissue cultures."

"The seeds from which form one of the two effective barriers to the spread of Cirenaica."

"If there is still a God in heaven," Aravanis said, pressing the fingertips of his hands against his forehead and closing his eyes. It was a gorgeous afternoon, cool but not particularly windy, tranquil where they had chosen to sit on the long terrace of the house. Ourania was shopping in Corfu Town; the Leprechaun, who had struck up a friendship with Niko, was entertaining the boy in his room. The bleating of sheep in the olive groves, the singing of schoolchildren in the village two kilometers down the road, came clearly to them. There were numerous caiques and sailboats in the narrow strait between the island and the coast of Albania, where ugly blocks of gray and white vacation apartments lined the east shore of Lake Butrino. There was green peace in the cypresses and umbrella pines surrounding the villa, but McIver, staring into space, saw nothing but the haunted look of starvation in the faces of too many people in more places than he cared to remember, and he had the nerve-prickling sensation of a time bomb ticking almost under his feet.

"But there has been one other murder that, considering the method employed, probably involved Minotaur. Actium International's former chief of security, Joe D'Allesandro. Then your cousin Kris went to Austria to ski and has been missing for more than a month. When did D'Allesandro come here to talk to you?"

"That was in late November."

"After you first heard from Minotaur."

Aravanis nodded slightly, becoming visibly tense, hunching over to watch the progress of a beetle crawling across the olivewood floor of the terrace.

"What did you tell D'Allesandro about Cirenaica?"

"Everything I knew at the time. I showed him examples of its destructive potential."

"Who did D'Allesandro report to?"

"The family. It was right for them to know why I suddenly felt the need for protection."

"How many members of the family?"

"My uncle Argyros Coulouris, my cousins Kris Aravanis and Plato and Theos Melissani. George Melissani, their father, is very ill in Athens and no longer plays a part in managing the business. And then—perhaps Joanna was there too."

"Joanna Coulouris?"

"Yes. The notorious one. Always in the gossip columns. Poor little rich girl. She does nothing, really, with her life. I suppose she can't be blamed. Joanna has a history of—severe emotional problems."

"Is she under psychiatric care?"

"At the moment?" Aravanis shrugged. "I couldn't say. I know there have been many analysts in Joanna's life."

"Of all the family, if it came down to it, who would you trust with *your* life?"

"That is difficult to say. They have always been—respectful of me, but we have seen little of one another. Kris is closest to me by blood—"

"Leaving Kris out for now, since we don't know what's happened to him."

Aravanis rubbed his bloodshot eyes and stared bleakly at a trio of hummingbirds around some early blooming mimosa. "Plato has always seemed to me the most solid and dependable—not like Theos. My cousin Theos is fully afflicted by the family curse: the desire to conquer merely for the sake of conquest."

"Plato will be here tomorrow."

"Yes, and I have much to do before he arrives." Aravanis stood and stretched, his neck creaking audibly; he looked down at McIver with a tired smile.

"I know what you wish to say. If Minotaur knows so much about Cirenaica, there must be a connection between Minotaur and a member of the family."

"It could have been Joe D'Allesandro."

"No, I don't think so. He was here for nearly a week. If he had wanted the spore, it would have been simple for him to take it from me then, along with all of my research. I placed myself in Joe's hands. I was defenseless. When he understood the potential danger, the guards were here the next day."

"I wonder how many of them we can really depend on if we have to."

It was a new thought to Aravanis; he laughed uneasily.

"You are the least trusting man I have met in my life."

"I've learned the hard way."

"There is no one to whom you feel you can commit yourself wholeheartedly, without fear of betrayal?"

"Just two. There's Viola. I told you about her. She's been my surrogate mother, and without her I wouldn't have outlasted puberty. But she's been dying for a long time. And the Leprechaun. Look at him. Too much terrible booze in places where the people go blind staring at the sky for rain and they dig in their own shit for seeds to eat. He's dying too, but he won't leave me; he believes he was ordained by the god of fools and knaves to keep me out of harm's way. And part of it is that goddam romantic melancholy that gets nearly all Irishmen in the end. I trust them. I love them. And I'm going to lose them, because the Great Betrayer is death."

"There has never been a woman for you? Other than the valuable Dr. Purkey?"

"I've had infatuations and affairs on five continents. But I usually had to pick up and leave at an inopportune time."

McIver absently rubbed behind his right ear, where there was a sizable scar from the stitches inserted after Blaize Ellington had nearly bitten the ear off. And he smiled ruefully, wondering where she was now and if the residual effects of the overdose of DMT were still zapping her at unexpected times. McIver knew it could take up to a year before the chemical imbalances in the brain were fully corrected. He wondered if Blaize had changed her mind again about trying to kill him. He wondered why he'd sort of like to see her once again, just to find out what *was* on her mind.

"I've been fortunate," Aravanis said. "There has always been Ourania. There never was anyone *but* Ourania."

"Good fortune indeed. The right woman. Your son. Your work. This great piece of countryside. I could envy you, my friend. But right now I just want to make sure we keep your lucky streak going."

The Leprechaun had a sketchbook under one arm when he sat down at a table in the *taverna* where McIver had spent the better part of two hours. McIver barely glanced at him. He was drinking beer and watching the flies buzz around the crumbs that remained on a plate of fried *kalamari*. Two old men were quarreling over their game of dominoes. A radio played behind the bar. A dog with a skin disease got up from where he had been napping in one corner and slunk around the room to the opposite corner. The sun had faded from the open doorway, and it was chilly and growing dim inside the *taverna*.

"I wondered where you took yourself to, Lucas."

"The peace and quiet up at the house were getting on my nerves. So I moved to where the action is. Stick around. There'll be some entertainment later. The proprietor, Mr. Stavropoulous over there, has spared no expense importing the entire cast of the Nude n' Naughty Revue from the King Tut Hotel in Vegas."

"Well, well."

"I keep telling Stavro what he needs in here is a talking Coke machine. I'm for anything that enhances the quality of life. You drinking? That's a silly-ass question, when did you ever stop?"

The Leprechaun stiffened slightly, but his voice was gentle when he replied, "Perhaps you're not in the proper frame of mind for company."

"I'm sorry. I could cut my tongue out. I mean it."

"Conversations with our host seem to depress you more and more as the days go by."

"The human race is in for a lousy time, Leprechaun. We've been cooking the books for too long, and God just finished his millennial audit."

"Not a shred of hope from Aravanis?"

"Oh, he's more optimistic than I am. But then he has more to lose. How is Niko feeling?"

"The fever broke. He should be fine by morning. He did a drawing of you, would you care to see it?"

"Sure," McIver said, suppressing a gloomy yawn.

The Leprechaun opened the sketchbook and went through the crayoned pages. There were just a lot of scrawls, typical of what the average five-year-old could do; but Niko was twelve and engaged in a lifelong struggle, forcing his brain to communicate accurately what he wished his fingers to do.

"Not bad," McIver said, giving the stick figure a glance. "Looks as if I've lost a little weight."

"The beard, Lucas," the Leprechaun said patiently. "He colored it correctly. Yellow. And he gave you eyebrows. That's a significant detail, an advance in ability. Who knows, in a few years he may become quite accomplished. His will to learn is not diminished by his failures."

"Look, I know what Niko's up against. And he's a marvelous kid. But maybe you shouldn't get too attached to him."

"Because we'll always be moving on? In a few days, or possibly even five minutes from now?"

"Correct."

"I discovered something about Niko today that is quite out of the ordinary. Perhaps the phenomenon is unique."

"Mr. Stavropoulous? Another beer, please. Ouzo or *Soumáda*, Leprechaun?"

"Ouzo."

"You got it," said Stavropoulous, who had spent twenty-three years driving a cab in Flatbush, U.S.A., before retiring to Corfu.

"What about Niko?"

"Ourania has explained his audiological problem to me in great detail." McIver nodded. "By accident, while I was with him in his room this afternoon, I discovered what may be a limitless ability on his part to repeat long passages of conversation, dialogue, recitation. In more than one language. Today I heard Gaelic, English, German—it didn't seem to matter."

"Niko *talks*?"

"Fluently, when properly cued. And, I believe, without the slightest understanding of what he is saying."

"How do you mean, properly cued?"

"He listens to music constantly, as you know. His favorites are the abysmal, manic rock groups children everywhere seem to find fascinating. Today, immediately after making a change of cassettes in the player in his room, he suddenly began to speak. You could have tipped me over with a feather. Particularly since the language was not Greek. It was German, with a marked Hamburg accent."

"You speak German. What did the kid say?"

"I quote, 'They spy on us again, little Niko. At this range I could shoot them down easily, before they knew what was happening to them. It would be good to finish off the helicopter. But we will find another—' "

"Another *what*?"

"That's all he had to say. But he said it twice, word for word."

"Twice?"

"When the cassette he was listening to had finished, instead of letting him play a different one, we listened to the same music again."

"What was the cassette?"

"Something of Elton John's. That isn't important. As soon as the first number began, Niko promptly spoke up in German."

"Did you ask him any questions in German?"

"Yes. He did not indicate comprehension."

"That's interesting, all right. You also tried him in Gaelic?"

"A language I'm confident he has never heard. We played a little game. As soon as a different cassette began playing, I quoted a short passage translated from Yeats. Then I played the tape back from the beginning. He repeated the poem without flaw, with my every inflection. It bristled the hairs on the nape of my neck. I'm quite sure I could have read the *Collected Works* to him and he would have been able to repeat every poem back to me."

"There's a term for that kind of specialized memory. Grown men who can't button their shirts can add long strings of numbers as fast as a computer."

"They were once known as idiot savants. Obviously, in Niko's case, the music he's listening to acts as a cue for whatever verbal input he receives simultaneously."

" 'At this range I could shoot them down easily—' Maybe he got that from the TV, some grade-B spy flick dubbed into German."

"Except for the odd fact that Niko was addressed by name. And we have a helicopter on patrol here twenty-four hours a day, infuriating nearly everyone in the vicinity."

Stavropoulous brought a fresh beer for McIver, ouzo and water for the Leprechaun, who added a few drops of the water to cloud the clear spirits. McIver sipped slowly and stared out the door at a small flock of goats herded down the unpaved village road in the dusk by a barefooted boy.

"We're under surveillance," McIver concluded. "From where?"

"The most obvious site is the mountaintop. I understand Niko has gone up there frequently, and alone. This time of the year few tourists make their way up Pantokrátor. But from someone—Ourania can't say who—Niko has learned to make paper airplanes."

"So whoever he is, he speaks German and he's become well-enough acquainted with the boy to call him 'little Niko.'

Great. I've had that buzz at the base of my spine for a couple of days now. It's trouble, and it's going to be bad."

"Perhaps it would be prudent of you to tell Ourania that Niko needs to be confined to his room for another day or two."

McIver finished his beer in a couple of long swallows. "I'd better have a few words with Ed Nikitiadas. He needs to get a couple of his men up on top of Pantokrátor right away. Maybe I'll go with them. It's something to do."

Chapter 24

The Gulf of Corinth

The steam yacht *Archimedes*, owned by Argyros Coulouris, was one of the largest of its kind ever to cruise the Mediterranean. At three hundred thirty feet from its clipper bow to the stern flag mast, the yacht was five feet longer than Onassis's fabled *Christina* and gave away no points in overall luxury. The three-room master suite, Olympia, was on the bridge deck. There were ten main-deck staterooms, each also named for a great city-state or religious shrine of the ancient Hellenic world, double cabins that were furnished with antiques and other works of art. Whenever the *Archimedes* sailed from the port of Piraeus or the family owned island of Iconis, there was a crew of fifty aboard, including chefs and stewards, maids and valets, a doctor and two nurses who staffed the ship's hospital.

Despite the presence of the large crew, Blaize Ellington had never felt more alone. She was Joanna's only guest; and Joanna, never an easy person to be around for any length of time, was in a peculiar emotional state, swinging from giddy elation over the gift Blaize had brought her (a beautiful set of gold lion-and-bull staters from Lydia, minted during the reign of Croesus) to sullen anxiety once they had cleared the long and narrow Corinth canal and were steaming west a mile from the Peloponnese coast. After she had expressed, for the sixth time, her delight in having Blaize aboard, Joanna suddenly had nothing else to say to her.

The wind was high after sunset, the gulf choppy, and despite the efficient roll stabilizers aboard the yacht, Blaize felt queasy; she retired to her stateroom to lie down for an hour before dinner. She was in a low mood herself: the fogbound morning that Joanna had met with the Marquis de Rienville was still very much on her mind.

At seven-thirty, Blaize changed into a simple black dress and heels and went forward to Joanna's stateroom. She knocked at the door. "Joanna?" There was no reply.

The door wasn't locked; none of the doors aboard the yacht, even the door to the bedroom where Argyros Coulouris slept, had locks. After calling again and waiting a few moments, Blaize let herself into Joanna's stateroom.

Next to the Olympia suite, Joanna's accommodations were the most impressive aboard. Like her father, she had a fireplace of lapis lazuli that had cost six dollars a square inch; she had an El Greco above the mantelpiece, carpets that had been a gift from the wife of the late Shah of Iran, seventeenth-century French furniture. A part of her enormous collection of gold and porcelain and jade bulls took up six shelves of a lighted breakfront. All the lights had been left on, and there was a cannel-coal fire in the fireplace, but Joanna, although she and Blaize had arranged to meet here, was missing.

While Blaize was deciding whether to wait for her there or go on to the dining saloon, the phone rang.

Blaize let it ring twice, then picked up the receiver and said briskly, "Hi, I'm waiting for you. Where are you?"

She heard nothing but the flurry of static common with an old-fashioned ship-to-shore connection in the Greek islands. And then a man said in heavily accented English, ponderously choosing his words, "This is not Joanna's room?"

"Yes, it is. But she's not here right now."

Apparently the caller wasn't far away. For international connections, the yacht relied upon Actium's privately owned satellite relay communications; talking to New York from the Mediterranean was like talking to someone in the same room.

"You are knowing where she is?"

"No, I'm sorry, I don't know. I was supposed to meet her here." Then, before she could think about the possible implications, Blaize asked, "Is this Axel?"

There was a long pause, long enough to make her uneasy and sorry she had asked. Then he said, "Do I know you?"

"I—I don't think so. I'm a friend of Joanna's. Listen, I'll tell her you called. Is there any message?"

"I will ring back later. Good-bye."

Blaize hung up slowly, her mouth dry. And she was suddenly jumpy. Which was ridiculous, she thought. She hadn't found his voice, a low, rasping monotone, appealing; but neither the long pauses nor what he'd finally had to say could be considered intimidating. He was just a man trying to express himself in an unfamiliar and difficult language. But he had not liked it that Blaize had called him by his name. Not liked it at all.

Blaize took a couple of long breaths and stared at the flames in the fireplace, then twitched all over like a nervous horse and put the telephone call out of her mind. She left Joanna's stateroom and went up a curving flight of stairs enclosed in a vitreous material like art-deco glass to the upper deck, where the main saloon, the dining saloon and a spacious drawing room were located. The main saloon doubled as a screening room, with the most modern thirty-five-millimeter projection equipment available. There was also a stereo-equipped television in the drawing room with a forty-five-inch screen, and that was where Blaize found Joanna, sitting on the carpeted floor in front of another fireplace, absorbed in home movies that had been transferred to video cassettes.

Joanna was aware of Blaize's presence, but she didn't look up when Blaize took a seat near her. She was so absorbed in the movies that Blaize didn't want to say anything to break the spell. Most of the fragments of silent color film featured Joanna as an awkward and pudgy adolescent at her own birthday parties, then as an unkempt young adult. And Blaize found it difficult to understand how she could find any pleasure in seeing herself like that. But pleasure was not evident in Joanna's face. And Blaize soon realized that Argyros

Coulouris was in nearly all of the shots of this wordless, forlorn odyssey of Joanna's. Here they were, seated at a big table with friends in a Paris nightclub on New Year's Eve; and there they were at the Great Wall of China. Then, without transition, Joanna was staring at a downed buffalo in Kenyan bush country, her father posing with his foot on the trophy head. The two of them in full morning dress at a lavish lawn party on an English estate; attending a dignified function with heads of state in a marble palace.

Then there was extensive footage of family and guests relaxing on the sand beach of Iconis or aboard the yacht, where they were all very dark from the high-season sun and wore little clothing, and a few of the women in the background were bare-breasted. In some shots, Joanna was at her most grotesque in a string bikini, and her morose expression indicated that she was aware of it. She was slack and humid and well-buttered, as if she'd just been prepared for a sacrificial pit of fire. Her father, by contrast, was heroically photogenic: he had a swagger of kingship; his mouth was fierce in laughter. Someone always to be reckoned with. He had his arms around several entrancingly lovely women. And equally lovely men. There were many of these celebrities ("Sonofabitch big shots," Argyros called them all, usually condescendingly), with Joanna invariably hovering at the fringe of any grouping, as if she'd inserted herself into the frame without anyone noticing or caring. And Blaize saw, unhappily, that even in those films where she posed alone with her father, Argyros seldom looked at Joanna, never embraced her, and smiled less often, enduring the moments of being photographed as if he knew his duty as a father but was bored by it.

Why, Blaize wondered, did Joanna, who had to be extremely sensitive to this lack in the familial relationship, torture herself with such blatant reminders that it was her fate to be shunned by her father? Or was it torture she both wanted and needed, concomitant with her need for revenge?

Suddenly there was a face on the screen Blaize had seen only a few days ago; and as Argyros Coulouris inclined his large head to kiss Elizabeth Roger de Rienville (the sexual avidity in the Greek's face was enough to give Blaize an erotic wallop, and there could be no doubt about what Elizabeth was feeling as their lips touched), Joanna picked up the remote-control unit and cut the VCR off. When the picture on the TV set vanished, the lights in the drawing room came up automatically.

"I never watch the wedding," Joanna said.

"Wasn't that—"

"Yes. Dear Elizabeth." Joanna got up from the floor with a litheness that surprised Blaize, who was accustomed to seeing her friend blunder into furniture. But Joanna, since they'd last seen each other, apparently had shed pounds and pounds in the right places; she wore a close-fitting bolero outfit showing off a figure that had never been in evidence in all the home movies. Joanna still had the morbid-looking tea bags under her eyes, and the hereditary family jaw did not flatter. The old adolescent whining still crept too easily into her voice ("I never watch the wedding."). Yet there was something so startlingly different about her that Blaize, in her presence, felt a psychic disturbance that conveyed a slight undercurrent of fear.

"It was really tragic what happened—"

"Elizabeth got what was coming to her," Joanna said with judgmental authority, crossing to the bar. "Would you like some Brouilly, Blaize?"

"Oh—sure."

"Then let's have something to eat right away, I'm famished. What would you like to do after dinner? I'm just mad about 'Trivial Pursuit,' aren't you? But I have Al Pacino's new movie, if you'd rather."

"I—I'm not sure. 'Trivial Pursuit' sounds like fun."

"But you don't get to answer any questions on archaeology or history! That's taking unfair advantage."

"Whatever you say, Joanna."

Joanna laughed. "You always know how to make me happy. You let me make the rules. Wasn't I an awful mess in those movies? Didn't you think?"

"You, uh, you've certainly been to a lot of places."

"But there's no place like home." Joanna came ebulliently back to Blaize, up from the dumps and astride Mt. Everest.

Blaize wondered if she'd been popping anything. But she had taken so many different kinds of pills for so long, probably nothing really worked anymore. "I love the *Archimedes*. I love the sea. I love Greece. New York is perfume and piss. Why does Papa spend so much of his time cooped up there? Oh, well. I'm so glad you finally decided to come cruising, Blaize. We'll have a good time tonight, won't we?" She clinked her wine glass against Blaize's. "*Pánta chará*, darling."

"*Epísis*," Blaize responded and smiled faintly.

Joanna drank a great deal more wine at dinner; her tongue was on the loose, and for a nonstop half hour she delivered herself of most of the pornographic gossip she'd been saving for such an occasion. Her jabber became assaultive while Blaize tried to enjoy her seafood mousse and squab. Joanne ate only a salad, declaring that she had become a vegetarian. For some reason this innocent assertion triggered an emotion that upset her; her mood turned as black and cold as the sea through which they steamed, and she sat staring at Blaize until Blaize was forced to ask her what the problem was.

"I've always thought of you as my dearest friend," Joanna said petulantly.

"Well—I guess that's true."

"Then why do you hide things from me, Blaize?"

Blaize glanced at the three stewards in the large dining saloon; they had no eyes and no ears. She shook her head slightly at Joanna, puzzled and feeling in her lowest depths that cold current of fear again.

"I don't know what you mean."

"Hmm," Joanna said with a sly smile, and she reached inside her bolero jacket for a folded sheet of paper. Looking at Blaize again through half-lowered lashes, her mouth still plumped up in an insinuating partial smile, she slowly unfolded the heavy paper as if she thought she was being tantalizing. Then she got up from her damask-covered seat, a steward rushing forward to give her an assist with the chair, and marched around the table to where Blaize was sitting with a forgotten forkful of pigeon halfway to her mouth.

Joanna thrust the likeness of Lucas McIver in front of her. "I mean *him*. You haven't said *one word* about him."

Blaize put her fork down with a slight clatter and pulled her shoulders together. She said evenly, "Where did you get that, Joanna?"

"I found it when I went through your luggage."

"You—when you—did *what*?"

"Went through your luggage this afternoon," Joanna said indifferently. "Now don't try to tell me he's not somebody special to you. You can't fool me. Who *is* he, Blaize?"

"You went through my luggage?" Blaize said, as if she were trying to memorize a difficult lesson. Her face was heating up with every accelerated breath she took. She placed her hands in her lap, where they trembled out of sight. "How could you do a thing like that, Joanna?"

"What do you mean? I go through everybody's luggage." The old nerve-racking whine. "I *always* have. Why shouldn't I? I just want to find out things, that's all. And I can do anything I want to on my own fucking yacht!"

Some of the heat left Blaize's cheeks and she gazed sorrowfully into Joanna's drink-fevered eyes until Joanna jerked her head aside defiantly. Then Blaize reached up to take the copy of McIver's picture from Joanna's outstretched hand.

"He's so good-looking," Joanna said. "I just—wanted to know about him, that's all."

"All right, Joanna. I'll tell you about him. In a little while. But I want you to promise me something. If we're going to stay good friends—*true* friends, Joanna—then you can't ever do anything like this to me again."

Unexpectedly Joanna collapsed to her knees beside Blaize's chair, sobbing.

"I'm sorrrryyyy!"

"Joanna, it's okay, this time. You don't have to apologize because I know we understand each—"

"*They've* always spied on me! All my life! Is that fair? Is it right? In that *place*, they were always watching me. It's true." She began to shiver as if she were freezing. "Switzerland. Staring at me through the peephole in the door, twenty-four hours a day. What difference did it make? Couldn't they see I was dead? I didn't move. I didn't even breathe. But it wasn't enough that I was already dead; they, they, cut me open! They stole parts of my body! Papa made them take everything out. I didn't deserve *that*. You understand, don't you?"

Joanna had crept closer to the chair and put both arms around Blaize. Joanna was so strong, hugging her, that Blaize thought her ribs would cave in. She couldn't breathe. She could barely speak.

"Joanna—it's all right, really. You just—caught me by surprise. He *is*—somebody very unusual, and I'll—tell you about him, only—God, let *go*."

"Do you still l-love me?"

"Yes. Yes. Don't—please—you'll break—"

Joanna released her then and sat back on her heels, tears running. "I'm strong, aren't I?" A flash of pride, but her mouth was quivering.

"Phewwww, say *that* again."

"Did I hurt you?"

"No, I'll be okay." Blaize pushed her chair back, waving off another steward, and found herself unexpectedly shaky on her feet. She leaned against the table for a few seconds. Joanna rose and stood at her side, downcast, sniffling, wiping the tears from her cheeks.

"You're never going to trust me again," she complained childishly.

"Joanna, it's a *little* thing, and I realize you can't—" Blaize stopped short of saying "help yourself" and refolded the picture of McIver, wondering just what kind of ordeal the rest of the evening would be. Joanna, it seemed to her, was so far 'round the bend, she was about to meet herself coming the other way. "Hey, let's go back to the drawing room. We'll have some coffee and play 'Trivial Pursuit,' and I'll try to explain what this is all about."

Joanna, instead of coffee, elected to drink another bottle of La Tâche '71 while Blaize related the long, long story of her life and her recent turnabout in favor of Dr. Lucas McIver. By then Joanna was nodding and swaying, making unintelligible comments and barely hanging on to consciousness. She had already gone twice to the toilet, and when the next urgent call came Blaize was forced to accompany her and hold her so she didn't fall off the seat.

"Do me favor? Put me bed?"

"It's about that time, isn't it?" Blaize said, thoroughly relieved. Her dinner hadn't set well because of the emotional turmoil Joanna had stirred up, and she had a crushing headache. Joanna expressed a desire to breathe some sea air, so instead of taking the little elevator down to the main deck Blaize helped her outside. The rush of cold air didn't revive Joanna, and Blaize tried not to look down at the dark water foaming past the yacht, knowing she would probably blow her cookies if she did. But Joanna decided to be difficult.

"No—no! Sleep in Papa's room. *His* bed."

"That's on the bridge deck, sweetie. Don't know if we can make it that far."

"C'mon," Joanna said irritably, pulling at Blaize and nearly losing her balance. Blaize had visions of them tangled together and falling into the gulf. She got a grip on the spraddle-legged Joanna and, pressed against the steel side of the upper-deck structure, inched toward the stairs. Mercifully they were met by a husky first mate ascending from the bridge following the watch change; he gave Blaize a hand. Five minutes later she was tucking the slumbering Joanna into an eighteenth-century Venetian bed.

As she was turning down the bedroom lights Joanna's lashes fluttered and she mumbled, "Don' leave, Blaize. Don' feel so good."

Blaize hesitated and then said with feigned good cheer, "Okay, Joanna, don't worry. Everything's okay."

"Don' worry," Joanna repeated and smiled blearily: she had lipstick on one cheek. A few seconds later she was snoring, her body twitching beneath the coverlet. The ship plowed on through the night. Blaize took a turn around the Olympia suite, which she had never visited before. In addition to the large bedroom, dressing room and bath, there was a library paneled in soft tan suede, with a fireplace like the one in Joanna's stateroom. There were two paintings from Picasso's blue period, and the famous portrait of Coulouris at forty, done by Andrew Wyeth. On the small writing desk the magnate had placed a framed, yellowed photograph of himself with his mother, taken when he was about twelve years old. He'd been on the small side then, but already he had good shoulders and a calm way of looking at the camera, as if he were confident of a destiny yet unclaimed.

The only other photograph in the library was more recent, showing Coulouris and Elizabeth Roger de Rienville in profile, their faces an inch apart.

"Elizabeth got what was coming to her," Joanna had said.

It was no surprise that Joanna had hated her father's bride, that she still made no bones about it thirteen years after the fatal accident. Or Elizabeth's suicide, if the Marquis's version of events was correct. But it gave Blaize a creepy sensation to think of Joanna wallowing drunk in her father's bed at this moment . . . did she make a habit of sleeping there when he was not aboard?

Blaize's headache was still grinding away. Looking for a remedy, she went into the bathroom. It was one of the more opulent studies in luxury she had come across in her lifetime. There was an octagonal bathtub carved from a single block of aquamarine onyx, with milky veins and touches of reddish-gold running through it; the tub was edged in gold, and there were horse-head faucets of solid gold. One wall of the bath was a seven-foot-square mosaic that duplicated a mural of dolphins and mythical beings from the palace of King Minos in Knossos. Looking down on the tub was the brown-eyed head of a *Kore*—a maiden—from the temple of Pallas Athena, and a bronze youth taken from the bottom of the sea, where he had left his right hand. His delicate penis was of shiny metal in a bluish-green patina, as if Argyros and others used it as a handhold for climbing in and out of the tub.

Blaize yearned for a hot soak and thought, *why not*? She looked into the bedroom where Joanna was alternately snoring and moaning softly in her father's bed, a shadow behind sherry-brown silk. Then Blaize stripped and ran the onyx bathtub chin-deep, adding herbal essences and oils from the collection of jars in gold-mesh baskets hanging from the wall above the tub. The hot water and steam and fragrant oils were more soothing than a handful of Excedrin, and a lot easier on her stomach.

The tub was equipped with a telephone and a remote-control panel for a TV set hidden behind sliding doors above the darkly mirrored toilet cabinet. Blaize played with the controls and got *Cagney and Lacey* off the satellite receiver.

Half an hour passed. Peace at last, thank God.

She was just beginning to feel drowsy when she heard Joanna scream.

Blaize scrambled out of the tub, sloshing water everywhere, and grabbed a bath sheet, wrapped it around herself as she ran through the dressing room. She pushed a flimsy drape aside and saw Joanna gasping and thrashing, struggling to get out of her tight toreador pants. She had vomited on one side of the bed. Her face was misted with perspiration.

"*Kathigumeni Kekilia . . . Kathigumeni Kekilia . . . !*"

"Joanna, what's wrong?"

Joanna's eyes were tightly closed, but she responded in English, "Pain—the contractions—they hurt so bad!"

"What hurts you?" Blaize asked. Bewildered and frightened, she reached down to help Joanna pull off the pants, which were now down around her knees. Joanna wasn't wearing underpants. Earlier, Blaize had removed the velvet bolero jacket for her; now Joanna was dressed only in a sheer silk blouse and bra. Her gently rounded belly was bare. Arching her back, spreading her knees, she gripped her belly tightly with both hands.

"The pains! Oh, *Kathigumeni Kekilia, Aja Panagía*, spare me!"

"Joanna, can you hear me? Do you want me to call the doctor?"

Joanna lay panting for breath, temporarily quieter but unable to speak. Blaize quickly toweled herself dry, staring at her friend. And then it seemed to her that she must be having another hair-raising bad trip.

Because, in a matter of moments, she had seen Joanna's belly swell hugely, her breasts engorge until they were ready to pop through the wispy bra; she was just inflating like a bladderfish, while simultaneously her shut labia opened like the claret-colored petals of a flower in a time-lapse, nature-study film. Joanna's head came up sharply from the vomit-smeared pillow, the cords in her neck stood out, the pain was irresistible: she screamed again.

Blaize grabbed the receiver of the antique-replica telephone on a secretary nearby, consulted the directory on the console. She found the number for the infirmary.

"Yes, this is Blaize Ellington. I'm with Joanna in, in her father's—the master suite, and she's having terrible pain. I don't know what's wrong! Could you get the doctor up here right *now*?"

"*Ajjjaaaaa Pannnaggíaaaa*!"

And suddenly Blaize knew what it must be as she stood there watching helplessly with the telephone receiver in her hands.

Joanna was trying to give birth.

Which was impossible; she could not have been pregnant, not in the form-fitting costume she'd had on all evening.

Yet the distended, blue-veined belly was that of a woman at full term, her womb contracting in birth-giving waves. The tremors in Joanna's well-muscled thighs, the agony in her bloodless face, the gaping vagina opening, none of this could be faked.

And Blaize, fingernails digging into her cheeks, fighting waves of nausea and increasing faintness, knew she wasn't tripping out. This was happening. This was real. She dropped the receiver and fell down on the carpet, Joanna screaming as more contractions hit her. Blaize had never seen a baby born, didn't know what to do—but there *couldn't* be a baby. *What kind of horror show was this?*

She was not aware that the doctor had entered the bedroom until he lifted her head gently and popped a capsule of amyl nitrite under her nose. Blaize came stingingly back to life; the black fog surrounding her thinned to a barely perceptible mist.

"Why don't you sit there for a few moments until you're feeling better?" he suggested. He was a small, elderly man in a neat black suit; he had melancholy eyes and a white mustache that did not conceal all of the scarring from long-ago operations to correct a harelip.

Joanna gasped, screamed, gasped.

"*Help* her."

"Joanna will be all right. You must not excite yourself."

"She's in such pain!"

"I've already given her a muscle relaxant and a strong sedative. They will take effect very soon."

"Is she having—but she can't be—"

"No, Joanna is not pregnant. There is no baby."

Blaize got up unsteadily on one knee, holding the towel around herself. She looked at the bed. Behind the brown silk drapes Joanna was breathing hard, but otherwise she barely moved. Her belly still seemed hideously swollen to Blaize.

"How can you be so goddam—"

He wasn't going to reply, but Blaize put a hand on his wrist as he turned away from her.

"Doctor, she's a friend. I mean I'm not a—I'm not somebody she just picked up in Piraeus. I was taking a bath, that's all. I couldn't resist that fantastic tub in there. I would never do or say anything to hurt Joanna; but you've got to tell me what's going on with her."

The doctor pressed a finger against his right eyelid to quell a nervous tic. "Joanna may never have another—what you have seen is the result of a deep-seated hysteria. A psychosomatic disorder. We have all—been through this before. That is all I care to say. In the morning she will not remember. Do you want to be of some help to her?"

"Yes—of course."

"Joanna will need her nightclothes, and the bed linen must be changed. I would rather not call in one of the maids."

"All right. I have to get dressed."

"I am Dr. Patacas."

Blaize offered her hand as she was getting up. "Oh . . . I'm Blaize Ellington." She couldn't keep her eyes off the bed. "My God—so incredible."

He tapped his temple with a forefinger. "It is all from the mind. The power of the subconscious mind caused the gross distortions of her body."

Blaize began to blubber uncontrollably. "The poor girl—the torment she goes through. I'm so *sorry* for her."

"I know. I have wept for Joanna too. Unfortunately it may be too late for tears. So. I am old and have no one to talk to, and now I talk too much. Go and dress yourself, please. See? Joanna already is resting more comfortably. And the swelling is not what it was."

"Maybe—do you suppose this happens because she really wants a baby? But you said she was pregnant once."

"No, I did not say that." Blaize, confused and weeping, started to object; Patacas, scowling, silenced her. "I am not a psychiatrist; I do not wish to speculate on her emotional needs. You will, I am sure, be wise and not mention to Joanna what you have witnessed tonight."

"I may be dumb—but I'm not stupid." Blaize managed to cap the flow of tears gushing from the deepest well of her soul. "Joanna said something to me, in Greek, before I called you. '*Kathigumeni Kekilia.*' What does that mean?"

He looked at her queerly. The tic in his eyelid was worse. "She said 'Mother Superior.' "

"Mother Superior? Was Joanna ever in a convent?"

"I can't answer that," Patacas replied. And Blaize couldn't tell from his tone or his dark, introspective eyes if he just didn't know, or was afraid to say.

While Blaize was in Joanna's stateroom picking out fresh undergarments and a nightgown, the telephone rang. Unthinkingly she was about to answer; then an ugly pulse began knocking in her head. Instinctively she felt it was him again. Axel. She was unwilling to say anything at all to him, to listen to his slow guttural struggle with the English language. She let the phone ring and got out of there.

Chapter 25

Ithaca

At daybreak the *Archimedes* was off the coast of Cephalonia, largest of the Ionian islands, and five miles southeast of the smaller island of Ithaca, which was like a piece of jigsaw puzzle separated from Cephalonia by a two-mile-wide natural channel. Blaize was on the bridge drinking coffee and watching the blue of the calm sea deepen, the shadowy cliffs of Ithaca emerge in a stunning golden light, when Joanna joined her.

Blaize looked at Joanna's face and found her serene, not in the least hung-over. Blaize felt as if she'd spent the night like a fly in a bottle, bumbling from one smooth glass side to another, condemned to puzzle over her own stunned reflection.

"We had a good time last night, didn't we?" Joanna said, linking arms companionably.

Blaize almost spilled coffee all over the sonar screen. "Oh—yeh—it sure was fun."

"I'd like some coffee, Stefanos," Joanna said to one of the crew. "Have you had breakfast?" she asked Blaize.

"No, not yet. I read most of the night, then I came up here when it started to get light."

"Oh, couldn't you sleep?" Joanna asked sympathetically.

"Well, you know, I'm not much of a sleeper. I doze, half an hour at a time."

"Have you ever been to Ithaca?"

"Uh-uh."

"Not that many people go there, but it's charming. There are some ruins that might interest you—a Doric temple that's supposed to be as well-preserved as the one in Aphaia. I don't know about that. The earthquake in '53 probably didn't do it much good."

"I've never heard of a Doric temple in the Ionian islands."

"It's in a pine grove near the convent of Aja Karía. You can just make out the convent from here—those white walls at the edge of the cliff, and the blue chapel dome." Joanna opened a locker and took out binoculars, handed them to Blaize. "You can see it better with these."

"Thanks." Blaize focused on the island of Odysseus, then the steep cliff and the convent buildings at the top. They looked freshly whitewashed, as if the convent had been completed recently.

"How old is Aja Karía?"

"Oh, thirteenth century, I think. The earthquake did a lot of damage there too. Papa paid to have it completely restored." Joanna yawned. "But most of the nuns are gone. And the *Kathigumeni Kekilia* is ancient, if she's still alive."

Joanna had turned to take a mug of coffee from Stefanos and didn't see the sudden startled look in Blaize's eyes as she lowered the binoculars. "They built them like fortresses," Blaize said. "Guess they had to. Or the Sisters wouldn't have been virgins for long."

"Why don't we run over to Ithaca after breakfast?" Joanna said casually after a couple of sips of coffee. "Maybe the temple is something you don't want to miss. Captain Anavatos has to take the *Archimedes* to Iconis today—Theos and all his brats are there—but we can have the big powerboat. You can spend all morning at the temple if you want to, and we'll still be in Levkas before dinner."

"Well—that sounds okay."

"When you get bored with Levkas, I'll have Captain Anavatos pick you up, or I'll run over myself from Iconis. Papa should be here soon. I think." Joanna grimaced at her father's tardiness. "But you never know, with Papa. I call him every day, but he always makes excuses. And he used to spend at least eight months a year aboard the *Archimedes*."

"He's not sick, is he?"

"There's nothing wrong with Papa! He must have a new girlfriend he doesn't want anyone to know about. That's why he won't leave New York."

"But that doesn't sound like your father—I mean, keeping an affair secret."

"Then maybe it's something else," Joanna said with a slight huffy sigh that indicated the subject was closed.

By eight o'clock the *Archimedes* was moored inside the deep-water harbor of Vathi, and members of the crew had off-loaded the yacht's principal powerboat, one of seven aboard. This one, the *Phaistos,* was twenty-seven feet of vacuum-molded Kevlar, Airex and epoxy, very light and strong, capable of getting better than fifty miles an hour from twin two-hundred-sixty-horsepower stern-drive gas engines. The luxury cruiser was tied alongside the yacht's Mediterranean gangplank while Blaize's gear and a picnic lunch was placed aboard. Joanna took the controls. It was going to be just the two of them today, Blaize observed, and she worried about that. Approximately two hundred yards from the *Archimedes* to quayside. No problem. But there were at least twenty-five miles of open water from Ithaca to Vassiliki, a hamlet on the lightly populated southern coast of Levkas, where she had planned to spend a couple of nights. And Blaize, although she was never really uncomfortable aboard a yacht that qualified as a small cruise ship, had always been a little afraid of the water. For that reason she had never learned to swim. Give her a horse, any horse, and she would ride it or die trying. But Blaize disliked toy boats, especially powerful toys that went very fast across the bounding main. She knew from experience that Joanna would have the *Phaistos* at full throttle as soon as they cleared the harbor.

Joanna, detecting an early case of nerves, was at her most persuasive, with an underlying tone of scorn. "Really, Blaize, I've spent half of my life in these islands. I grew up on boats. The weather couldn't be more perfect, the sea should be glass all the way across. What do you have to worry about?"

Nothing Blaize could express very convincingly; there was no room for argument anyway, she had already placed herself in Joanna's hands.

Although Ithaca was a mountainous place, renowned for its seafarers and its stature as the seat of Homeric legend, it was not popular with tourists at any time of the year. The day was slowly warming up, but there was little activity in the town square. The three taxi drivers at quayside had raised their rates three hundred percent when they saw who was coming. Joanna singled out a spindly old man in a lime-green shirt and haggled spiritedly while Blaize checked out her cameras and lenses, snapping a few pictures at varied distances.

A man stood near the window of his second-floor room at the Odysseus Hotel, leisurely buttoning the cuffs of his light-blue shirt, which was so well-fitted Blaize assumed it had been made for him. He had the wide, sloping shoulders and wedge-shaped torso of the dedicated body-builder. His hair was curly, brown shot through with premature gray. He had a wide shelf of brow and a full, handsome jaw and would have been absolutely smashing, except for a rather bitter, old-maidish set to his mouth, as if all he had tasted thus far of life were ashes. Still, she hadn't found anything better in town to look at and she continued to study him through the 135-mm. telephoto lens while he placed a couple of gold chains around his neck. His shirt was unbuttoned over his tanned chest. His hands were enormous. Almost a Teutonic dream-prince, a mate for a Valkyrie; but that twisted, brutal little mouth—

"Blaize?"

She jumped guiltily and lowered the heavy camera. "Oh, are we all set?"

The roads of Ithaca were fair to bad; the way up the partly wooded mountain to the temple ruins was a jolting ordeal. The driver kept the radio up high and occasionally they heard snatches of music through squalling static. He and Joanna argued above the noise, in Greek and in English, about the efficacy of various folk remedies. The interior of the evil-smelling English Ford was filled with bottled nostrums, as if the driver operated a traveling medicine show on the side. There were powdered herbs and the all-purpose absinthe;

some scorpions pickled whole in eucalyptus oil; dried scarab beetles and twisty ginseng roots.

But the remains of the temple in the hillside pines were worth the trip. It was, of course, of the Ionic and not the Doric order, as Joanna had carelessly proclaimed. Despite earthquake damage over the centuries a number of columns were still standing, and it was possible to envision the classic peripheral layout with the aid of the maps sold at the little souvenir kiosk. Joanna and Blaize were the only visitors this morning. They strolled around a broad concavity, now overgrown with brambles, where a shallow lake once had reflected the full glories of the temple.

"Papa remembers when there was water in the lake," Joanna said. "But the last earthquake drained it through the caves to the sea."

"What caves?"

"There are caves everywhere in the mountain. Most of them are connected by passages. I think a couple of the caves beneath the convent are used for storing religious relics."

Joanna stopped suddenly, a stricken look on her face.

"What's the matter, hon?"

"Oh, Blaize, this is *so* stupid of me." She began pawing anxiously through her purse, then looked up at Blaize apologetically. "I'm getting my period. And I didn't bring any—would you happen to have—"

"No, I don't think so. Let me look."

Blaize didn't have any tampons with her. "Well," Joanna said, "I'll just have to go back to town."

"Do you want me to—"

"Oh, no, we just got here! Both of us don't have to go. I'll send Petros back for you at noon."

"Okay."

"Enjoy yourself." Joanna walked briskly back along the path they had followed and was soon out of sight. Birds chirped in the pines and stunted chestnut trees on the hillside. Blaize felt momentarily forsaken, which she knew was foolish of her. She picked her way carefully down to a level place from which she had some good photo opportunities—the widely spaced columns and capitals, the blue water in the distance, the mainland—and snapped away. But gradually something, half-swallowed, began to choke her. It wouldn't go down, it wouldn't come up. Joanna, anxious to get back to town. *I'm having my period.*

Joanna, down on her knees and right out of her mind in the dining saloon of the *Archimedes,* shrilly hysterical:

Papa made them take everything out.

They stole parts of my body.

Hysteria.

Hysterectomy, Blaize thought, and the unswallowable lump suddenly plummeted straight to her belly; she felt a pang and then a cramp.

But was it possible, from one moment to the next, to believe anything Joanna said? Particularly when she was in one of those phases when the emotional gears were shifting out of control, the engine seemed about to explode?

Blaize sat down on a gnarled windfall in the sun, noticing belatedly that she was sharing the Judas tree with a gimlet-eyed brown lizard. He kept his distance, his bubble throat swelling and receding rhythmically. Like the bloated belly of Joanna in her father's bed.

A sunbeam shot through gently wavering cypress smote her like a lance in the temple, and Blaize had to steady herself with both hands on the windfall until she recovered from a brief but potent spell of dizziness.

Hysteria or hysterectomy? Or both?

If Joanna's uterus had been removed, then she couldn't be having a menstrual period; therefore she had told a lie so that she might return to Vathi by herself.

Why, because she was bored? Joanna was easily bored.

No reason for her to suggest a visit to the temple in the first place.

So there had to be a compelling reason why she wanted to be on Ithaca today, and Blaize's interest in archaeology had provided a convenient excuse. An excuse that Joanna felt she needed because she was up to something and didn't want anybody to know about it.

She was meeting Axel, Blaize concluded. He had been waiting in Ithaca for her to arrive.

Standing at the window of his hotel room, perhaps, buttoning his cuffs, gazing down at the two of them on the quay.

Why was it necessary to be so secretive?

Blaize was frustrated at that point; she couldn't stretch the already thin fabric of speculation she was weaving to fit a reasonable hypothesis.

Basically it was just none of her goddam business, she thought. Whatever trips your trigger, Joanna; and have fun.

Blaize got up, shouldering her camera case and colorful woolen bag. She trudged uphill, through the terraced stones, tumbled in anemones, of the ancient temple. She had lost interest in vaporous gods and further explorations.

But this conundrum of the present still intrigued her; it was like a boil on her body she couldn't leave alone. Sore as the sun, and very touchy; but she needed to squeeze and squeeze, ignoring pain, until suddenly all the corruption spurted out and was replaced by a flow of clarifying blood.

At the souvenir kiosk there was a signpost, in English and Greek: it indicated the road to follow to the convent of Aja Karía. Three kilometers up the mountain. Not a long walk, but the road that remained would have been difficult for goats.

Nevertheless Blaize set out to find the convent. It was only nine-thirty in the morning; Joanna had said noon. She could be back at the temple site in plenty of time.

The convent was more extensive than it had looked from five miles at sea. Where the road ended there were high walls, steeping in myrtle, broken by ironbound wooden gates. They enclosed in a zigzag course the windowed aerie at the cliff's edge. It was a place dead silent except for the mild bluster of morning wind, the far-off cry of a predatory bird. Lengthy shadows of cypress writhed around Blaize in the rock-studded dust as she approached the main gate, limping a little to favor a stone-bruised foot. There was a small sign in Greek she couldn't read. A bellpull. She rang and rang. No one came.

Blaize went up on her toes to peer through the spokes of the half-moon opening at the top of the gate. Inside there was a courtyard, a single huge-spreading plane tree rising from earth baked to the consistency of brick, stone pathways and steps, shadowy galleries. There were many seams showing where walls had been ruptured, repaired and mortared over. Earthquake damage.

"Hello! Is anybody here? I would like to speak to the *Kathigumeni Kekilia*!" Her voice echoed, and before it faded she repeated herself, louder than before. "I'm a friend of Argyros Coulouris! Coulouris! Is anybody inside?"

Coulourislourislourisssss . . .

Blaize stayed on her toes until she felt the pain of stretched tendons, then settled resignedly to the ground and backed away from the gate, to where she could see the highest windows of the convent, the Coptic cross on the dark blue dome of the chapel. She unslung her camera case and decided the walk wouldn't be wasted if she took a few pictures.

She was focusing on the little wayfarer's shrine in the wall beside the gate when she heard a rattle of chain and a creaking of hinges. The gate opened slowly, about a foot. A very small nun, like an overgrown mouse, only eyes and a pale blur of face showing within dark cowling, looked out and around until she located Blaize. The nun spoke to her in Greek.

"I don't understand what you—"

The nun nodded vigorously, beckoned with one hand.

"*Óchi Angliká*. Coulouris. Coulouris. *Ne. Ne. Parakaló*."

Blaize knew enough Greek to interpret that. Any friend of Argyros Coulouris was a friend of theirs. She was welcome to enter.

"*Kathigumeni Kekilia*?" Blaize asked as she walked through the gateway. The gate was closed and padlocked behind her.

"*Ne. Ne*." And then what might have been the Greek for "Follow me."

Blaize followed, looking around as she tried to keep up with the scurrying nun. The entry courtyard was rather plain, as she had already seen, but through an open door as they passed the chapel, she glimpsed the dramatic fresco of an overseeing Christ on the vaulted ceiling, a richly appointed altar. To one side of the chapel was a tiny walled cemetery and next to that a flourishing vegetable garden that smelled of manure. There were goats in an enclosure, and two nuns were at work tending an arbor against a sunny wall. Small oblong buildings housed a library, a cloister. They turned down a long gallery with a low wall at the very edge of the cliff, and Blaize looked out on islands, the sea, the Greek mainland, dry as bones in the winter sun. A dim passageway took them back toward the interior of the convent, to an archway framing blue sky and the strong green of fruit trees. At the top of a short flight of steps, the nun left her and hurried back the way they had come. Blaize found herself facing a cul-de-sac, the sunken garden of the Mother Superior.

"*Kaliméra.*"

She was seated, in mountainous folds of black cloth, on a small bench near a thick wall with a lancet opening that afforded a glimpse of the outside world. She had one hand on the silver-clad knob of an olivewood staff, another on the back of the tortoise-shell kitten in her lap. The silver crucifix that adorned her habit looked as if it might weigh almost as much as the Mother Superior herself. The garden was only about twenty feet square. It was half in shadow from the angle of the sun. The high wall to seaward and the adjoining cloister kept the wind out.

Her dark eyes moved inquiringly. "You may come down," the Mother Superior said in a thin, cracked voice.

Blaize nodded and walked down the steps into the garden. There was a hothouse fragrance at ground level, of mandarin orange and jasmine, of nespole blossoms.

"*Kaliméra,* Reverend Mother. You speak English very well."

The kitten raised its head somnolently to gaze at the visitor, then batted a pink ear with one paw and rolled over under the yielding hand of the Mother Superior.

"I speak many languages. Eleven in all, though I have never traveled. Berlitz has excellent courses available on records, and there is the short-wave radio. Might I ask your name?"

"Blaize Ellington."

"Blaize," the Mother Superior repeated, sampling it. "I

have never heard of anyone named 'Blaize' before. As in 'conflagration,' perhaps?"

"No, I don't think so. It's just an old family name."

"Most interesting. Won't you please sit down? I find it difficult to look up to you. Many years ago there was an earthquake here; my back was broken and I have never fully recovered from the infirmity."

Blaize sat on a bench opposite her. The Mother Superior's face was like a cameo in Parian marble, worn down evenly to nubs of features, colorless except for a tint of purple in her thin lips. Her eyebrows and lashes had vanished long ago. The wry angle of her head spoke of suffering; the smooth, white brow was untroubled by mortal pangs, and told a different story, that of the serenity that develops from long contemplation of a higher plane of existence.

"You do not wear a wedding ring, so you are not of the family of Coulouris by marriage."

"I'm a friend of Joanna's. She told me about the convent of Aja Karía, and I wanted to see it."

"Ah, yes. Joanna. She is well?"

"She's had her ups and downs. Then you haven't heard from her lately."

"Not for many years," the Mother Superior said, stroking the belly of the kitten. "She is remembered in our prayers. And also her father, our benefactor, who, as you may know, saved the Order from extinction."

"It must have been a terrible earthquake."

"Yes. Millions of *drachmae* were needed for restoration. He heard of our plight; he gave freely to us, without solicitation. His generosity surely will be remembered in heaven for all eternity. Perhaps you would like to see more of our little convent; I will arrange that for you."

"Joanna told me about the caves underneath."

"Yes, there are caves, all the way down to the sea. Unfortunately, they may no longer be visited. Since the earthquake no one has attempted to find his way through the passages; I have no doubt that many of them are blocked by rock slides."

She turned her wan face away from Blaize, gazing through the narrow opening in the wall at blinding blue. Her eyes watered and closed slowly, squeezing tears down her cheeks. She seemed to be falling asleep.

"Mother Superior?"

"You must excuse me now. I would accompany you, but I have so little strength these days. You will please convey my continuing gratitude to Argyros Coulouris."

"And Joanna?"

A slight nod. "I will pray daily, as I have always done, for her salvation."

"Reverend Mother, there's something I have to know, and I think you're the only one who can tell me."

"It is tiring for me to talk so long," the old woman whispered.

"Did Joanna have a baby here?"

The Mother Superior reached up slowly to caress the crucifix she wore. The kitten squirmed in her lap, as if disturbed by the energy generated from her act of reverence. Again there was a nod, but whether it indicated weariness or assent Blaize couldn't tell.

"If you must ask such a question, then I am certain—that you have neither the right nor the need to know."

"I already know. I mean, I can't prove it, I just guessed. Reverend Mother, Joanna's in a terrible bind—"

" 'Bind?' What signifies *bind*?"

"Since I've known her, Joanna has never been very stable emotionally, but now I have reason to believe she's—under the influence of a man who wants her father dead. Joanna's obsessed with Argyros, but it isn't love, not anymore; she must really hate his guts, because of something he did to her after the baby was born. She told me last night that her father had her sterilized, probably by a doctor in Switzerland."

The Mother Superior's head sagged a little more. Folds at the corners of her mouth deepened. She spoke, in Greek, to herself; from the tone of her voice, it was either a lament or a malediction.

"But why would he do a thing like that?" Blaize persisted. "Because she got pregnant? Because he didn't approve of the father and couldn't persuade Joanna to have an abortion?"

The Mother Superior drew a sharp breath at the thought.

"This thing you say—cannot be true. The man could not have done such a terrible thing to his daughter after all she had suffered. He is a man who has made many mistakes in his life, committed sins common to all men, yet this I know: he is not evil. Perhaps—there were complications following the birth. Perhaps it was necessary to remove the womb to save her life."

"I don't know. I hope that's true, but I doubt if it changes how she feels about him. Was the baby born alive?"

"Yes. It was a healthy child."

"Who delivered it?"

"I delivered the child, with the assistance of Sister Theodora, who died last year."

"Did Joanna have a boy or a girl?"

"It was a boy."

"What happened to him?"

"I do not know. Three days after the birth, the *Papas* came. The child was—taken away. I assume he was to be adopted. Please. I am so—very tired."

"I'm sorry, Reverend Mother. But I had to know. I'm scared. For Joanna, don't you see? And her father. I don't know what's going to happen."

The mouselike nun had appeared silently at Blaize's side; she put an imploring hand on her shoulder. Blaize shook her head rudely. The Mother Superior's eyes were closed again. She sat slumped on the bench in a state of suspense, as if every breath might be her last.

"One more question," Blaize pleaded. "Do you know who the father was? That could be important, Reverend Mother."

Now the little nun was tugging at Blaize, trying to get her to move. Blaize resisted and stared anxiously at the still, sorrowing face of the old woman in front of her.

The kitten rose and stretched, then looked up and struck at the silver crucifix with a tiny paw. The crucifix trembled, as did the Reverend Mother's lashless eyelids. She raised her hand a fraction and looked out at Blaize from a vale of meditation. A tongue as arid as the tail of a lizard appeared between her lips and tried to moisten them.

"It never mattered," she said. "They needed our help. Only God may forgive them, as He chooses." With her right hand she made, weakly, a sign of benediction over Blaize. "May it please our most loving Lord that you—have come to us today; may He grant you success in your efforts to assist the family Coulouris in their time of greatest trial; in the hour of their undoing."

Blaize got out of the smelly taxi in front of a *taverna* on the square at half past twelve. Joanna was sitting alone at a table under the awning, reading a tattered copy of *Elle* she had picked up somewhere. She was surrounded by parcels and a straw carryall, as if she'd been on a shopping spree. When Blaize pulled up a chair, Joanna took off her reading glasses and looked at her as if she were trying to remember what Blaize was doing there.

Blaize wanted to say, *And how was Axel?* but she wasn't feeling particularly bold or sure of herself; nor could she say any of the other things that had been going through her mind on the long, winding way down the mountain. She was tired and rather depressed, and it showed.

Joanna wasn't talkative either. "Well, we should be going. Unless you need a drink."

"No, thanks."

Joanna paid for her coffee and rose, gathering up her packages.

"Buy something pretty?" Blaize asked.

"I'll show you later."

"Okay. Let me carry that for you."

Joanna snatched the carryall, styled like a shopping bag, away from Blaize's outstretched hand.

"It's all right. I can manage."

They walked silently together toward the quay. The bright sun reflecting off the water was hard on Blaize's eyes; she stopped to put on her sunglasses. Joanna kept going. There were several ragged kids chasing a puppy on the quay, and as usual, when kids were having a good time, they weren't paying attention to anyone else. One of the boys ran into Joanna from behind, a perfect example of a blind-side block in football, and Joanna took a nasty tumble; packages and the carryall went flying. Blaize hurried to help her. She was already getting up; shouting epithets in Greek at the fleeing children.

"Are you all right?"

"Oh, look at my knee." It was bleeding. "Damned little brats."

Joanna retrieved her handbag and pulled out a wad of tissue, sat on a low railing to apply pressure to the cut. Blaize gathered up everything that Joanna had dropped.

"I'll put these on the boat for you."

Joanna nodded, peering at the cut. It was shallow; the bleeding had almost stopped. She shook her head, exasperated. "I'll be right there."

Blaize went down the gangway to the speedboat, stepped into the rear lounge area. The boat was steady against the fenders hanging along the stone side of the quay; there was little wind and only a slight swell shoreward across the deep harbor. She opened a locker to stow everything away.

A gray envelope she had stuffed back into the carryall was torn; several eight-by-ten color photos were spilling out. Blaize opened the envelope, intending to straighten out the pictures. There were at least two dozen of them. Many of those she glanced at appeared to have been taken at a great distance, with a 300-mm. lens or better. There were photos of a village, a church, a farm, a helicopter; of men carrying automatic weapons. Curious now, she sorted through the lot, uncovering some macrofocus portraits, exceptionally fine detail. She saw a bearded Greek carrying a young boy on his shoulders. The face of the boy was almost out of the frame. A pretty woman with an adoring smile was partially visible behind the bearded man.

The boy was also in the last of the photos she looked at, and, full-face, he was eerily familiar to Blaize. Also familiar was the face of another bearded man, who stood beside the boy. It was Lucas McIver.

Blaize thought her heart had come to a full stop.

It started again when Joanna jumped down into the speedboat and stood in the cockpit, hands on hips, watching Blaize.

"What are you doing?" Joanna demanded.

"I was—putting your things away for you, Joanna."

"Spying on me, you mean?"

Blaize realized the *Phaistos* was moving, slowly drifting away from the quay. Joanna had cast off both lines before boarding. Now she settled into the bucket seat behind the wheel.

Blaize said quickly, "Joanna, I don't want to go with you."

They were already six feet from the quayside steps; Joanna turned the key in the ignition, the stern-drive engines roared.

"Joanna!"

"Sit down!" Joanna yelled, gesturing curtly; and without waiting for Blaize to make a move she gunned the *Phaistos* toward the harbor entrance, careless of the small caiques lined up against the quay.

Blaize sprawled backward onto the striped sun bench in the lounge, hitting her head hard against a chrome stanchion of the rear grab-rail. The photos she had been holding flew up and were scattered in the wake of the swiftly accelerating boat.

By the time they had reached open water and Joanna had set the automatic pilot, Blaize was sitting up, holding her head with her hands, tears of pain on her cheeks.

Joanna sat down beside her and stared silently.

"Joanna—take me back."

"No, I can't."

"Oh, please! What are you going to *do*?"

Joanna looked a little flustered by the raw panic Blaize exhibited, and possibly contrite. Then her mouth firmed.

"You know how much I love you, Blaize. We've been friends for a long time. You always brought me nice things. So thoughtful. You're the only person I've ever cared about who didn't want or try to take something from me."

"If I'm your friend, then you'll listen to me, won't you? You'll let me help you, Joanna."

"I don't need any help."

"But you do! Joanna, I went to the convent this morning. I talked to the *Kathigumeni Kekilia*."

Joanna accepted this news with a slight narrowing of her eyes, an expression of bitterness as she reached up to pull away the hair streaming across her face.

"Axel said you would probably cause trouble."

"I don't know who Axel is or what you're planning, but you just ca-can't—"

"Did you look at them, Blaize? The photos Axel took?"

"I wasn't snooping! The envelope tore, I was only—"

"*All* of them?"

"Yes, goddammit, yes, yes, I saw them all! Where is he? Where's McIver?"

"On Corfu. With my cousin Demetrios Constantine Aravanis. Don't tell me you didn't know that."

"Of course I didn't know!"

Joanna thought about Blaize's denial, her spray-misted face tilted downward. One cheekside brilliant from the sun, her eyes in oceanic shadow. After a while she said, "I believe you, Blaize. It's too bad you won't have the chance to see him again. I really feel bad about that."

"Why? Why won't I see him?"

Blaize got up, holding tight to the grab-rail, and leaned over Joanna, who raised her head slightly and stared noncommittally into her eyes.

"We're going thirty-five miles an hour, Blaize. If you don't sit down you might fall in the water. Do we want that to happen?"

"What I want is for you to turn this boat around now and go back to Ithaca or, or, *anywhere*. Just let me off."

"No. Sit down, Blaize."

"I won't sit down until you—"

"Blaize, I'm stronger than you are. I'm much stronger. I said that I want you to sit down. Otherwise I'm afraid that you'll have an accident. Do you know what I mean?"

Blaize said in a shocked voice, "Joanna, that would be *murder*. I can't swim."

"I know you can't. Now just sit there. Don't be a bother. I have to think about this."

Joanna gripped Blaize just above the elbow on her right arm. The pain was instant, awful, terrifying. Blaize sat down immediately, sobbing. Joanna's expression didn't change. As she had said, she was deep in thought. She looked once more at Blaize, a little vaguely, then got up and went forward to the starboard seat behind the wheel. She sat there, her back to Blaize, hands in her lap, while the speedboat hurtled on, slapdash and fancy, bow half out of the water, the automatic pilot correcting for wave action, the island of Ithaca now half a mile to port, smaller islands appearing in their path. There were other boats in the vicinity, fishermen, a big ferry steamer southbound. They were not alone out there on the populous Ionian; but who could help her now?

Blaize touched the lump on the back of her head where it had hit the stanchion. Her hair was damp and bedraggled from the spray of the waves. What could she do? Try to take control of the boat from Joanna? She didn't know a hell of a lot about operating a boat, and the only way she could accomplish this mutiny would be to sneak up from behind and hit Joanna with something heavy from the mid-cockpit locker. Blaize had trained herself with a .45 automatic in the west Texas desert to kill a man she thought she hated, but she was not trained to batter a woman whom she knew well with a steel wrench or a hammer; her gorge rose at the thought. And still she could not believe, despite Joanna's dementia, her behavior so far, the subtle threats, that she was in mortal danger. Joanna had to come to her senses sooner or later.

Whatever Joanna was going to do, she had now decided. She took the speedboat off automatic pilot and headed toward a chunk of rock looming up fast off the starboard bow.

"Where are we going?" Blaize shouted, but Joanna didn't turn around.

As they continued to approach the small island at a fast clip, Blaize panicked again. She forced herself to get up and go forward to the portside buddy seat near Joanna. What was she trying to do, crash into the rocks, kill them both? Joanna, in and out of hospitals for years, the constant drugs: Thorazine, even worse junk than that. Blaize had heard how the psychoactive drugs could mess up your frontal lobes. Cause permanent disorientation or derangement.

"Joanna—stop!"

Joanna made a sweeping turn around some barren pinnacles that rose fifty feet above the sea; Blaize was thrown sideways and almost out of the boat. She rebounded from the padded edge of the lounge gunwale and lay stunned on the teak deck, looking up, seeing nothing but sunlit cliff dead ahead. They appeared to be seconds away from smashing into it. She couldn't move or scream. She closed her eyes just as Joanna backed off hard on the throttles. The sound of the engines reverberated from the cliff's face; waves broke against the rocks all around them. Then the sun disappeared and they glided into darkness.

Blaize got up slowly, her twisted back aching, and looked around. They were in a broad channel of some kind, a sea-filled cavern that went deeply into the rock. The island that had seemed solid from a mile away was almost hollow. The vaulted roof of the grotto was broken in a couple of places; sunlight streamed down and sizzled on the surface of the black water, hot spots in this Stygian hideaway. They intersected one of these blinding pillars of light, and Blaize glimpsed Joanna's face as something whitely burnt, with only the crisps of eyes showing above one shoulder.

Now what?

Still looking back at Blaize, Joanna navigated with one hand. There were, Blaize saw, small islets, some only a few feet above water level, within the cavern.

"This is the best I can do, believe me, Blaize!"

"What? What do you mean?"

Their voices, distorted by the acoustics of the cavern, sounded foreign to Blaize, a consequence of the developing nightmare. Joanna had throttled down until they were nearly adrift. A large chunk of stalagmites, shaped somewhat like the Enchanted Castle at Disneyland, had appeared to starboard; Joanna eased the boat toward it.

"Get ready! I want you to jump!"

"Jump? To *there*? Joanna, have you gone totally—"

"I said jump, Blaize, jump, get off the boat!" And Blaize saw the little nickel-plated automatic pistol in Joanna's free hand, pointing back at her.

"Oh, come on now, Joanna, you wouldn't—"

Joanna did it. She shot her.

What Blaize saw was a reddish spurt of flame from the muzzle, and what she felt was a pinch of something fiery against her left side, almost as high as the armpit. She couldn't say it hurt, really, but then the realization that she had missed being killed by perhaps an inch hit her harder than any bullet could have. The rocks were now only two feet away, and without conscious thought she scrambled over the grab-rail of the speedboat and landed hard, cutting her elbows and banging her forehead. She kept going, clawing for purchase at the bare, steeply angled rock that was her only refuge, looking for a crevice big enough to hide in. But there was no hiding place. She turned, shuddering, spread-eagled, toward the boat and saw Joanna standing in the cockpit, looking back at her as the boat pulled away slowly.

"Blaize, I'm sorry! Did I hit you? I didn't mean to. I was only trying to get you to jump!"

A red rage came flooding from the region of Blaize's solar plexus and she shouted back, "Why don't you shoot me again? Get it over with!"

"I don't want to hurt you, Blaize! You're my friend!"

"Hurt me? You're leaving me here to die!"

"I said I was sorry!"

The boat circled and came back, six feet abeam of the islet in the middle of the huge cavern, which was not unlike the eye socket she had once envisioned as the dwelling place of Godtherat.

Oh, God, Blaize prayed, *let her change her mind. I'll do anything, God, but don't let her leave me here!*

"Blaize, do you want the TV? I could leave you the TV."

At first Blaize didn't know what Joanna was talking about; then she remembered that there was a little Japanese color set with a miniature screen mounted on the cockpit console of the *Phaistos*.

"A TV? What good is a fucking television set? I don't even have any water to drink!"

"I'm just trying to think of ways to make you more comfortable," Joanna said with a hint of petulance. Keeping one hand on the wheel, she pocketed her pistol, took a lap robe in a plastic case from beneath the right-hand seat of the cockpit and pitched it toward Blaize.

"You'll need that. It gets cold in here. And—wait a minute, I've got an idea."

"Damn it, Joanna, come to your senses! Get me off this rock pile!"

"I *can't,* Blaize," Joanna whined. She had opened a console locker as the boat drifted nearer. "Here. You said you needed something to drink. Can you catch it?"

Blaize saw a wink of light on something shiny arcing toward her like a missile; she reached up blindly with both hands and came down with a full bottle of wine, vintage unknown.

"That's all there is. I have to go now. Are you sure you don't want the TV?"

"God damn you to everlasting hell, Joanna!"

"Oh, Blaize. Don't *say* a thing like that. You know I love you, Blaize! Good-bye!"

"Nooooo!"

The echo of Blaize's voice drowned in the busy thrum of the Mercruiser engines. Joanna sank back into her seat and piloted the boat between the rock outcrops, the pillars of light. Blaize got up and stumbled a few feet down to the water's edge, numbly clutching the bottle of wine to her chest. But there was nowhere else to go, and all she could do was stand there getting wet to her knees from the backwash as she watched Joanna and the speedboat pull steadily away; watched in disbelief until the boat was indistinct at the far side of the cavern, a mote in the pale blue opening at the edge of eternity. And even when the *Phaistos* had disappeared altogether, when there was no further sound from the engines, Blaize continued to stand there rigidly, eyes fixed on the jagged hole in the rock, trusting that at any moment now the prank, Joanna's bum joke, would wear thin and Joanna would be back for her.

It was a very long time before she was willing to acknowledge the reality of the bullet-burn on her side, to admit to herself that Joanna was not coming, that she probably already had put Blaize out of her mind forever.

Blaize knew she could save herself—the way out was obvious. All she had to do was to learn to swim.

Or teach herself to fly. It amounted to the same thing.

She was shaking out of control. Deliberately she bit her tongue several times, but that did no good. There was a bad trip coming, the great-granddaddy of all bad trips, and the destination this time was permanent insanity.

If she were to have any chance at all, there was only one thing to do, and Blaize did it quickly.

She found a sharp edge of rock and knocked the top off the bottle of red wine, wrapped herself in the lap robe and sat down on the tough plastic case, a cushion of sorts. Then she proceeded to drink steadily, until she was in a state of wretched apathy.

Chapter 26

Athens

The telephone in Pard Randolph's suite at the St. George Lycabettus rang a few minutes after five.

It was answered by the billionaire Texan's traveling secretary, a redheaded niece from Concho County. Leila turned the call over to Pard with a wince but no audible comment.

"Pard, this's Buford Ellington."

"Figured I'd be hearin' from you, Bewf."

"You know where my daughter is?"

"Not right this very minute I don't, no."

"I want to see you, goddammit! Right away."

"Expected you would," Pard said dryly. "Come ahead on, I'll be waitin'."

Pard, wearing his at-home serape of fringed buckskin and Navajo beading, delayed the start of his bath. Buford Ellington was ringing his chimes eight and a half minutes after their phone conversation had ended. Leila let them in. Buford on his aluminum hand crutches, with that swinging sideways kick that eventually took him in the direction he wanted to go. He looked angry as an ape. His companion was Bealer Stout, whom Buford had hired to track down Lucas McIver. Stout, well turned-out in brown tweed, coolly surveyed Pard and the six-foot-one Leila, then measured the living room of the suite as if he were thinking of redecorating it.

"How you makin' it, General?" Pard said. He knew that all the employees down at Bealer's shop in Miami had strict orders to always address him as "General." Pard had quit soldiering with one more star than Stout had to his credit, but soon after the last shot was fired along the 38th Parallel, Pard wanted no more of that "General" crap for himself. "Leila, fix these men whatever it is they're drinkin'."

"This's no social call," Buford snapped, and he didn't look for a place to sit. Bealer Stout walked to the windows and looked down at the rush-hour traffic in Dexaméni Square. He had that expression, Pard observed—jut-jawed, tight-lipped—that in some men passed for thoughtful when in fact they really didn't have a hell of a lot to think about. Buford continued, "What I came up here to find out is, what's turned you against me all of a sudden?"

"You don't even know what you're talkin' about, Bewf."

"Shit if I don't! You're takin' sides in this highly personal matter, Pard, and it's the wrong side!"

"Now looky here, Blaize asked me would I do her a leetle favor—" Bealer Stout turned from the windows and snorted softly; Pard gave him a glance that would have cold-cocked a mule. "All she's lookin' for is some peace and quiet and time to get some things sorted out. So I promised I'd help her skip town"—he let his eyes linger for an extra second on the general—"because I still do get some kind of kick from outfoxin' the sniffer dogs."

"You know where she's headed, don't you? Straight to Lucas McIver!"

"I don't know any such a thing. I asked Blaize did she know where she could find him, but she didn't."

"I don't happen to buy that load of bull crap."

Pard took a soft step toward Buford, but he seemed to grow an extra foot or so in the process. Buford Ellington sagged back on his crutches and the general frowned, patting his jacket near one arm as if to check on the availability of his piece. Pard took a deep breath; his eyes cleared, but their temperature had plunged to absolute zero.

He said, carefully, "Regret that I ain't had as much time to spend with your daughter as you have. But there's two things

I know for sure about Blaize Ellington. She can sew a mean stitch with a .45 auto, and she's no liar. Ought to know that yourself by now."

The phong rang, interrupting an edgy silence. Leila answered, murmured something, turned and said, "It's for you, General."

"I left word I could be contacted here," Bealer Stout said.

"Why don't you take that call in my bedroom there if you require some privacy," Pard advised him. The general nodded and crossed the living room, shutting the bedroom doors behind him.

Leila brought Pard his George Dickel on the rocks. Pard said, "Aw, listen, Buford, we been too good friends to carry on like this now. I don't think I done anything I need to feel ashamed of. Why don't you just give the girl a chance to go off on her own and get her head straight?"

"You don't know what could happen! What the consequences might be if she meets up with McIver again." Buford shook his head sorrowfully. "I just don't understand Blaize anymore, and that's a natural fact." He looked up, regretting his lapse, stoking his fire again. "What I want to say to you is, don't get yourself mixed up in *my* business, in *family* business, anymore!"

"Ain't aimin' to. And that's as close to a threat as you're allowed, Buford."

"We understand each other, then?"

"Yeah."

"I'll take that drink now. Bring any Black Label with you?"

"Wouldn't set foot outen the house without a quart or two. Leila!"

Buford had tossed down his two ounces of whiskey by the time Bealer Stout finished his phone call and came out of the bedroom.

"You do one thing for me, Pard?" Buford said. "And I won't call it meddlin'. You hear from Blaize, I want to know. Just tell me, dammit! She called, she's okay."

"Got my word on that."

Buford nodded wearily and they went on their way. Leila

rinsed out Pard's glass and poured another shot of the Dickel for him.

"Run your bath now?" she asked.

"Yeah, that'd be okay. And see if you can get *Rawhide* again on the TV. I don't care if it is dubbed in Greek."

"Want me to pull the bug the general left in the telephone in the bedroom?"

"No, just leave it," Pard said after a moment's reflection. "Then they don't have to go to the trouble of sneakin' somebody up here to the suite to plant another one. Blaize and I already worked out how she was to get in touch if she needs me in a hurry."

Chapter 27

Corfu

"It is essential," Demetrios Constantine Aravanis explained to his cousin Plato Melissani, "that *Niko-B* and *El Invicto,* along with the data I have accumulated on the Cirenaica spore, be made available to *all* companies presently involved in plant genetic research and recombinant agricultural technology and not be limited to Actium International's bioengineering group. There is too much work that must be done quickly for me to entrust the fate of millions of people to a single company. I appeal to you, Plato, because I believe you are, above all, a man of conscience. There surely will be enough profits in the future to satisfy those who think only of profits."

"Of course, I agree," Plato said. "The fact remains that the results of your research are licensed to Actium. It will be more difficult to convince our Uncle Argyros and my brother. But you leave them to me."

"Thank you, Plato."

Lucas McIver had observed, upon meeting Plato Melissani, that the man was ill; probably he was continuing chemotherapy on an outpatient basis after a course of radiation treatment. He had the febrile eyes, the telltale lesions around his mouth. He had lost weight recently, judging from the poor fit of his expensive clothes, and his close-cropped gray hair was wiry and sparse. But there was no fear in Plato. You could always tell the fearful ones; the first sting of the radiation lash also burned out their guts. But Plato would be a fighter until he took his last breath. McIver wondered where the cancer was, and how much time it would give the man. But it wasn't his business, unless Plato Melissani asked for or required his help.

"How do you want me to proceed?" Plato asked Demetrios Constantine.

"Arrange a conference for one week from today, in New York. I will furnish a list of those who must be there."

After dinner that evening the botanist returned to his laboratory with his son Niko for more hours of work; Ourania Aravanis had come down with a cold and retired early to her room. McIver, the Leprechaun and Plato strolled down to Stavropoulous's *taverna,* where the Leprechaun had promised to work off a debt incurred at backgammon by singing "Come Back to Erin, Mavourneen, Mavourneen" and two selections from Gilbert and Sullivan, accompanied by Stavropoulous himself on the squeezebox. Halfway down the road, Plato excused himself and went off into the trees to vomit up his dinner. The Leprechaun, after a glance from McIver, continued on to the village and McIver stayed behind, perched on a low stone wall, watching the lights of fishing boats in the strait between Corfu and Albania. There was a chill in the air, a light mist forming in the groves. It took Plato a considerable time to pull himself together.

"I'm sorry," he murmured when he rejoined McIver.

"Why should you apologize? Are you sure you want to go down to the *taverna*?"

Plato said a bit stiffly, "I go where I want, when I want. Now I will have a drink."

"What do your doctors have to say? I assume you didn't put up with the usual bullshit."

"I have had prostate cancer for several years. I refused an operation that would have ended my already limited ability to have sex. I have been in remission twice. Now the cancer is in the pelvic bone. Lytic metastases, I believe they are called. Inevitably my kidneys will be affected."

"I see."

"I have faith in my God, and faith in the strength of my body. Neither has ever failed me. I will live to see my children grown." That ended the conversation about his illness. After they had walked a little farther in silence, Plato asked McIver, "Do you have any conception of what Minotaur is, or means?"

"I think it could be a terrorist cell; political in nature, with Libyan or Turkish or Bulgarian financing. But there are pathological elements that don't fit the profile of political anarchists. Blowing up airplanes is consistent with terrorist activity; but ritual murder is not. The psychomyth of the legendary minotaur may well explain Minotaur's actions better than standard terrorist ideology."

"My brother has also come to this conclusion. I share it, but reluctantly."

"Why reluctantly?"

Plato's face was lined with anguish. "He is convinced that one of us—one of the cousins—is deeply involved."

"Excluding the two of you, and Aravanis, and Kris, who is missing, who does that leave?"

"No one but Joanna."

"Coulouris's daughter? Why?"

Plato explained. They had reached the edge of the village, and paused in front of the small church. McIver listened with interest and then with a sense of excitement, feeling the warning tingle at the base of his spine.

"The girl ought to be taken into somebody's custody, and right now."

Plato shrugged. "We don't know where she is. Joanna was due to arrive in Iconis today aboard the *Archimedes*. But she left the yacht in Ithaca harbor at eight-thirty this morning. She had a companion with her, a young woman."

"Who?"

"We don't know. Someone she took aboard yesterday in Piraeus. No doubt she is one of Joanna's casual *inamoratas*."

"So they're somewhere on Ithaca. How big a place is that?"

"Quite a small island; but no, they left in the early afternoon aboard one of the powerboats which Joanna borrowed from the *Archimedes*. I talked just before dinner with my brother Theos, but Joanna has not been seen or heard from. This is not unusual, of course. She has been known to disappear for days, popping up in out-of-the-way places.''

''Maybe she's coming here.''

''Why would you think so?''

''I'm certain Minotaur has been around already, on reconnaisance of the estate, sizing up Ed Nikitiadas's defenses, looking for a point of entry. I don't know how many of them there are, but I'm expecting a hit, and soon. Your arrival probably assures it.''

''I know nothing that is of value to Minotaur. My brother's suspicions I have shared with no one but you.''

''Minotaur has killed a lot of people in order to grab all of the *El Invicto* tissue cultures available. Considering what's in store once Cirenaica has riddled the food chain, *El Invicto* may be worth a billion dollars; or any terms Minotaur cares to exact. All that remains of the cultures are in Aravanis's keeping. Your presence will indicate to Minotaur his decision to release *El Invicto* and his own discoveries to his colleagues. Minotaur will take any measures to prevent that.''

''Yes, I understand.''

''I think you should make every effort to track down Joanna Coulouris, even if you have to alert the Greek authorities. Ed Nikitiadas has done a damned good job of securing the estate, but it's still vulnerable to certain kinds of weapons. RPGs, or even field-grade, one-man missile launchers. Minotaur could have Stingers, or Hots, or Rolands. One direct hit on the lab would wipe out Aravanis and all his research.''

Down the street, Stavropoulous had appeared in the doorway of his *taverna*, waving an untidy apron in their direction.

''Hey, Lucas! You tryna avoid me tonight? Church don't open until five-thirty in the morning. So get your ass down here and have a drink. First one's ona house, pal.''

McIver signaled that they were on the way and turned back to Plato Melissani, who laid a heavy hand on his shoulder.

''Of course you are right. Joanna must be found. We'll talk to Theos. But I think we both need that drink before we call him.''

Chapter 28

New York City

In his large library on the fifty-second floor of Actium International's building on Fifth Avenue, Argyros Coulouris stood alone, staring at the ancient astrolabe in the center of the sea-green onyx floor. Smoke from the cigarette in his palsied right hand curled slowly up past his face. He still wore the pin-striped gray business suit he'd had on for most of the day, but his feet were in slippers.

The pieces of the photographs he had received twenty minutes ago by courier pouch were scattered on the low round table in front of his favorite chair. The wine that had spilled from a smashed glass was as dark as blood on the polished floor. His heart was quieter now, and only now was he afraid of the delayed stroke that his rage might have precipitated.

What difference does it make if I live or die? he thought. *What is there to live for after this?*

A telephone was ringing. Not the console on the worktable, but the ultra-secure line, the scrambler telephone in another part of the library. Because of his speedboat accident long ago, Argyros was unable to move his head more than half an inch to either side. He turned slowly, with an elderly shuffling of his feet, as each imperative ring sent a new shock through him.

He knew he could not ignore her. The telephone would ring all night until he answered.

It took him a long time to cross the library to the scrambler phone. Physical weakness was a further humiliation. He picked up the receiver but had to hold it in both hands.

"Can we talk, Papa?"

"I am alone," Argyros said, his normally sonorous voice degraded, lowered to a whisper.

"Good. Do you have the photographs? They should be there by now."

"Yes—I—they came."

"Isn't he cunning? Isn't he a little bull?"

"Do you want me to fall down dead from a stroke? Is that why you are doing this to me?"

"Oh, no, Papa! I miss you. I want to be with you. I want us all to be together."

His face darkened. He swayed. "Never!"

There was a significant pause. Joanna said, "Yesterday I went to visit Uncle George. He looks very bad. He never leaves the bed. Such a frail old man. I could have reached down and pinched his nostrils together. In less than a minute he would have been dead. No one would suspect me. Did you want me to do that for you, Papa?"

"You must—stop this—crazy talk. You must get away from that man!"

"From Axel? But we are the same person. We can't be separated. Didn't Dr. Hoelscher explain that to you? Papa, are you crying? Don't cry, Papa."

"In God's name, Joanna—!"

"But Papa. You are *my* god. You always have been. All I ever wanted was to please you. Now I have a gift for you. A gift for a god of this earth."

"I don't want—"

"You must come. I've been waiting much too long. Come right away."

"I *can't*! Joanna, will you tell me—"

"Papa, what's the matter with your voice? I can't hear you. Speak louder."

Pitching his ragged voice above a whisper, Argyros said to his daughter Joanna, "Where is Kris?"

Joanna sounded mildly vexed that he should ask about Kristoforos Aravanis. "Kris is asleep, Papa."

For a moment he had hope. "Asleep? Where?"

"In the glacier in Austria. Where we put him. Isn't it interesting? If Kris should be found, even ten thousand years from now, there will be no change—he will look the same. Ice is better than memory, don't you think? Memory rots. It disfigures what was beautiful. I don't like to remember things. I only think of how perfect it will be when we are all together."

"But what is it—you are plotting now?"

"I told you about Kristoforos. I don't want to tell you all of my secrets, Papa. We'll talk when you join me. You'll come tomorrow, won't you? Say yes."

"Yes, yes, *yes*. I'm coming! Where will I find you?"

"Oh, don't worry. I'll find *you*, Papa." There was a quiet note of exultation in his daughter's voice just before the connection was broken.

Afterward he did not recall hanging up, nor making his way back to his favorite chair. He was not conscious of the passage of time until the cabinet clock in the library struck one-thirty. It was then he blinked awake as if from a somnambulist's trance and gathered up the pieces of photographs, trying not to look at them again. When he had stuffed them all back into the envelope and marked it for the shredder, he reached for the other telephone, his private line, and dialed the one number he had never written down anywhere.

The woman named Petriades answered, as she always did, on the third ring.

Argyros Coulouris found himself unable to utter a word. His throat had closed. It was all he could do to breathe.

After waiting for a decent interval, the woman prompted him.

"Do you want the Actors, sir?"

He felt watched and looked up, startled, to glimpse a shade of himself as a younger man, vigorous and full-bodied, smiling at him from across the room. Nervelessly, curiously, he studied the apparition.

"Kill her," said the ghost.

Then with a little formal nod the ghost turned and walked through the closed doors of the library, and he was alone again.

The guilt that had crippled him like a wasting disease vanished with the ghost. Now that it was gone, he could acknowledge the logic of the proposed solution. He sat back deeply in his chair, feeling the crack and stretch of muscles long unused, appreciating the strong and steady beat of his off-threatened heart. His voice was loud and authoritative.

"There will be no more performances. I will not need the theater any longer. Tomorrow it will be in your name. Sell it. The money is yours to keep."

Chapter 29

Corfu

At seven forty-five a.m. on the third of March, a Sunday, Axel Stroh and Joanna Coulouris drove up the unpaved main street of the village of Portais, one kilometer below the estate of Demetrios Constantine Aravanis, and two and a half kilometers from the corniche road. Joanna was behind the wheel of a rented Fiat. Axel had a Hasselblad camera case on a strap around his neck and a MAC-10 with a Sionics noise suppressor between his knees. He was looking at a folded road map.

Two of Ed Nikitiadas's security guards were across the street from the Church of St. Spyridon. One sat behind the wheel of the armored Chevy Caprice sedan, the other was on a balcony overlooking the entrance to the church.

Joanna drove abreast of the Chevy Caprice and stopped. Axel held up the road map in one hand and said to the driver, "Can you tell me where is the best road for to get to the summit of Pantokrátor?" The guard didn't hear a word. His bulletproof window was rolled up; the engine of the Caprice was running. Axel hung out the window and smilingly repeated his question, gesturing with his map toward the Mountain of Christ. At the same time he got a good look at the second guard on the balcony, who was looking down at him from twenty feet away. He had a walkie-talkie in one hand.

The guard behind the wheel of the Caprice lowered the

window about four inches, which was all the space Axel needed to blow the top of his head away with a burst from the MAC-10. The windshield looked as if it had been spray-painted, badly, on the inside. As soon as the guard on the balcony saw the MAC-10, he raised the walkie-talkie to his mouth and went for his weapon, holstered beneath his jacket, where he also was wearing a Second Chance Deep Cover vest. But Axel was out of the Fiat and into the street like a panther pouncing from a treetop. As Joanna accelerated and made a quick turn to come up in front of the church doors, Axel went for another head shot, destroying the walkie-talkie and obliterating most of the man's face.

Joanna left the Fiat's engine running, got out and walked briskly into the church. The seven-thirty mass was in progress. She was wearing tinted shooting glasses, earplugs and a safari jacket, the cargo pockets of which were filled with three-inch Magnum shotgun shells. She had altered her face, with latex and paint, into a death mask. She was high, just high enough, on poppers. She was carrying a semiautomatic, twelve-gauge combat shotgun by its pistol grip.

There were only half a dozen pews in the little church. The family Aravanis were kneeling in the second pew, Niko between his father and his mother. Plato Melissani was on the aisle.

The third security guard assigned to the family this morning was in the back of the church and to the left of the doors as one entered. His location was a variable that Axel had carefully worked out after making two visits to the church. The brilliant early light of morning streamed in through the open doors onto the stone floor; the rest of the interior was, in contrast, rather dim. Joanna took three steps into the church, soundless in nylon running shoes, the shotgun in her right hand and at her side. She turned smoothly and brought the weapon up and fired at the guard, who was standing just where Axel had theorized he would be, a fresco of the Last Judgment at his back. Despite her strength it was hard for her to resist the kick of the miniature cannon. The fully choked round of shot took him in the chest, where he wore a protective vest, but although he wasn't killed or even seriously injured, he was slammed against the wall. Before he could recover Joanna took a step forward, braced herself and pulled the trigger again; she shot him in the side of the neck and he slid down the illustrated wall, spouting like a whale.

Now there was a lot of screaming. Axel had sprinted across the street and joined her in the church. While the booming of the shotgun still echoed around the vaulted cloister, Joanna, with her gun leveled, a third shell in the chamber, approached the pew her cousins occupied and demanded, "I want the boy."

"Joanna?" Plato Melissani said; he was still on his knees, looking around at her in disbelief through the maze of gunsmoke and incense. The muzzle of the shotgun was only a couple of feet from his forehead.

Joanna ignored Plato. She was looking at Demetrios Constantine.

"Pick up the boy and carry him outside. Quickly. Do what I say or I will kill the *Papa*."

"No!" Ourania shrieked and wrapped both arms around Niko.

Joanna swung the shotgun toward the altar and gunned down the black-robed priest. He lay open-eyed and shuddering violently beside the altar table, blood streaming into his gray beard. The altar boys dropped their censers and fled.

Plato Melissani lunged to his feet, intending to snatch the shotgun from Joanna's hands. She moved more quickly, clubbing him in the temple with the hot barrel, knocking him down again. She aimed the shotgun again, this time at Ourania.

With a glance at Aravanis she said, "Pick up the boy and carry him outside. If you don't do what I say *now*, your wife is next."

Demetrios Constantine looked dumbly at his crouching wife and son. His mouth worked. Joanna, because of the earplugs, could not have heard him even if he'd been able to speak to her. She did not care what he had to say, what protests he wanted to make. And Demetrios Constantine saw in her eyes that she was about to murder Ourania.

He reached down, pried the struggling boy from his wife's hands and stood up, holding Niko tightly, staring in terror at his cousin. Plato rolled ponderously onto his side in the aisle of the church, holding his bloodied head. He tried to get up and fell back.

Joanna edged away from the pew, motioning slightly with the muzzle of the shotgun.

"Go!"

Aravanis stumbled out of the pew with Niko, ignoring the hysteria of his wife, her clutching hands.

"Shut up!" Joanna snapped at Ourania. The church was filled with outcries, with lamentations. Axel sprang to the doorway, looking cautiously outside. Perhaps fifty seconds had elapsed since Joanna had walked in and killed the security guard, a minute and a half since their arrival in the village. Joanna marched Aravanis and the furiously kicking boy outside.

"Not much time," Axel warned, indicating the Chevy Caprice a few yards away.

"Quiet the boy down," she said to him.

Axel put the MAC-10 on the hood of the Fiat. He took from his coat pocket a can of ether and a small rectangle of artificial sponge, the kind used for cleaning dishes in the kitchen. He soaked the sponge in ether and pressed it against Niko's nose while Aravanis continued to hold him. Aravanis turned his head sharply aside but got a few whiffs of the fumes, enough to further cloud his brain.

"Please, I know what you want. Take me instead!" he pleaded.

Axel threw the can of ether ringingly down the street and, still holding the sponge against Niko's nose, pulled the slumping boy away from his father.

Plato Melissani came running from the church with blood dripping down one side of his face and knocked Joanna down with a glancing blow. He leaped on Axel Stroh, who dropped the boy.

Demetrios Constantine went for the MAC-10 lying on the hood of the Fiat.

Joanna got up, slowly, dazed from hitting her head on the hardpan of the street. One ear was scraped raw. She realized that she couldn't shoot Aravanis without disabling the getaway car as well. She trained her shotgun on the boy, who was lying in the road beside the car, nearly unconscious from several deep breaths of ether. Plato had thrown Axel over his hip and fallen on him; he was grappling for a submission hold.

"Put the gun down," Joanna ordered Aravanis. "The boy will die before I do."

Aravanis dropped the MAC-10. Axel rose slowly to his feet, grunting and straining, Plato's muscular arms around him. He placed a palm beneath the older man's chin and began to pry himself out of the crushing bear hug. They were almost equal in size, but Axel Stroh was much younger and Plato had been seriously weakened by chemotherapy. Desperation was not the ultimate advantage against someone of Axel's strength and quickness.

"Put Niko in the car!" Joanna shouted at her cousin.

Demetrios Constantine turned as if he were half asleep. He opened the rear door of the Fiat. Joanna jumped on him while his back was turned and broke the shotgun against his head. Plato was groaning in agony as Axel got the better of him. Now Axel had both hands free. Muscles tore in Plato's neck and right shoulder as Axel brutally twisted his head far to one side. And then suddenly Plato's neck snapped and he pitched over backward, a startled, fixed look in his eyes. Axel walked away, flexing his long fingers, smiling a little; he snatched up Niko by the hair and the seat of his pants and hurled him into the backseat of the Fiat. Demetrios Constantine was lying face-down and half under the car, but Axel didn't trouble to move him. He climbed in after the boy.

"It is going to blow," he said calmly to Joanna as she slipped in under the wheel, laying her useless shotgun in the seat beside her. She released the brake and jammed her foot on the gas.

The car jolted hard over Aravanis's outstretched left arm and upper body and sped down the street as Stavropoulous appeared in the doorway of his *taverna,* wearing only a pair of undershorts. He raised a long-barreled side-by-side to his shoulder and fired a charge of birdshot at the Fiat, taking out the back window and spraying Axel, who had ducked low, with ground glass and spent shot. In the next moment the charge of C-4 plastic explosive Axel had placed beneath the Caprice, along with a crude timing device consisting of acid and some phosphorous in water, went off. The blast overturned the armored car and disabled it without doing much structural damage. A lot of glass in the vicinity, including every window in the church, was shattered; the shock wave flattened several parishioners who had come crowding hysterically to the doorway.

Ourania was one of those stunned by the explosion, but she recovered soon enough to crawl over the sprawled bodies of the others and into the dust-shrouded, littered street. She reached her husband. She had been temporarily deafened by the explosion and couldn't hear a sound. There were figures running back and forth across the street, shadows in the haze. She turned Aravanis toward her and, in a state of mind that was close to full detachment, noted the splintered bones of his wrist, blood trickling from his nose and ears. Looking at him, she could not tell if he was dead or alive. She lifted his head into her lap and began, delicately, to brush the dirt from his lips, his beard. When the helicopter from the estate landed thunderously at the end of the street, kicking up a storm of dust, she bent over Demetrios Constantine to shield him.

Ed Nikitiadas walked out of the church of St. Spyridon and watched as Lucas McIver supervised the placement of Aravanis on a hard stretcher. McIver had made the most of the crash-survival medical kit aboard the helicopter. Aravanis's left arm was encased in an inflatable splint; there was a padded collar around his neck to keep his head motionless. He was receiving oxygen from a bottle in Stavropoulous's hands. McIver could only speculate on the nature and extent of internal injuries—to the brain, the spinal cord, vital organs. Aravanis might slowly and invisibly be bleeding to death; there was nothing any doctor could do under the circumstances.

Four volunteers lifted the unconscious man and carried him uphill to the waiting helicopter. McIver turned and came over to Nikitiadas.

"Really fucked it up, didn't I?' the security chief said angrily.

McIver wiped muddy perspiration from his forehead and cleaned his hands on a pad of gauze soaked in alcohol. "What else could you do to protect them? If one man can penetrate the defenses around a head of state or the Pope, two fanatics can pull off almost any outrage, as long as they're willing to die in the attempt."

"What are his chances, Lucas?"

"His skull is fractured. If it's a cominuted fracture, there's bone pressing against or into the brain. Too spongy back there for me to tell. He isn't leaking cerebrospinal fluid, which is a hopeful sign. And he's breathing on his own. But his next breath could be his last. With serious head injuries, you just don't know. You can't quote odds. Aravanis could walk out of the hospital good as new a month from now, or he might be brain-dead already. We'll know when we get him to the machines. What did you find out from the hospital in Corfu Town?"

"It's ten minutes away by chopper. They'll have a portable respirator waiting and the drugs you asked for. But if he's going to need sophisticated diagnosis and then surgery, your best bet is Andronicos Hospital in Athens."

"That's what I figured. Are they sending an emergency medical team from Corfu Town?"

"They just left." In the church behind them, women were sobbing as they prayed. "We've got five dead. Three of my men. Plato Melissani. The *Papa*. The injured aren't hurt too badly, they'll be all right until we get more help. Listen, Lucas. The Greek government is going to be very difficult about all this. I'll have some of our people waiting at the hospital in Athens, they may be useful to you. Your best bet is to say you were just passing through, you don't know a thing. Okay, on your way."

Ourania was standing with the Leprechaun near the Gazelle helicopter when McIver got there. Aravanis's blood was on her dress, on her face. She had a silver rosary in one hand, and there was cold courage in her eyes. She reached for McIver.

"Save him," she said.

McIver put his arms around her. She almost yielded to her grief, trembling momentarily. But they were a people who had endured centuries of cruelty and oppression, and always they gave as good as they got. Ourania held her head high. "I will never rest until that woman is dead. I swear an oath now. I will kill her myself if I must."

"We'll get her—and we'll get Niko back too."

"But why won't you let me go with my husband?"

"It's almost certain that Minotaur will contact you. Soon. They'll want to exchange your son for Demetrios Constantine's research. I know how you feel, but for everyone's sake, it's important that you deal with Minotaur. Give them anything they ask for—as long as they return Niko to you."

Ourania nodded. It was difficult for her to keep her eyes off her husband, whom she could see lying inside the helicopter. She said, "You will call me as soon as you know? You will tell me everything—even if the news is not good?"

"I promise."

The turbocharged engine was turning over. McIver had a good grip on Ourania; otherwise she would have bolted to the open doorway of the helicopter.

"It isn't good-bye," McIver said. "He's coming back! But every second is important now, Ourania!"

Her tears were whipped from her eyes by the wash from the twin rotor blades.

"God bless, Lucas!" the Leprechaun said, and he led Ourania to a safer distance from the chopper. McIver ran to the chopper and climbed in over his patient. As he shut the door and they lifted off, it seemed to him that he had done this too many times, evacuating the critical and the hopeless from scenes of carnage in almost every corner of the world. But never had a single life mattered so much, and never had he felt this sick and helpless.

"Pour it on!" he yelled to the pilot. On his knees, he looked out as the Gazelle rose swiftly and turned due south. He saw among others Ourania's steadfast, upturned face, her black veil licking across one cheek.

For the next five minutes he gave all of his attention to

Demetrios Constantine, whose respiration was shallow but steady. McIver counted his pulse, which had weakened slightly, and periodically opened in turn each of Aravanis's eyes. The pupils remained equal in size, but they did not react normally to the bright sunlight that filled the cabin of the helicopter.

McIver took a break and looked out, seeing the sharp-edged mountain behind them, the fleet shadow of the helicopter on the blue surface of the gulf of Kerkyra a thousand feet below. The hills of Corfu Town were in sight, and the gulf was filled with boats. If they had planned it carefully, he thought, they were on the water now, having driven with the boy to any of the numerous small coves and inlets that were only minutes away from the village of Portais. Even if the police on Corfu were effective—and they were not, according to Ed Nikitiadas—there was virtually no chance of learning where Minotaur had gone after the raid. The car would be found, of course, abandoned. But the small Greek Navy would have to board and search every boat in the Ionian Sea within a matter of hours, an impossible task even if it could be mobilized in time. There were too many islands, too many hiding places, even on Corfu itself, where long stretches of coastline were unvisited at this time of the year. The advantage was Minotaur's.

Vidos Island had appeared on their left; the long breakwater and anchorage on Corfu Town's north shore lay just ahead. Behind the anchorage was the fort on the low hill called Mount Abraham. The hospital was just on the other side of the hill, on Ioulias Andreadi Street. One minute away, no longer. And Demetrios Constantine Aravanis was still breathing. If the good-bad scenario McIver had constructed was accurate, the balance had tipped slightly to Aravanis's favor. But Athens, and the intensive care he badly needed, was still far away.

The Marquis de Rienville's chartered yacht *St. Affrique*, out of Tangier, had taken the powerboat *Phaistos* in tow three kilometers south of Kalami Bay in the Gulf of Kerkyra. The unconscious Niko had been lifted aboard, concealed in a small wicker trunk that was carried below to the master stateroom. The drug Axel had administered earlier would not begin to wear off until eighteen hours had passed.

Joanna and Axel joined their host under the awning on the stern deck for breakfast. Joanna had brushed her hair so it covered the ear that had been bloodied in the street outside the Church of St. Spyridon, and Axel had attended to the minor nicks received when Stavropoulous blew out the back window of the Fiat. Aside from these slight wounds, they showed no signs of having just murdered several people. They seemed without nerves and in a chummy mood, nuzzling each other as they shared a tall glass of fresh orange juice. Rienville could not imagine the devastation they had wrought in the village of Portais, and he didn't care to hear about it. The boy was aboard; he would be most useful until it was time for him to die. His revised plan, the Marquis reflected, dovetailed nicely with the grand strategy he had carpentered these past few months.

When he heard the helicopter coming from the direction of Pantokrátor, he felt a twinge of concern. He got up from the table and ventured out of the shade into the unfriendly light of day. Shielding his eyes against the glare from the cloudless sky, he located the Gazelle less than a kilometer to starboard, southbound, heading away from the *St. Affrique,* no doubt bearing the most seriously wounded to Corfu Town. Satisfied that he and his guests were not in jeopardy, he returned to his breakfast. It would be best to scuttle the powerboat, he thought, where it could be done without arousing the curiosity of his six-man crew. Joanna was looking at him, just a trifle maliciously it seemed to him, her demeanor that of the Queen of Hell. He smiled back at her, determined to rise above the ordeal of being civil to his guests. For the last time, Rienville assured himself. A matter of a few days, and then he would rid himself forever of these monsters.

Chapter 30

The Grotto of Marathía/Antipaxos

Blaize was not aware of just when she came to the conclusion that it was going to be sink or swim. But after one night of drunken discomfort and a second night of ten thousand bats and terrifying dreams, after many wakeful hours staring remorselessly at the small day-glow aperture of the cavern in which she had been stranded and seeing an occasional boat pass by the little island, of growing so thirsty her lips had cracked and the cracks had filled with dried blood that was as hard as nail polish, she realized that death by drowning could not be such a bad thing. Her fears of a smothering death were dulled by the reality of slow torture on a rock pile, surrounded by water she couldn't drink. Either leave her bones among the stalagmites or beneath the black waters of the grotto; there was no other choice.

Swimming wasn't what came to mind, however; Blaize couldn't swim, but she knew she could at least dog-paddle, navigate her way to the open sea if she had something to hold on to that would keep her afloat. Out there her chances weren't exactly golden that a passing ship would pick her up. But there might not be any visitors to the grotto until the high season. If ever.

She had folded the lap robe and crammed it back into the

tough polyethylene carrying case. Then she stripped down to her panties. Her butt was so sore she found only little relief in standing. The makeshift flotation cushion was approximately two feet square, eight inches thick. Because there was a zipper down one side, it wasn't going to be watertight. Water would seep in—slowly, she hoped. When the blanket was soaked, then the loaded cushion would sink under her weight and down she would go, futilely holding on—

Fuck it, Blaize thought irritably, but she was so close to tears she nearly broke down. Without her clothes she was shaking, a mass of gooseflesh. She concentrated on the nearness of another islet, a jagged crown of rock only a few feet above the waterline. Not too far away. So close, really, a baby could make it. And once she was there, she would be just that much closer to getting out.

Somewhere in the cavern, Godtherat, who hadn't been much company during the first part of her ordeal, was keeping an eye on her, his whiskers twitching expectantly. She would show him.

Blaize held tightly to the handle of the case with her right hand, pressed it to her breasts and stepped down, water closing over her right ankle until she found a submerged ledge to balance on. She took another tentative step, sinking deeper. Another, the cold water creeping shockingly up past her knees. She was quivering all over; she began to bawl. She leaned over and pushed off, balanced on the slippery case, her chin held desperately high.

And it worked: she was floating.

But it was more difficult than she had expected; the makeshift flotation cushion tended to slide buoyantly out from under her. She had to move very carefully, just kick gently to steer herself in the direction she wanted to go.

With the eyes of Godtherat boring holes in the back of her head, she pleaded, *"Don't let me die!"*

Kick. Kick. A little stronger.

Moving, uneasily but steadily. The crown of rock closer. Fifty feet away? She could make it. Then there was that other little piece of rock sticking up at the edge of one of the blinding shafts of light that came from holes in the roof of the grotto. Beyond the light, the entrance. The sky. A chance to live.

When she reached the crown, she rested, lips stinging painfully from the saltwater. The rock was so jagged that she couldn't pull herself out and examine the blanket to see how much, if any, water had leaked past the zipper closure. Maybe better not to know. She was going to pull this off. The entrance, beyond the shaft of sun like a pillar of heaven, was looking larger now. She was getting used to the water temperature but still shivered. The radiance just ahead inviting, biblical in portent; she felt that if she could paddle straight through the light she would be magically endowed. This was a fringe effect of delirium, but she didn't recognize the state she was in.

Now!

There were currents in the cavern she hadn't reckoned with. She had to kick harder to reach the sunbeam. And it was obvious by the time she was bathing in its brilliance and crucial warmth that the cushion she rode had settled lower into the water. How much farther? Blinking, edging out into the darkness again, she tried to estimate the remaining distance to the grotto entrance, and open water. There were no more little islets to grope for if she began to go under. Kick. *Kick*. The current carried her sideways despite her efforts to stay on course. Blaize could hear the waves breaking against the rocks outside the entrance to the cavern, but, this close, she knew she was in danger of being swept back in a wide arc, winding up even farther away than from where she had started. She fought the current, her legs tiring. She couldn't use her hands, needing to keep a tight grip on the submerged cushion. Twenty yards from the entrance, maybe less; but the strong inflow of the sea kept her bobbing against an invisible wall. Not losing yet, but running out of strength.

So close. She knew what she had to do, no matter what the risk.

Blaize caught the handle of the case between her teeth, freeing both hands; she paddled furiously, kicking despite a cramp in one foot. The action of her arms and hands freed her from the drag of the current and she popped out of the cavern like a cork from a bottle.

And went under immediately, swept at an angle and tumbled hard toward the cliff's face by an incoming wave. The wind of the Ionian was blowing fiercely.

She grabbed the cushion, but there was little bouyancy left. Her head broke the surface and she gasped. She screamed. She was carried down and banged against the rocks beneath the surface. She lost her grip on the cushion. The sea rolled back; she was above water and flailing, choking, in a panic as the trough deepened and then another wave began to swell, carrying her toward the cliff. Her vision had blurred: a salty smear of brown rock, dazzling sun, the churning white water.

And something bright orange hurtled past her head as the velocity of the wave rode her toward a bone-crushing finale against the rugged cliffs. She reached out instinctively, too choked to breathe anymore. Her fingers slid over tough Dacron line and her arm shot through the opening in a life preserver. Holding on to it, she was snatched back as the wave exploded over and through the rocks; she was inundated but pulled steadily backward, towed toward open water.

When her head came up again she saw through matted hair a striped, multi-colored spinnaker, the sun of late afternoon glaring through belled fabric; she saw the looming white bow of the twenty-three-foot sailboat, the man at the tiller wearing a Van Gogh peasant's straw hat that shaded all of his face. He tacked smartly to keep from going aground on the off-shore rocks and headed away from the island, Blaize hanging exhaustedly at the end of his line.

In easier waters he came about and alongside and hauled her aboard. She lay nearly naked at his feet, puking salt water copiously while he wrapped her in blankets. He gave her tepid tea in a thermos. The wind whistled and the sail cracked like gunshots.

"Thank God you're alive, daughter," the Marquis de Rienville said.

Blaize, sitting up, looked at him with stinging reddened

eyes as he sat in the stern with the tiller in one hand, line in the other, changing to a northwesterly course.

"Only Joanna knew—where I—"

"Yes. She told me what she had done with you. I came as soon as I could. Just made it, didn't I?"

"You're telling me," Blaize said fervently. She fought a tendency to dim out. She hung her head for a while, bracing herself against the motions of the sailboat as it clipped along in the brisk wind. Every time she moved, she was aware of a different bruise. She hurt all over. "Where—did you come from?"

"The *St. Affrique*. A chartered yacht. I have it moored off Antipaxos."

"Is Joanna there?"

"Not at the moment."

"I'm going to—use a skinning knife on her. I know how. Jordy showed me once. Squirrels, people—the technique's the same."

"You needn't bother. Joanna's life expectancy is very short as it is."

"You know—all about her?"

"Oh, yes, everything."

"I figured out—it had to be Joanna who went to bed with her father. The night he married Elizabeth."

"Yes. It was Joanna."

"Couldn't bear to—give him up. Looneytunes. But how drunk can a man be, doesn't know his own daughter? Roast in hell, the two of them. But the baby. Jesus. Why did she—have the baby?"

"A form of revenge. She hid the fact of her pregnancy from Coulouris until it was too late for him to do anything about it, short of having them both killed. So the unfortunate child was born."

"She'll do—worse. I don't understand—why you have anything to do with her."

Rienville glanced down at Blaize. His eyes swarmed in the deep night beneath his tied-down straw hat.

"She is going to kill her father for me."

"You're crazy too," Blaize said bitterly. "Why save me?"

"I had no reason to let you die, Blaize."

"I know too much."

"In a few days that won't matter. You will believe in my cause as I do. Because we are alike, my daughter."

"I'm not your daughter. I already have—all the difficult men in my life I can handle."

"You won't betray me," Rienville said calmly. "We can't hope to raise Antipaxos before dusk. Why don't you go below? There's food—clothes that should fit you. Fresh water to wash your hair."

Blaize the survivor, she thought. Abandoned by one maniac, rescued by another. What she most needed now was sleep: oblivion. But she couldn't give in to that need, she must stay awake. Because she didn't trust Rienville anymore than she trusted Joanna. She thought about food but wasn't hungry. She had kept down a pint of the sugared tea, but it had bloated her, given her gas. Washing her hair wasn't such a bad idea, though. At least the Marquis would be staying topside to handle the boat; she wouldn't have to talk to him. She got up, weary and wobbly, slid back the hatch cover, shed a couple of damp blankets. She glanced back at Rienville, fully expecting him to be staring at her ass, it was going to come to that sooner or later; but no, he was watching the sea and not her. He seemed almost to have forgotten she was aboard.

The clothes he had brought with him weren't much: a sportsman's medium-blue shirt with a lot of pockets and zippers and epaulets, a red windbreaker, some designer jeans with a man's button fly. Deck shoes a size too big. No underwear, of course. The clothing was laid out on one of the two small bunks built into the forward area of the hull. The galley in the cabin was small, but there was a stainless-steel sink, and hot water. A bottle of shampoo. She got suds all over everything with the boat skipping around the way it was, but the feel and scent of clean hair was luxurious. So was a generous shot of Chivas Regal from the master's locker. Blaize farted until her stuck-out abdomen returned to a nearly normal size and she was able to button up the French-cut dungarees. By then she was falling asleep on her feet and the light of day through the small ports was a vivid orange.

"Blaize?" Rienville called. The boat seemed to have slowed; wherever they were going, they were almost there.

Reluctantly she went topside and saw, across the darkening sea, a rim of sun; and, closer, only a hundred yards away, the stately three-masted schooner *St. Affrique,* moored in a crescent cove, olive groves and cypresses on the heights of the small island behind the ship. The scene was an all-too-trite picture postcard except for the boil of black smoke rising amidships on the *St. Affrique*. Rienville was frowning, standing up in the stern, the lines in his right hand.

"What in the name of—"

Blaize was looking at his face and not at the *St. Affrique* when she said, quietly, "Joanna." She had just gotten the word out when the yacht exploded, was engulfed in a fireball that gave back to them the glare of mid-afternoon and, two seconds later, a hot hurricane wind littered with shrapnel.

The shock wave hurled Blaize back and down into the cabin almost hard enough to break her neck. The little sailboat nearly rolled over. Everything that wasn't stowed away in the galley crashed on top of her. Debris from the explosion thudded and whanged against the hull.

When the violent rocking and pitching were over, she crawled painfully up the steps to the stern deck, saw a smoldering sail, saw what was left of the *St. Affrique* burning feebly on the beach. She did not see the Marquis de Rienville.

All she saw was his Van Gogh straw hat floating a few feet away in the water.

She remembered where he had put the boat hook after using it to help pull her aboard. With the boat hook she fished for the hat and brought it, limp and soggy, to the side of the boat, where she could reach down and pluck it off a swell.

There wasn't much light anymore, but she could tell the hat was soaked in blood as well as seawater. She felt something lumpish in the crown, turned the hat over and saw what must have been a full quarter of his head welded to the straw, a brackish lump of scalp, skull bone, macerated brain tissue.

Blaize put the hat carefully on the bench seat beneath the tiller and didn't look at it again. She had the presence of mind to throw out the anchor, which stopped the seaward drift of the sailboat. That exhausted her knowledge of boats. She stood quietly as night fell, watching lights bob in her direction, caiques from the islands of Paxos and Antipaxos, filled with the curious or would-be rescuers.

Chapter 31

Corfu

When Lucas McIver got back to Aravanis's farm estate, he fell into bed and slept for twenty hours straight. On Friday afternoon, five days after Joanna Coulouris and Axel Stroh had walked into the Church of St. Spyridon and snatched Niko, he came up from the depths to find the Leprechaun sitting on the side of his bed in the darkened room, looking somberly at him, rattling ice cubes in a tall, nearly empty glass.

"You don't put ice in your whiskey," McIver said.

"Of course not. This is *tzinzerbíra*, Lucas. Corfiote ginger beer, and quite good. I *have* managed to draw a few sober breaths this past week."

McIver sat up slowly, groaning. "Bad news?"

"Oh, no. We've been receiving hourly bulletins. Demetrios Constantine's condition remains the same. He is in a coma but responds to vigorous physical stimulation, to bright lights, to sharp sounds. Encouraging."

"It was a hell of a big blood clot. But that's what saved his life. The clot formed just in time."

"Perhaps when Ourania speaks to him—"

"Is she there now?"

"She leaves tonight."

"What about the boy?"

"There has been no word from Niko's kidnappers. Plato Melissani was buried yesterday. Argyros Coulouris was not present at the funeral. He took a flight from New York to Athens, alone, on Monday night. No one has seen or heard from him since his plane landed at Hellenikon Airport. Can you get up? Stavropoulous the landlord has been asking for you."

"Why?"

"He has been more than mildly agitated, awaiting your return." The Leprechaun did Stavropoulous with eerie precision: " 'Tell Lucas I gotta see him. Maybe it's important. But I dunno.' "

McIver groaned again. "Okay. Twenty minutes."

Walking down the single street of the village of Portais, McIver could see that considerable scarring remained from the raid. The blown-up Chevy Caprice had been towed away, the bomb crater filled in, but buildings opposite the church were smoke-blackened and windowless. Scaffolding had been erected over the entrance to the church. The doors were closed. Tourist police stood guard, for what reason he didn't know. Perhaps just to keep the curious from trying to enter, to stare at blood-drenched stones.

He stepped over the twitching mangy dog in the doorway of the *taverna* and called Stavropoulous, who came through a curtain of hanging plastic beads from a back room, munching on a sandwich.

"Whaddya say, Lucas? Hey, it's good to see you. Fix you one of these? Ever so often I get the urge, you know? Bacon, lettuce, mayo, white bread."

"No thanks, Stavro. You could pour me a drink."

"Somethin' heavy-duty? You're lookin' a little peak*ed,* you don't mind my sayin'."

"Retsina's okay."

"Yeah, grab a seat. I'll bring it over to you, pal."

"Where is everybody today?"

"Well, you know, officially the village is in mournin', and I ain't open for business yet. So I hear Demetri, he's gotta chance maybe."

"It's tricky. I couldn't make any predictions."

"This friggin' business, you know, it's got the wife half crazy. What kind of lunatics walk inna church, croak a priest like that? I mean what the fuck, I seen a few things in Brooklyn, like you are takin' your life in your hands goin' to some of the neighborhoods. Sure, I had 'em inna cab, guns against the back of my neck, fuckin' ice picks, sharpened screwdrivers. Gimme all you got, hopheads, crazies, the whole zoo. But this little place, hey! No way, you think."

Stavropoulous brought the remains of his BLT and two glasses of retsina on a tiny tray to the table McIver had chosen; McIver was staring at the flies wheeling almost at stall speed above the head of the pink and white mutt in the sunlit doorway.

"This business, what I regret *deeply*, you know, did I get one of 'em or not, him ridin' in the backseat of that Fiat. Make me feel better know I did the motherfuck some damage, right?"

"Yeah. *Pánta chára.*"

"*Epísis.*" Stavropoulous drank, finished his sandwich, licked an excess of mayo from his fingers. "What I need to see you about, Lucas, Demetri came to the *taverna* couple-three nights before this business, middle the night he shows up, lockbox only with no lock on it under his arm. About so big, big enough for a lunch, right? Don't say nothin' much, I pour him a drink, he's like too whipped to talk even. Sittin' right over there, that lockbox in his lap, and I'm thinkin' like, what's he got in there, a king's ransom or somethin'?"

"Maybe," McIver said, a glint of interest in his eyes. "Did he show you?"

"Nah, never did. Just kind of went to sleep there sittin' up; then his hand gave a jerk, you know, real spastic, knocked his glass ona floor, which woke him up. I told him, why don't you go home, catch some Z's, you're all in, Demetri. And he nods, like he don't have the stren'th to make it up the hill. But he gets as far as the door with that lockbox and then he turns like he's kinda forgot, gives me a little smile and holds the box out. 'Want you to keep this for me, Stavro,' he says. Yeah, sure. Then he goes, like, 'Anything happens to me, give it to Lucas, he'll know what to do with it.' So I go

Whaddaya mean, anythin' happen? But Demetri, he don't say nothin' else except—oh yeah, he's leavin', see, walkin' up the street, just draggin' ass is more like it, then he turns and says like how it's slipped his mind but it's important, 'Don't open the thermos, Stavro; your fingers'll fall off.' "

"What thermos?"

"In the box, I guess. I stashed it behind the bar, and then all this bad shit comes down, and you're flyin' off in the chopper with Demetri, and I don't have a chance to tell you what he wanted me to tell you."

"Why don't you get that box?" McIver said.

It was enameled gray metal, with two chrome catches and a little chrome handle that lay in a depression in the lid when it wasn't needed. Like a lunch box, as Stavropoulous had said. McIver undid the catches and lifted the lid. Inside there was a Duraflask; McIver had seen several of them in Aravanis's lab and knew what they were used for. There was also a cassette tape.

"That's all?" Stavropoulous asked, disappointed.

McIver was very quiet for a couple of minutes, looking contemplative, a trace of awe in his expression. "What I think is in that bottle will save—maybe—half a billion lives over the next three years."

Stavropoulous whistled; the dog in the doorway gave him a look.

"Jesus! How do you know so much about what it is?"

"Because Aravanis explained it to me. It's dried embryonic tissue cultures. For new types of blight-impervious corn and wheat seeds." McIver put the cassette tape in his jacket pocket and closed the lid of the box. "Here, Stavro, put it back."

"Behind the bar? What're you, kiddin' me or somethin', Lucas? Half a billion lives, that's valuable shit."

"The cultures will be as safe here as anywhere I can think of. Until I know what I'm supposed to do with them. I'll be back later. I need to listen to this tape."

McIver and the Leprechaun both listened.

"Play this for Niko," Aravanis's voice said at the beginning of the tape. "Record what he has to tell you."

There followed numerous brief musical selections, each a few bars in length, from fugues, concertos, operas. The Leprechaun identified the overtures from *Samson and Delilah* and *Tannhaüser*, and the "Ritorna Vincitor" aria from *Aïda*. He recognized most of the Bach chamber music and the first notes of "The Rites of Spring." Other pieces were more obscure. But it was obvious what the musical selections were for.

"These are the passwords," the Leprechaun said.

"Yeah. Everything Aravanis knows about Cirenaica, *El Invicto, Niko-B*. He stored the information where he thought it would always be safe. How could he figure they'd take Niko? You know something? I'm not so sure now why they took him either."

"For a trade, obviously."

"Then why hasn't Minotaur been calling?"

"That too is obvious. Aravanis is in a well-publicized coma and unable to deal with anybody. We know that Minotaur already has a stock of *El Invicto* tissue cultures, stolen from Aravanis's colleagues. It should bring a fancy price from desperate world governments once the destructive potential of Cirenaica becomes reality."

"If all Minotaur wants is money, they don't need the boy. Unless of course they know what he's carrying around in his head and have the key to retrieve it." McIver thoughtfully weighed the tape cassette in one hand.

"No," the Leprechaun said after a few moments. "I can't accept that hypothesis. I don't think either Demetrios Constantine or Ourania have discussed Niko's remarkable mnemonic ability with anyone. I found out about it quite by accident, if you recall." The Leprechaun went to the window of the bedroom in which they had been listening to the tape, stood gazing out unseeingly at the hillside vineyards, hands clasped behind his back. "I've come to be very fond of Niko," he said, a catch in his voice. "We must, I assume, prepare ourselves for the possibility that he has been disposed of."

"I don't think he's dead," McIver objected. "In fact, I

have a hunch that Niko ties in with Minotaur in a way we don't know a damned thing about yet."

"Should we bring this tape to Ourania's attention, then?"

"She has enough on her mind already. She's flying to Athens in a couple of hours. She's a damn fine woman, but she's never been the star of a circus before. Actium has two lawyers for every government investigator on the case, but nobody'll give her a minute's peace. And when she sees her husband—I've tried to get her ready for that one, but—"

"Shouldn't you accompany her, Lucas?"

"So far this is just a kidnapping by suspected international terrorists, an oblique shot at the Actium oligopoly, which is a concept the press is familiar with and therefore can handle without difficulty. I was just an innocent bystander. I used my Robert B. Painter alias. I didn't give the guys with the motor-driven Leicas and the minicams any good angles on me. But if I go back I'm going to arouse suspicions somewhere; one of the journalists will start digging and before you know it, I'm blown. Maybe, if I were the clever fellow I like to think I am, I'd take this opportunity to say good-bye and get the hell out of Greece."

"But you want to get Niko back as much as I do. If there's any chance he's still alive."

There was a knock at the door. Ourania called, "Lucas, are you sleeping? There is someone here who insists on speaking to you."

"Tell him I'm coming," McIver told her. To the Leprechaun he said, "The government of Greece never sleeps. Once you kick it awake." He held out the tape. "Better make a safety of this. Probably some blank tapes in Niko's room."

Ourania was waiting for him in the hall. She was on Valium; her mother and a sister were staying with her in the house, and neither was the type to wring her hands or moan a lot. They kept Ourania occupied.

"It's good to have you back," she said to McIver.

"It's good to see you again, Ourania."

"Will the doctors lie to me?"

"No."

"Will my husband know me?"

"I think he'll recognize your voice. There'll be a reaction. The more you talk to him, the better."

Ourania nodded, said, "The man is waiting on the veranda." She hesitated; sometimes her mind stalled that way, for four or five seconds; her gaze just drifted. "Oh! I know what I should tell you. He knows you by your correct name."

"Not from the government?"

"A friend of a friend, he says." Ourania stood on her toes and held a hand high above her head. "*This* tall. And from Western movies, I think. Not a cowboy, but the one who owns everything. The town. The water rights."

McIver went outside. Pard Randolph turned from admiring the view of the strait and smiled. He was wearing a twill suit with leather piping and fancy-stitch boots. He held a tan dress Stetson in one hand. McIver noticed the canary-yellow pinkie diamond. For sure he owned the water rights, McIver thought.

"Had a sight of trouble gettin' up here. All the roadblocks. Good thing I carry credentials for all occasions, includin' my diplomatic passport."

"From the sovereign State of Texas?"

Pard laughed. "Pard Randolph's my name. Can I call you Luke?"

"Supposing we get on a first-name basis, then what do you want?"

"Be at ease, young fella." He had a slight chronic wheeze, or maybe it was the altitude. "I don't mean you any harm. I come up here at Blaize's request. She wants to see you."

"Blaize Ellington? Where is she?"

"Waitin' down in Corfu Town."

Jesus Christ, McIver thought. *What next*? "I don't think she'd better wait any longer for me."

"Blaize allowed you'd be a leetle difficult. But she's there by herself, ain't no thunderin' herd behind her. Pure luck she happened to discover your whereabouts. She'll explain later."

"I don't want to see Blaize Ellington. So long, Pard. I've got a lot on my mind."

"Don't we all. I've been followin' the whole rumpus in the newspaper." He patted a folded copy of the international *Herald-Tribune* in a pocket of his Western-style suit jacket.

"That explosion in the sea south of here? Blew up the yacht *St. Affrique* and killed all hands, 'cludin' that big grain dealer, Rienville from France? Maybe you heard about it. But I don't believe anybody's made the connection yet."

"Connection with what?"

"Those two loonies call themselves Minotaur. Snatched the boy up this way Sunday last? Won't mention any names 'cause I don't think it's common knowledge yet who the woman is."

McIver just stared at the big man for a time, out of reach although not out of range of the quick-draw knife; but his suspicion of an assassination attempt had faded slowly. Pard just stood blue-eyed easy and continued to smile. He had a lot of confidence in himself, and an uncanny ability to communicate trust.

"Blaize just missed goin' up with the yacht herself. Seems like she's had a rough week. And it ain't over yet."

"So what's the connection you're talking about?"

"They did it. Minotaur. The big one, he goes by the name of Axel Stroh. The woman, she was a friend of Blaize's for years until Blaize accidentally got a little too close to findin' out what they were up to. Anyhow, Blaize says she thinks she knows where they're holed up at, probably got the boy with 'em too."

"Where?"

"Reckon you'll need to come on down to Corfu Town with me, ask her that yourownself."

Chapter 32

Corfu Town

She was waiting for him on the Listón, a long building with an arcade façade; the French had built it to resemble the Rue de Rivoli in Paris. It faced the bay-side esplanade, a sizable park with a scruffy cricket pitch the British had left behind after their colonial period. Just north of the esplanade was the Venetian-built quarter called Old Town. The Venetians had been around for more than four centuries, so a couple of hundred years later a lot of the Corfiotes still looked more Italian than Greek.

Blaize Ellington looked like she had been out in the sun too long. But it wasn't sunburn. Her eyebrows had been singed too. Although the sun had set a few minutes ago, she was still wearing dark glasses.

McIver said, "How far were you from the *St. Affrique* when it blew?"

"I think about a hundred yards. It was like a war movie. A mushroom cloud. But seeing a movie doesn't give you any idea of what it's really like. All of a sudden there's this wind, and it's red-hot. And big pieces of junk, traveling so fast you don't even see them. I landed on the back of my neck on the cabin floor. I don't know what hit the Marquis. His body hasn't turned up yet. If there's anything left to find."

"How's your neck now?"

"It hurts like hell. At the hospital they gave me muscle relaxants. But I don't want to take anything that might make me groggy. I've got a score to settle."

They were sitting at a small table outdoors on the Listón, McIver with his back to the wall and with a view of the old fort in Garitsa Bay. There was no wind and it wasn't chilly yet. There were a lot of strollers on the Listón, good smells from the food shops. Some pretty girls in blue-plaid school blazers giggled at a table near theirs. Blaize sat with the immobility of the aged, but her head moved slightly to track the progress of a horse-drawn carriage on a nearby street. She winced. She turned back carefully to look at McIver. She might have been staring at him or she might have fallen asleep, he couldn't tell. The dark glasses.

"I feel like I've borrowed a couple of lives I'm going to have to pay back someday," she said.

"You've had your share of luck, that's all."

"How do you feel about luck?"

"Wouldn't be here without it."

"I don't know if I should press mine now, or forget it."

"Where do you think they are?"

"Ithaca. The convent of Aja Karía. It's where she had Niko. Now she's got him back. Outside of the fact that it's a perfect place to hide for a while—hardly anybody goes there—it seems like the logical place to complete the psychodrama she's been acting out for most of her life."

"Let the Greek government take it from here, Blaize."

"Uh-uh."

"Why not?"

"In addition to the Mother Superior, there are maybe a dozen nuns in the convent. The least little thing goes wrong, they could all be killed. This guy Joanna's with, Axel Stroh? I've seen him once, through a telephoto lens. I don't know his history, but sometimes you can read everything you need to know about a person in one glance. Look at the job that was done on the *St. Affrique*. They've had plenty of time to rig the whole convent with explosives. Don't think they won't gladly die if they're cornered, blow that whole cliff into the sea."

"What do you want to do, then?"

"I think seeing me might throw Joanna off, just enough. I ought to have time for one shot. Through the head."

McIver let it ride for a time, sipping coffee, watching a married couple having a spirited but not heated argument as they walked along. McIver felt, strangely, envious. He looked again at Blaize.

"It's not for me," he said.

"Okay. I'll go with Pard."

"I presume he gets to handle Axel Stroh while you're croaking his schizo girlfriend. Little long in the tooth, isn't he?"

"Pard's been there before, at nut-cutting time. I might worry about me, but I wouldn't worry about him. He's one of two people in this world I trust completely."

McIver was going to let that one ride too, but he couldn't resist. "I'm the other one?"

"You're it, friend."

"Blaize, I think—"

"What?"

"I think this whole business is so bizarre that neither of us can look at it objectively. And then there's the problem of what went on between us for so many years. Our perceptions of each other aren't all that accurate. Neither of us is the hero we feel we should try to be. The bad guys win too often in real life, Blaize. Maybe you can get closer to Joanna than a Greek SWAT team; but then the gun doesn't go off or you drop it on your foot or you just stand there aiming and can't pull the trigger because you're too busy chewing crap. I'm not much of a fighter and I don't give a damn what happens to Axel Stroh, really. I do care about Niko. His origins are sad, but there are two people who don't have to know where he came from. All they know is they love him and he needs them. And if I do something dumb or don't think fast enough on my feet, the boy could die. Do I want that responsibility?"

Blaize slowly took off her dark glasses and folded them, laid them on the table. She looked up at McIver, her eyes, hazel, paled further by the brick tones of her skin but picking up from somewhere a patina of gold, an inner light of conviction that could send armies marching.

"Yes," she said, "I think you do. So why don't we get on with it?"

Chapter 33

Ithaca

There were six of them, finally, in the Gazelle helicopter that flew south at two thousand feet over the dark sea of Poseidon: the chopper pilot; Ed Nikitiadas; the Leprechaun; and Blaize and Pard and McIver. Between Ithaca and Cephalonia, they followed the long channel to Ithaca's south coast, where the convent of Aja Karía, highest point of the island, was a gleaming bone-white against the midnight sky. The nearly full moon, by contrast, looked like a dried cake of goat cheese, grayish with curds of yellow. By the time they were in sight of the convent they were down to two hundred feet, a hundred feet off the cliffs, close enough to see the shadowed pockmarks and wavy striations in the dun-colored rock, the bitten-off places where tons of cliff had cascaded into the sea during the last big earthquake, the many small cave openings where waves dashed up in spume. There were offshore rocks and sheltered coves where a boat the size of the *Phaistos* could safely be moored, unnoticed unless someone was making a dedicated effort to locate it.

Ed Nikitiadas operated the powerful hot-blue spotlight under the helicopter, aiming it at water level along the cliff at the base of the convent.

"There it is," Blaize said on the second pass. They had missed it the first time because the dark-hulled speedboat was anchored stern-to on a small wedge of protected sand beach and rode so low in the backwater there that it looked like one of many chunks of rock that had fallen from the heights.

"Okay," Nikitiadas said. "What do we do about it? Blow it now, or wait?"

Pard said, "Best you wait 'til we give you the word to go after it. Like Blaize says, there's nuns in that convent could be in a bad hostage situation."

The Gazelle flew around to the west side of the island again, then headed inland and up the mountain, landing in a clearing near the temple ruins Blaize had visited less than a week earlier. The area was deserted; there was not so much as a cottage along the road to the convent. Pard and McIver carried walkie-talkies. Under her sweater Blaize wore, courtesy of Pard, a version of the .45 ACP that she had lost in Chicago.

The Texan's choice of weapon was a Micro Uzi machine pistol. McIver took a .38 Special loaded with Hydra-Shoks; he was no marksman. They each had a thirty-thousand-candlepower Mag Lite. Pard carried sixty feet of coiled Dacron rope attached to a Teflon-coated grappling hook.

"Perhaps I should go along," the Leprechaun ventured.

"Why?" McIver said. "The last thing we need is a crowd."

"It *has* been a considerable time—but I believe I am the only one amongst us experienced at second-story work. From the looks of the place, it is a skill that may prove useful. So may my modest knowledge of the Greek language."

"That's not bad thinking," Pard allowed.

They walked up the rocky road in single file, not using their flashlights, guided by the moon, by the emerging walls of the convent shining through dark cypress. The wind was loud enough to cover the sounds of their progress. But McIver doubted that the helicopter scouting the cliff had gone unnoticed. It would be exceedingly dumb to hope, at this point, that they were not expected.

The Leprechaun had borrowed a dark-blue knitted cap from the chopper pilot. He turned his windbreaker, which had a dark lining, inside out. Beneath the high outer wall of the convent he took off his shoes and socks.

"I'll do the climbing," he said. "I'm a smaller target, if it comes to that. Wait there in the shadows of the trees. Give me a few minutes."

With a penknife the Leprechaun cut eyeholes in the fabric of the cap and pulled it down over his chin. He had found a tin of powdered graphite in the helicopter's tool case and used some of it now to blacken the backs of his hands, his throat and his feet. He took the grappling hook from Pard and swung it neatly up over the ten-foot wall. The Teflon barbs dug deeply into the soft limestone. The others retreated to the stand of cypress opposite the gates and the Leprechaun went boldly up the wall, flattened against the top for a moment or two and then dropped into the courtyard. McIver's teeth were on edge as he waited for a rattle of machine-gun fire. But they heard nothing.

"What I haven't figured out," Blaize said in a low voice, "is why they decided they didn't need Rienville anymore. His motives were as important as Joanna's. He did more than just encourage Minotaur. Hell, he was in control, a psychological force, the authority figure Minotaur needed to obey."

"Maybe," McIver said, having already given the matter a lot of thought, "the acting-out of ritual and myth created a power that was greater than his power over Minotaur. Separate the two of them, you might be able to deal with each one. Together, they don't think, they act from impulse; and that impulse is to destroy whatever might threaten Minotaur's notions of immortality. I don't know what motivated Minotaur before, but I think now all it wants is to live forever."

"Why did Joanna take Niko?"

"I don't know. Try this: he was born of an incestuous relationship with her father. Maybe that gives Niko symbolic value to Minotaur."

"I think you just got tangled up in a big snarl of complexes."

"What the hell, maybe she just wanted to give him back to her father. What's keeping Leprechaun?"

They waited tensely for another full minute. McIver had made up his mind to follow the Leprechaun over the wall when they heard the gates of the convent creaking open. He appeared quickly, motioning to them. They ran over and joined him.

"What's going on?" Blaize whispered. "Where are they?"

The Leprechaun just shook his head. "Follow me."

He led them beneath the huge plane tree to the chapel on the other side of the courtyard. Candles flickered inside. Nuns were praying; some wept softly. One of the Sisterhood approached the Leprechaun, glanced at the gun in Pard's hand and began to protest. The Leprechaun quieted her.

"Where's the Reverend Mother?" Blaize said, looking around.

"They have her," the Leprechaun said. He spoke again, in Greek, to the tall nun, listened to her reply, frowning, not understanding every word. He turned back to the others. "This is what happened. They came by boat, as we know, with the boy, who was bound in some kind of hamper or wicker trunk. They came up through the caves that form a continuous passage from the sea to the ossuary beneath the museum across the way. They will kill the *Kathigumeni Kekilia* unless the nuns provide them with food and give them full protection. The Sister is trying to persuade us to leave before they find out we're here. They will be merciless, she says. Already they have taken the silver coffin that contained the remains of the sainted founder of this Order, dumping the bones on the floor of the ossuary."

"Took a coffin?" Pard said. "What for?"

"We don't know."

"So they're holed up in a cave with the Mother Superior as hostage," McIver said. "Now what?"

"Maybe this wasn't such a great idea," Blaize said.

"Now wait a minute," Pard objected. "We're here, so let's think this thing out."

The tall nun was talking again, arguing, using her hands to get her point across to the Leprechaun. Blaize watched her, then said to McIver, "Sister Blaize is going down in the cave to see Joanna."

"What?"

The Leprechaun turned his head, leaving the tall nun speechless in mid-sentence. Then they were all looking at Blaize. It was enough to give her stage fright, but she said, calmly enough, "The Sister's about my size. Tell her I need a habit like hers."

"Big chance, Blaize," Pard said doubtfully.

"I know, I *know*. Leave me alone and let's get it over with. I want to get out of this place."

Blaize was dressed in fifteen minutes. She felt awkward and strangely intrusive in the costume she had borrowed from the tall nun. There was no place for the .45. She had to carry it in one hand, concealed inside the full sleeve opposite.

As soon as she was ready, she joined the others outside the museum. McIver was talking to Ed Nikitiadas on the walkie-talkie. Blood was pounding in Blaize's ears and temples; her face felt hotter than ever. But the steel of the automatic was reassurance, of a sort. If she could bring herself to use the weapon.

The Leprechaun talked again with the tall nun. "The ossuary lies below the museum. There's an opening in the cave wall, a barred gate. But it wasn't padlocked earlier today when two of the Sisters took food and medicine down to them."

"Where are they?"

"In a big chamber at the base of a rather steep passage; no more than a large wormhole, actually. You'll have to stoop and feel your way along. But there are torches in the chamber."

"Take a walkie-talkie with you," McIver said.

"How the hell am I going to carry a walkie-talkie too? Thanks, I'd rather have the gun."

"Soon as you signal us, we'll come runnin'," Pard assured her.

"How do I do that?"

"Shoot somethin'," Pard said.

The hole in the ground called the ossuary was bad enough, smelling mustily of religion, of candle wax; in addition to being a burial place it was a treasure house of icons and old triptychs that had weathered the centuries well in the cool dry air. But there was a pile of rusty cloth and bones in one corner, a limestone pedestal for a coffin that was missing. Blaize shuddered, but what really gave her the horrors was the route to the lower depths, a dark, gated crevice in one wall. She would have backed out, but the men were right behind her, expecting her to do just that. And she knew it was the best chance they were going to have, without sacrificing several lives.

But it's *Joanna*. Poor hopeless blundering Joanna Coulouris, with the droopy eyes and the pouts and the knack of always saying something malapropos. The girl with the daddy complex she couldn't get over or around.

"Blaize?" Pard said softly.

"I'm all right," she told him, clearing her throat so she could breathe. She opened the gate slowly and entered the passage. Looking down, she couldn't see a thing at first. The nun's black shoes were too narrow and pinched her feet. She bumped her head against the ceiling of the passage and was forced to hunch over painfully as she edged her way down.

After about fifteen seconds of what she had perceived as total darkness she was able to make out a flickering yellow light, the opening of the cavern that lay a hundred feet below.

It was quiet down there, so quiet she was conscious of the sound of every pebble dislodged and sent rolling by her feet. Her throat was parched from fear, she needed to cough. The footing was so uncertain she lurched from one side of the cramped passage to the other. "Wormhole" described it perfectly. She had a sudden, chilling flashback to her nightmarish time in the hospital in Chicago. Visions exploded and fizzled in front of her eyes. It wasn't Joanna she was going to meet in these lower depths, it was her brother Jordan with the red pucker on his forehead. Blaize felt as if she were twelve years old and cringed at the expectation of her brother's wrath. Because she'd had the chance to kill Lucas McIver and hadn't done it. She'd betrayed the family honor.

She could no longer control her breathing; she inhaled and exhaled with noisy fervor. The walls had been tight before, but now they really closed in. Almost no elbow room. And instead of getting closer, the chamber toward which she was nearly crawling had receded to the smallness of a star in space.

I am Sister Blaize, I am Sister Blaize, my god is not Godtherat, my God is just; surely His goodness and mercy. . . .

She tripped and fell and went howling painfully head over heels to the floor of the torchlit chamber, where she lay on her back trying to see through a whirling mass of fuzzy stars, afraid she had broken something. Or lost something. But what was it she had lost?

Small hands touching her face, her shoulders. Trying to help her up.

Blaize turned her head. The pain brought jets of tears. She saw the bloodless face of the *Kathigumeni Kekilia*, reminiscent of all the praying saints in the triptychs upstairs but without the obligatory golden halo.

"Reverend Mother, are you all right?"

A slight nod. "But who are you?"

"You don't remember me? I was here just—"

Blaize sat up then, more or less with the Mother Superior's frail assistance. The cavern was an uneven place, roughly oblong, the size of an airplane hangar, stalactites like massive stone chandeliers. There were torches in iron brackets near the entrance, deep shadows elsewhere. Many braziers stood smokily upright around a massive silver coffin. Above the coffin, mounted on a pikestaff, was the horned mask of the Minotaur.

But who was that in the coffin?

Blaize got to her feet. As she took a step toward the coffin her foot hit something on the floor, and metal clinked against stone. She bent over to look at it. That was what she had lost: the .45 automatic. She picked it up, looked back at the Mother Superior.

"Where's Joanna?"

The old woman shook her head slowly, gesturing toward the back of the big cavern.

"They went to their boat—for supplies. They will return."

Blaize walked unsteadily across the rough floor to the coffin, gun in hand. Now with a jolt she recognized the corpse.

"Our benefactor," the Mother Superior said in her faint voice.

"Good Lord! When did he die?"

"Two days ago. He came here. He waited. He said he knew his daughter would come too. He had a pistol with him. But when Joanna appeared and he saw her—" The Mother Superior clutched her habit at the level of her heart, head nodding forward.

"Heart attack?" Blaize turned back to the coffin. The resting place of the sainted bones on the floor of the ossuary upstairs. The ornate coffin must have weighed several hundred pounds, she thought. How had Joanna and Stroh managed to move it down through the tight passage? It was a feat of strength for six strong men.

Closer to the coffin, to the body of Argyros Coulouris, she could smell the smoke from the coals of the braziers. A good thing. Because there were patches of spoilage already on the once-handsome face. Now all that she found recognizable was the hawkish nose. His eyes were closed, but there was a grimace of terror etched in the meager flesh.

"Fire, fire," the Reverend Mother croaked, but Blaize was too absorbed to pay much attention to her. Her eyes were attracted to the shaggy bull's mask, the head three times the size of a human head, that loomed over the casket. The realistic glass eyes reflecting torchlight: a fearful, pagan thing. From his expression Coulouris's final sleep could not be restful. What hell did he find himself in now?

"*Fire*!"

Blaize frowned, and then she got it; the Reverend Mother was calling *her*—but she hadn't gotten the name quite right.

Trying to get Blaize's attention before it was too—

Blaize jerked around, ignoring all the shooting pains in her abused body.

And there was Joanna, coming toward her, dopey Joanna all dressed up sort of like Wonder Woman, except that she was bare-breasted and oiled all over and shapely with iron muscle like the just-crowned winner of a, what did they call it in body-building, a pose-off? Painted, too, stripes and curlicues and deep dark-blue pockets around the eyes. She wore feathers, and a fur-trimmed gauntlet on her right hand and sandals that laced to the knees. A little gold loincloth on a G-string completed her costume.

Unless you counted the double-bladed ax in her hand as part of the costume.

Blaize didn't; or at least instinctively she knew a lethal weapon when she saw one, and she backed off even as her mind tried to grapple with all aspects of this incredible getup and the sheer size of the *labrys,* which was, judging by the bulges in Joanna's right forearm and biceps, God knew how heavy.

"Joanna," Blaize said, "I'm sorry about your father."

Something about the way Joanna had been moving, light-footed, supernatural in her confidence, should have told Blaize it wasn't any use to try to fuck around, stall, be reasonable. She saw no mourning in the woman's eyes, no spark of human response. Joanna leaped at her, the ax coming around in a big flashing arc above her head, and down.

Blaize fell behind the coffin, and the ax whanged through an inch of solid iron, decapitating a brazier, showering Joanna with red-hot coals.

The oil on her body made excellent fuel; she was instantly outlined in blue flame like a tidbit in a chafing dish. Her abundant hair flashed, exploded, and was consumed. She whirled around once, soundlessly, the huge ax falling from her hands and ringing against the side of the casket. For a moment she hung over the edge of the casket, her roasted, hairless head an inch from the dead face of her father. Then she began an aimless, hissing flame-dance around the cavern, flinging out a blackened arm, a fire-tipped foot. The hissing now a thin, drawn-out screech of rats.

Blaize took aim and shot her dead. But it took three shots, the last one in the center of her face, to put Joanna Coulouris down for good.

Blaize was still standing near the coffin with the .45 in a double grip when the Mother Superior gained her attention by pulling at her habit. She pointed.

On a dark promontory at the far end of the cavern, Axel

Stroh stood looking down at the smoldering body. He had Niko clutched in both arms.

Lucas McIver came up behind the motionless Blaize and together they watched what was left of the pathological entity known as Minotaur.

Dimly they heard the sounds of the helicopter.

Stroh turned and stepped down out of sight with the boy.

"I'm going after him," McIver said.

Blaize followed, but the voluminous habit slowed her, tripped her. McIver was far ahead, climbing up to where they had last seen Axel Stroh, when the potent blue spotlight of the helicopter flashed inside the cavern. The racket of the rotors was deafening.

When she reached McIver, who was crouched atop a slab of quartz, he put out a hand to stop her. Blaize knelt shivering beside him and looked down.

Axel Stroh was only about fifteen feet away, standing at the very edge of an opening in the cave wall, a seven-foot doorway above the slash of the sea below. Filling that doorway, almost, the boy quiet against his chest. Blue light poured on them from the helicopter hovering fifty feet off the cliff's face. Axel Stroh's eyes were half-closed, his face bluntly shadowed in a way that reminded Blaize, unpleasantly, of the face of the monster in the old Frankenstein movies that still turned up on the late late show.

"My God," she said in McIver's ear. "He'll fall!"

"Maybe he thinks he can fly," McIver said as Stroh's shoulders lifted and he craned his neck, trying to get a look at the bothersome helicopter directly behind him. With Stroh's head turned, McIver took the opportunity to slide down the quartz ledge. His hands were free.

"No, don't, don't!" Blaize pleaded, but she couldn't be heard above the noise of the chopper.

Axel Stroh took a half-step backward, all the space he had left.

In the blinding light, something came dangling down from the wall of the convent above Stroh, like a big squat spider on invisible silk.

Stroh stepped off into space with Niko.

The grappling hook took him under the chin as he started to fall, and he hung there, feet kicking.

McIver jumped and was at the edge of the doorway, reaching out with both hands as Stroh let go of Niko. He caught the boy by one arm and did a precarious balancing act as Stroh twisted in the air, the prong of the grappling hook stabbing through the soft underflesh of his chin. Blood gushed from Stroh's open mouth.

Fifty feet above him, where the snubbed Dacron line crossed the parapet, the Leprechaun looked at Pard Randolph and said, "Lucas has the boy. What do we do with Stroh? Pull him up?"

"Be at it all night," Pard grumbled. "And I don't think it's gonna matter to him nohow." There was a Bowie knife in Pard's hand. He brought it down smartly on the taut line, which parted.

"Fish food," Pard said. He picked up a walkie-talkie in his other hand. "We're goin' below to see if we can be of any help!" he said to the chopper. "Pick us up outside the convent gates, time we were goin' home."

In the cavern McIver checked the dazed Niko. It was obvious they had kept him drugged. He would be able to walk, McIver decided, as long as someone kept a tight grip on him.

"He'll be fine," McIver said to Blaize. It was quieter now, the helicopter having flown up and over the convent to land. "Niko can go home. With a little luck, he won't remember much of this."

"That's it, then?" she said.

"It's over, Blaize."

She drew a deep breath.

"Then I guess the only thing left is to settle up with you, McIver."

When he looked at her, he saw that she still had the .45 in her hand. She wasn't smiling.

But then Blaize never had been one to smile a lot.

Epilogue

Singapore

The operation was more complicated than the surgical team had anticipated. It lasted a little longer than four hours. The waxlike tumors, clustered around the breastbone, were laced with neurofibromas and aberrant blood vessels. Epinephrine constricted the blood vessels, which slowed the copious bleeding. But the heart of the small fourteen-year-old girl was not strong. A ganglionic blocker helped to reduce her blood pressure, minimize the risk of cardiac arrest, while the surgeon tirelessly snipped away at the rubbery tissue. It had not been possible to tell from the X rays if the vital nerve complex of the solar plexus had been invaded by the rioting cells that had produced the mass of bone and cyst deforming the patient's chest. An added complication: one imprecise cut in the area where he was working could maim or kill the girl.

She had come from a Kuala Lumpur slum. A charity case, of course, chosen for the rarity of the affliction. It was a teaching hospital, and Singapore, a flyspeck of an island at the tip of the Malay Peninsula, was a rich place. Sebarok University was well-endowed. It could afford the latest in high-tech equipment. But in this case, it was old-fashioned skill with scissors and scalpel that counted.

In the OR locker room afterward, he reviewed the operation with the half-dozen surgical residents who had been on the floor with him. "Nice work, doctor," they said. They were respectful. He was one of the best.

Yeah, McIver thought on his way from the hospital complex in Queenstown to his hillside home in Fragrant Isle. I do nice work, don't I? Traffic, as usual, was heavy around Tiger Balm Gardens, Singapore's Disneyland, and on the West Coast Road. One of the fastest-growing cities in the world, and one of the best-managed, but still, there probably wasn't any place on earth that could keep up with the demands the automobile made, particularly where several hundred thousand prosperous families could afford two or three of them.

He liked Singapore. It was clean. Because of the nearness of the sea, the equatorial climate wasn't a burden. This was the longest he had been in one place since he was a child. Singapore suited his needs. And it was a hell of a long way from Lexington, Kentucky.

Four years.

The world had settled down from the near-fatal shock of the Cirenaica spore. There had been crop failures. And riots, and insurrections. And during the darkest time, a three-month period when surplus food had been as scarce and valuable as gold, there had been three hundred thousand deaths a day from malnutrition, in all of those marginal countries where subsistence was the rule even when conditions were good.

Then the new crops had ripened, grown from the new strains, *El Invicto* and *Niko-B* and their many cousins. And cropland had been developed from land previously too poor or too salty to support growth. Heroic work by Demetrios Constantine Aravanis and his colleagues had prevented the ultimate disaster.

This past year, Aravanis had been rewarded for his work with a Nobel prize.

He'd had a little something to do with that, McIver thought, and it felt good. Although not as good as being in the operating room. Learning every day. Getting better. A surgeon.

He turned onto the Rainbow Serpent Road, looking forward to that first cold drink of the day, gin-and-bitters, on the garden terrace of his Indonesian-style house. There would be time for a jog down the road to the simmering sea, a sunset swim in his pool.

Four good years. And maybe he'd become a little too complacent, careless as well.

They took him as he walked into the breezy bamboo house, across the teak-paved entryway. Two big revolvers on either side of his head. He didn't have a chance to call to the Thai houseboy to get his drink ready.

"Welcome home, Dr. McIver."

He didn't try to get a look at them; they didn't matter anyway. Only their guns mattered. He willed himself to relax. "Just take it easy. Where is he?"

"In the garden room," one of them said. An accent. Chinese, maybe.

"Okay." If all they wanted to do was kill him, they would have shot him down as he stepped out of his car in the parking circle. So Buford wanted to talk. To gloat over his long-delayed triumph. "Let's go," McIver said to the gunmen.

The Leprechaun was in the shady garden room bound to a chair. High ceiling fans enhanced the incoming breeze. The little man tried to smile when McIver was escorted in.

"Sorry, old sweetheart. Let my guard down, didn't I? Growing flabby upstairs."

"Forget it," McIver said. Suddenly he had no patience with the men who had entered his house with guns. He was sick of the sight of guns.

A peacock screeched by the fish pool outside. Buford Ellington clumped in from the deck that overlooked the garden. Behind him there was a tranquil blue line of ocean visible through purple bougainvillea and pong pong trees. Buford set the rubber tips of his crutches on the terrazzo floor and leaned forward. The suit he wore was too heavy for this tropical climate. He was sweating. He looked old. He looked unwell. But this was the supreme moment of his life.

"Why," McIver said, "couldn't you just leave us alone?"

"You filthy son of a bitch," Buford said. "You think you got a right to live?"

"You're not going to kill me," McIver said. "So sit down and take a load off. Or get the hell out of my home."

"I'm gonna kill you, all right," Buford said. "Make no mistake about that."

"But you want to wait and do it in front of Blaize. Is that it?"

McIver looked around at the gunmen. Four of the bastards. One Asiatic he might or might not have seen in the vicinity of the hospital for the past week or so. He guessed there just wasn't any place far enough removed from Lexington, Kentucky.

He heard Blaize's Nissan wagon on the crushed-shell drive. They all heard it. Nobody moved. McIver clenched a fist, but he didn't know what he was going to do. The Leprechaun raised an eyebrow slightly. Four guns. Too many.

Blaize came into the house calling, "Mac?" And he answered, "Back here. There's company, honey."

Blaize walked in, a shopping bag in one hand. She saw her father first. The gunmen didn't seem to matter too much to her. She stared long and hard at Buford, who licked his lips and offered a smile.

"Oh, fuck," Blaize said.

The towheaded, three-year-boy at Blaize's side looked up at her, puzzled, and then at McIver.

"That's not a good word, is it?"

McIver smiled. "Mom just says that sometimes, when she's having a bad day."

The boy looked at Blaize again, uncertainly. "Is it a bad day?"

"Why don't you go over there and ask your grandfather that, Jordan Lucas?"

The boy's freckled face opened up in a big grin. "Jordan Lucas! How come you call me that?"

"Go, Jordy Luke," Blaize said in a gentler voice.

But the boy wouldn't budge. Shy now, and the grandfather he'd never seen was red in the face, and there were all those guns.

"Why do they have guns, Mama?"

"They were just going to put them away. Isn't that a fact? Have I got that right, Buford?"

Buford Ellington said, "Four goddam years I don't hear a word." He was crying.

"Tell them to put the guns away; I don't want Jordy Luke to have anything to do with guns. Then, unless everybody's staying for supper, send them back to wherever they came from. I know what you'll do and what you won't do—Daddy. And one thing you won't ever do is k—is bring harm to the father of your only grandson. Now have I got *that* right, Daddy?"

"You—you got that right," Buford said, now looking at the handsome towheaded boy.

Jordy Luke said, "Why did they tie you up, Leprechaun?"

"It's a magic show," the Leprechaun said cheerfully. "Now I'm going to show everybody how long it takes me to get untied." And with that, he held up his hands, which had been behind the chair. He winked at Lucas. "Maybe not so flabby upstairs after all, hey laddy?"

"I'm dying to know what else you had up your sleeve," McIver said.

"A blessing we'll never have to find out. Why don't I show these gentlemen the high road, as I'm sure none of us want to intrude on a family reunion."

"Get out," Buford said to the hired hands. They put their guns away. Jordy Luke looked a little disappointed. The Leprechaun undid the knots that bound his ankles together. The four men left the house. Blaize came up behind McIver, who slipped an arm around her waist.

Jordy Luke ventured a little closer to his grandfather. "Why do you have crutches? Did you hurt yourself?"

"A long time ago," Buford said.

"I've got a seashell collection, would you like to see it?"

"Would you like to see it, *Grandpa*," Blaize corrected.

"Grandpa," the boy said.

"Jesus Christ," Buford said.

Jordy Luke looked to his mother for guidance. "It's all right," she said. "He can talk that way if he wants to. Go get your seashells."

When the boy had left the room, Buford looked at McIver.

"So you named him after Jordan. That doesn't change

the way I feel. I just might hate your guts till the day I die.''

''Yeah, you might,'' McIver acknowledged. ''Want a drink?''

''Hell yes, I want a drink,'' Buford said.